Shaving the Bear

The Twelfth Otto Fischer Novel

Jim McDermott

Copyright Jim McDermott, 2024

All rights reserved

Abbreviation and Acronyms

BCP - *Bund Christlicher Pfadfinderinnen*: Bavarian Girl Guides Association (before 1973)

BND – *BundesNachrichtenDienst*: Federal counter-intelligence service of West Germany (from 1956; formerly the Gehlen Organization (or 'Org')

CIA – *Central Intelligence Agency*: US foreign intelligence service

GdP - *Gewerkschaft der Polizei*: West German (national, following reunification) police trade union

GRU - *Glavnoye Razvedyvatel'noye Upravleniye*: Soviet military intelligence directorate

HIAG - *Hilfsgemeinschaft auf Gegenseitigkeit der Angehörigen der ehemaligen Waffen-SS*: Mutual aid association of former Waffen-SS members, dedicated also to rehabilitating their wartime reputation

KGB - *Komitet Gosudarstvennoy Bezopasnosti:* state security agency of the Soviet Union, formed in 1954 by the amalgamation of former domestic (MVD) and foreign (MGB) security agencies

MfS - *Ministerium für Staatssicherheit*: DDR's Ministry for State Security; colloquially, **Stasi**

MGB - *Ministerstvo Gosudarstvennoy Bezopasnosti SSSR*: Ministry for State Security, counter-intelligence successor organization (from March 1946) to the former **NKGB**, forerunner of the counter-espionage section of **KGB**

RONDD - *Rossiyskoe Obschenatsional'noe Narodno Derzhavnoe Dvizheniye*: Russian All National Popular State Movement: Russian anti-communist émigré movement

SIS – *Secret Intelligence Service*: British counter-intelligence service; known also as **MI6**

Sovmin – *Sovet Ministrov SSSR*: Council of Ministers of the USSR

Stille Hilfe - *Die Stille Hilfe für Kriegsgefangene und Internierte*: 'Silent Assistance for Prisoners of war and Internees', organization originally providing 'rat-lines' to assist the escape of Nazi fugitives from occupied Germany; later a holocaust-denying operation. It exists still today

1

The lane was a whim of long-dead field owners, their mutual boundary drawn back slightly to preserve an ancient right of way. A single horse, or two slim humans walking side-by-side, might have passed its half-mile length untroubled other than by the uneven, rock-embedded surface. Anything wider would have needed to hold its breath, or find a different route from high to higher.

The track was bordered on each side by a steep, grassed bank and mortar-less stone wall, the eastern one suffering a collapsed section of about two yards' breadth. This was being given some attention by a man wearing a heavy sweater and British Army-issue leather jerkin, through both of which a biting wind (having taken a long run-up from the Urals) passed almost unhindered. He shivered occasionally, or beat his upper arms to restore circulation to his hands, or glanced to the northeast to monitor the inexorable approach of a rain front. Otherwise, he applied himself to the missing section of stonework.

Squatting at the base of the opposite wall, a second man smoked a cigarette and cast a critical eye over the same area. Already partly sheltered from the wind, he was further warmed by an expensive camel overcoat, its seat and lower hem stained by the damp grass beneath. When his companion picked up a stone from the dwindling pile that had almost entirely blocked the track a few hours earlier, he sniffed but said nothing. The other man paused and turned.

'What?'

The fingers clamping the cigarette pointed at the newly-laid second course of facing stones.

'You want a through-stone about there.'

'Another one?'

'Yep. It's a steep gradient, so better to overdo it or the thing will shift again. Pretend it's the Atlantic Wall, and you're Rundstedt.'

'Alright.'

'How much is he paying you for this?'

'Materials and nine shillings an hour. He does the haulage'

'That's an unskilled labour rate! You're a fucking artisan!'

'I'm a beginner.'

'No, you're not. This is your tenth job.'

'Sixth. And the others were minor repairs. This is my first collapse.'

'Still, nine shillings. You'd be better off as a pit-pony. At least it's warm at the coal-face.'

At the wall-face, the Artisan shivered. He enjoyed this work, but every job so far had been undertaken at impressive altitude, without the distraction of tree-cover or nearby shelter. He hadn't thought himself particularly sensitive to cold, but when it arrived at speed, carried horizontally by the wind and almost invariably laden with moisture, it seemed to find every decrepit joint in his body and stab it. There were plenty of dry-stone walls in lower, kinder climes, but down there the competition was fierce, and probably competent.

The Camel Coat stubbed out the last of his smoke. 'They're a breed, hill farmers. They all drop into the world as tight as a nun's … someone's coming.'

A Morris Minor crept up to the southern extremity of the narrowed track and wheezed to a halt. A woman in rough work-clothes climbed out, reached into the rear seat and removed a small package. She placed this carefully on the wall, waved at the two men, got back into the car and reversed back the way she had come.

Camel Coat watched all of this without apparent interest. His companion had returned the wave, and now he turned back to his repairs.

'Who was that?'

'My landlady. She told me she might have to go into Aysgarth this morning, and that if she did she'd drop off a sandwich on the way.'

Camel Coat perked up slightly. 'That was nice of her. What d'you think's in it?'

'Almost certainly fried blood sausage.'

'Urgh. Then you needn't share it with me.'

'I hadn't intended to.'

'Ungrateful bastard. Who taught you these valuable skills?'

'You did, but I need the sustenance. All you seem to need are coffin-nails.'

The other man giggled. 'I like that. Where'd you hear it?'

'It's what they call cigarettes in these parts.'

'See? You're learning the vernacular. You'll pass for an Englishman, soon.'

'It's too late for that. I'm known as The Kraut, locally. To the younger ones, at least.'

'*Bosch* to the elderly?'

'Hun.'

Camel Coat sighed. 'They really should read up on which barbarians are which.'

'They don't seem interested in any history that isn't theirs.'

'That's what a moat does to a national perspective. When your home gets invaded constantly by passers-through you need to know whose boots you're kissing. Hell, it's cold.'

'As my landlady's fond of saying, I don't know where that wind comes from, but I know where it's going. I'm running out of the raw material.'

'We can knock off, then. The pub?'

'I can't. He'll be bringing more stone in a couple of hours.'

'Well, you can't wait here – your arse will freeze. I'll get you back in time, I promise,'

'Where's your car?

'Down there, on the road. It's not far.'

When the work was snug beneath its tarpaulin the men walked down the track. At the gate the Artisan picked up his lunch, unwrapped it, examined the contents and held out half.

'Ham.'

'Lovely.'

By the time they reached the road the sandwich was a fond memory. On the verge, an almost-new Rover P5 was parked badly, its gleaming chrome shaming the bleak surroundings.

'Hired?'

Camel Coat stroked the bodywork. 'I bought it. Now that you're in t'North I thought I'd need something that can carry me long distances in comfort.'

'How do you do that?'

'What?'

'The gutteral 'T'. I've tried, but it sounds forced.'

'Practise – long, cold, miserable practise. If you make an effort to parrot them they tend to laugh and think better of you. Back then, a skinny kid in a *Heer* uniform needed all the *better* he could find.'

'Your camp was well to the south of here. Was it really that cold?'

'There isn't anywhere in the Pennines that isn't. Some of the other prisoners were lucky – they'd been captured during the winter months, and had their coats still. I was taken in early May, during my epic dash from the Rhine. Put your tools in the boot and get in.'

The other man looked doubtfully into the plush leather interior. 'Are you sure?'

'Yeah, I've got parcel paper for the seat. Wash your hands in the pub, though. I don't want dirty fingerprints on my new darling.'

'Have you given it a name yet?'

'Of course. She's Brünnhilde.'

'Wouldn't Mavis or Deirdre be more diplomatic?'

Camel Coat grinned. 'I lost the uniform years ago. Why would I still care what they think?'

The pub - a stone hovel at a trough head, perched upon a slight, further ridge to get the best of the weather - was only a five-minute drive away. The Artisan emerged carefully from the Rover, trying not to put his dirty hands on the fuselage, and studied the small faded sign above the low door.

'*The Shoulder of Mutton*. Where do the English find these names?'

Camel Coat locked his door, peered at a small smudge on the car's roof and rubbed it gently with his sleeve.

'I'll remind you that Berlin's oldest, most famous drinking hole is called *The Last Instance*'.

'But that's romantic. A sheep's shoulder isn't.'

'It is to another sheep, I expect. Come on.'

The bar was a hatch, behind which several barrels sat on a low shelf. In a fireplace that was much too large for the room it graced, a small fire was flanked by two old men in flat caps, sat upon stone benches set into the inner fireplace wall, sipping dolefully from their pints as they stared into the struggling flame. Neither seemed to notice that the tally of customers had just doubled.

Camel Coat produced his wallet. 'What will you have?'

'Pale ale, please,'

'That's your tipple now, is it?'

'I don't take to bitter or mild, and any kind of stout makes me fall down.'

'And vomit, I recall.'

'Liberally.'

The landlord poured their drinks, barely reacted to the unusual face in front of him, took money and returned the change with a single nod that might have been a greeting, thanks or the most conversation he was willing to deploy on a cold midweek afternoon. His new customers retired to a small table closest to the fire, whose radiation failed to reach either man. The camel coat and army jerkin continued to do duties.

The Artisan added the entirety of *The Shoulder of Mutton* to a list of incomprehensible aspects of Britishness he had never intended to compile. If this was to be his homeland he wanted to see the best in it, but the tradition of self-flagellation that had allowed Britons to forge an empire in the World's least pleasant climes continued to perplex him. A larger fire would have cost next to nothing to feed, but choosing the comfortable option – even if it took no more effort than the unpleasant alternative – seemed to be regarded as unmanly, or even degenerate.

'So, why?'

Camel Coat's bitter paused halfway to his mouth. 'Eh?'

'Don't think that I'm not pleased to see you. God knows, there are few enough faces in this landscape, so a familiar one's a treat. But we're hundreds of kilometres from central London, and even your nice new car couldn't make that journey less than an ordeal. Why are you here, Jonas?'

'Can't a friend want to see how a friend's doing?'

'Of course he can. But you arrived as I pulled the tarpaulin off the wall this morning, so you knew where I'd be, and when. You can't have spoken to my landlady because when the sandwich arrived you didn't know who she was, and I don't tend to put my movements – or address - in the local newspapers. This has the faint smell of a planned encounter.'

'Christ, Otto. Don't you ever get tired of thinking things through?'

'Not really. So, how did you find me? I last called you a week ago, to say that I'd taken on a new job. I mentioned the farmer's amusing name, didn't I?'

Camel Coat sighed. 'I asked a contact at the Agriculture Ministry to check the National Farming Register. Actually, there are six Ramsbottoms on it, five of whom work farms in Lancashire.'

'Which leaves my new employer, Arthur. So, that's *how*. I asked why. And don't tell me you miss me.'

A thick envelope was plucked from a coat pocket and pushed across the small space between them. The Artisan glanced down and closed his eyes. His young friend cleared his throat.

'It's from ...'

'I know.'

'You do?'

'Only one man would address me as Major. I don't suppose you know what he wants?'

'No. I imagine you'll find out when you open it.'

'That would be to take a first step, and I'd rather keep my feet where they are.'

2

After a second round of drinks, Jonas Kleiber returned Otto Fischer to his ailing wall and drove off to find a hotel room for the night (a quest that was likely to stress-test his new car's fuel efficiency). Farmer Ramsbottom arrived a few minutes later to announce that they had both been *let down* by his stone merchant, and that the promised delivery would happen the following Friday at the earliest. He must have felt the disappointment keenly, because he departed without thinking to offer his hired help a lift to the nearest bus-stop.

The breeze from the Urals was blowing side-on still, but the rain-front had moved off. After a moment weighing the likelihood of rural thieves making an epic trek from their warm lair, Fischer tucked his tool bag beneath a suspended through-stone and descended the hill to the road once more. His landlady would be returning by the same route, and though he had no idea when that might be he was content to enjoy the fine, slightly less wind-scoured view in the meantime. He perched himself on a farm gate, pulled his jerkin tightly around his body and only then turned his mind to the item that Kleiber had conveyed to him.

Why had it required an expedition to northern parts, when the United Kingdom had a perfectly adequate postal service? His friend had gone to the trouble of tracking down the correct Ramsbottom, so he might easily have made the further, slight effort to telephone the farmer and ask if had an address for the *Hun*. Considerable time, petrol money and inconvenience would have been spared, the seat and hem of an expensive coat preserved and a night in a dreary provincial hotel avoided. Even the opportunity to test-drive a nice new car couldn't have made the ordeal any less than …

The answer volunteered itself the moment Fischer's fingers prised open the envelope and parted its edges. A single sheet of paper was wrapped around a banker's draft for £500. Dumbfounded, he failed to resist the urge to glance around in all directions, but when he had satisfied himself that no highwaymen loomed he put the draft back into the envelope, the envelope into a pocket, unfolded the paper and read the familiar scrawl.

Dear Major,

I assume that I have managed to engage your attention. Let me first offer my hearty greetings after several months of silence (for which, my apologies). I trust that life on the English steppe is not proving too onerous, and that your walls fully meet local expectations.

That said, I wonder if you might enjoy a short break from your duties? As you will have noticed, the remuneration – for what I anticipate to be no more than 3 – 4 weeks of your time - is quite substantial, and likely to provide a comfortable shield against the vagaries of your new profession. At the least, it would allow you to remain indoors during the worst of the coming winter weather.

I assure you that the size of the payment does not reflect any danger from, or illegality concerning, the job I have in mind, but you will understand if I not commit any details to paper. I asked your friend Kleiber if he might attempt to secure your agreement to come to London to discuss the matter, and perhaps offer you a lift in his motor car. If, after hearing my 'pitch' (as Americans say), you decide not to take up the task, I shall ask for the return of the banker's draft but be happy to pay you £100 for your trouble.

I look forward to seeing you.

Sincerely,

S.A. Zarubin

ps. I wish I had known previously of your willingness to heave large stones in inhospitable conditions. My *homeland offers infinite opportunities in that line of work.*

Fischer folded the paper and placed it in his pocket. Several thoughts occurred, none of them any less troubling for the speed with which they presented themselves. First, he didn't for a moment believe the assurance. In his world, five hundred pounds wasn't the going rate for three weeks' safe, respectable work. Secondly, he was perfectly aware that the intelligence supplied by former KGB General Sergei Aleksandrovich Zarubin to British Intelligence had proved to be only mildly valuable, for which he had been paid accordingly (that is to say, hardly at all), offered a low-ranking role in their Sovbloc directorate (which he'd refused) and then been set loose upon London's streets to fend for himself. If he was now in substantial funds, he had either sold himself to a competing party, robbed a small bank or was pimping for several young ladies on the five-star hotel circuit. None of these possibilities made the offer more attractive. Thirdly, and not least, a firm resolution never again to put the Fischer fate in hands other than the proprietor's own could hardly be kept if he were to take up something – *anything* - proposed by this most sinning of his acquaintances.

On the other hand, Kleiber had taken directions to Fischer's lodgings, told him that he would return the following day for a reply to whatever the letter proposed, and, as Zarubin had requested, offered a lift to London if he wanted it. A comfortable trip south in a new Rover, a brief discussion, a polite refusal and one hundred pounds to sweeten the ordeal didn't strike him as the worst way to spend some time in which he wasn't going to be working anyway. The tiny stab of guilt that might otherwise have accompanied this cynical thought was deflected by the prospect of a falling Russian face and the deflation of a monstrous ego, a tableau that could only add to the attraction of the (what was the English word?) *jaunt*.

He was trying to spot potential landslides in this pleasant vista when the battered Morris Minor chugged into view. He climbed down from his perch and raised a hand. Being a little shortsighted, Laura Braithwaite had almost passed by her lodger before she recognized him; fortunately, the brakes were sufficiently spongy not to send her through the windscreen when she stamped on the pedal. Fischer walked the short distance to his lift and climbed in.

'You've finished early, Mr Fischer.'

'We're waiting for more stone. Arthur thinks it may be next Friday before his supplier delivers.'

'Oh, dear. What will you do?'

'I need to go to London for a few days, so I suppose this is con …'

'Convenient.'

As usual, she jumped into a hesitation before he had time to find the word he was seeking. It was well-meant, but he would have preferred to explore the beauties of the English language without a tour guide forever waiting to pounce.

'Yes, convenient. I may go tomorrow. I'll pay for my room while I'm away, naturally,'

'You pay for what you get, Mr Fischer. Don't worry, the room will be waiting.'

He thought for a few moments about how or why a room might *wait*, but then her meaning came to him.

'Oh. Thank you.'

Poor man. To have a face like that, and slow-wits as well.

She half-turned and smiled. 'Will you be visiting some German friends? In London?'

'Actually, a Russian.'

'Not a Soviet secret agent, I hope?'

The previous week, she and her friend Margery had been to the cinema in Appleby to see *Spy in the Sky!*, an overheated drama about the Soviet space-satellite programme, so her nerves were still unusually attuned to eastern treacheries. She put the question in a bantering tone, but her lodger didn't seem to realize that he was being teased. He cleared his throat.

'Not these days, no. He *was* KGB, but he defected to the British.'

A cousin who'd been stationed in Hamburg once told Laura that German humour was unfathomable, so she didn't even try to understand the joke. A treacherous, winding section of un-metalled road kept her attention for a few moments, and she had to remember not to call it any of the names she usually employed when she had no company. Her passenger braced himself discreetly, a hand on the dashboard and his left knee pressed into the door. When she spoke again it was too brightly, as if to dispel both spies and her potty-mouthed habits.

'Would you like me to give you a lift to the station tomorrow? I assume you'll be taking the train?'

'That's very kind, but the man I was with this morning has a car. *He's* a German – a journalist. He writes about England, for German newspapers.'

'Nothing bad, I hope?'

'No, he's an anglophile. He has fond memories of being a prisoner of war here. Or at least, of the English girls he imp … importuned.'

It was a delicate subject, but a landlady had certain inquisitorial rights. 'Were *you* …?'

'No, I managed not to get caught by anyone. Perhaps they didn't think I was much of a threat.'

His bad hand waved in front of his worse face as he said it, and Laura wondered if she was being given permission for an even more delicate line of questioning. Fortunately, her gate loomed before she could test the ground.

The further track up to High Scar Farm required concentration if the Morris Minor were not to arrive with a tyre or even wheel missing. As a newly-wed, Laura had imagined a touch of the Brontes in her new home's wild, inconvenient situation, but familiarity had soon bred a weary resentment for the accident of geography that made a hard way of life even less glamorous. When her husband died (much too soon but thankfully covered by life assurance) she decided that the work was beyond a widow and had built a modest living doing local farmers' accounts, so income from the occasional lodger went straight into the bank. She should have been content, but a former farm wore its redundancy heavily, and a persistent local suitor was dangling the lure of autumnal romance and Middleham's frantic urban lifestyle. If she hadn't raised three daughters and buried a husband here the offer might have been seized upon by now.

She pulled up, and her German lodger climbed out and went to close the yard gate (though the last of her sheep had long ago escaped to the slaughterhouse). He'd told her that he had been a farmer too, for a while, but of grapes, tomatoes and other exotica, and no doubt the weather had been a lot less punishing in Portugal than here on the fell. He didn't look to be the farming type (Lord, what *did* he look like?), but for a skinny bugger he was surprisingly strong. The previous week, her dog Benny (a big, stupid lump) had slashed open his paw on barbed wire at the bottom of her furthest field. His distant howls had made her frantic, but Mr Fischer had gone on manoeuvres and brought him home, cradled in his arms. Benny now had a new very best friend, whether or not the other party was agreeable.

She had made stew and dumplings that morning, and they ate it at her kitchen table. In his six weeks' residency, Mr Fischer had neither refused nor complimented her cooking a single time, but she took his consistently hearty appetite as a sort of approval. Her initial uneasiness – at his mutilated features, his nationality and complete lack of small talk – had faded, and she no longer slept with her husband's shotgun beneath the bed (not that it was ever loaded anyway). He paid his rent promptly, always offered to washed the dishes, didn't snore loudly and never splashed around the toilet. A little more casual conversation would have made a model guest.

The thought had only just broken surface when he placed his knife and fork together and cleared his throat.

'I shall miss your cooking. My friend's idea of cuisine is to be found in a heated display case at the end of a bar.'

Pleased, she took away the plates before he could volunteer. 'Well, it's only for a few days. If you know exactly when you'll be back I can have something ready for you. A steak and kidney pie?'

'I don't, unfortunately.'

'I'll give you Margery's number, then. She'll pass on the word, if you call her before you leave London.'

High Scar should have had a telephone, but it lay too far from and above the nearest march of cables to tempt the GPO into extending its empire in that direction. The same logic made modern plumbing a fond ambition (water came pure but unhandily from an ancient well beneath the farmhouse, and a septic tank took it the other way), though a nearby wooden pylon allowed the frivolous luxuries of a washing machine and radio. To most lodgers the arrangements would have seemed spartan; to a man who had experienced Germany's smashed cities in the war's immediate aftermath they were the epitome of comfort.

'Yes, I'll do that. Do you need anything? From London?'

Surprised, Laura thought about what the Wen might offer that North Yorkshire didn't. Her only indulgence was knitting, and though she would have loved to tour the city's vast range of haberdasheries there was a perfectly serviceable wool-shop in Leyburn, with a selection that quite exceeded her ambitions.

'I don't think so, but thank you.'

'If I can find a German delicatessen, I'll buy some *blutwurst*, and you can compare it to your black pudding.'

She smiled. 'I've never been to Germany, so that'll be nearly a holiday. It's nice, isn't it?'

'What is?'

'That we're not killing each other any more.'

'A peace is of the nature of a conquest; for then both parties nobly are subdued, and neither party loser.'

'Who said that?'

He returned the smile. 'A very famous German, Wilhelm Shakespeare.'

Not so slow, then.

3

'Why are they doing it like this?'

Jonas Kleiber shrugged. 'They're trying to relieve the most badly congested bits first. I suppose they'll join them all up later.'

Since leaving the Dales, the Rover had made good and bad time in equal measure. Their journey down the Great North Road was akin to a beginner's dance class, a series of stop-starts as the single carriageway blossomed briefly into more modern, dual capacity stretches and then, just as a sense of momentum took hold, converged once more to give everyone a chance to admire the passing countryside in slow-motion. Four hours after commencing their odyssey, they were no closer to London than southern Lincolnshire.

'I don't see why they can't decide which two places need connecting and then push through an autobahn in one campaign, as we did.'

'Ancient property rights, something the Führer never needed to fret about. Every inch of every planned route in England has to be wrestled from the hands of folk whose way with a compulsory purchase notice is to wipe their arse with it.'

'Speaking almost of which, I need to piss.'

'Again?'

'The last time was two hours ago. An old bladder doesn't hold much.'

'We'll stop at Stamford, get a coffee and loosen our limbs. It's a pretty town.'

Pretty didn't do justice to the elegant old burgh, but Fischer was too eager to finish the journey to enjoy their brief visit (it would have been briefer still, had not Kleiber been ambushed by an elderly gentleman, a fellow P5 driver who insisted upon rehearsing the car's virtues at great length). Fortunately, traffic eased south of Biggleswade, and some daylight remained as they reached London's northern outskirts. It was the first time that Fischer had passed through the capital by road, and his sense of its drab vastness was magnified. Several times he was at the point of asking Kleiber if he had lost his way, but he needed a bed for the night and didn't want to cause offence. Like ships' masters, some motorists had great regard for their navigational skills.

It was fully dark when the Rover pulled up in a mews yard in what Kleiber claimed to be an up-and-coming part of South Kensington.

In the previous year he had moved out of his old flat above the Kennington bakery, crossed the river and taken up lodgings more appropriate to a foreign correspondent's dignity. Here, he was handy for the Albert Hall (though he didn't like classical music), any number of museums (for which he had no time whatsoever) and some of the prettiest girls-from-good-families that an aspiring social climber could wish for (and he wished very, very hard indeed). Fischer, while acclimatizing to English ways and planning out a new life to suit a former *kriminalkommissar*, paratrooper, clock- and gramophone-repairer, reluctant politician, hapless spy and failed farmer, had helped his friend to move homes and then, as a house-guest, spent three tiresome months getting daily reports on the 'skirt' hereabouts, a subject that in no way assisted him in absorbing the theory and practise of dry-stone walling.

A pretty young woman stepped out of the door immediately in front of the Rover and waved, Ironically, Kleiber's strenuous attempts to net an Arabella, Pandora or Sybilla had landed Maisie, sister of one of the barmaids in his new local, *The Flowers*. Maisie was from peasant stock, but her profession - she was a nurse at St Thomas' Hospital – made the matter of pedigree irrelevant. It was, or had been, Kleiber's confident opinion that daily exposure to illness, physical disintegration and the surgeon's gruesome art had the effect of putting social mores (particularly those that determined how *nice* girls should behave) into perspective. Hence (he had explained to

Fischer), all nurses possessed robust sexual appetites, very few inhibitions and were inclined to live for the moment.

Maisie was a statistical anomaly, though. She had taken up Kleiber's invitation to share his home at the first time of asking, but they held very different views on a tenant's obligations. She did more than her share of cleaning and cooking, and even darned both men's socks as necessary; but the nominal rent she paid gave her no further sense of obligation regarding her landlord's baser needs. When Fischer had packed his things and moved north at the end of the previous year, she moved from the sitting-room sofa to the vacated spare bedroom, seemingly unconvinced by glowing testimonials as to the excellence of the obvious alternative. He hadn't since bothered to enquire whether the situation had changed.

'Hello, Otto. You look dashing.'

'Hello, Maisie. Do I?'

He was wearing a tweed jacket, rummaged from a second-hand stall in Sedburgh market, and a pair of forgettable grey trousers. His brogues were well-polished but old, so he supposed that it must be the almost-new white shirt that was propelling him out of the sartorial traps.

'Very elegant. How was the trip south?'

'Interminable. Is that the right word?'

'I think so. Hello, darling. I've made up the spare bed.'

This last, and the brief hug and kiss she gave Kleiber as he climbed out of his car, handily summarized the current state of things.

'Thanks, sweetheart. Sorry we're so late. We can grab a bite at *The Flowers*.'

'No, you can't. I've made a *chasseur*.'

Proudly, Kleiber wrapped an arm around her waist. 'Maisie's taking a cookery course, at Le Cordon Bleu.'

She pulled a face. 'I had to, or starve. I didn't realise when I moved in that he could hardly boil a kettle. I hope *you've* been eating, Otto. You look thinner.'

'Very well, yes. It's the work that keeps me svelte.'

Kleiber waved Fischer through the hallway and into the sitting-room, dropped his overnight bag on the floor and stood back to allow his friend to admire the extensive changes since his last visit. Moving from a furnished flat to an empty house, he had bought quickly, indiscriminately and by the tonne, sweeping up items that would occupy the most space for the least outlay. A few of them remained, but the majority had made way for a much smaller selection of tastefully understated pieces that didn't look to be sharing a furniture warehouse. A framed Mondrian exhibition print hung over the fireplace, replacing a bucolic daub that had made Fischer shudder slightly on the day it went up, while the floral wallpaper that once had provided an equally unpleasant backdrop was now snug beneath a neutral shade of emulsion.

'This is very nice. Maisie's doing?'

'Yeah. It's strange how girls can see what we can't.'

She ate with them but went to bed soon afterwards, being on an early shift the following morning. Her parting *don't be long* to Kleiber (and the meaningful look that accompanied it) told Fischer that he had very little time to broach the subject of the moment, a moment he'd been putting off all day. As they began to clear the table he put the question.

'Did Zarubin say anything to you about this business?'

The plates paused on their descent to the draining board. Kleiber half-turned and looked blankly at his friend.

'How could he? I've never met the man, or spoken on the 'phone, even,'

'Then how could you know …?'

'The envelope I gave you came in another one, with a note … why don't I fetch it?'

The note was brief, and asked only two things: that Kleiber undertake to deliver the envelope personally to Fischer, or, if this proved impracticable, impossible or just too inconvenient, to return it to Zarubin, who could be found every weekday morning in the London Library, and, for an hour thereafter, at a café in Crown Passage, off Pall Mall.

'How did he get your address?'

'No idea. You'll have to ask him.'

'*Which* London library? There must be a few, at least.'

'No, *The* London Library – the first ever British lending-library. It's in St James's Square. I assume that's where he wants you to go.'

'I doubt it. We'd be overheard in a library, or told to shut up. Remind me where Pall Mall is.'

Kleiber fetched an A to Z and pointed it out. 'The passage is at its western end, north side. You should get the tube to Green Park – it's five minutes' walk from there. I wonder what he wants you for.'

'He writes that it's neither dangerous nor illegal, so it's probably both.'

'You're not going to oblige him, are you? He's persuaded you to do dumb stuff in the past.'

Fischer took a plate and applied his tea-towel to it. 'It was never quite *persuasion*. Usually, I had little choice. Unless this business turns out to be as bland as he claims, I'll refuse and go straight back North, to my walls. He's offered a hundred pounds for my trouble, even if I say no.'

'And if you say yes?'

'Five hundred.'

Kleiber blew out his cheeks. 'That's ... a lot. For a man in your line of work, I mean.'

'It is, for something straightforward and legitimate. If it puts my rear end in a hot pan, not so much.'

'You don't think it's …?'

'What?'

Kleiber reddened slightly, and shrugged, 'Something about Cuba?'

Fischer laughed. 'That mess is over now. And even if the world was on the brink still, who'd want to use Zarubin? The Americans think he's a snake, the Ivans would shoot him on sight and the British have made it clear that he's as useful to them as socks in a sauna. Whatever advice he had to offer on the Cuban business went into Khrushchev's ear long ago, and it was ignored. In any case, what the hell use would *I* be?'

'None, I suppose. But he *was* KGB …'

'They're not all top spies or deadly assassins. Zarubin was paid to think through possibilities and options, put them on paper and make recommendations. The only reason he was ever considered dangerous was that he took care to know what his rivals didn't want him to know. And he lost that battle, didn't he?'

'I had to ask. It's been worrying me.'

'If I'd thought for a moment that it was about Cuba or any other political catastrophe, I'd be in the north still, hiding in my landlady's cellar. A man can have only so many stark lessons thrown at him before he takes the hint. My skin – what remains of it – is now my most precious possession.'

'Not before time. I'm off to bed. Sleep well.'

'I will, if you grip a pillow between your teeth until she's finished with you.'

Kleiber's grin almost reached his ears. 'Are you jealous, Otto?'

'Nostalgic, Jonas. In that I may recall the act as being more wonderful than it ever was.'

4

Just before eleven-thirty the following morning, Fischer stepped into Crown Passage, having successfully negotiated three stops on the Piccadilly line and a brief, pleasant stroll down St James's street. He found no café along its narrow span, but an establishment whose garish plastic sign proclaimed a 'Restaurant-Sandwich Bar' seemed to fit the bill. It was directly opposite – and almost touching – *The Red Lion*, apparently one of the oldest licensed premises in London (this according to Kleiber, whose knowledge of public houses within a kilometre's radius of Whitehall was encyclopaedic). A floor-standing sign outside the premises alleged *good food always available*, something that Fischer's much lesser experience of British pubs made him doubt greatly.

The restaurant, or sandwich bar (*how could it be both?* he wondered), was staffed by Italians, one of whom offered a hearty greeting and addressed him as Boss. He ordered a double espresso and took a small table facing the door. The coffee arrived in the grasp of a girl with film-star features and cascades of curly black hair, restrained by a long pony-tail. She, too, called him Boss, and seemed equally oblivious to his war-wounds. It took an effort of will not to turn and dwell upon the rear view as she returned to the kitchens.

An abandoned copy of that day's *Daily Sketch* sat on the next table. He requisitioned and read it slowly, pausing at the occasional unfamiliar word or term, to reacquaint himself with current events off-moorland. The most interesting home news – or rather, fevered speculation - continued to be about the War Secretary Profumo's alleged romps with a young prostitute, interest in which had only been stoked by his threats to sue anyone who repeated the accusation outside the House (to Fischer's mind this was as much as an admission of guilt, if such a pastime could constitute a crime). On the foreign pages, Khrushchev was going to China to patch up relations before the two Communist mastodons could declare war upon each other; San Francisco's Alcatraz Prison, an expensive, underutilized facility (lately it had held just twenty-seven prisoners) was being shut down; in Iran, the Shah's police had beaten to death several students of an obscure Shi'ite cleric named Khomeini; and, as ever, De Gaulle was saying *non* to something…

'Are you having lunch, Boss?'

The starlet was leaning closely, and a slight hint of her sweat stirred something in him that definitely wasn't nostalgia.

'Just another espresso, for the moment.'

'Double?'

'Please. Do you know what time it is?'

Her pen pointed to a clock on the wall directly in front of him. 'It's five minutes fast.'

Which made it almost twelve-thirty pm, and a certain former General of KGB had yet to show his face. The lunchtime trade had filled every other table by now: an assortment of shoppers, workers and at least one family of tourists, loudly reprising their attempts to make the bearskins twitch at the entrance to St James's Palace, just across the road. The busyness reminded Fischer that his coffee and otherwise unoccupied table constituted an impediment to trade, so he drained the cup quickly, stood, nodded to a hopeful trio of women loitering by the door and went to the counter to pay his bill.

'Two and six, Boss.'

The old man's cheeriness encouraged Fischer to push his luck.

'I was supposed to meet someone here. He comes in for his lunch most days – a very blond man, quite good-looking. He has an accent. Is he sometimes late …?'

The man winked, turned and shouted into the kitchen.

'Giulietta!'

The starlet pushed through the bead curtain. 'Si?'

'This gentleman's looking for your fancy man. E's a friend, 'e says.'

The girl blushed. 'He isn't my …'

'I don't think 'e was in yesterday either, but she knows better than me.'

'No, he wasn't. It's the first time he's not eaten here in weeks.'

The old man winked again. 'He makes you laugh, doesn't he? And he tips well, always ten percent.'

Giulietta sniffed and folded her arms. 'He's nice. He talks to my face, not my breasts.'

That wiped the smile from her boss's (her grandfather's?) face. He lowered his head and applied himself to buttering a pile of bread rolls. Fischer, who feared that he may have addressed at least one comment to Guilietta's plunging neckline, cleared his throat and held her gaze firmly.

'When you last saw him, did he mention that he wouldn't be coming in?'

'No, he said nothing about that.'

'Has he ever come here with anyone else?'

Giulietta looked sideways at the roll-butterer. A policeman or creditor might have asked the same, and she seemed reluctant to put one of her favourite customers against a wall.

'Just once, I think. A small man with a bad limp.'

Fischer nodded. 'He's a friend. If he comes it later, would you tell him that his other friend – the one from the North - was here?'

'Yes, of course. Otto will be sorry he missed you.'

The old man looked up and smirked. 'Only this customer she calls by his first name.'

I'll kill him.

Ten minutes and only one minor detour later, Fischer found St James's Square, and, in one of its corners, the London Library. The modest but elegant facade, stained by decades of airborne city-dirt, led immediately into a large, pillared room. Its central space, filled with reading desks, was a well, overlooked by an upper storey of bookshelves. On the ground floor, a reception area stood to one side of the inner entrance, where, behind a high desk, a cardigan'd young man sorted index cards and talked quietly either to them or himself. Fischer advanced, took up a supplicant's position and waited for his presence to register.

Eventually, the man looked up, started slightly and smiled. 'Oh! Sorry. These things are never in the right order. You wouldn't think an alphabetic system could be confusing, but … may I help?'

'Yes. I'm looking for one of your members, who …'

'Readers. We call them readers.'

'Except when they don't put the cards back in the right order. Then you call them something else, I suppose?'

'Ha, yes.'

'I was suppose to meet him nearby, but he didn't arrive. I wonder if you could tell me if he's been in today? His name is … Fischer. Otto Fischer.'

'I don't think he has. Give me a moment, would you?'

He went to consult a grey-haired lady sitting at a desk in the well. She looked up, shook her head slightly then leaned back to peer across at reception. Fischer nodded to her, hoping that the gesture conveyed at least a hint of innocence (though he couldn't say why he felt guilty about having had his identity purloined). She climbed to her feet and returned with the Cardigan.

'No, and he wasn't here yesterday, either. He's a relatively new reader, but I think he's been in almost every day since he first subscribed, a few weeks ago. Until yesterday, as I say. You're a friend, I take it?'

'His brother. I've just arrived in England, so I'm anxious to see him.'

What might have been a *you don't resemble each other* died on her lips. Of course they didn't. One of them was a handsome blond devil who could attract girls half his age; the other was a cautionary tale about what war did to human tissue when it didn't duck. But at least they sounded alike. When he wished to be mistaken for a German, Zarubin's accent was almost pure Berlin, with tiny hints of Pomeranian usage from his brief service in Stettin. Fischer's carried the reverse proportions, but no-one who hadn't lived for years among his compatriots would hear the subtle differences.

The Cardigan seemed politely concerned. 'What bad luck you should arrive now, and he not. Do you have an address for him?'

The woman opened her mouth to head off a kindness that almost certainly broke confidentiality rules, but Fischer spoke quickly.

'Yes. I'll go there this evening. No doubt he has a good reason for being somewhere else. I'm sorry to have bothered you.'

'It was no trouble. Do you need directions?'

Incredulously, the woman gaped at her colleague.

'No, you can't …'

To spare the young man further embarrassment, Fischer removed Kleiber's A to Z from his coat pocket.

'I have this, thank you.'

Outside, he paused on the corner of Duke of York Street and pretended to tie his shoelaces. Zarubin was a clever man, and usually very careful to get his fish on the hook before he yanked the rod. Five hundred pounds was shiny bait, but identity theft was a taunt, the disappearing act gratuitous and both of them reminders that everything he plotted came in layers. If he wanted something from Otto Fischer – the *real* Otto Fischer - this wasn't the way to do it.

The sensible thing would be to return to South Kensington, put the banker's draft into Kleiber's hand, navigate his way to King's Cross Station and find the cheapest ticket to Middleham. If Zarubin was being evasive the consolation prize couldn't be collected, but the hurt to Fischer's pocket wasn't going to be nearly so painful as that to his self-respect. It seemed that he had been played yet again, and by the man he most expected to do the playing.

Damn.

A few paces up Duke of York Street he came to a pub (yet another *Red Lion*, what were they thinking?), where he squandered money he could no longer spare on two bottles of pale ale. That indulgence made the tube too expensive to consider, so he consulted his borrowed traveller's bible and discovered the route back to base to be mostly a straight line, with one left-turn at the Albert Hall. It turned out to be pleasant exercise – a saunter past grand edifices the length of Piccadilly, a fraught dodge through traffic into Hyde Park and then all he needed to avoid were loose footballs and soldiers exercising their horses from the local barracks. With frequent halts to take in the sights (not least, the imposing memorial to one of the very few Germans of whom the British were genuinely fond), it took him less than an hour to return to *Chez Kleiber*.

He let himself in with the spare key and found his friend at the sitting-room table, frowning at an Olivetti.

'Ah, Otto. What's a polite way of saying *fucking*?'

'I doubt that there is one. And why would there be?'

'The verb I mean, not the expletive.'

Fischer pondered the carpet for a few moments.

'Being intimate with?'

'Yeah, too prissy.'

'Engaging in the lists of Venus?'

'My arse.'

'Well, I don't know then. The act tends to be described forensically or circumspectly. There's not really anything in between.'

'I suppose not.'

'What's the article about?'

'Profumo. Again.'

'The War Secretary?'

'Yeah. I could refer to his 'affair', but the girl's a tart …'

'What's the latest on the epic?'

'Not much. German interest is mainly in the English reaction to it, not the story itself. Hell, if he were a French politician no-one would have blinked; banging someone who isn't your wife's almost part of the job description for the Assemblée Nationale. Did you refuse your mate Zarubin?'

'He wasn't available to refuse.'

'Eh?'

'He wasn't at the cafe, or the Library.'

'Fuck him, then. I mean, *be intimate* with him.'

Fischer sighed. 'My first, strongest instinct. But …'

'There's always a but.'

'It doesn't make sense. Why would a man go to the trouble of arranging a banker's draft, get you to drive hundreds of kilometres to deliver it, offer some sort of job, have you drag me to London and then take pains to ensure that he wasn't where he said he'd be? Even Zarubin was never so whimsical as to waste his own time and money.'

'He's ill?'

'Possibly.'

'Dead? Arrested? He's met a young lady and they're busy profumo'ing the derrières off each other?'

'Or he's been called away on some other business. But then, he would have left word with you. He knows where you live.'

'You don't have an address for him?'

'No. I know someone who does, though. Which tube station would be best for Cecil Court?'

'Leicester Square – is, was and ever will be. Who lives there?'

'Another KGB man.'

'Christ, Otto. Don't go jumping into all that shit again.'

It's alright. He's a fervent capitalist these days.'

5

The sign above the shop-front was in Latin script, of course, and as far as Fischer could recall from the Russian he'd imbibed during his years in NKVD Special Camp no. 1 (known also as Sachsenhausen), *Proshlyye Vremena* meant something like Old, or Past, Times. The display items in the window suggested that the *times* predated the October Revolution, though of course many communists had since proved to be as fond of relics of an imperial past as their dispossessed owners.

Fine furniture, jewellery, porcelain and even two ball-gowns: it was an upmarket pawn shop, though Fischer doubted that many of those bringing their treasured possessions here would ever find the means to redeem them. Their diaspora had endured for almost half a century now, a wandering in a western desert without promise of a land to relieve the ordeal. Reminders of a privileged past couldn't fill stomachs, or sentiment generate calories. It was sad, he supposed, but that was the elegant symmetry of Russian history. *Everyone* suffered, sooner or later.

He stepped inside, a bell above the door rang once and an elderly lady emerged from behind a tall mahogany armoire. It wasn't difficult to guess why she had been employed here. A front-of-house needed to reflect the nature of the business, and she had a lugubrious air that someone seeking a good price for an heirloom might mistake for sympathy, or regret. It was also less likely that an (inevitably disappointing) offer would be met by harsh language if the desperate party was minded to recall a dear grandmother.

'Good morning. May I help you?'

French, or Belgian. He tried to smile with the good side of his face, and make it seem more than a sardonic smirk.

'Is Mr Levin available, please?'

'He's on the telephone at the moment. An international call.'

'When he's done, would you tell him that Herr Fischer is here? The *actual* Herr Fischer?'

She disappeared behind the armoire, and less than a minute later the proprietor emerged. He was wearing a suit – a nice suit – with a pink shirt, burgundy silk tie and a markedly guilty expression, to which Fischer attached no meaning. Boris Levin had a face that always seemed ready to admit to something.

'Ah, Herr Fischer. How are you?'

'Puzzled.'

'About ...?'

'I was invited to London, to hear a proposition.'

'Yes, he said he might do that.'

'But he's not here. That is, not where he said he'd be.'

'Really?'

'I looked for him at the library, and the Italian place at which he eats. I found that he's been using my name as his own. What game is he playing, Mr Levin? I should say, what game is he playing *this* time?'

'He regards his own name as unhelpful in certain circumstances. He's pretended to be *me*, on occasion.'

In addition to his MGB and KGB pedigree, former General Zarubin carried uncomfortable family history. His father had joined the Mensheviks and paid the price, but his uncle owned such few and twisted principles as to have become a close friend of Josef Stalin (until the monster decided that friends and enemies were equally inconvenient). Fischer could see how the name might be a burden, occasionally; but not why Smith, Jones, Brown or Bolkonov couldn't have served just as well as Fischer.

'Do you know what business he has with me?'

'I'm afraid I haven't spoken to him in more than a week.'

Which doesn't nearly answer the question. Fischer looked around the shop.

'How's business these days?'

'I'm doing very well, thank you.'

'This is hardly a thoroughfare, is it? I wouldn't have thought the passing trade was that healthy.'

'I sell very little to browsers. Most of my buying customers are dealers themselves.' Levin lifted his walking stick and waved it at the armoire. 'That ugly thing, for example. It's French, early 19th century. Somehow, it found its way to Minsk – probably pillaged during the Russian occupation of Paris. After the Revolution its owner managed to get it out of Russia and brought it here, but hard times have made it currency. I bought it from the family last year, thinking it might well become a fixture, but recently a gentleman with premises in the 5th Arrondissement came into the shop, saw it and made me a very pleasing offer. Tomorrow it ends its long exile and goes home. I find it pleasing that a Russian could help in that process.'

'And make a profit from it?'

Levin shrugged. 'Profits put food upon the table. And you'll recall that I wasn't enthusiastic about coming to a place where they're essential to life.'

'Forgive me. I'm glad that you're doing well. At least one good thing came from your boss's plots.'

'I'm grateful to him. It was his money that seeded this.'

In fact, it was misappropriated Kremlin funds that had provided, planted and watered the seeds, but Fischer didn't think it politic to say so. He needed Levin's help to make sense of his predicament, and was beginning to suspect that the man's anxiety wasn't on the usual point of life and everything. The frank approach had met a carapace, so he circled instead, hoping to find a way in.

'Your assistant's from France, isn't she?'

'Sandrine? From Chartres, yes. She fled when the Nazis reached Paris, and stayed on after the war. I don't speak the language, so she's very helpful with some of my foreign clients.'

'Don't introduce her to Zarubin. He'll probably borrow her identity, too.'

That raised a faint smile. 'I'm afraid he's met her already. She was quite overcome when he kissed her hand.'

During an earlier exile in the Unites States, the penniless, younger Zarubin had briefly found employment as a companion (a gigolo, rather) to an heiress, an occupation that had honed valuable skills. Young waitresses, elderly shop assistants, more or less anyone lacking a Y chromosome – their barricades invariably toppled when he deployed his glib charm. It seemed both ironic and faintly wasteful, that a man possessing such a gift almost certainly had never experienced ardent feelings for another human being.

But then, almost everything about the visible Zarubin was a deflection, a misrepresentation or a half-glimpse through frosted glass. Fischer glanced at Levin, and, playing for time, removed a handkerchief from his pocket and blew his nose. He wasn't going to be offered coffee, or a seat, or any other reason for extending his visit, which suggested to him that the proprietor – an otherwise hospitable creature, always happy to hear the latest news or rumours – knew at least enough about this business to wish that he knew nothing at all. Short of threatening to kick away his stick, there was no way to prise out more than what couldn't be refused.

'Do you have an address for him? A telephone number?'

Levin swallowed. 'Not a number, no. His apartment has no 'phone.'

'Well, then. Where does he live?'

'I don't know if he'd want me to …'

'Come on, Mr Levin. If it's a secret, you're going to have to tell me why. If it's a secret only from me, I'm going home on the next train. Would he want that, do you think?'

'I … suppose not.'

Levin found a pen and notepad, scribbled briefly and parted reluctantly with the information. Fischer glanced at the address – he had never heard of Bishopsgate, but the postcode, E1, suggested that it was part of the inner city. He was about to offer his thanks when a very necessary thought occurred, and he held up the paper.

'I don't suppose you know what name he's known by at home?'

'His own. He complains that his landlord pronounces it *Zaroobin* some days and *Saroobeen* others.'

'I'm surprised he remembers the correct pronunciation. He uses it so infrequently these days.'

'He's a man with enemies, most of whom have the resources to scratch their itch. He feels the proximity of the Soviet Embassy very keenly.'

'Then why has he remained in London, given that SIS have made their indifference to his talents so obvious?'

For a moment, Levin looked as if he might risk an opinion, but it passed. He shook his head.

'It's a shame they won't use him. The General has the deepest understanding of Kremlin politics of anyone who isn't *in* the Kremlin, but you can guess how it is. Intelligence agencies prefer to have their traitors *in situ*, not offering opinions or advice from a safe distance.'

'If he hadn't upset so many people, *all* our circumstances might be less of a shame. You must miss Moscow as much as I do Berlin.'

Levin's face showed the pain only for a moment, but it couldn't be mistaken for indigestion. Whatever he had made of his brief time in the West he was an outcast, an exile who could expect no remission of his life sentence. Like Fischer, his only crime had been one of proximity to Zarubin, for which he had exchanged a comfortable apartment and privileged access to foreign consumer goods for political freedoms he didn't want or need and the absolute human right to starve if his business failed.

'Well, never mind. How far are you going to pursue this?'

It was put as a question, but Fischer knew Levin just well enough to suspect that he was hearing as close to a warning as the other man dared or cared to offer.

'Not very. If our friend stays out of view for even a few more hours I shall take the hint and give up. There's a matter of returning a banker's draft, though. A substantial amount.'

'May I ask …?'

'Five hundred pounds. It was to be my fee, if I accepted the work. A hundred, if I said no.'

Levin could hide shock no better than pain. He swallowed, tried to speak and then glanced around his shop as if to find a means of sending the conversation elsewhere. When nothing obvious presented itself, he leaned further into his walking stick and waved the free hand.

'If you don't manage to speak to the General, I could return that to him. I have enough cash to compensate you to the agreed amount.'

Now why would you do that?

'That's very kind, and tempting. Do I sense that you'd rather I didn't find him?'

'No, I … don't know exactly what he's doing, and I prefer it that way. I promised that I wouldn't repeat anything of the little he *has* said to me, but …'

Fischer waited, letting the thing tease itself out. His own history with Zarubin was an epic cautionary tale, one that had brought a single, wonderful gift but was otherwise a manifest of betrayals and carefully-staked pits. That they had all been intended to snare or confound someone else was a small consolation, given that the hapless bait had ever been likely to be consumed also.

' … just be careful, is what I mean.'

'If he ever reveals enough that I can guess what care to take, I shall.'

6

After leaving Levin's shop, Fischer consulted his A to Z, re-entered London's bowels at Charing Cross and rode the Underground to Liverpool Street, It was almost lunchtime and he was hungry, but by now he had as little money remaining as he had patience with Zarubin's latest game. A growling stomach could be ignored for a while; the thumping headache needed flushing as soon as possible.

The eastern side of Bishopsgate immediately north of the railway station was a messy mix of old stone and new concrete, the former almost certainly scheduled to be converted to the latter. The address he had been given belonged to a narrow, Dutch-gabled edifice, its ground floor and two storeys above occupied by a wholesale textile business (presumably the landlord's), with a top floor punctured by two wide, bow windows. In bright sunlight, their curtains were closed.

Fischer entered the premises and presented himself before a middle-aged man at a counter. Since arriving in England he had been pleased at how little visible reaction his face elicited from most strangers, a phenomenon he attributed to the national reputation for reserve, or perhaps politeness. Today, however, he confronted an untypical specimen.

The man looked up, half-looked down again but then came to attention when the damage registered. He made no attempt to hide his shock, which shaded quickly to mild outrage, as if an unwanted interruption and the harvest of long-ploughed-over battlefields were conspiring to ruin his morning.

'May I 'elp?'

'I'm here to see Mr Zarubin.'

'Oo?'

'The tenant.'

'Oh. Outside, turn left, the first door in the passage. It shouldn't be locked. 'E's three flights up.'

Fischer felt the indignant gaze warming his neck as he retreated. He hadn't even noticed the passageway, a hint of how he'd allowed himself to become distracted by this ridiculous situation. He took the stairs (elegantly carved but ramshackle) two at a time at a run, and reached the apartment door almost out of breath. It had a security spyhole but was otherwise ordinary, and certainly not capable of stopping a determined shoulder-charge from large men who might think to visit with a view to terminating the occupant's pension rights. He knocked twice, firmly, and stood back.

Five minutes and several sore knuckles later he retraced his steps to the ground floor, rehearsing several of the fruitier expressions he'd picked up during his English exile. At this time of day his hopes had been thin, but their disappointment left him without any further ideas on what next. Clearly, Sergei Aleksandrovich Zarubin was not in a mood to receive the company he had invited, and an unwanted guest had few options other than to retire, hurt.

All obvious options had been exhausted, Levin's offer of recompense-by-proxy pressed its attractions strongly, and Fischer told himself that even his tender conscience could be satisfied by the efforts he had made. And yet something held him at the passageway's mouth. He couldn't pretend to guess at what Zarubin was doing (who could, ever?), but no rational being handed over a deal of money and then tried to avoid the rest of the transaction. As far as he knew, a banker's draft couldn't be cancelled remotely, so the moment it had been posted the thing was done, the arrangement set into motion. At best, a Russian exile with no steady employment or known wealth had made himself a hundred pounds (and possible five) poorer, and unless he rematerialized it was money spent for nothing, nothing at all.

Fischer sighed, rubbed his head and challenged it to argue him out of this. Obligingly, it threw out plenty of attractive options – northern walls in need of tender care, the hearty fare that Laura Braithwaite put on her table each morning and evening, an honest, mostly safe employment (the occasional crushed finger and frequent dousing apart), a modest but regular recompense, and, best of all, the utter want of former or serving intelligencers in the wilder parts of the Pennines. He could fault none of its logic, but the small, poisonous voice wasn't stilled. Something was wrong, and though he was exonerated by his absolute ignorance of what it was, who was responsible and what consequences might fall from it, the fact that he had been unable to reject Zarubin's proposition out of hand gave him a perverse sense of being morally indebted.

Idiot.

He re-entered the wholesaler's shop, ready to further spoil the offended party's morning. There was now a different face at the counter, however, one that didn't react noticeably to his own. The man closed a ledger he had been consulting and smiled.

'May I help you?'

'I've been upstairs to see your tenant, but he's not in. Do you know when he might return?'

'I don't, I'm afraid. Are you a friend? You could leave a message with me.'

'I'm a friend, yes, but I'm due to return to the north of England this evening or tomorrow, and I need to speak to him. May I ask when you saw him last?'

The young man frowned at his ledger. 'I couldn't say. Having his own entrance he comes and goes as he pleases. I don't see him more than once a week, usually.'

'Would any of your colleagues have spoken to him recently, do you think?'

Another, more rueful smile. 'I doubt it very much. They're mostly veterans, and have particular opinions regarding foreigners. I always have a few words with Mr Zarubin if we cross paths, but I'd be surprised if he gets more than a nod from the others.'

'And yet he's a Russian, a former ally. How would they feel about a German?'

'Oh, they don't discriminate – 'the wogs begin at Calais', as they're fond of saying. Have you tried his church? They might be able to point you in the right direction.'

'His *church*?'

Fischer didn't even try to disguise his astonishment. Most members of the Soviet *Nomenklatura* were atheists by conviction or political necessity, but Zarubin's impiety was built upon broader foundations. The only true faith he possessed was in his own cleverness.

'The Orthodox Cathedral. In South Kensington, I believe.'

What was it about one small part of London, that was attracting shards of the Fischer Past? Kleiber and Zarubin may have passed each other in the street, oblivious to their proximity, both wondering (one hopefully, the other fearfully) if their mutual friend was going to be so ill-advised as to fall into yet another game of mirrors. Murder, politics, espionage and assisting a defector in his flight out of the Soviet Union – he had been dragged into and through every lunatic stratagem short of declaring war, and if it turned out that the latest was further polluted by some matter of religion, he wouldn't need to worry about finding his train-fare home – he'd abscond with Kleiber's A to Z and sprint northwards until he reached fields or collapsed.

The pleasant young gentleman was consulting his own copy of the invaluable tome. 'Yes, it's in Ennismore Gardens, W1. Do you .,.?'

'I know the area quite well, thank you. If by any chance you see Mr Zarubin today, would you tell him that Otto Fischer called?'

'Of course. Does he know where to find you?'

'He always seems to, yes.'

'Oh, hang on a minute. Derek?'

From a large rack at the rear of the room a brown-coated employee was loading a roll of what looked to be cotton on to his shoulder. He paused.

'Alan! 'Ow can I brighten your day, mate?'

'This gentleman's looking for our tenant. Have you seen him?'

'Nope. But I wish I 'ad a pound for every time I've bin asked today.'

'How many's that?'

'Twice. A rum 'un was in earlier, all but demanding that I produce him. 'E went away disappointed.'

'How rum?'

''E 'ad a face that could sour milk.' Derek paused and glanced at Fischer. 'No offence.'

'None taken. Did he ask for Mr Zarubin by name?'

'Yeah. An' then 'e flounced out. I 'ad to laugh.'

'Why?'

'Wot a sight 'e was – long black frock an' a big, fancy cross dangling 'arfway down 'is belly.'

'He was a priest?'

'Didn't I say?'

7

'Jonas, will you lend me fifty pounds, please?'

'I will, Otto, if you can give me a word. I'm still struggling for something better than *affair*. As in illicit fucking.'

'This is for your German readership?'

'I have no other.'

'Tändelei?'

'Um. That translates more or less as affair, or dalliance. I want something meatier that still has a chance of getting past the editors.'

'Mauscheleien, then.'

'Too slang'y. like hanky-panky. There isn't anything really, is there? What do you want the money for?'

'I need to return Zarubin's bank draft, and it looks like it's going to take longer than I thought.'

'Why not leave it with me? He'll come looking for it eventually. Then I could get your hundred smackers from him, deduct my fifty and send on the rest.'

'Smackers?'

'More slang.'

'Boris Levin's already offered to give me the hundred and return the draft himself, but I don't want to involve him more than necessary. Or you. And I have a mind to hear from the object itself why I'm being jerked on strings - again.'

'You promise you won't agree to whatever it is he wants?'

'Willingly. Heartily, even.'

'Alright, then. We'll go to my bank now. And you can buy me a pint with your new wealth.'

Inevitably, the recompense was poured in *The Flowers*, where several barstools now retained perfect profiles of the Kleiber fundament. It was almost last orders for the afternoon session, so he ordered two pints for each of them, and, with a hand, referred the barmaid to Fischer. Usually, he would have settled himself where he could best appreciate her in motion, but today he led his friend to a corner table, well away from interested ears.

Fischer had intervened swiftly to halve his own order, but even a solitary pint threatened to cloud thoughts he would have preferred to flow like a mountain stream. The priest had asked for Zarubin by name, which meant, presumably, that it had been offered previously to someone in or associated with the Orthodox church. That was surprising. Members of the Russian Communion abroad were routinely spied upon by KGB personnel assigned to Soviet embassies, while their domestic colleagues were usually made to spy for KGB as a condition of being allowed to travel overseas. It was hardly likely that a former General in the organization could keep his secret from the London congregation if they knew his real name, so why hadn't he played to form and adopted a pseudonym? Was it likely they'd trust him a centimetre, once his identity and record was known?

Was that why the priest had been in a milk-souring mood? Had he and his colleagues discovered who they had welcomed into their congregation, and was he conveying instructions as to where their new parishioner could go next? That possibility provided the neatest, quickest exit for one Otto Fischer, so the pessimist dismissed it immediately. It was just as likely that one or more consequences of yet another tortuous game were making themselves felt, and the priest – like so many before him – was coming to terms with the flypaper to which he had attached himself. Or even that the man's *mood* had been something else entirely – not anger but anxiety, or trepidation, or concern for ...

'... keep your ears warm.'

'Sorry?'

Kleiber's pint halted halfway to his lips. 'The tits on the new barmaid. I said they could ...'

'Listen, Jonas, this might sound mad, but I'm worried about Zarubin.'

'You needn't be. Bankers' drafts can't bounce. Unlike those tits ...'

'No, I mean *for* him.'

'Why? He's a lizard, a greasy sod, a triple-dealing swindler, a ...'

'He is, but until now I've always managed to catch at least a glimpse of what he might be about. My head must be entirely full of wool, because I'm – buggered, is it? - buggered if I can see why he's doing this. Which makes me think he might not be.'

'Eh?'

'What if he isn't avoiding me?'

'You think he's in trouble?'

'I don't know what to think, it's just too strange to see. *And* he's found God, apparently.'

'Sounds more like a nervous breakdown. He might be hiding in a hole somewhere, gibbering.'

'It isn't unknown for someone who's come through great changes to point himself in new directions, but Zarubin? I can't see prayer being the answer to any sort of question he'd have. Which leaves …'

'What?'

'I don't know. I started the sentence to encourage something to occur, but it hasn't.' Fischer drained his glass and looked around, resisting the urge to survey the new barmaid's alleged bounty. 'How do I get to Ennismore Gardens from here?'

'I'll show you – it's only five minutes away. Wait 'til I finish this.'

Kleiber's second pint was despatched with speed, and he punctuated its passing with a loud belch. Two young ladies at the next table turned and frowned. Fischer sighed.

'You're becoming very *English*, Jonas.'

'Thank you, Otto. Come on.'

They made a small detour to allow Kleiber to purchase cigarettes and the *Manchester Guardian*, but within eight minutes they stood outside the handsome facade of the Church of the Dormition of the Mother of God and All the Saints, a dedication that caused the younger man some amusement.

'Covering their bets, are they?'

'You can go now. I'll see you later.'

'At least it doesn't have a big onion on its roof, like the one in Chiswick.'

'Jonas, go.'

'You don't want me to hang around and be the muscle?'

Amused, Fischer gave his friend a quick up-and-down. An English diet and lifestyle had worked a little magic over the past half-decade, but even now Kleiber wouldn't look fleshed-out in a tuberculosis ward.

'I think I'll be alright, thank you.'

Inside, Fischer paused for a few moments to allow his eyes to adjust to the ambient light. No service was being held, and the pews contained fewer than a dozen people, all of them making private supplications. From a side door at the eastern end of the church a priest emerged and carried something to the altar. Fischer moved as quickly as wouldn't seem disrespectful to intercept him before he could withdraw, but then the thought occurred that the most sacrosanct spot in the church wasn't the ideal location to interrogate a cleric. He slowed at the crossing, and was rethinking his approach when the priest was joined by a colleague carrying a shallow box of candles, which complicated the task considerably. While he pondered his advance, retreat or flanking manoeuvre a couple of elderly ladies looked up from their devotions and peered suspiciously at him. Their pinched faces stirred a memory - of his childhood attendances at his village's Moravian Church; of the feckless local wastrel, Ulrich Grabow, waiting for their minister at the entrance to the Preparation Room, hoping to tap God for beer money at the end of the service. Fischer adjusted his course, took up a blocking position at the door from which the priests had emerged, folded his hands and waited. Gratifyingly, the two provisional glares that had followed him there strengthened considerably, and a third old lady shook her head with unchristian emphasis.

After some minutes, the priests bowed to the altar, turned and retraced their path to the Sacristy. Fischer smiled and stepped out of their way but caught the door before it closed behind them. The younger man turned and lifted a hand.

'You're not allowed …'

The words were English, the accent heavily French. Fischer smiled.

'I'm sorry to trouble you, Father. I'm trying to find one of your congregation, a man named Zarubin – Sergei Aleks …'

The priest's elder colleague spoke over him, loudly. 'We don't know him. Please leave this room.'

Not being of a pious disposition, Fischer didn't know if it was likely that a member of a Cathedral's large complement would be familiar with every one, or even most, of its regular worshippers. He did, however, retain enough of his *kriminalkommisar*'s nose to sense when a question was being stifled before a lie became too obvious. In any case, the other priest's reaction was almost a confession –

surprise, shock, sudden reddening and the half-opened-and-then-clamped-shut mouth reflex – which Fischer affected not to notice.

'Of course. Forgive me.'

Outside the Cathedral, several benches stood against its northern flank, facing into the garden square. Fischer sat down on the first of them, resting his legs and putting his out-of-practise mind to work. The force of the rebuff had been unexpected but encouraging, and he took it to mean one of two things. He was a stranger, asking questions of men who had probably been told to be wary. Their flock was composed substantially of émigrés, some of whom, even now, remained of interest to the revolutionaries they had fled half a century earlier. Lying to protect a parishioner from a potential threat was sensible and even laudable, but didn't explain the brusqueness (which almost begged to be noticed). Was it then a specific, involuntary reaction, to the name Zarubin? If so, it strengthened his suspicion that his KGB past had become known, and that they had shunned him as they might a leper.

No, not a leper, Priests gave succour to lepers, didn't they? A nasty, ambulant rash, then - Zarubin the infection, a pretend, born-again sinner, come to London on State business but recognized and ejected. To where, though? Fischer scratched an itch on the damaged area of his scalp that the sun was goading. If the man was no longer welcome here, why wasn't he visible anywhere else in his known habitat?

Perhaps a posse of local clergy had panicked, hit him with a spade and buried him among the flowerbeds that surrounded their cathedral. It was hardly likely, particularly as one of their number had turned up subsequently at his lodgings and made a scene - a clever enough deflection in theory, but inevitably, it would draw attention to where it wasn't wanted. From whichever direction he came at it, he couldn't convince himself that Zarubin was hiding from the Orthodox Church, so ...

Another possibility: he might have sought sanctuary, in which case the Chapter might be protecting him against some threat, and by following the trail here and asking questions, Fischer had only confirmed their fears. He could hardly go back inside and make another attempt, try to convince them that he was a friend, not an ill-wisher blown in from the East. Hell, he didn't *look* innocent, so why should they believe him?

He was pondering the employment of Jonas Kleiber as a (probably inept but undoubtedly handy) surrogate when he felt a presence by his left shoulder. It was the blushing priest, the silent but helpful young man. He paused, looked down, opened his mouth once more, thought better of it and then strode off at a healthy pace towards the corner of the Gardens that led to Ennismore Street. Fischer gave himself enough time to ensure that no-one had witnessed the encounter and then followed.

He found him leaning against the wall at the corner of Rutland Mews, trying to light a cigarette. When it had caught he dropped the match and drew in deeply; his cassock, lying snugly against his angled body, gave little hint of a chest, much less one that had expanded to accommodate the smoke. He was a tent-pole loaded with too much canvas, as if appetite was one of the earthly indulgences he'd abandoned for the calling.

He turned as Fischer approached, pushed himself upright and nodded warily.

'Karpenko, Artem.'

'Fischer.'

'Who are you?'

A French accent, attached to a Ukrainian name – probably a second-generation exile, a son of aristocracy, or a mercantile dynasty, or just people with the wrong views on what should have succeeded the Romanovs.

'An acquaintance of the man I asked about. The one that your colleague doesn't know.'

'He knows. Everyone in the chapter knows or knows *of* General Zarubin.'

'How was he discovered?'

'What do you mean?'

'His rank. His past.'

'He admitted it, freely. He asked for an interview with the Archpriest, requested that he be allowed to join our congregation and offered a full – a damningly full – account of his career with KGB. He wanted to know whether atheism and abetting the persecution of Christians could be forgiven, in the next life if not this one.'

'And was he reassured on that point?'

'Of course, if he was sincerely regretful. But then, we all wondered why would he have confessed to such damaging things if he wasn't.'

'When did this damascene moment occur?'

'I couldn't say. He came to us a few weeks ago. He stayed for Divine Liturgy on the first day, and then attended at least twice a week, until …'

'Yes?'

Karpenko took another deep drag and surveyed the view to either side. 'Until everyone took care to forget about him.'

'Which was …?'

'Five days ago. We were summoned by the Archpriest and told that Sergei Aleksandrovich Zarubin was a matter not to be discussed, ever. That, if asked, we should deny any knowledge of the man.'

'Did he tell you why this should be?'

'He didn't need to. By then, we'd all heard the terrible news. A few of us were curious as to why we shouldn't go to the police with what we knew; but then, we thought about KGB and their undying interest in the exiled Church, and how silence has always been our best defence, so …'

'Why should the police be involved?'

Father Artem looked at Fischer, searching for reassurance in a stranger's ruined features; perhaps asking himself if it were likely that KGB or GRU would employ a face that could hardly be forgotten or misdescribed. Or perhaps the same ruin was evoking pity, which tended to smooth the sharper edges of anxiety. Either way, a war's terrible luck seemed to be paying out a small peace dividend once more. The hand dropped the cigarette and addressed itself to the air between the two men.

'General Zarubin made a friend among our congregation. And then murdered him.'

'His name was Stanislav Kudrin, a parishioner for many years. I didn't know him well – I've been in England only eighteen months – but his reputation was high. He fought under Yudenich when the Whites almost took Petrograd, and afterwards under Denikin in the south. When the Bolsheviks won he went into exile, first in Paris and then England. After more than forty years he was a patriot still. He never doubted that the communists would get kicked out, eventually.'

'Strange that he should make a friend of a former KGB man, one who had worked his way up into the Kremlin itself.'

If you *are* acquainted with Zarubin you know how disarming he can be. In any case, they had a prior connection of sorts.'

'How …?'

'Kudrin knew his father – at least, they met on several occasions, when the Mensheviks were fighting alongside the Whites on the Southern Front.'

'A remarkable coincidence.'

'I was told not. Apparently, there were many strange alliances during those months, as the Fronts shifted like sands. I understand that the elder Zarubin, being both a former aristocrat *and* a socialist, was involved in a great number of negotiations to bring together coalitions that might turn the war. But then the Reds captured him, and …'

'I know. A bullet to the back of the head.'

'Perhaps their history made Kudrin think too sentimentally of the son. I understand that he offered him accommodation for a while, and some money. He was a very generous man – he gave funds to the Eparchy to help build our Cathedral.'

'He was rich?'

'Apparently, yes. When my brethren speak of his donation I get the sense that they're using an upper-case D.'

'What was his business?'

The priest looked blankly at Fischer. 'I don't know, something important. I'm told that he was a personal friend of de Gaulle's, though I don't know if it's true. Priests are great gossips, and don't like to understate things.'

'It seems despicably ungrateful, to murder a man who's been such a good support.'

'You think Zarubin didn't do it?'

'I don't know enough to form an opinion. It seems out of character, but he's a man who hides a great deal, even from his …'

'Friends?'

'I doubt he regards anyone as such. I've known him for almost twenty years, and in that time he's been responsible for the death of only one man, a monster, and even that was a betrayal rather than a hands-on execution. My feeling is that he would regard the deed as demeaning.'

'Perhaps it was an act of desperation, or momentary passion.'

'Possibly. How was Mr Kudrin murdered?'

'By strangulation, according to the newspapers.'

'A very physical method.'

'Zarubin was strong enough to choke an old man, surely?'

'No, I meant that it's an extraordinarily intimate way to murder someone – literally, *hands-on*. How certain is it?'

'The building porter told the police that a well-presented man with very blonde hair visited Kudrin's flat on the afternoon of the crime, and left several minutes later. He also claimed that there were no other visitors that day. I don't know what else he said.'

Fischer tried and failed to decide what he thought about this. He couldn't see Zarubin as a murderer, but then he couldn't quite see him as anything else, either. Everything the man appeared to be was a conscious construct, an artful moulding that said only what the artist wanted said. Without more information, it wasn't clear what quantity of trouble might fall upon anyone trying to unearth the truth. Which, of course, was an excellent incentive to allow the police to do their work untroubled by an amateur.

The young priest was watching him carefully. 'Do you think we should have told the authorities what we knew?'

'*You* seem to think so. Otherwise you wouldn't have spoken to me.'

That earned a *moue* and a gallic half-shrug. 'A murder isn't a little thing. We – the Church - should have done something more than nothing at all.'

'Well, you have. I was a policeman once, a long time ago and a great distance from here.'

For the first time in their brief acquaintance, Father Artem smiled. 'Then I must congratulate myself. I've eased the burden on my conscience without putting it anywhere near harm.'

'Was it you who tried to speak with Zarubin?'

'What?'

'This morning. A priest visited the business premises below his flat, and asked for him.'

'I'm sorry. I know nothing about that.'

Fischer thanked him, shook hands and walked away, southwards along Rutland Mews. He had awoken this morning in a state of irritable confusion, and what he had learned since had added to it ten-fold. Zarubin the disappearing act was now the least of his worries. If the man stayed disappeared there would be few consequences for Otto Henry Fischer, other than the hole in his pocket that he'd expected to be filled. *Finding* Zarubin, in contrast, might well put the finder squarely in the sights of the Metropolitan Police Force. His conscience was clear, but that hardly mattered. The alleged perpetrator had a talent for dragging hapless bodies into a tainting, decaying orbit, and Fischer had crashed too many times to hope that the mere fact of his own innocence might cushion the next landing.

9

'Jonas.'

'Mm?'

'Stanislav Kudrin.'

Kleiber looked up from the small pile of English newspaper clippings he was sorting into various degrees of potential interest to his German readership, and squinted at Mondrian Over the Mantelpiece.

'Um, old fellow, a Russian émigré. Discovered dead a few days ago, in his home. He wears his neck-ties much too tightly, apparently.'

'What have the police said about suspects?'

'Nothing yet, other than they're following leads. There's a witness to some part of it, but they won't release a name.'

'Where's the scene of the crime?'

'Kensington Gore, the east side, just next to the Albert Hall. You know where that is, I expect?'

'Know? Seeing Malcolm Sargent conducting Mozart, Schubert and Brahms there last August was one of the great moments of my life.'

'I'm sure those words mean something, Otto. I just haven't a clue what.'

'I bought a ticket for you that evening. You went to *The Flowers* instead. Sometimes I'm not convinced that you *are* German.'

'Why is this poor old sod of interest to you anyway?'

'One of the police leads is almost certainly pointing in Zarubin's direction.'

'Oh, fuck.' Kleiber closed his eyes and rubbed his forehead. 'I *knew* I should have stuffed a hundred quid into your pocket and carried you to King's Cross. Whether he was involved or not, it isn't your business. You can't investigate and you can't pass unnoticed. If you start asking questions the police will have a dual-carriageway of a trail to follow.'

'When did it happen? The murder?'

A long, deep sigh accompanied a brief scramble though the newspaper clippings. Kleiber lifted one of them and scanned it.

'The fourteenth, sometime between midday and six pm, they think.'

'And the package from Zarubin. When did you get it?'

'About then.'

'No, *exactly* when?'

'Christ! It was … the day I took Maisie to Liverpool Street. She was off to see her parents for the weekend. The thing was on the floor behind the front door when I returned. That was a Friday, so …' Kleiber glanced at his desk calendar; '… the fifteenth.'

'Do you have the outer envelope still? The one you showed to me?'

'I suppose so.' A brief rummage through two drawers unearthed the object. Fischer examined it.

'It's addressed to you but not franked. He must have delivered it himself.'

'Why would he do that?'

'To save time, I assume So, you didn't do anything about it for … what, three days after that?'

'I was busy. And his note didn't suggest that it was desperately urgent, did it? He gave me the option of doing what he asked or returning the inner envelope to him unopened.'

'And yet he didn't provide a return address. You were supposed to meet on neutral ground – the cafe or the library, yes?'

'That's … right.' Kleiber frowned. 'It was very hopeful of him, given what he must have known you've told me about your past dealings.'

'Not really. He was confident that you'd do what he asked, one way or another. He must have been watching you, because he knew about your new car. Perhaps he assumed you'd take any chance to open her up on an an English autobahn – what there is of one. Still, this is all very strange.'

'Which bit of *all*?'

'He'd just killed a man – allegedly – and the next day he took the trouble to hand-deliver a package intended to entice me south to do some work for him. For at least two days after that, he continued to visit the London Library and have his lunch in Crown Passage, to be seen about town even as the police hunt a murderer for whom they have at least a physical description. And *then* he disappeared, before he had an opportunity to tell me why I'm in London.'

'All excellent reasons to become less, not more, interested in what he's up to. Take the hint, Otto.'

'You're right, obviously.'

'I don't care for that *obviously* - it has the odour of *but*. How many times has this man led or pushed you into the proverbial?'

'I'd need to borrow more fingers.'

'Exactly. And you told me you were done with all that. Listen to your own excellent judgement.'

Fischer couldn't quite place what was giving him pause. Everything Kleiber had said about his relationship with Zarubin was forensically accurate. Since their first encounter in the rubble of Stettin, through the Berlin Blockade, the '53 Rising, the years of the *Wirtschaftswunder* (whose *wunder* hadn't quite stretched as far as *Fischer's Time-piece Repairs*, Curtius-Strasse 23, Lichterfelde), a pleasant but aborted retirement in northern Portugal and then an enforced British exile, most of the turds in the Fischer firmament had been provided by or by reason of Lieutenant, Major and, eventually,

General Zarubin. And now it seemed that their civilian iteration had bagged and delivered a fresh batch.

But. Zarubin always had reasons for his games, yet this one couldn't be guessed at. Its logic, purpose, rules and structure were not so much opaque as missing in action, much like the player himself. If he had killed the generous, welcoming Mr Kudrin, what had been his motive? If he hadn't, why flee (and in doing so more or less confirm his guilt in the minds of the local Russian Orthodox Church and Metropolitan Police Force)? And why had he attempted to recruit his long-term kicking fool for a task that he was doing his absolute best not to put into motion or even explain? Obtuse though it was even to deploy the word with respect to Zarubin's Gordian world, this wasn't *usual*.

Kleiber was pretending to sort his clippings still, but the air between the two men might have been charged directly from the St Pancras sub-station. There remained an easy, broad, well-paved way out of this. He had come south to hear a proposal, ostensibly with an open mind (and ironically, if Zarubin *had* appeared and presented it, his intended recruit would already be back in North Yorkshire, a hundred pounds wealthier and with a conscience as clear as a moorland stream). The fact that he remained ignorant of what this proposal entailed was in no way his fault. He had done his best to locate the elusive article, even to the point of blundering into a situation that, had he known of it previously, would have kept him as far from London as this little island permitted. Now, having been made aware of the consequences of poor Mr Kudrin's association with Zarubin, he had an unarguable reason for allowing himself to be put over his young friend's shoulder and carried to King's Cross Station. With luck and a quick telephone call to Mrs Braithwaite's friend Margery, there might yet be an excellent steak and kidney pie for that evening's supper and nothing more to fret about than whether Farmer Ramsbottom's stone merchant had stepped up to the crease.

But.

'You're still playing with *but*, aren't you?

'I'm searching for some sense in what's inexplicable.'

'An effort that makes trying to knit fog seem worthwhile. Go home, Otto.'

'I will, Jonas.'

'But not yet.'

'Your spare bed is very comfortable. I might have just one more conversation with Boris Levin. He was reluctant to tell me something, but this killing changes things. Unless he's as tired of Zarubin's manoeuvres as I've become, he must be worried.'

10

The large armoire was there still, almost blocking access between the shop and back room. The doorbell brought Sandrine from behind it; she nodded once and reversed like a hermit crab, a hollow thud flagging her failure to avoid the impediment as she withdrew. Several moments later the proprietor emerged, pushing his stick ahead of him so as not to repeat her vandalism.

'You've not gone home, Herr Fischer.'

Fischer couldn't swear to it, but Levin seemed somewhat short of delighted by that prospect. He was also considerably less presentable than he had been two days earlier. The smart suit and tie were elsewhere, and his shirt lacked a collar; its sleeves were rolled up unevenly, one of his braces hung by his side as if he had been caught half dressed or undressed (Fischer had to suppress an ugly mental image of employer and sole employee entertaining themselves between customers) and he appeared not to have shaved that morning.

'Nor has your largest item. Wasn't it supposed to be in Paris by now?'

Sadly, Levin regarded the armoire. 'I'm afraid the gentleman from the 5th was wasting my time. He called on the morning I last saw you to tell me that the piece wasn't what he'd been expecting, which was nonsense, because he almost kissed the thing on his first visit. Perhaps one of his own customers had withdrawn in the meantime, I don't know.'

'You must be disappointed.'

'It would have been one of my best sales to date. Never mind. Would you like a cup of tea?'

'That would be nice.'

Levin beckoned and shuffled behind the unsold item. Fischer followed him into a spartanly-furnished office and sitting area (the latter occupied by a solitary armchair, which in turn had occupied hurriedly by Sandrine). A small desk – heavily marked by evidence of hot cups placed directly upon its once-varnished surface - held a typewriter, a notepad, a mug half-filled with an assortment of pencils, ball-pens and plastic drinks-stirrers, what was probably a day-ledger in a cheap, marble-effect binder, and a tea-caddy. Underneath a stand-chair, next to the only visible wall-socket, an electric kettle kept company with two further, tannin-stained mugs. The whole was one doorway and half a world away from the elegant fittings of the shop, a contrast that reminded Fischer very much of his own, now-atomized home and business premises in Lichterfelde.

Levin stooped carefully, lifted the kettle and carried it through another doorway into a tiny utility area. Fischer felt a surge of pity for the man. The ravages of childhood polio had kept him from the fighting war on the Eastern Front, but a series of posts serving the Red Army's General Staff establishment must have polished the fastidious, detail-poring temperament that had caught Zarubin's attention and wafted them both into the Kremlin thereafter. If Fischer sometimes felt the pain of his own dislocations, he could only imagine that of Boris Levin's translation from Communism's Elysian Fields to not-so Merry England.

Two lives, gifted by the same man, whereabouts unknown but whose presence filled this room. The kettle, watched, was slow to boil, putting off the moment when the matter could be raised once more, and in the meantime his unwelcome guest could almost feel Sandrine's eyes boring into his visible wounds. He half-turned, offered a smile and got nothing in return. He kept it in place, in the hope of irritating her sufficiently to drive her back into the shop.

The strategy hadn't succeeded by the time that Levin returned, without the kettle but bearing a teapot. He filled a mug and handed it to his unwanted guest.

'Aren't you having some?'

'Herr Fischer, I could be floated on the amount of tea I drink during my working day. Our lavatory is upstairs, two flights, so I'm trying to be sensible.'

The tea – black, unsweetened - was better than expected, and Fischer took several sips before coming to the point. Levin waited, apparently patiently, using the time to adjust his errant braces.

'Tell me …' Fischer cleared his throat of a stray tea leaf and continued, '… about God.'

'Not required KGB reading, I'm afraid.'

'I mean personal faith. General Zarubin's, for example.'

'You've heard, then?'

'From the experts, so to speak. I visited his Cathedral.'

Levin pulled a mildly disapproving face. 'I was surprised when he first mentioned it, but it seems a sincere change of heart.'

'Of temperament, I would have said. You worked with him for years; was there ever any hint of a higher calling?'

He used the Lord's name only as an epithet.'

'Perhaps his exile has encouraged reflection.'

That earned a sniff. 'He spent three years in America at the turn of the 'fifties. I would have thought that the land of the self-consciously Godly would have uncovered any latent piety in him. It certainly did in his former boss.'

'Colonel Shpak? He became an Amish, didn't he?'

'Mennonite. It's almost the same. The thing is, Zarubin didn't. He tried the life of a male escort instead, and then worked for the CIA. I can't think that two years in London has managed to wreak what three in the US couldn't.'

'Age mellows, Mr Levin. Some of us begin to consider the nature of eternity.'

'He's a young man still. Have *you* become spiritual, Herr Fischer?'

'No, but my agnosticism is intact, so there's hope yet. Did this apparent revelation bring any noticeable change in his behaviour?'

It's hard to say. I saw less of him for a while. He made a new friend, an elderly fellow-worshipper who offered him a room rent-free. I suspected the worst, of course, but apparently the gentleman has no unchristian intentions.'

Has? 'Do you have a name?'

'No. The General has mentioned him only twice so far, the second time when he moved out of the gentleman's apartment to new lodgings in Bishopsgate. I think he's embarrassed to have fallen upon the charity of others.'

'You don't know, then?'

'Of what?'

'The old man is dead, murdered, quite brutally. And I believe that our mutual friend is a strong suspect, though the police haven't yet named him.'

Fischer's instincts told him that Levin's shock was unrehearsed. Mouth half-open, he clutched at the edge of his desk and lowered himself slowly into the stand-chair. The room, Sandrine and Fischer were blinked at in turn, the eyes settling on nothing for more time than it took to find the next unseen object. He tried to speak twice but found nothing more than a grunt of pain or incomprehension, so for a while after that he waited for some thought to occur.

Sandrine seemed uninterested, or perhaps oblivious. The two men had been conversing in German (Levin was fluent, while Fischer's Russian was execrable and English was a language-in-progress for both of them), and her wartime flight to England had probably saved her from needing to understand the conquerors' tongue. Her attention had flickered momentarily when Zarubin's name was first mentioned, but since then she had subsided into a semi-torpor (a state that carried her through the shop's slow days, probably).

After several minutes, Levin looked up. 'It's … unlikely.'

Fischer shrugged. 'So is finding God, yet he seems to have done that. We may have underestimated his taste for novelty.'

'How did the old man die?'

'His name was Kudrin, I was told he was strangled.'

'Well, then. It could hardly have been done by a man who's always done his best to avoid physical contact with others.'

'That was my first thought, but desperation breeds desperate acts, and a sufficient motive can bring out the best or worst in any man.

Consider the timing. You said that he'd needed the charity of his host, yet a matter of hours after the poor bastard's death our friend was able to arrange a banker's draft for five hundred pounds to entice me to London. *That* goes a long way towards wiping any other names off the suspect list.'

'He might have asked his friend for a loan. It's at least possible.'

'Of course it is, and the police will do their best to dismiss it. The thing is, Zarubin disappeared. To the minds of even the best investigators, you don't do that if you're innocent of the crime. *And* he was seen visiting the victim at some point on the day of the murder. No-one else was, though we can't ignore the possibility that the building's porter turned his back or had to drop his trousers at some point during his shift. Even so, when a hare breaks cover the dogs' attention tends to be upon just the one thing.'

'What can we do?'

'An excellent question. It would be very useful for you to tell me what you wouldn't say when I last visited.'

'I …' Levin thought about it for a few moments, sighed and looked pointedly at Sandrine. She pouted, pushed herself out of the armchair, lumbered into the shop and took a sentry position at the window, flanked by a pair of Kronilov vases on low pedestals. The proprietor waited until she was as distant as the premises permitted and then turned to Fischer.

'I really don't know why he asked you to London. He came here most recently a few days ago, and it was obvious that something had changed.'

'In what way changed?'

Levin grimaced. 'For quite some time now he's been … subdued. I think he found it hard to accept that he wasn't useful to SIS. It's not that he particularly wants to be a traitor to his own, more the hurt it did to his high opinion of himself. The money thing hasn't helped with that. What little the British gave him had gone by the end of last year, by which time the funds he'd gifted to me had been invested in this business, otherwise I would have forced them upon him. At one point he left most of his personal effects here and had a bed at the YMCA hostel in Crouch End, which must have been humiliating.'

'You couldn't offer him accommodation?'

Levin looked up at the ceiling. 'My own bed is in the storeroom upstairs, which is against the terms of my lease. I take a shower three times a week at a bath-house in Long Acre. Until business improves I can't afford a shop *and* a home.'

'I didn't know anything of this. A man of his peculiar talents - I'd always assumed he could transmute dirt into truffles.'

'In his own element he might, but this is alien territory. He has no spies here, no intelligence that can be bought or buried for a price, no allies with resources …'

'Until Mr Kudrin appeared.'

'A God-send, literally.' Levin smiled sadly. 'When the General told me that he had found spiritual comfort, my first assumption was that the Cathedral had a soup-kitchen, or priests with open pockets. But it seems that he persisted with his devotions, and when he was introduced to this poor man his situation changed markedly.'

'How did the Bishopgate flat come about?'

The gentleman had an acquaintance, a businessman with premises in the east of the City who was looking for a tenant. I don't know what financial arrangements were made, but ...'

'He *must* have accepted money from Kudrin.'

'He admitted to me that he was indebted to the man. I assumed he was speaking literally.'

'So that solved the matter of a roof. What put him onto his subsequent scholarly lifestyle?'

'I … don't know.'

'I think you know something.'

'I *suspect* something.'

'What?'

Levin examined the dregs in his teacup, as if seeking the consequences of what he was going to say. The message appeared to be inconclusive; he rubbed his eyes with the back of a hand and deflated slightly.

'While Zarubin was a guest of YMCA he had his post directed to me. He would telephone from Crouch End, have me summarize the contents of whatever arrived and decide whether it was worth a trip to Central London to retrieve it. As you may imagine, there was nothing worth spending a tube fare upon, so I threw it away daily. The arrangement stopped after he found his new friend, moved to South Kensington and then Bishopsgate, but one further piece of correspondence was directed here. We hadn't seen or spoken to each other for several days, and he had no telephone at his new address, so I opened it.'

'Why? If nothing else that had arrived for him was important, couldn't it have waited?'

'That would have been my assumption, but the postmark … it was from Munich.'

'Who does he know there?'

'E.N. Artsyuk, for one. The gentleman addressed himself to Sergei Aleksandrovich, so they must be more than casual acquaintances.'

'And the matter?'

'Opaque, which worried me. One doesn't dance around a subject unless it's allergic to full daylight. He expressed gratitude for the General's interest in his work, invited him to Munich as soon as might be convenient but cautioned that he was often called away at short or no notice on a business he was certain didn't need to be spoken of. That being the case, he suggested that Zarubin contact him through 'K', who knew the people he dealt with.'

'Kudrin?'

Levin shrugged. 'Possibly.'

'I was told that he was often abroad, on unspecified business.'

'Probably, then. I'm worried, Herr Fischer.'

'Because of his death?'

'That, yes. And the fact that this Artsyuk may be a part of the problem.'

'You know him?'

'I know the name. It isn't a common one, though I'm sure there must be several in a country as populous as mine. The particular E. N. Artsyuk I'm aware of has a substantial file in the Lubyanka.'

'KGB don't like him?'

'They've watched him, intermittently, for at least fifteen years. His name appeared sometimes in status reports on overseas operations. General Zarubin was on the circulation lists, of course, and I routinely read what was sent to him.'

'Is Artsyuk a foreign agent?'

'Not that I know of, though I'm sure he'd welcome assistance in his endeavours from any source that volunteers itself. His particular field of interest is how the overthrow of the Soviet Regime may be effected.'

'As you'll imagine, there are plenty of Russian émigrés who yearn for the same thing.
Over the decades since the Civil War ended, groups of them have coalesced into organizations of varying degrees of unrealistic ambition. A few of them are faintly admirable - the Solidarists, for example, whom one might almost regard as liberal-democrats. They reject class hatred in whatever direction it travels and want a Russian society based upon tolerance of other points of view. They claim that they're willing to accept almost any political system that's not coercive and has first been authorized by a popular plebiscite.'

'They sound too good to be of this world.'

'Yes, don't they? Then, there's the Russian All-Military Union, who are – I should say *were* – dedicated to more practical means of removing the Bolsheviks. They and the Russian Imperial Union Order are the ragged descendants of the White Army, and can be distinguished from each other only by the relative strength of their monarchism. Both twisted themselves inside out during the Great Patriotic War on the question of whether that should ally with the Nazis or stand aside from the whole mess. In fact, many individuals from both factions took the decision into their own hands and served with the Wehrmacht. I needn't tell you what happened to them when they were caught. Both organizations still exist on paper, though most of their leaders have retired or been assassinated by KGB. I could also mention the *Evraziitzi*, or Eurasianists: exceptionalists who believe in Russian evolution, not revolution; the *Smenovekhovtsy*, who appear to be so pro-Soviet one wonders why they exist at all; and, most absurd of all, the *Mladorossi*, who could never decide whether they were Monarchists or Mensheviks, who adopted the Mussolini salute because it looked good and who finally joined the French Resistance for want of a coin to flip. They're long-gone, having been sold out to KGB by their own leader, Kazembek. Finally, there's the Russian All National Popular State Movement.'

'A clumsy name.'

'Not catchy, is it? Commonly, its Russian equivalent is abbreviated to RONDD. The organization differs from its fellow-travellers, and is more dangerous.'

'They have an actual plan?'

'You're being snide, Herr Fischer, but yes. RONDD have been trying for some years to reunite various émigré factions into an effective umbrella organization – theirs, obviously – and to that end are extremely industrious publishers of pamphlets, magazines and other instruments of political propaganda. They may be characterized as occasional monarchists, but more particularly as fascists.'

'The Soviets accuse everyone to the right of themselves of the same vice.'

'Yes, but in RONDD's case the epithet is quite accurate. They are based in your Federal Republic, and are in close, fraternal contact with a number of secretive German bodies that hold a degree of affection for their own good old days.'

'Pleasant people.'

'No, but quite committed. Their founder and leader is one E.N. Artsyuk. If, in addition to the minor matter of an alleged murder, our friend General Zarubin is involved with this man, I fear that nothing less than disaster can come of it.'

'Can the man be that dangerous? Even if his organization is a little more competent than the others, it's hardly …'

'It isn't what his organization is – it's what the *man* is.'

'What? A sadist? A butcher?'

'Worse than either, Herr Fischer. Like Kazembek, betrayer of the *Mladorossi*, he plays a double game. He dedicates himself to the ending of the Soviet regime, yet also obliges KGB with occasional intelligence regarding his own people. Of course, it's the nature of such arrangements that no-one can ever know exactly what motivates the man. It may be that he does it only to keep KGB off his back, and that his gifts to them are threadbare. Equally, he may indeed be another Kazembek, in which case there may already be a spot on a Lubyanka mantelpiece reserved for the General's head'

'But … surely, Zarubin's aware of this fellow's treachery already? From *his* Kremlin days?'

Levin blushed to the roots of his few remaining scalp hairs. 'The KGB situation reports could be interesting, sometimes. Most of the time, not so much. The General had me sift what came in and summarize what, in my judgment, he needed to know. His own duties had nothing to do with countermeasures against émigré organizations, so I don't believe I ever felt the need to mention the name.'

'You're not certain?'

The misery was tinged with guilt, as if the model secretary would have anticipated every permutation of future risk. 'Fairly certain, yes. He didn't enjoy being bothered by irrelevances.'

Fischer made an effort to put himself into the mind of Zarubin, and failed. Again, the questions flooded in. Why would the man seek the company of failed counter-revolutionaries, much less a group at the fascist end of that rainbow? Had he been coerced into it by his benefactor Kudrin, or had he seen an opportunity in diving into a rats' nest of self-deluding plots and rivalries? Had he somehow discovered Artsyuk's betrayal of RONDD, or was he wandering blithely into a trap already laid by KGB to catch an entirely different prey? Most importantly, what part had he seen in all of this for someone whose life was now devoted to repairing dry-stone walls and preserving his fingernails?

The practical possibilities were a little easier to tally. Zarubin was missing, so he was either hiding, abducted, dead or had set about his new, mysterious business. If hiding, he should have ensured that he retained some means of contacting his few friends (particularly the one to whom he had offered a large bribe), but there was nothing in the ether beyond static. He had no secrets to barter, no value to exploit and plenty of unexpunged marks against his record; so if someone had abducted him he would be deceased already or on his way to where the job could be carried out semi-judicially. In either case, there was nothing to be done. Otherwise, it seemed likeliest that he was in motion, and as capable of being tracked as a spore in the wind…

'Munich.'

Levin frowned. 'What about it?'

'We know that this Artsyuk's based there, and that he's invited Zarubin.'

'Yes, but I haven't been able to pass on that message.'

'No, but the letter's mode of address and its invitation suggests that Kudrin – if 'K' in the letter *is* our man – may have effected some form of introduction to our mutual friend before he was murdered.'

'Um ... yes, that seems right.'

'*If* Zarubin is the killer, he'll need a friend - preferably one who's distant from the reach of British justice. If he didn't strangle Kudrin, he may still need protection from whoever did, or at least time to gather evidence that exonerates him.'

'These are substantial *ifs*.'

'I know, but what else do we have? Zarubin isn't at his home, or anywhere that he's known to frequent. He hasn't fled north to hide with me in the Dales. He hasn't come to you, the only other person on this island he can trust absolutely. So, what's left? He's dead, snatched and returned to Moscow, or he's elsewhere.'

Levin turned to his desk, opened a drawer, removed an envelope and handed it to Fischer, who glanced at the frank and experienced a brief stab of homesickness. The short note inside was scrawled in Russian. Helplessly, he returned it to Levin for enlightenment.

'It gives an address - Prinzenstrasse 46. Do you know Munich?'

'Hardly at all. I did some training at Oberschleissheim before the war, but I recall visiting town on just one occasion. Needless to say it was dark, and I got as drunk as was expected of me.'

'What are you going to do?'

'As little as possible. I'll go to Munich, enquire after him, and if he condescends to appear I'll return his draft, ask for one hundred pounds plus the expenses I'm about to incur. If I'm in the mood I might ask him if he murdered Kudrin, and, if he did, why. And then I'll bid him a final, definitive farewell.'

'And if you can't find him?'

'I shall be able to reassure myself that no-one, including *WASt*, could have done more.'

'Wast?'

'An organization that traces and identifies Wehrmacht's missing or dead personnel.'

'The Red Army doesn't have one of those.'

'I'm astonished to hear it.'

'You're being snide again, Herr Fischer.'

'Technically, I was being sarcastic. Which no graduate of a military establishment that somehow misplaced five million men has a right to be, of course. I apologize.'

'Well, it's all water under the bridge now.'

'What worries me is that too much of it isn't. And that out friend has decided to cast himself into the torrent.'

12

Fischer felt slightly deflated as the BEA Trident began its descent into Munich-Riem. This was his first ever flight as something other than a target or supercargo, and he had enjoyed almost every moment of it. An English businessman sitting next to him had found a dozen shortcomings in the service and comfort offered during the too-short journey, but complaints about leg-room (Fischer considered it to be magnificently generous), refreshments (perfectly adequate for a two-and-a-half hour trip), punctuality (they had departed West London airport six minutes later than scheduled) and the attitude of cabin crew (less than utterly obsequious, more than adequately helpful) had received neither sympathy nor even acknowledgment, and after a few minutes the injured party had applied himself to his other neighbour.

Unused to being pampered, Fischer thanked a hostess effusively as he exited the fuselage without having to duck or check the location of his rip-cord, and followed his fellow travellers into the Tempelhof-styled terminal. At passport control he presented his old Portuguese passport (SIS's thin generosity hadn't extended to arranging British nationality for him), was congratulated on his fluent German and waved on without any interrogation as to the reason for his presence in the federal Republic. Baggage reclamation – another novelty – was swift, though identifying Kleiber's loaned suitcase (a generic item, in plenty of like company on the carousel) was harder than he'd expected. Less than twenty minutes after landing in his homeland he was at the rear of a queue for a taxi into the city.

He had considered joining the plebian clench at the bus-halt, but a taste of the high life had given him an appetite for more. He reasoned that this was a legitimate expense, and that he was far more likely to glean useful local information from a taxi driver than a bus passenger (who might want to ignore him entirely). It was flimsy, but he was in no mood to economise with Zarubin's money. In any case, the man might be dead, in which unfortunate eventuality the whole five hundred pounds was destined for a bank account in the name of O.H. Fischer (the probability that the money had been the legal property of the definitely deceased S. Kudrin in no way altered that destiny). When he reached the head of the queue, a Mercedes-Benz 190 purred to a halt beside him and removed any lingering doubts regarding his the decision.

The journey into Munich took fifteen minutes, during which time he managed to glean nothing more from his driver than the edited highlights of TSV 1860's brilliant season to date. He was deposited at his hotel, a three-star establishment off Marienplatz (optimistically, he had booked a room for just two nights), where he checked in, deposited his case and stepped out to recce the local terrain. Inevitably, that useful occupation ended at the first café he encountered, a small establishment with an outdoor terrace of just three tables. He took a seat at one of them, ordered a coffee from an elderly waiter and examined the view.

Like most Germans he was familiar with the story of the city's reconstruction, but even so, the view struck him forcibly. In contrast to West Berlin's determined march from rubble into futurity, central Munich had turned her back upon the twentieth century and its brutalities. Blessed by one of the Führer's few rational decisions – to have the streets of the old city photographed in minute detail before the Allies could flatten it – the inheritors of a ruined landscape were able to effect a gargantuan, near-perfect restoration in just fourteen years. Scrutinizing the nearby buildings closely he was able to make out sections of repair-work only because they had yet to acquire the grubby patina that time alone would bring. Like all illusions it bore an inevitable taint of dishonesty (however well-intentioned), but he couldn't disapprove of the principle or its results. To his mind, the world needed very little more concrete than it endured already.

It was pleasant to see it all, to be where he was, waiting for what, undoubtedly, would be his first decent coffee for a great while; but even the sense of enjoyment jarred, and brought him back to his purpose, to what the hell he was going to do next and how the hell he was going to do it.

For years, Zarubin had pulled the strings, but now they lay limply in the marionette's hand. Initiative was good if it came with accurate data, a view that wasn't occluded by fog and at least an ally or two. Without any of those necessary foundations it was at best a step into darkness, and that's where he was now. He knew nothing about E.N. Artsyuk, other than that he had the gift of terrible handwriting and either was or wasn't a fascist or double-agent. Either way, a stranger turning up on his doorstep, unannounced and without references, asking for a former KGB General (whom Artsyuk had met - if at all – only very recently and knew previously only by name and reputation), wasn't going to receive an open-armed welcome and asked if he preferred tea or coffee. The organization he headed was one of Moscow's prime targets, and even if he was content to have it exterminated the presence of Zarubin in his house must complicate things. Certainly, it would light up the nerve-endings of Artsyuk's comrades, should they realise who he was. And, if word of Kudrin's murder had reached Munich by now, they would very probably detonate.

So, what to do? *Good morning, I assume I'm speaking to Mr Artsyuk. Is General Zarubin in, please?* would get him a gun-muzzle in the mouth, or at least a comprehensive slapping from the household help. He had neither time nor resources to watch the premises, hoping to catch Zarubin on the way in or out; he was entirely unfamiliar with Artsyuk's daily routine (or even whether he risked moving outdoors in daylight without a phalanx of body men), so an 'accidental' encounter in the street couldn't be arranged; and if there was an entry for the gentleman (in his real name) in a Munich telephone directory he would almost certainly be dead already. There was only one way to effect an introduction, and that was to put himself entirely at the mercy of the other party.

He drank his (excellent) coffee and a refill and then returned to the hotel. His room was pleasantly furnished, comfortable and large enough to accommodate an armchair and desk. Upon the latter sat several brochures and a pad of headed notepaper. He tore off a sheet, removed Jonas Kleiber's second-best ball-pen from his jacket pocket and committed himself without further pause to ponder the suicidal possibilities.

Dear Sir,

My name is Otto Fischer. I am an acquaintance of General Zarubin, formerly of Party Secretary Khrushchev's personal staff, who, I believe, travelled from London to Munich some days ago in response to an invitation from yourself (my source for this information is Boris Levin, whose name you may know).

It is important that I speak with the General regarding a personal matter, and hope that you will be able to facilitate a meeting, or at least to pass on this message so that he may make his own arrangements. I am in the city, staying at Hotel Alte Freundschaft (room 9) on Sporerstrasse, and will be here for the next two days only, so I would very much appreciate an early response.

I apologise for the inconvenience this may cause, and shall make myself available upon whatever circumstances you regard as most convenient for yourself and the General.

Sincerely,

He placed the note into an envelope and addressed it to Artsyuk, sealed and took it downstairs to reception, where an offer of ten marks to have it delivered immediately (half to be paid upon return) was taken up enthusiastically by a boy wearing the hotel's dark green livery. He departed like a hare, leaving Fischer with an unsettling sense of having committed himself to a high dive into an emptied pool.

He would be obliged to wait for the next few hours at least, so he enquired after a good restaurant nearby. The desk manager recommended three, of which a Greek establishment seized his interest and appetite for purely historical reasons (Hauptman Fischer having invaded Greece, shot several of the locals, almost died in a ditch and yet never managed to sample the cuisine). It was only two hundred metres from the hotel entrance and more than half-empty, even at noon. He took a table near the window, ordered a glass of wine and asked the waiter to recommend a two-course lunch.

The food was excellent, the wine (a Naoussa, entirely unfamiliar to him) extremely drinkable, and the restaurant's copy of that day's *Suddeutsche Zeitung* helped the time pass pleasantly enough. No doubt directed by the duty manager of the Hotel Alte Freundschaft, the lobby boy arrived during the main course to confirm that the message had been delivered (that is, placed in an external post box, the property's walls being high, the gate locked and the bell unheard or ignored) and collect his five marks.

Slightly troubled, Fischer ordered a second glass of wine and did a quick calculation to reassure himself that his funds could stretch to a longer stay in Munich. Why hadn't he considered the possibility – the likelihood, even - that Artsyuk would make himself difficult to reach? A man in his line of work must look over his shoulder constantly, searching for the too-casual glance or choreographed innocence of passing strangers; so why wouldn't his home be as much of a fortress as he could make it? Did he even check his post every day? Was he even in the city at present?

'Was everything alright, *patriótis?*'

An ancient waiter was removing his plate deftly, a dessert menu ready to take its place.

'It was excellent, thank you. The beef …?'

'Stifado.'

'That, especially. And the wine.'

'Good. I'll tell the Boss. Would you like to see …?'

Fischer held up his empty glass. 'Another one of these will do.'

The waiter beamed. 'The best dessert! Have you ever been to Greece?'

'Yes, but not in ideal circumstances.'

'Ah. I fought your lot at Epirus. You?'

'The Corinth Canal. And then Crete.'

'Still, we're all friends now.'

'It's nice that you think so.'

The old man shrugged. 'You Germans were murderous bastards, but afterwards we had the communists. They were murderous, thieving bastards. Was it our boys who did that to you?'

'No, the Soviets.'

'More bastards, but with a proper alphabet at least. The same wine again, or you try something different?'

'The same, please.'

The bottle returned quickly, and it was poured with a knowing wink. 'This is a better year. When we open one, the Boss likes to drink whatever's left. He's going to be disappointed today.'

'Thank you, um …?'

'Denis.'

'Otto.'

Denis nodded and shuffled away, leaving Fischer with a thought that had surfaced almost unnoticed. *A proper alphabet.* He had needed Levin to translate the contents of Artsyuk's letter to Zarubin, and what he'd heard had been almost entirely anodyne. So had it been coded in some way? A melodramatic thought, but someone in fear either of KGB or his own people (it might be both, but it was at least one) would take steps not to make his intentions too obvious. Committing something to paper and then surrendering it to several postal services was not the most secure method of communication. That being manifestly apparent, wouldn't he take steps to misdirect a hostile eye?

So, what if the recipient of the letter was expected to know that *Munich* really meant Frankfurt? That *come and see me* meant *stay away at all costs, I'm being followed*? That *K.* referred rather to an M., or B., or L.?

Christ. If he allowed every possibility to play through his head he'd either put himself on the next 'plane back to the Yorkshire Dales or remain, paralysed at this table, like the proverbial badger in headlights. Of course he could be mistaken. A best guess about anything to do with Zarubin was a ten-sided coin, flipped in half-light. He was doing all that could be done on the basis of almost no hard, reliable information, and if that led him nowhere, well …

He signalled for his bill, which Denis brought on a silver dish in the company of a pistachio-studded biscuit. He ate it without thinking, ruining his palate for what remained of the wine, and left a generous tip. Outside, sunshine warmed his neck as he walked back to the hotel, lifting his mood as far as it was willing to be lifted. Once more, the imp on his shoulder (possibly his vestigial common-sense) did its duty. It reassured him that he could stop this at any time he chose to. He could go home, forget Zarubin, deluded Russian émigrés and anything else not to do with dry stone walls (or food, or music, or the quiet passage of uneventful days), and no-one would ever think any less of him for it. He might even come to think the same, eventually.

At the hotel entrance he paused to give this easy option the space it deserved, an occupation aided considerably by the wine he'd consumed. Whatever he had owed Zarubin had long been repaid with compound interest (not to mention blood, sweat and jail-time). Even a conscience as easily pricked as his own could find no shard of outstanding obligation that required him to press on into this fog. A wise, well-grounded man (call him Other-Otto) would forgive himself for not feeling a weight of guilt he hadn't earned, remove the well-fitting crown of thorns and drop it in the gutter. It was, after all, what he had resolved to do when the prospect of a long English exile became a near certainty, a small moral consolation for having been plucked from his Portuguese *heimat*.

His sense of weightlessness was no less pleasant for being unfamiliar, and he almost floated to the hotel reception to inform the duty manager that he would be leaving the following morning. The news was met with a practised look of regret, a hope that he'd enjoy what was left of his time in Munich and that business or pleasure would bring him back soon. Some glib but obliging reply was forming on his lips when the other man frowned suddenly, flicked his fingers, turned to the rack of pigeon-holes behind him and removed an envelope. For Fischer, gravity returned brutally, and as much as he yearned to back away, to ask that the fucking thing be ripped up and burned, his betraying hand reached out and clasped it.

Weakly, he nodded his thanks and went up to his room. The message was brief, but amiable. Mr Artsyuk was pleased to receive his note and regretted to say that, although General Zarubin was presently staying as a guest at his home, he would be away for the next few hours. In the meantime, Herr Fischer must be entertained. Perhaps tea, at four pm?

One couldn't have hoped for a better welcome from a complete stranger who might also be a fascist or KGB pensioner (or possibly both), and Fischer was acutely disappointed. A cold rebuff, a hardly-veiled threat to mind his own business, a bare-faced declaration of complete ignorance of anyone named Zarubin or the simplest option of no reply - each would have set him on his way, back to the relative safety of High Scar Farm. But a polite invitation kept him exactly where he didn't want to be, waiting for his exposed head to draw fire. He shouldn't have written the note, shouldn't have tested his thin luck …

He sighed. Convincing Kleiber and Levin that he would do only so much and then bail out of this burning aircraft had been necessary to curtail their nagging, but trying to convince himself of the same was an exercise in futility. In any case, having invited the invitation (so to speak), he could hardly ignore it. At least Zarubin seemed to be in the world still, and he was pleased about that, in principle. A conversation with the man would dispel much of the mist, perhaps allow him to gauge how much shit he'd waded into this time. At best, he could find some form of words or a pretence of iron will that would lift him from the ordure, though long experience told him that any easy option was unlikely to advertise itself. A blunt refusal to consider any proposal would have been feasible, had it been delivered several days ago over a cup of coffee in an English sandwich bar, but Zarubin was now a fugitive and keeping company with someone – perhaps a number of someones - who might not be agreeable to a manly handshake and clean farewell.

So much for weightlessness. He rubbed his face, consulted the price-list on the inside door of something labelled a 'mini-bar' and added a whisky to the growing list of expenses he was going to present to the founder of his predicament. He had almost two hours to waste before his appointment and had already memorized the route between his hotel and Prinzenstrasse, so he pulled off his shoes, laid on the bed and pinned his hopes on a well-thumbed copy of *Down and Out in Paris and London* that he had lifted from Kleiber's bookcase. He wasn't going to rehearse his plan because he didn't have one; he wasn't going to consider every possible eventuality because he couldn't conceive where they began and ended; and although a credible, innocent explanation for why he was tracking Zarubin might well be needed at some point later that afternoon, he suspected it would require several more visits to the mini-bar to put flesh on its bones.

Prinzenstrasse was a well-to-do thoroughfare of detached houses, a church and a striking number of medical practices, advertising their services via discreet brass plates. Along its easternmost stretch, trees promenaded down both sides of the road, their upper branches arching over substantial walls and making leafy glades of the pedestrian footpath below. The iron gate to number 46 was two metres high and locked, but a button-pad set between two of its bars hinted that callers weren't necessarily to be shot. Fischer pressed it twice, and stood back.

Through the bars he had an imperfect view of what seemed to be a considerable, turn-of-the-century house, the lower storey of which was almost entirely shielded by cherry trees. Its situation reminded him a little of the property in Lichterfelde that Kleiber had inherited from his former editor, Herr Grabner: an edifice hinting to the passer-by that its owner was a person of substance who either enjoyed the bucolic illusion in a large city or (as had been the case with Grabner) didn't want the inconvenience of company as he drank himself to death. Boris Levin's allegations regarding RONDD also brought to mind the Führer and his afternoon-tea guests, playing out monstrous imitations of bourgeois normality at Berchtesgaden.

He was about to try the bell again when an athletic young man in a black turtle neck sweater and matching slacks (a badge identifying him as The Muscle wouldn't have been more obvious) emerged on the path from between two shrubs and advanced to a blocking position immediately behind the gate, as if its bars weren't doing their job adequately. No smile was offered by way of welcome.

'Your name, please.'

'Otto Fischer.'

The young man grunted, produced a large key, unlocked the gate and stood to one side. Fischer thanked him and stepped in, submitted to a brief, perfunctory frisking and was pointed toward the house. The path turned severely to the right and then corrected itself, ensuring than the front door couldn't be observed from the street.

Waiting in the doorway was an elderly maid in all the trimmings, who gave her guest a minor curtsey and waved him inside. The hallway provided an immaculate first impression – a dark wooden floor (polished to perfection), two marble-topped console tables facing each other beneath gilt mirrors, and, reflected to infinity in each, twin vases half-full of fresh white roses, arranged with the sort of artifice that seems anything but. The visitor was intended to be impressed, and Fischer didn't resist.

He was led into a sitting-room and told that Herr Artsyuk would be with him in a few moments. When the maid disappeared he examined the terrain, a markedly less elegant prospect than the hallway. Piles of leaflets had made themselves comfortable on every flat surface (including the floor), and more substantial newsletters – or perhaps copious copies of the same edition – were similarly stacked in one corner of the room, almost concealing a small bureau. A tall, wide bookcase was a further crash-site for books, papers, pamphlets and several box-files, none of which lay in any discernible order that might have allowed an impulse or enquiry to be satisfied. Only two armchairs and an occasional table, grouped together in the middle of the room, provided a small polynya of neatness, and it was at this haven that the maid aimed a large tea-trolley when she re-entered the room.

Fischer had no idea how long Artsyuk had been a guest of the Bavarian state, but the man seemed to have adopted its afternoon refuelling protocols in their entirety The trolley was laden with *donauwellen* squares, creamy slices of *bienenstich,* slivers of *butterkuchen,* and, lording it over all, a *prinzregententorte* of sufficient proportions to make a platoon costive. Helplessly, he glanced at the maid to enquire how many dozens of fellow guests were expected, but she was already retreating to fetch the liquid element of the bacchanalia.

In the quiet that descended upon the room he heard for the first time a clock, though he couldn't pin its location amid the general disorder. He had assumed that his host, a would-be consolidator of conflicting émigré ambitions (as well as a potential target), needed to keep a punctual schedule, and with this in mind he had timed his journey to Prinzenstrasse precisely. He was about to check his watch when the hidden timepiece chimed the quarter hour and the maid, pushing a second, smaller trolley, returned as the vanguard of a small column.

Its rear was brought up by the young athlete, who was now wearing glasses and peering distractedly at a piece of correspondence. Between the two, a smartly-dressed gentleman of indeterminate age, his hair cropped with almost Prussian brutality, folded his own piece of paper, placed it into a breast pocket and swapped a preoccupied frown for a welcoming smile.

'Herr Fischer? You haven't taken a seat! Please …'

The man whom Fischer took to be E.N. Artsyuk dismissed his colleague with a nod, turned to the larger of the tea-trolleys and rubbed his hands.

'Etiquette allows me to break my strict diet when I have a guest, so thank you for your letter! Ellie, if you would?'

As the maid began to pour tea he sat, reached across to his already-seated visitor and shook hands. 'Artsyuk. Please, call me Evgeny. I see that you're a veteran of our late misunderstanding. I hope one of my compatriots wasn't responsible for the damage?'

To be interrogated on the genesis of his wounds twice in the same day was unusual, but Fischer was grateful that his host had the time and inclination for small talk.

'Yes, but innocently so. The gentleman was in a cockpit, and expired as he showered his blessings upon me. I doubt that he even realised I was between him and the ground.'

Artsyuk pulled a face. 'How absurdly haphazard it all was: every hope, ambition and expectation thrown into a vile game that made flung dice seem like a plan. One of my childhood friends was killed during the operation to retake Rostov by a mere ricochet, and from a Soviet rifle!'

'You seem to have come through it unscathed.'

'Fortunately, I was in exile in Paris long before your Führer made his greatest strategic blunder. May I call you Otto?'

'Please.'

'Here, have some tea. It's Darjeeling, I think. You wrote that you need to see our friend Zarubin as a matter of urgency. May I be curious?'

Fischer had spent most of the journey between his hotel and Prinzenstrasse thinking about how to answer that question. Something trivial wouldn't do, of course, but neither would spilling some great secret, however plausible he might make it, to a man he had just met. *Mind your own business* wasn't likely to get him far either, which seemed to leave only a brush with the truth.

'He wrote to me recently after months of silence, inviting me to London on some unspecified business. When I arrived he wasn't where I expected to find him, and there's been a suggestion of his involvement in some trouble, though I don't know what it is. I'm anxious to find out why he contacted me, and if he needs help.'

'And you decided he was here, in Munich.'

'As I mentioned in my note, I spoke with Boris Levin. Your letter to Zarubin was the only clue we had as to where he might be. You've confirmed that our guess was the correct one.'

'Yes. He arrived a few days ago but had another task to discharge, in Koblenz I think. He should return either this evening or tomorrow.'

'It's a relief to hear it. Would you tell him where I'm staying, so that he can get word …?'

A small plate, holding a heroic portion of *butterkuchen*, almost landed in Fischer's lap. 'Please, try some of this, it's delicious. Why don't you return and speak to him in person? We can have a proper lunch, another treat for me.'

'You wouldn't mind? I don't want to impose.'

'Absolutely not. I get very few visitors who aren't pestering me on official business, so this will be a rare pleasure.'

Fischer sipped his tea, played with the *butterkuchen* and wondered how much of Artsyuk's magnificent hospitality might come with teeth. They didn't know each other, had no connection that wasn't Zarubin, and even if he hadn't been someone for whom mistrust was a tool of survival his open-handed welcome was beyond any call of etiquette. Had this been an entirely innocent encounter, Fischer's next question would be *what business is that?*, but he didn't want or need to force his host's hand. In fact, he didn't care if Artsyuk was himself a fascist, a mere friend of fascists or a KGB double-agent. He neither admired or deplored his aim of toppling the Soviet system (not that it didn't need to be toppled, only that what replaced it might be worse); nor did he have any interest in whether RONDD survived to see it. In a narrow sense he was being entirely honest with his amiable host. His only purpose was that which he'd stated – to get into Zarubin's presence, speak to the man and then go back to his exile's home before KGB, Gehlen's people, Willy Brandt or anyone else who retained a grudge against Otto Henry Fischer discovered that he was presently within reach. By the same token, he imagined that the majority of those who chose to step into bears' caves had every intention of stepping out again, and with their body parts mostly intact. Unfortunately, intention wasn't always (or even usually) the mother of success.

'Well then, I'd be delighted.'

14

Fischer walked back to the hotel, checked his messages (none), asked if it were possible to hold his room for a second night after all (it was), and, as it was only early evening, gave some thought to whether he needed further distraction before he retired. The *butterkuchen* lay heavily on his stomach still, and conspired with the day's early start to make him feel dull; but his intrepid explorer's spirit (as he like to think of it) told him that there much of Munich yet to be seen, and this was his first, and, probably, final opportunity. The S.A. Zarubin expense account could bear the weight of another couple of drinks, at least.

He asked the duty manager about wine bars in the centrum, which earned him a sad gaze.

'This is the beer capital of southern Germany, and you want wine?'

'It's my Portuguese blood, I suppose.'

The young man gave him his best *It takes all sorts, I suppose* face and scribbled something on the back of one of the hotel's courtesy cards.

'Your German is very good, almost like a native. There's the *Pfälzer Weinstube*, on the corner of Residenzstrasse and Odeonsplatz. It's not far from here, a big place, not intimate, and they serve wine in beer-sized glasses I'm told.'

Fischer took the card. He wasn't looking for *intimate*, not if he was going to act upon a sudden thought (one that should have occurred at least an hour earlier). The duty manager's directions were offered slowly and then repeated for the benefit of the foreigner, who thanked him and went up to his room to shower and change. The wine bar was about a kilometre to the north of the hotel, and the two thoroughfares that connected it with Marienplatz – Theatinerstrasse and Residenztrasse – were almost arrow-straight. Together, they would do perfectly.

Maisie's recent praise of his dashing taste made his only white shirt obligatory, and when he had dressed he checked the pitiful result in a full length mirror. A large, hungry mammal would find him attractive, he supposed, but he wasn't going to be fighting off the ladies, much less squandering the Zarubin benefice on prophylactics. But why should an old man care, anyway? He reminded himself that it was only the physical damage that made him think too much of what might have been, otherwise. Long before he reached his sixties, an unmutilated Fischer (handsome devil though he'd been) would doubtless have settled happily into the golden state of not having to bother any more; content merely to recall his many splendid bouts and make passers-by wonder why he was dribbling. *This* Fischer, given a head start in becoming an unattractive proposition, perversely cared still. For want of a better cause he blamed Jonas Kleiber, for reminding him how it felt to be with a woman. And, of course, for diagnosing a case of jealousy.

Having worked himself into this low mood, he departed the hotel and turned into Theatinerstrasse. Plenty of people were out, enjoying a pleasant evening in their own or others' company, making his task more difficult than he'd hoped. Even so, he had been walking for less than ten minutes when he spotted his first suspect. The movement of pedestrians between them rendered casual what might have been deliberate and suspicious, and he couldn't be certain; so he paused, pretending to find a shop window interesting, and was almost disappointed when the man walked briskly past him without the slightest hint that he knew Otto Fischer to be in the world.

The *Pfälzer Weinstube* was a barn-like venue, stuffed with garishly expensive fittings. The place was busy, but its capacity was such that he had no trouble finding an unoccupied table. He sat, and picked up a large menu-type card. There were in fact a number of local beers available, but the wine-list was vast. At an adjacent table he heard a man order by number, so he hurriedly scanned the modest French section, and when a traditionally-dressed waitress turned to him he was ready with his own number. She nodded, made a note and went back to the bar.

He looked around. It was effort wasted to attempt to do here what he had done on the street. Anyone might be watching him, and only a fool would allow himself to be betrayed by a caught gaze. He told himself that he might as well relax, people-watch, drink his two glasses of wine and then ...

One glass, he decided suddenly. The waitress had returned quickly, with a heroically-proportioned vessel that was almost overflowing. He gave her money, told her to keep the change and wondered how bad he was going to feel later. He had already consumed more that day than his average intake for three, and if this latest consignment hadn't drained an entire bottle it must have been poured from a barrel. Feeling ridiculous, he raised it to his lips and sipped.

It was as good as any he'd tasted of that type and vintage, but his enjoyment was interrupted when he noticed the face of the man who had passed by him in the street, who was now keeping company with three women at a table not too nearby. That in itself was hardly suspicious – he had been walking in the same direction, so why wouldn't he have been coming here? But a minute's carefully casual observation told him that this was a party of three and a further party of one. The gentleman may have asked if the seat was available, but no further conversation was passing between them, and Fischer didn't believe than a man in the company of three pretty young women wouldn't be at least slightly interested in what they were saying. He was nursing the smallest beer in the room, taking in all the sights except those that would have required him to look in the direction of a badly-wounded war veteran, while they talked loudly, and then very quietly, and then burst into giggles. Not everyone was interested in salacious gossip, but a polite smile was the least reaction that they might have expected from a bored, male friend. This fellow wasn't hearing – wasn't even pretending to hear – a word they said.

Satisfied, Fischer applied himself once more to the stemmed goldfish bowl in his hand. Finally, Artsyuk was acting rationally for a man in his position. A potential risk had appeared from nowhere, and he had been presented with three options. To have done nothing would have been unthinkable. The most prudent option – a quick, clean excision, putting the risk face down on asphalt – must have been tempting, even if it meant that tomorrow's pleasant lunch had to be forgone. Thankfully, prudence had been tempered by caution, perhaps because Artsyuk wanted to consult Zarubin before addressing a potential problem decisively. Being watched could never be a pleasant experience, but after several days of trying to negotiate seemingly inexplicable events, Fischer took comfort from any logical process that didn't wound, maim or remove him from the firmament.

He tried to put his new friend from mind, and turned his attention to the busyness around him. For a former cradle of National Socialism,

Munich seemed a jolly place. Bavarians played loudly and less self-consciously than their northern, Protestant compatriots. A normal conversation couldn't be had here, secrets couldn't be told and remain so; it felt safe, an illusion that lasted almost as long as his wine. He was about to break his pledge and order a second when he noticed that the gossiping women were alone now at their table. His friend must have noticed the emptying glass, assumed that his man was not a raging drunk and taken up position outside the hall. Being as he was a part of this little theatre, Fischer finished the dregs and, dutifully, rose to leave.

It had been his intention to go back to his hotel via Residenzstrasse, but having already identified his follower he was under obligation not to make things too difficult, or suspicious. Consequently, he turned into Theatinerstrasse once more and walked slowly, peering into shop windows on the way and trying to give the impression that he had all the time and inclination to dawdle that any stranger to the city might.

He was almost two hundred metres into his return journey when he realised that traffic moving in the other direction wasn't, so to speak. A single horn alerted him to this, and then another, and then a ragged chorus of outrage from drivers wanting to get home, or to the theatre, or anywhere that wasn't precisely where they were. He glanced back, looking for the source of their troubles, and saw a ribbon of flashing lights almost entirely blocking ingress to Odeonsplatz.

It's not my business. The thought was one of his more perceptive efforts, yet despite its wisdom he turned and retraced his steps as far as he could before a policeman's arm denied further progress. By then he was close enough. Two men were stood beside an ambulance, donning whites, while a third was photographing Fischer's new friend from several angles. Blood was pooling outwards from beneath the victim's head but his face was in perfect repose, the bullet having approached from behind and caused no apparent discomfort before its destination passed beyond such things.

Christ.

Left as it was, the situation was a death sentence. Artsyuk had put a man on to him, and if that man didn't return to Prinzenstrasse to make his report there would be no need to test possibilities of varying remoteness. One suspect, one perfectly clear solution to the problem; Zarubin would return to hear bad news about his old glove-puppet and sometime-comrade, or, more likely, left to wonder how and why he had disappeared without trace, never again to be seen in this life. A strong urge to run, out of Theatinerstrasse, Munich and southern Germany, needed a deal of willpower to ignore. Something better was required, a deflection that would convince the world (or at least one man) of Otto Fischer's babe-like innocence.

The policeman whose arm was a makeshift barrier had his head half-turned towards the corpse, not wanting to miss any of what was probably his year's most exciting shift to date. Fischer coughed politely, to catch his attention.

'You can't come through.'

'I know. It was me.'

'What was?'

Fischer nodded towards his deceased shadow.

'Him. I did that.'

15

He was released just before one am, with instructions not to waste police time (this from the investigating officer) and to fuck off smartly if he didn't want his arse kicked from here to Vaterstetten (the duty sergeant). He went meekly, after apologizing for having given an unfortunate impression.

Of course he hadn't mean for a moment that he'd *done* it, just that he was responsible, in a way. Being a stranger in Munich he'd lost his way and needed to ask directions back to his hotel. The victim had been standing on the pavement just outside the *Pfälzer Weinstube* and happily obliged, taking his time to ensure than his directions were clear and then offering to walk that way if he wished. He had refused, thanking him for his kindness. If only he had bothered someone else, perhaps the fellow might have had a head start on his assassin and escaped his terrible fate.

No, he hadn't heard a shot. He'd only retraced his steps because he'd heard the sirens, so many of them, and a terrible premonition had taken hold of him. He'd had them before, his wife had often said that it was a sort of clairvoyance. Yes, he was a Portuguese citizen, though he'd spent some time in Germany immediately after the war and loved the country. This was his first visit to Bavaria, a holiday. Yes, he'd been told that his German was very good.

They had examined his passport carefully, not caring to hide their irritation, and at the station door he was intercepted by the investigating officer's colleague and given a lift back to his hotel, where his occupancy was confirmed and his room searched perfunctorily. When the detective had departed Fischer went down to reception and breathlessly recounted the evening's principal event to the hotel's night staff, who congregated from all corners of the establishment to hear it. He spoke loudly, drawing into his audience two blank-faced gentlemen who had been sitting in the lounge area when he arrived with the detective and had since not moved nor ordered any refreshments. When he had finished his near-forensic description of the corpse he answered a couple of questions from the duty manager (who required a little more red sauce to give depth to the mental image) and then noticed that the blank faces were out of their chairs and departing. He felt himself relax slightly, mentioned to the manager that he would definitely be needing his room for at least one more night and went upstairs.

He could feel the effects of an untypical day's consumption of alcohol in his gut still; even so, he opened the mini-bar, removed a tiny bottle of scotch and threw it back without bothering a nearby glass. His hands were steady, but his heart was working as if he had jogged through a series of swimming pools, and it took a while to slow. Frustratingly, an adult life lived largely in the midst or wake of an impressive variety of unpleasantnesses hadn't in the least prepared him for every next one. His stomach continued to turn over, his head clear of useful thoughts at precisely the wrong moment and a vague sense of outrage sour whatever scrape of good fortune had carried him through each new misfortune. Examining that legacy through the rosiest lens he could congratulate himself on an excellent constitution (an infarction or brain aneurysm would have carried him off by now, otherwise), but the thin prospect of a resuscitated sex life aside he was more than content to forego further excitement. Over the years he had heard countless grumbles about lives half-lived, of the curse of days that blended into a seamless mid-shade of grey, and wondered what it was about safety and security that made people squirm. Had the terror-bombings, the Soviet rape-wave, near- or actual starvation and atomization of German society not been enough excitement? Hell, why was scuba-diving now a leisure activity and not just the worst, most parlous method of sinking enemy ships?

He managed, just, not to make a bad day worse with more alcohol. Instead, he showered once more, hoping to wake himself sufficiently to be able to sleep, and then spent the hours until dawn poring over the implications of what he had witnessed.

Otto Fischer had fallen among serious people, for one. He couldn't think that the victim had been anyone other than Artsyuk's man, so who had killed him? KGB were obvious suspects, but where was the utility in putting themselves at odds with someone who was alleged to be their agent in RONDD? And yet if not KGB, who? From what Levin had told him, he doubted that any of RONDD's erstwhile competitors in the émigré-recruitment market were sufficiently competent (or sufficiently alive, for that matter) to mount a nerveless assassination on a busy Munich street. To his groggy, sleep-deprived mind, that left three other possibilities - another intelligence organization with a dog in this race, a faction of the German fascists with whom Artsyuk was said to be in some form of alliance, or, improbably, someone with a deep personal grudge, satisfying it at the most inconvenient moment imaginable. None recommended themselves loudly, which, given his lack of data, was to be expected. Who could say who Artsyuk's enemies might be, except the man himself?

At first light he shaved, dressed and read a little more Orwell to pass the time until breakfast. He might have taken it in his room, but the charms of his own company were beginning to pall. The prospect of a few strange faces around him, the obligatory nods and good mornings, was not one that he relished, normally; but a growing sense that the cosmos comprised himself, an indeterminable number of malignant wraiths and no visible signs to Elsewhere needed exorcising, even at the risk of conversation.

He was in his shoes and jacket at two minutes to seven, ready to seek the company of others, when he first saw the folded note that must have been slipped under the door at some time after 2 am. He opened it, read it in less than ten seconds, slipped it into his pocket and recalled nothing of his journey from his room to the breakfast area two floors below.

No table was as yet occupied, and a waitress who was putting the finishing touches to a well-stocked buffet gestured widely, offering him his choice. He filled a plate without noticing what he was about to eat, took a coffee and sat as far as possible from a large window offering an unimpeded shot from far too many buildings nearby. He ate slowly, tasting nothing, trying to order his thoughts.

He recognized the hand, of course, and that was as far as his wits took him. What the message *meant* was beyond comprehension, though the arrangement of words was admirably unambiguous. He glanced at his watch. Two hours to wait, to torture himself with questions that would circle for want of answers. Something rose in his throat, but he stifled it quickly; an anguished moan, probably, but he wouldn't have bet against a scream.

Concentrating upon his food distracted him only slightly, so he caught the buffet re-stocker's eye and asked directions. She offered them and told him it was at most ten minutes' brisk walk from the hotel. The last had been intended to reassure him, but he had to make an effort to hide his disappointment. A substantial trek, garnished with a couple of wrong turns, might have eaten time and exhausted his anxieties. Then again, the previous evening's ordeal suggested that walking was probably not the healthiest mode of getting around Munich.

He helped himself to another coffee (though it wasn't of a standard to encourage gluttony), took his seat once more and was grateful to be distracted by a neighbour, who had overheard his request for directions and assumed that he required a comprehensive visitor's guide to all of Munich's attractions. This took up another twenty minutes of the morning, but then the gentleman was joined by his wife, a single frown from whom entirely quelled the flow. After that, all conceivable diversions exhausted, Fischer went to the hotel reception and asked that a taxi be arranged for him, the pick-up half an hour hence, if that were possible. It was indeed, the duty manager assured him, and asked the destination.

One end of the buffet table had been adorned by a stack of fold-up tourist maps of the city. Fischer had helped himself and examined the terrain while waiting for fresh coffee to arrive from the kitchens. It was cartoon-simple, a graphic display for near-idiot tourists, and told him what he needed to know in seconds.

'The Bavarian National Museum, please.'

Twenty-five minutes later, Fischer was in his outdoor coat and at the front door. A taxi pulled up before he had time to check his wallet. Having his destination already the driver pulled away as soon as the rear door closed, and his passenger waited until the car was almost at Dienerstrasse before he spoke.

'Do you know, I've changed my mind. The Stadt Museum, please.'

'Right, mate.'

The driver took a right and then another right, and the taxi was heading south. Fischer forced himself not to look out of the rear window until they reached the junction of Rosental and Oberanger, where a quick backward glance confirmed that they had no close pursuers. As the taxi slowed to turn into Klosterhofstrasse he had his wallet ready, over-estimated the fare and told the driver not to worry about change. The effusive thanks followed him out onto the street, but his attention was entirely upon the passing traffic – which, gratifyingly, continued to pass along Oberanger. He walked towards the museum entrance, turning every few moments, but no vehicle or pedestrian entered the street before he was inside.

He was further reassured by a sign greeting the visitor, boasting that this was the largest stadt museum in Germany. It was now almost the designated time, so rather than explore he asked a receptionist for directions to the Armoury, was told that he was almost there and had a floor-plan thrust into his hand.

In thirty seconds he was among a remarkable collection of pikes, glaives, swords, halberds, arbalests and sundry other means of inflicting catastrophic damage upon bone and soft tissue. Having been given no further instructions than to be in the room, he positioned himself beside an entire suit of horse-armour (the fifteenth-century equivalent of a *panzerkampfwagen*, he supposed) and waited. Two other visitors were perusing the exhibits already, an elderly couple he assumed to be man and wife, but neither seemed interested in an ambulant example of what weaponry did in expert hands. He checked his watch, loosened and re-fastened its strap (it was a recent acquisition, and chaffed still), and felt the man's breath in his ear before he heard a single footstep.

'You daft cock! What d'you think you're doing?'

Quelling his own, considerable ire, Fischer turned and barely managed a smile.

'Much the same as you, I imagine. How are you, Freddie?'

16

It was not quite two years since they had last met, but Freddie Holleman's unmanageable shock of black hair was now shockingly grey, and cropped so closely that he resembled a shaved boar (a boar's mother might have disagreed). He was angry, and almost grinning, and one of his hands moved as if it might thump or squeeze a portion of its target.

Fischer's good shoulder took the blow (it was only mildly painful, being pulled at the last moment) and he grasped the hand before it could have another go.

'Zarubin?'

Holleman nodded. 'He said you were likely to be heading for shit.'

'If I am, he's the one who's pointed me towards it.'

'That's what I thought. And you let him.'

'It's not quite that simple.'

The words had hardly met air before Fischer realised it might very well be that simple; that this path (wherever it led) had been laid out from the moment the banker's draft first went into its envelope. If Freddie Holleman was here it was because Zarubin must have had a strong conviction that Otto Henry Fischer would be here also - a man so transparent, so predictable, that a modest moral shackle could be relied upon to drag him from bleak, windswept safety to a well-appointed Bavarian mine-field.

'You look like you've just wiped your arse on broken glass.'

'It feels like that. Why are you here, Freddie, other than to tell me I'm an idiot? Which I am, of course.'

'I …' Holleman paused, his face reddening slightly. 'I'm not sure. All he said was that you might need help if things went wrong.'

'I don't suppose he defined *things*?'

'Zarubin? Is it likely? Though …'

'What?'

'It's something he said. I thought he was making conversation – I mean, we hadn't spoken since just before you went off to Portugal. But why would he be interested?'

'In what?'

For a few moments Holleman didn't speak. He glanced at the horse armour and raised a hand as if he might test its strength, or the noise he might make with a thump. It came down again, rubbing his nose as it passed by.

'You know I'm retiring from the police?

'I know you've been saying you are, for some years now.'

'Well, it's official. Kristin and me are going to travel a little, see stuff before we're too old and addled to care. I've told my Direktor that I'll be going in September, after I hand over my case work and liaison role.'

'Who do you liaise with?'

'Interpol, mainly. Though liaise is probably the wrong word. It implies that I'm of some use to them.'

'And you aren't?'

Holleman grinned. 'Not very. But my Direktor's complimented me on how I manage to seem more willing to help than I am.'

Fischer could hardly imagine Freddie Holleman in any role that involved a degree of collaboration or even pretence of it, but then he knew almost nothing of what his friend had made of his third police career. A decade had passed since the Holleman family fled East Berlin and found a quieter life in Trier, while Fischer's own voyage had, by contrast, taken him from calm harbour out into rough seas. Much distracted during these years, he'd made only the occasional polite enquiry as to how work was going. Invariably, it met with *tedious, unchanging, an adventure in paperwork* or *Christ, Otto, don't ask me about fucking work*. But if the *Landespolizei* trusted Holleman sufficiently to represent them in dealings with Interpol, some aspect of life in Rhineland-Palatinate must have allowed him to become at least semi-domesticated.

And *role*. It implied an ongoing process, and there was only one matter of cross-border criminality that abided longer than the crime itself – at least, one which the *Landespolizei* would want to stifle, slow or otherwise confound.

'You're not chasing Nazis?'

'Not as much as I'm glancing into long-interred files and then reporting to Zurich that no recent information's been received. Which, usually, is the stone-cold truth. They don't call very often. Once in a while some eager young things gets the feeling that another Eichmann would be just the coup to kick off careers, and their enthusiasm lasts about as long as the first disappointment. Otherwise, most of what I do in that particular line is make a note of any piece of news on what HIAG or *Stille Hilfe* are doing.'

'I'm surprised your bosses let you do *that*, even. Aren't some of them members of one or the other?'

'Most of them, probably. I just want to leave paper to show that I bothered, occasionally. For posterity, when I'm gone.'

HIAG's efforts to rehabilitate the reputation of Waffen SS were no secret, nor was their enduring failure to do so. Many former senior officers had found their way into industry, government and regional police forces, though, so every time that someone made a noise about it there were plenty of august witnesses to jump forward to testify that Herr A. had been an exemplary officer who'd only ever fired upon enemy soldiers and never even thought of lining up civilians over a trench. Those who wanted to believe it did so; everyone else laughed into their hand and tried to forget about it as they did everything else about the war. *Stille Hilfe* were a different case. Their days of running rat-lines to help men disappear to Spain or South America were long over, but a different sort of work continued. If time couldn't be reversed, at least the story could be re-written, so the organisation had put its revisionist pen to work, particularly with respect to the Auschwitz 'Lie'. It was their aim to convince Germans, but more so the world, that millions of Jews,

Roma, homosexuals and other non-viable human beings hadn't died in death camps but merely been put to useful work for the Reich in challenging but healthy surroundings (following which, presumably, they had conspired to disappear en masse in order to stain the reputation of their fond overseers).

Stille Hilfe were persistent, which meant that they had funding. Who provided it was a mystery, though certain elements of German industry in the Catholic south were strong suspects (the organization's founder and principal adornment, Princess von Isenburg, was a staunch Romanist). To date, no-one had tried to move against them, and not only because they had powerful allies. From a legal perspective they were committing no recognizable crime, other than against the truth. Furthermore, the dead couldn't sue, and the survivors had little incentive (and even less desire) to return to Germany to avenge their relatives in the courts. Only a few Israelis and the occasional Interpol initiative attempted to keep a terrible crime in the light, and only a rare tactical victory illuminated their struggle. Even then, for every gentile who applauded an untypical instance of justice seen to be done, another two or three regarded Nazi hunters as attention-seeking troublemakers. The world was moving on, striding away from an ugly past.

On the whole, Fischer couldn't get too exercised about any of it. He didn't believe, or want to believe, any of what the revisionists said, couldn't feel more than vicariously ashamed of the truth (he'd played with war-guilt but never been burned by it) and had few opinions on what should happen to individual perpetrators of historic mass crimes. If the Allies had decided that Germany had paid a sufficient price by now, he wasn't going to argue the point. He had always known much of what was going on in the East during those dark years, but also what British and American had done to German civilians with their fire-bombs and what Soviet soldiers did with their cocks in '45. War was war, and it had always been the case that some of those who jumped into the mud-pit did so because they enjoyed getting extremely dirty.

He wondered if Holleman felt the same about it. They hadn't discussed it, not the matter of how much of a burden each German in uniform did or should bear; but *his* fighting war had been clean and brief, and he hadn't begrudged losing a leg to it. He had readily and often – too readily, too often - expressed his opinion of OKW and the Party, and none of it had been flattering, then or later. But iconoclasm does not necessarily make a rebel, nor indiscretion a martyr. Germans were extremely good rule-takers, and both Fischer and Holleman were good Germans.

'Anyway, Zarubin said that this – whatever *this* is – might be a bit of a busman's holiday for me. I had to ask what that meant.'

'It's a British …'

'Yeah, he told me. But when I asked how it might be that, he changed the subject to what he wanted me to do.'

'Which was?'

'Pass on a message. ... I have no idea what it means.'

'Tell me.'

'He said don't mention Kudrin. That's it.'

'I hadn't intended to. Not in Artsyuk's presence, at least.'

'Who?'

'You really know nothing?'

'I was hoping you'd switch on the light.'

'Kudrin's dead. Zarubin may have killed him. That's all I can tell you.'

Holleman snorted. 'He wouldn't kill someone. Fit them up, perhaps, or hand them over to proper executioners. He's always kept his fingernails clean.'

'He no longer has fingernails.'

'I was speaking …'

'Metaphorically?'

'Yeah, that.'

'You may be right. When did he bring you here, to Munich?'

'I came in this morning. I was in Koblenz yesterday, at headquarters, making my quarterly non-report. He ambushed me outside, told me he needed me. How he knew I'd be there I can't say, but he was.'

'Needed you? That was all?'

'That, and the bit about you being in the shit. Naturally I told him to fuck off, but he seemed serious, nervous; so I did an Otto, parked my common-sense and came.'

'He should certainly be nervous. If he didn't kill Kudrin he may be next on a list. He's been making some strange friends recently.'

'Strange?'

'God, for one. He's joined the Russian Orthodox Church. And he's now a chum of E.N. Artsyuk.'

'Chum?'

'Another Anglicism, meaning friend, or fond acquaintance. Artsyuk heads a Russian émigré organization – one, incidentally, that may have links to HIAG, or *Stille Hilfe*, or both. He may also be a KGB double-agent, intending to betray his own people.'

'Jesus. That explains the holidays of bus drivers. And you've been recruited into this mob, have you?'

'Zarubin offered me money, for an unspecified job that wasn't dangerous, he claimed.'

'And you believed him, you senile fucker.'

Fischer sighed. 'I know, I know. I convinced myself that I could bail out at any time, but to do it at the *right* time I would have needed far more information than I have.'

'All the more reason to walk away before you had to be carried.'

'Jonas Kleiber said something similar.'

'He's a clever boy. One to listen to.'

'And you? You've warned me about Kudrin. Is that it?'

'I don't know. He said I might be needed for two or three days.'

'And your sole incentive to come was that I might be in trouble? I'm touched.'

'Well …'

'He paid you?'

'In a way. ' Holleman glanced around, but the elderly couple had moved on to a section displaying a comprehensive collection of morning stars, flails and bludgeons. 'He arranged a strange and wonderful present – said he did it before he fled Moscow.'

'What is it?'

'Peace of mind. He asked a favour of the cousins at Ruschestrasse,'

'To forget one Kurt Beckendorf?'

Holleman nodded. 'As good as. He told them that KGB had an interest in me – well, in my alter ego - not getting cacked, and, to head off any bursts of initiative that couldn't be undone, would they mind removing his name from any active operations lists until they heard otherwise.'

'That would have required … pull.'

'He had it back then, didn't he? Even Eric Mielke sits up straight when a direct call comes through from the Kremlin. Still, he didn't have to do it. In fact, I wonder why he did.'

Fischer scratched his cheek. 'He was torn apart by guilt for what he'd put you through over the years. Or, he thought he might need as many friends in the West as he could hang on to.'

'Yeah, what was I thinking? Anyway, that's what dragged me here. That, and needing to make sure that you don't do anything dumb – I mean, really Otto-dumb.'

'Where are you staying?'

'There's a GdP hostel near the river. I might be the most senior police who's ever had a bed there.'

'Will they put flowers in your room?'

'A turd under the pillow, probably. Still, they're said to do a nice stodgy breakfast. Speaking of food, you have a lunch date, don't you?'

'Not for a few hours. Let's move – we're beginning to look planted.'

They had walked around the armoury and almost into the textiles collection before Fischer noticed it.

'Freddie, you're not limping.'

'I'm not, am I?'

Has it grown back?'

Holleman reached down and lifted his trouser leg to the knee.

'A new model, cost me a fortune. Kristin saw it in a prosthetics catalogue and insisted
I get it. It's American, of course, though without fins or chrome options. I can walk almost as far and sweetly now as when I had two pins.'

'Can you run?'

'You think I might need to?'

'There was another killing, last night, here in Munich. And Zarubin may have had something to do with that one, too.'

17

Fischer presented himself at the Artsyuk's front gate at 2pm, and was met by the athletic young man, still dressed in black and adorned by the same air of intimidation. Given that a murder – possibly of an acquaintance or colleague – had occurred since they had last faced each other, the visitor took the unchanging vista as a hopeful sign.

He wasn't frisked this time, but Surly followed him every metre from front gate to hallway, where the elderly maid took charge once more. She led Fischer into the study-cum-distribution warehouse, though some effort had been made to tidy it since the previous day. The small table and chairs now had room to stretch out, and upon the former sat a filled wine decanter and four glasses.

The maid waved at the ensemble. 'He said you should have some while you wait.'

He recognized her accent immediately. 'You're from the *Drei Kaiserbäder?*'

Surprise, she nodded. 'Bansin, your honour. You?'

'I was born in Koserow. On the very last day of 1898.'

She smiled, and shook her head. 'A better time.'

'A harder life, but …'

'… our holidays were cheap, and long!' She clapped her hands, pleased to be able to deliver the venerable line. With surprising agility (she must have been in her mid-70s), she crossed to the table and poured a glass for him. 'He says it's one of his best, a French wine. You must be a special guest, he doesn't offer it to everyone.'

'Four glasses. Do you know who else is expected?'

'More Russians, I think. There's a handsome blond one, he arrived a few days ago. I don't know the fourth man, but I was told he's a friend of … the organization.'

'Ah.' It was an effort not to ask more of someone who wanted to be an ally, but he was supposed to be a lunch guest, not a spy. He took a sip from his glass and held it in his mouth for a few moments.

'So, Bansin. Where the naughty ladies and gentlemen bathed together, the first time ever in Germany?'

Even more pleased, she wagged a finger. 'It was a scandal! All our young men were at the beach the day after the new permits were issued. Even my son, the little …'

She paused, her eyes filling, another little slice of tragedy finding the light. Hurriedly, he broke the silence.

'I would have been there myself, ogling with the rest of them. But I'd started my police training only a few weeks earlier, in Stettin.'

She wiped her eyes with the back of a hand. 'I went there once, to see my aunt. It's not even Germany now, is it?'

The door opened. Artsyuk (wearing a different but equally fine suit) peered around it, and the maid came to attention.

'Herr Fischer. Good, you're punctual. General Zarubin is here also, but we're waiting for one more guest. Bring your glass, will you? Magda, we'll have the rest of the wine in the library, please.'

Fischer followed him almost to the end of the hallway, where several delicious odours had mingled into a welcoming whole. Turning right, they entered a large room whose walls were entirely hidden by floor-to-ceiling fitted bookcases, none of which appeared to have space for a single further volume. As in the study, other furniture was sparse - a desk and captain's chair, a small sofa, an armchair and an occasional table didn't begin to fill the large central space, but the busy boundaries kept the room from seeming under-furnished. The armchair was turned almost entirely away from the door, but Fischer didn't need to guess who was occupying it. The hint of blond was as good as a confession.

Zarubin stood and turned. He was dressed elegantly as always, and conspired with Artsyuk to make the new arrival feel wretchedly shabby. His face, however, was not as always. Fischer couldn't ever recall it not being in want of a punch, but today the familiar urge was stilled by a strange hint of human frailty. It might have been uncertainty - an *imbalance* in the mechanism that, usually, maintained an insufferable equanimity. Had it not carried implications for anyone dragged into its radius of instability, the prospect would have been almost pleasing.

The strangeness persisted as Zarubin lunged forward and grasped Fischer's hand in an awkward attempt at bonhomie.

'My dear Major! How good of you to find me. Evgeny Nikolaevich tells me you've had quite a time of it.'

Fischer smiled, his irritation soothed by the thought of how much of Zarubin's money he'd spent to date, having quite a time of it.

'I was beginning to think you were more of a rumour than a fact. I have the ... papers you sent to me. I wondered what you wanted done with them.'

Artsyuk poured and passed a glass of wine to his compatriot. 'No, no. You gentlemen can discuss your business after lunch. For the moment, *Zum Wohl!*'

Twenty minutes later, Magda announced lunch. In the meantime, the small talk – the wine and its expensive provenance, the unseasonable Munich weather, that of the far north and south of the western Soviet Union (from which Zarubin and Artsyuk hailed respectively), English manners and eccentricities - was *very* small, and Fischer had the impression that the Russians were scripting it for his benefit. He didn't know if he should be pleased about that. If Zarubin was keeping him at a prudent distance from whatever was plot was brewing that was all to the good; if, on the other hand, he and Artsyuk were conspiring to tickle the piglet before dropping into a dog-pit ...

'Sergei Aleksandrovich tells me you've been of great service to him over the years, both to the advantage and hurt of our Mother Russia.'

Artsyuk said it without giving any hint of whether or not he approved of this, and Fischer decided that the truth would probably do.

'I wasn't ever given much choice in the matter. His persuasive skills are always supported by a cosh. Whatever good or harm your country derived was entirely incidental. To me, at least.'

The older man pulled a face. 'I wouldn't worry about it. The Nazis and Mongols were remarkable only because they managed to do more damage to us than we habitually do to ourselves. We are a great mass of sects, bound by an absurd idea that we constitute a nation.'

Zarubin, who had been peering into his glass, looked up. 'My family was the proof of that. I had a Menshevik father, an Imperialist mother and a Bolshevik uncle, each convinced that the others were in grave, heretical error. It taught me the value of holding few principles. I believe the Major here feels much the same.'

Fischer supposed it was meant as praise (in which case this might be a job interview). He shook his head. 'Regarding politics, certainly. As for the rest, a few less principles honoured only in the breach would be pleasant.'

'Ha! My moral compass, always pointing true North.'

It didn't sound as if he were being mocked, so Fischer took no offence. The conversation moved back to impersonal things, and then they went into lunch, the remaining guest still absent. Magda was assisted by a younger maid who helped to ladle *vichyssoise* from a silver tureen. Three bowls had just found their place on the table when the doorbell sounded. Artsyuk looked up and smiled.

'Good.'

A few moments later, Surly led into the dining-room a sleek, executive-type gentleman of about Fischer's age, and withdrew. Their host got to his feet, shook hands and gestured at the spare seat.

'Yet another Otto! I thought you might not come.'

The gentleman looked pained. 'Evgeny, I'm sorry. The telephone fired up during breakfast hasn't stopped since. I'm sure you have days like this.'

He sat down, smiled at his fellow guests and waited for his ration of wine and vichyssoise. No-one attempted introductions, which struck Fischer as odd. There was something else, too - a faint recollection, stirring but keeping itself out of the light. He tried to dismiss it. Following the thing would yield nothing but a headache, and he'd had too many of those recently.

The new arrival dominated the conversation for a few minutes with gripes about debtors, supplicants, a schedule that never quite found the time to expand into and a forthcoming meeting he was particularly keen to cancel, and it was only as his flow slowed that Fischer realised he hadn't mentioned what it was that he did to earn a crust. He might have been a goldfiner, industrialist or restauranteur, a stock jobber or importer, and nothing he had said would have seemed out of place. As his acquaintance, Artsyuk wouldn't have needed to be led through any of it, but two strangers, sitting at the same table, might have been offered at least cursory enlightenment as to what they were hearing.

Zarubin was eating his soup, glancing up occasionally to catch a little of this other Otto's conversation without apparent interest. He didn't look in his namesake's direction even once, so the spurned party applied himself to his own dish and to whatever occupation it was that preferred not to have itself named. And then the penny dropped.

He put down his spoon, picked up a piece of bread from his side plate, tore it in half and regarded the pieces. How could he have missed it? Life, new events and preoccupations held a man's attention, drawing him away from what was once to the fore; but some matters snagged in memory, and this man's life was one of them, surely?

He looked up, intending to say nothing, but half his face must have offered a hint of surprise. Artsyuk's face creased in a faint smile that could have been a mere acknowledgement of eyes having met, but wasn't. He dabbed his mouth with his napkin and nudged his neighbour.

'I think you've been made, Otto.'

If Otto cared about that he didn't show it. He glanced at Fischer and raised his eyebrows, more in amusement than shock. 'Dear me. Who is it that you think I am?'

Fischer cleared his throat. 'Probably the only senior NSDAP man who'll ever go to Paradise.'

The other Otto roared and slapped the table. Artsyuk frowned. 'What does that mean?'

'He's referring to my exile, Evgeny. I spent more than ten years in the wilderness of Nova Scotia, a farming community named Paradise - a rare example of Canadian irony, I suppose. Yes – Herr Fischer, isn't it? I am that man, now welcomed back to the bosom of my country, or what remains of it.'

Otto Strasser - an early member and bright light of the NSDAP, one of the three founders (with his brother Gregor and one Josef Goebbels) of its largest, North German branch. He and Gregor had led the left-wing of the Party, the one that treated seriously the word 'socialist' in its name. He had fought Hitler at every stage in the NSDAP's growth, but finally split with both man and Party in 1930, when the latter threw in his lot with (or rather seduced) Germany's industrialists. Forced to flee the country when Hitler became Chancellor, Strasser had avoided the massacre of the Nazis' left-wing during the Night of the Long Knives (unlike Gregor, whose lingering, naive hopes for reconciliation proved fatal). The Führer regarded him as a grave threat even in exile, and a reward equivalent to half a million dollars was placed on his head; but a series of quick-steps via Austria, Czechoslovakia, Switzerland (where he paused to drop off his family), France, Portugal, Bermuda, and, finally, Canada, kept him out of the Reich's clutches. Despite apparently remaining faithful to his own ideals of National Socialism, he had somehow managed to convince successive hosts, and, eventually, the West German Government that he had never agreed with the Hitlerite faction's racist policies – that he was one of the nice, embraceable Nazis.

Fischer had followed the news, of course. He knew that Strasser, a Bavarian, had settled in Munich following his return in 1956 and founded a new Party imbued with at least part of the spirit of the old: the Deutsch-Soziale Union. It had been a pleasant surprise when the experiment failed utterly, the pathetic results of its recruitment drive confirming that the nation was over that particular obsession. But the man was alive still, and seemingly prosperous, and how many sworn enemies of Adolf Hitler could claim as much?

The DSU had been wound up in 1962. Fischer doubted that the man was entirely done with his past, though, and it was a striking fact that some people continued to regard him as a considerable person. Why else would the DDR's ruling party, the SED, have offered him leadership of the National Front, an umbrella organization intended to give the (utterly false) impression that the East German Government was a broad church? To have made himself amenable to both post-war Germanies suggested he had a rare gift of plausibility.

Fischer glanced at Zarubin, whose face betrayed no surprise or interest at Strasser's outing. He knew already then, which added a further layer of confusion. What sort of occasion was this meal? Setting aside the nonentity at the feast, the table hosted the leader of an organization devoted to overthrowing the Soviet leadership (but who also might be an instrument of that same body); a relic of Nazi prehistory and natural (perhaps actual) ally of Russian émigrés, an honoured guest but possibly also an unwitting sacrifice to Artsyuk's friends-with-long-memories in Moscow; and a former KGB General whose head, presumably, the Lubyanka wished to ventilate with at least one bullet and who, having fled England because of a murder he may have committed, had willingly put himself close to two men upon whom KGB doubtless kept an interested eye. Either he was desperate, very bored or set upon some mad plan that would make his previous efforts seem like models of linearity.

Fischer had a sudden, strong urge to get out of the house, to drag Zarubin to some quiet place where he could interrogate him until the fog lifted; but Magda and her young friend had already removed the soup bowls and returned with a trolley upon which sat a magnificent rib of beef. Being in a mood to carve up something, Fischer was minded to volunteer. Surly's duties, however, extended to more than one form of violence. Wielding a large knife, he followed the two women into the room and immediately applied himself to the task.

Potatoes in (yet more) cream, spinach, butter-mashed carrots and two further bottles of wine arrived to reinforce the beef. Strasser, having been nudged by Artsyuk, was relating anecdotes from his fugitive years, and even Fischer had to admit that the man could tell a story well. He was witty, self-deprecatory, had excellent timing and didn't fail to pin the most comical characteristics of each nation that had sheltered him. An ingrate, certainly, but an amusing one.

Their host was, or seemed to be, hugely entertained by all of this, and led the laughter. Zarubin smiled politely at the correct moments but otherwise set himself to his plate. Fischer, who felt responsible for having breached the dam in the first place, managed to throw in enough questions about Switzerland and Bermuda, and to offer enough of his own experience of Portugal, to appear fully engaged. But all he really wanted to know was what business Strasser had brought here, and what potential it had to further darken a threatening horizon.

Artsyuk was a slow eater (which added to the torture), but eventually the plates were remove. Their host bent closely to Strasser and whispered something, looked up and gave the other two guests a courteously regretful face.

'Would you mind if Otto and I retire briefly? We have a little matter to discuss, but please, don't go. Magda has made her speciality, a *bavaroise*. Fifteen minutes?'

Christ. How much cream can the human body absorb?

Fischer smiled weakly. Zarubin cleared his throat. 'In that case, the Major and I should deal with *our* business. May we take a turn in your lovely garden, Evgeny?'

The pause was barely noticeable. Perhaps it required a moment for Artsyuk to bring his mind back from his own, imminent business, but in his present hypersensitive state Fischer thought he caught a glimpse of something else in the man's expression. It might have been disappointment, or even irritation, and because Zarubin had asked the question one thing occurred instantly. An organization that had survived KGB's efforts to expunge it could probably call upon a wide range of necessary resources, but electronically bugging the outdoors wasn't one of them.

'By all means. Don't omit to admire the dahlias. It's what they're there for.'

Behind the house, the shrubbery parted around a small lawn, bordered, as promised, by an impressively martialled collection of dahlias. Zarubin and Fischer paused in the middle of the open space, so that anyone peering out of an upstairs window could see them plainly.

'Why did you involve Freddie?'

Fischer had no intention of allowing Zarubin to control this conversation. A familiar whimsical smile had appeared - the prelude, usually, to a line being cast with fair certainty of hooking a fish.

'I have only one pair of eyes. I thought you might need some on you.'

'Why? You offered me a job that isn't illegal or dangerous. Why would I need watching?'

Zarubin sighed, and turned slightly so that his mouth couldn't be observed from the house.

'I lied, obviously. What I had in mind carried certain legal implications, but probably not for you. Unfortunately, events have moved on.'

'I assume the death of Mr Kudrin wasn't one of the *legal implications*?'

Zarubin almost winced. 'No. And no, I didn't kill him.'

'You were seen at his home that day.'

'Yes, the porter. I only wish he'd seen the murderer also.'

'The police think it's you.'

'As would I, given what little evidence they have. But I had no reason to kill poor Stanislav. In fact, I owed him a great deal.'

'He gave you shelter.'

'At his apartment to begin with, and then he arranged accommodation elsewhere.'

'Bishopsgate.'

Zarubin's eyebrows rose slightly. 'You *have* been busy, Major.'

'Boris Levin was very helpful; but then, he needed to be. I'd been dragged to London on a promise of good money and light employment, and the man who made the offer was to be found nowhere.'

'That was unfortunate. I'd conceived the offer to you and written the letter before Stan died. With his murder the thing became something else, yet what I'd originally intended for you seemed to serve the new purpose very well. It was just unfortunate that I had to flee London before we could speak.'

'And yet you remained in the city for two days after Kudrin died.'

Zarubin pursed his lips, but said nothing.

'According to Jonas Kleiber he got your letter the following day. Lacking a stamp, it must have been hand-delivered to his post-box. You were also noticed at the library and your sandwich bar. Or is it a restaurant?'

'Well, it was important that we speak. I was hoping Kleiber would move quickly. When he didn't, I felt I couldn't risk waiting any longer.'

Fischer's gaze rested on the pleasing prospect of the dahlias while he considered this. Zarubin thought best when he *needed* to think, when his arse was closest to the fire. He must have felt its heat fairly painfully during those two days, yet there were other means of contacting someone in a hurry, even a man who resided on a moor. It didn't seem likely that he would put himself so entirely in the hands of Kleiber, a man he didn't even know, if …

'You didn't just run to avoid arrest, did you?'

'Can you think of a better reason?'

'If I'd appeared at your library or lunch venue during those two days you would have put your proposal to me?'

'Yes, I …'

'And had it refused out of hand. Whatever your original intention, I would have said no, probably. With Kudrin's death clouding the business, *probably* would have become *definitely*. You thought about it, and decided not to allow me the option of refusing. You ran for safety's sake, but also to make me follow.'

'How could I know that you'd oblige me?'

'Because you know *me*, unfortunately. With your money in my pocket I had an obligation to find you, to return it – minus expenses incurred – and only then would I be able to tell you to go to hell and take your proposal with you.'

Zarubin smiled. 'And how could I possibly be confident you'd decide that Munich was where I was?'

It was a good point, but Fischer needed only a few more moments with the dahlias to pin it.

'You had an invitation from Artsyuk. You didn't get it, because like all your post it was redirected to Levin's address while you were in the Crouch End hostel. But as you *are* here, Artsyuk must have reached you through another channel – Kudrin, perhaps. He would have mentioned his letter, wondered why you hadn't received it, and you would have pictured it in your mind's eye, sitting on Levin's desk, ready to be shown to me when I turned up at his door. And as I had no other clue as to where you'd gone …'

'Life on the Yorkshire tundra hasn't dulled your mind, Major. I'm gratified. How is dear Boris, by the way?'

'A little down at heart. He didn't manage to sell a piece that his cash-flow had been relying upon. To flow, that is.'

Zarubin frowned. 'That hideous armoire? I thought the deal was sealed?'

'Apparently not. The gentleman from Paris changed his mind, though he was good enough to return to the shop in person to break the bad news.'

This very small piece of information gave Zarubin more pause than it deserved, but after a few moments he looked up and smiled. 'Well, I confess to hoping that you'd come. I'm entirely upon my own resources here, though Evgeny's been very kind.'

'Resources for what?'

'For the end I have in mind.'

Fischer breathed deeply. 'Look, the money you sent. I don't want …'

'Oh, please, keep it.'

'Keep it? I haven't done anything to earn it. I'll take the hundred pounds you offered, plus the expenses I've …'

'No, keep all of it. Money isn't important. Not that money, anyway. It wasn't mine, to be truthful.'

'Not Kudrin's? Please say that you didn't steal from the man the police think you murdered?'

Zarubin was hardly capable of being offended, but he acted the part well. 'You think that I could rob a man who held out his hand to me when I was on the floor?'

'Then who?'

'His Church. The Russian Orthodox Church in Exile, bless them.'

'Why?'

'Because I needed it to bribe you. That is, to tempt you'

'That's ... despicable.'

'Not to an atheist, it isn't. Besides, they have a lot of money, and some of it comes from very questionable sources. Really, you shouldn't worry for my immortal soul. Which doesn't exist, of course.'

'How much did you steal?'

'Little more than a thousand pounds. They'll hardly know it's gone.'

'I think a priest did. An angry one came to find you at your apartment.'

'That would be Father Kyril. I promised him half of the plunder if he let me into the Purser's office. He has gambling debts. Of course, I never intended to keep my word.'

'You've made yet another enemy, then. How many is enough?'

'I doubt that he'll ever betray me. He couldn't find the courage to do the job himself, and pointing the finger would advertise his involvement.'

'So, what next?'

'Next?'

'There's probably an arrest warrant out for you in England by now. If you can't prove your innocence, what will you do?'

'Remain here, for the moment. Artsyuk seems happy to extend his hospitality.'

'Why is that? Does he know you're a former KGB General?'

'He does. And that I've repented of my previous career.'

'That hardly explains his invitation for to you to be house guest. What's the incentive?'

Zarubin glanced at the house before answering. 'I've dangled a promising financial opportunity.'

'*You* have? A man who hasn't got two pfennigs of his own to rub together?'

'Naturally, it won't be my money. I just know of it, and may be able to arrange something to his considerable advantage.'

'Something you can't or won't discuss with me?'

'I don't see why not. You'll have heard of *Stille Hilfe*?'

'Strangely, Freddie Holleman and I were discussing them this morning.'

Fischer had the satisfaction of watching Zarubin's face fall.

'A curious coincidence. KGB became interested in them a few years ago, when they contacted a Russian émigré group here in Germany.'

'That would be RONDD, I suppose?'

This time the surprise was muted, but Zarubin regarded him carefully. 'You're extremely well-informed, Major.'

'Again, I have Boris Levin to thank. He recalled Artsyuk's name from a KGB briefing paper. But he thought you knew nothing of all that.'

'Poor Levin. He always imagined himself to be the gate-keeper of what I should or needed to know. He didn't appreciate that senior KGB men come to meetings with the same determination to impress as anyone else. I recall that the First Main and Seventh Directorates were always vying to take the most credit for penetrating or hurting the White exiles.'

'So you became interested in *Stille Hilfe*? Why? They're just apologists for National Socialism's record. Probably, they socialize with your émigrés only because some of them fought with the Wehrmacht back then. It'll be nothing more than drunken evenings reminiscing about the good times, surely?'

'I expect so. Occasionally, they may offer their Russian friends a little money to carry them through the thinnest times. I can't see it being much more than that.'

'So, again – why should you be interested in them?'

'I happen to know something of where their own funding comes from – that is, a particular, partial source. I plan to divert the flow, somewhat.'

'To RONDD?'

'That's what I told Evgeny.'

'Which doesn't quite answer the question.'

Zarubin smiled, a hint of his cockiness returning.

'His organization shall of course receive a sufficient proportion.'

'How sufficient?'

'Sufficient to quell thoughts of his having been under-compensated.'

'So, you're going to steal from someone who'll almost certainly have the means to punish you for it, and then screw the supposed recipient? Doesn't the threat posed by several thousand former colleagues in KGB provide enough excitement?'

'Major, have you thought at all about the future since we fled to England? Excuse me, of course you have. Already, you've embarked upon a new career, pitiful though it seems to me. Even our friend Levin has found himself a niche, relying upon the misfortune of others for his daily bread. I, though, have been forced to face a rather brutal truth – that ordinary occupations don't engage me sufficiently to allow me to do them well, or even competently. Curiously, it isn't their repetitive nature that repels me, nor their insignificance weighed against a man's former achievements. After all, Einstein was a mere Patent Office clerk at one point in his life, Engels a textile manufacturer and Marx a poet, for Christ's sake. No, what hurts is the reality that such employment would oblige me to face.'

'That you're just the same as anyone else. *Of* the herd.'

Zarubin chewed absently at his lower lip. 'I doubt that I could be content to accept the defector's usual fate and slide gracelessly into drunken oblivion, surrounded by alien mores and bad table manners.'

'A lot of very powerful men wanted you dead. Your drawing breath still must torment them every waking hour. Can't you draw comfort from that while you're packing boxes, or auditing ledgers?'

'If only I had an actual *talent* for something worthy, like bashing a piano. I haven't, though, and might-have-beens are the least nourishing crop of all.'

Fischer noticed a face peering from an upstairs window. 'Lacking a faculty for honest work, the alternative has to be theft, does it?'

'Call it unearned wealth, and I can't despise either it or myself for wanting it. Obviously, I inherited *something* from my Mother's side of the family. In any case, the persons from whom I intend to take my retirement fund will make the crime seem at least a little like the product of gainful employment.'

'May I ask …?'

Zarubin brightened slightly. 'Apart from half the boardrooms in the Federal Republic, who would want to finance apologists for National Socialism? Obviously, it's KGB.'

19

Not trusting himself to speak, Fischer waited. They were being watched still from the upstairs window, so he attempted (and probably failed) to convey an air of indifference. He also shuffled a little to his right, to keep a potential lip-reader from discovering anything of this extended suicide note. Zarubin didn't notice the manoeuvre, but he spoke quietly.

'As you point out, KGB want me dead anyway, so robbing them – or rather, diverting monies they've already allocated to a group of unpleasant Germans – is hardly going to make my present situation worse, is it?'

'Giving a further incentive to would-be executioners is *always* more dangerous. Does Artysuk know that his little windfall is coming from Moscow – from the pockets of men he's allegedly spying for?'

'Of course not. I was very vague about the source of his good fortune.'

'Well, vagueness is the best one can hope for, I suppose. If I might risk seeming self-centred, what role did you see me playing in this mad plan?'

'Originally, a very minor one. I've opened accounts at three unconnected London banks in your name. You were to await my confirmation that transfers had been made and then withdraw everything on the same day. You would then have returned immediately to your moorland realm with the cash. In a few weeks I should have journeyed north myself, taken charge of the monies and bid you a final, fond farewell. Of course, Stanislav Kudrin's murder changed things.'

'I'm not going to help you rob an armed convoy for *any* amount of money.'

'Don't be absurd, this isn't 1946. KGB finance their foreign operations – including payments to sympathetic partners – either through accounting arrangements with local Soviet embassies or via electronic transfers through certain disinterested Middle-European institutions.'

'You mean Swiss banks.'

'Why not? Their discretion is legendary. In any case, no-one in Switzerland knows that the ultimate account holder happens to be KGB. Except for the nominal customer, that is – the middleman in this transaction.'

'Who happens to be?'

Zarubin snorted, suppressing a laugh. 'This will amuse you.'

'I doubt that very much.'

'In return for being left alone in other respects, the Russian Orthodox Church.'

'Are they even *in* Switzerland?'

'They have been honoured guests there since the mid-19th century. Which is when their beautiful *Église Orthodoxe Russe* was built on Avenue Jacques-Martin, in the fair city of Geneva.'

'So that was how you were able to justify your robbing their London branch, was it?'

'Technically, they're different sects of the same Faith, but yes. It seemed an elegant irony, to be seeding my theft from an Orthodox bank account by thieving from the Orthodox Church.'

'And how might you possibly get at their – I mean, KGB's – money? Will you wander into the bank wearing a long black robe and ask to make a withdrawal?'

'Again, Major, your grasp of modern financial mechanisms is comically weak. To intercept the *swag* as it were, one requires no more than the customer identification and unique transaction codes. And I have those already. In fact, I've had them for almost two years now.'

'How ...?' Fischer paused. Zarubin had been KGB-but-not-KGB, a resented presence at Khrushchev's side, protected by (and only by) that proximity. The Lubyanka had manoeuvred constantly to loosen the Party Secretary's loyalty to him, to coax his head above the parapet and give them one clean shot. All the while, their intended mark had been scanning the terrain, making arrangements to flee the Soviet Union when his position became impossible. Why shouldn't he have been planning reprisals? He wasn't necessarily a vindictive man, but who could have resisted an opportunity to serve a tormentor the same dish?

Even so – and as ignorant of the world of banking as Fischer was – something sounded wrong. He looked at Zarubin, who had noticed the face at the window and was waving.

'It's one thing to discover KGB's account details, but transaction codes? Won't they be allocated or determined only when a transfer happens?'

'Actually, no. All foreign payments intended by KGB are reviewed and then authorized by internal committee, which sits four times each year. Every regular – that is, recurring - payment is considered separately, and has its own internal KGB accounting code, as does does the recipient bank in Geneva. Treatment of these payments is discrete at each stage, from the Lubyanka to Switzerland. There is no amalgamation of payments intended for different causes.

'One only needs to have the unique transaction code for the very first payment ever made to a particular foreign party, count the number of subsequent payments, and the current or next transaction code will have proceeded consecutively from that. It doesn't need to be more complicated because no-one in KGB would be so foolish as to dip their fingers into the till. And because these are discrete, hermetic payments, the Swiss bank also designates a consistent identifier code to the recipient's account, updated only by the final digit as transactions occur. Naturally, these banking codes appear on statements which are provided to the Church and then passed, clandestinely, to KGB.

'My most difficult task was to find someone in the KGB's Department of Financial Planning who might be amenable to a little light questioning. Research led me to a young gentleman who had a problem with the ladies – that is, he preferred men, and much younger men than himself. I arranged for him to be blackmailed, became his partner at the Services Tennis Club, waited for the inevitable admission and then offered to use my connections to deter whichever scoundrel was pestering him. He showered me with gratitude, and, upon request, sight of a KGB file, borrowed for less than half an hour.

'It told me that payments to *Stille Hilfe* were made four times each year, immediately after their confirmation by the committee. By my reckoning – and if payments have since continued - the thirteenth such would have been made almost three months ago, which means the next one will be due very soon. In three days, to be precise.'

'And if they were discontinued at some time since you defected?'

'Then, as the English say, I'm buggered. But why would they be? This is a relatively inexpensive donation, which has the potential to keep a terribly embarrassing chapter of German history alive and in the public eye. *Stille Hilfe* are notoriously secretive, but KGB hope eventually to be able to extract and leak to western newspapers a list of their domestic financiers, at which point huge damage will be done to the Federal Republic's international reputation. Why would they throw away such an opportunity, to save a little money?'

'I suppose they wouldn't.'

'No. In fact, quarterly payments to *Stille Hilfe* were increased significantly three years ago, from a little under the equivalent of fifteen thousand dollars to more than forty. I can't see that they've since decided to cut and run from that commitment.'

'Alright, you have the necessary codes. KGB transfer the money to the Orthodox Church's account in Geneva, the Church sends it on to *Stille Hilfe*. There remains the small matter of your diverting the transfer – and without it being noticed instantly.'

'Allow me to say nothing of that at present. A single further matter needs to be arranged. It won't be a problem.'

'I hate it when you even mouth that word. And I'll ask again – what part do you think I'm going to play in all of this?'

'Hm? We really should go in. I believe we're being beckoned.'

'When, exactly, did you invite him to sodomize himself?'

'I don't recall the moment clearly.'

'Otto, you're a prime tit. I may have had occasion to mention it before now.'

Fischer took another sip of coffee to avoid having to admit the point. He and Holleman had arranged to meet at a café with outdoor seating in Marienplatz, so that a report upon lunch – and precisely what the hell was going on - could be made, after which both men would (they had agreed) evacuate Munich and leave Zarubin to whatever fate he had constructed for himself. That Fischer had failed to take the initial step was something for which he had expected to be dragged over the coals.

'Who was the smart fellow who gave you a lift?'

'Mm? Otto Strasser.'

'Be fucking serious, will you?'

'No, really. He was the fourth at lunch.'

'Martin Bormann couldn't make it?'

Fischer had returned to Artsyuk's dining room with Zarubin and managed to eat a polite portion of the richest *bavaroise* he had ever endured. Coffee had followed, and then, excusing himself, he had accepted Strasser's offer of a lift back into the city centre. The ride was a surprisingly modest Opel Kadett, the conversation during their ten-minute journey pleasantly free of any hint of interrogation, and once the passenger had exited the vehicle and thanked his driver it u-turned and disappeared promptly down Kaufingerstrasse. Whatever Artsyuk's private business with Strasser that day, it appeared not to have touched upon the previous evening's deadly incident or Fischer's part in it.

Sensing that nothing more was going to be offered voluntarily, Holleman sniffed and scowled at a passing pram. 'What next, then?'

'I asked him that. He said we should meet tomorrow, at midday, the Viktualienmarkt. It's just around the corner from here.'

'You might be watched.'

'It's very busy, apparently, and big. He'll arrive about half an hour before me, and you'll be there already to check whether he's being followed. If he is, you tell me and then I'll meet him loudly, obviously, like an innocent man would. If not, we'll go into a church at the edge of the market, the Alter Peter.'

'And the point of all this will be …?'

'To be told what it is he wants me to do.'

'You really want to know?'

Fischer watched the pram's propulsion unit – a harassed young woman – pause at the edge of the road and attempt to place two large parcels into it without damaging the occupant while holding its handle with her other hand. His legs had only just flexed to go to her assistance when a much closer samaritan reached her. He settled back into his seat, trying to find a form of words that wouldn't make him seem as naive as he felt.

'He says that he didn't kill the old man in London. I believe him.'

'You're probably right. That doesn't mean he's owed anything.'

'No.'

'Particularly not a helping hand for something that's likely to sever it.'

'No.'

'And even if by some chance it doesn't, the fact that he's stealing from KGB, or *Stille Hilfe*, doesn't mean that the thing wouldn't be regarded as a crime by any passing police agency. Theft is theft, is how they'd see it. Did you enjoy your three years in Sachsenhausen?'

'Only the fine dining.'

'Hmph.' Holleman reached for his coffee, changed his mind and tugged an earlobe instead. Fischer played with his own cup and wondered why he couldn't ever strip down complicated matters to their component parts as his friend did.

'He's on his own here, and whatever I do or don't do he'll proceed with it, won't he?'

'I can't see that he wouldn't.'

'It's not as though he's going to wave a pistol in a bank, or fell a tree in front of a security van.'

'If you're reduced to listing the small mercies, don't bother.'

Fischer sat up. 'It all depends upon what he asks. If it's quick, clean and I don't sense that it has teeth …'

'Yeah, but *why*?'

'He …' Fischer paused, not wanting to say it. Freddie had never met his second wife, never known how she'd mended his broken soul. And it had been Zarubin who'd dragged her out of the pit, arranging the miracle for no more self-interested reason than that it had been in his power to do so. Her early, pointless death hadn't diminished the weight of his gift. It was a debt, an enduring debt, incapable of being repaid fully.

Holleman was looking at him severely. 'It's not still Maria-Therese, is it? How many of his shit-slides do you need to fling yourself down before you can consider yourself squared?'

'I don't know if there are enough of them. He needn't have got her out of Stettin.'

'It was a whim, mate. He likes to think he's wonderful. Or Christ.'

'It doesn't matter what it was. She might have been used, killed and thrown into the Oder, and Zarubin would have lost nothing by it. She *was* nothing to him, and nor was I. If anything that makes what he did even more deserving of … '

'Of what?'

'I don't know. I've never known, which is why he gets leeway.'

'You could park the *Tirpitz* sideways in the fucking leeway you've given him.'

'Well, there it is. Fischer the fool, or perpetual debtor, it doesn't matter.'

Holleman sighed and shook his head. 'Alright. What's your cut?'

'We didn't discuss it. I still have his banker's note.'

'What's five hundred pounds in real money?'

'About five-and-a-half thousand deutschmarks.'

'Nice, but not worth putting your cock in a mangle for. Negotiate. If he's planning to retire on what he filches, make sure that you can do the same. What does he think the take will be?'

'He says about forty thousand dollars. But he'll need to give Artsyuk enough to make sure than he's not chased. I imagine that would take ten thousand, at least.'

'Well, then. Tell him you want five thousand dollars from what's left or you're flying back to England.'

'What about you? He's dragged you here on the same business.'

'I only came because he said *you* might need watching. You can tell him that if Freddie gets five hundred dollars I might not point him out to Karlshorst.'

Fischer smiled. He wasn't going to negotiate, because he didn't want to be anywhere near KGB money. Still, it was a nice thought. With five thousand dollars he could return to Portugal, buy a small house somewhere near Zofia and her husband and spend his days renovating the place. An easy climate, kind company, a setting that would grace any chocolate box and the occasional visit from old friends wouldn't be the worst ordeal a man could face in his fading years. He might even try his hand at cultivation once more, as long as it went no further than pots on a patio.

But the means by which all of it would happen dragged a long, spiny tail. Given what he understood of Zarubin's original intentions, he could have seen himself excepting the banker's draft, if it required no more than the emptying of three bank accounts and then keeping the proceeds safe in Laura Braithwaite's now-redundant outside toilet, pending collection. He could have no moral qualms about being an accessory to the theft of monies intended for Nazi holdouts as long as it was only his conscience that was being pricked. But what new arrangement could adequately cover the new risks? He might negotiate a meatier reward for his help, do everything asked of him and come out of this without a scratch; but he could never know that in years to come there wasn't going to be someone on a hillside in northern Portugal, looking down on his property, waiting for a door to open and offer one clear shot. How much longer his body was going to allow him to repair broken walls in unforgiving English weather he couldn't say, but it was a better option than the twisted spine that looking permanently over his shoulder would gift him.

'I should hear what Zarubin has to say before talking money.'

Holleman groaned. 'You *know* you're going to oblige him, you soft bastard. So why not give his balls a half-turn at least?'

Fischer had no good argument for that. He had told Kleiber, Levin and now Holleman that he would be cautious, do the wisest thing, make no decision without first finding the thing's edges; but as each day passed without him refusing outright to be sucked into Zarubin's latest plot the centripetal forces increased. He knew more about the business than a disinterested party would ever want to know and less than was needed to provide a spur to flee. It was typical of the man's cleverness to dangle something so finely, keeping it just out of reach and clear sight until the hook slid in. A salmon with learning difficulties would have drawn a lesson from it by now, yet here was Otto Fischer once more, reduced to pretending that he had a number of options.

'If he snatches enough to retire upon, he won't bother me again. That's worth any amount of cash foregone.'

'Alright, I give up.'

For a while, both men enjoyed the warm evening, the artfully-reconstructed setting, the young ladies in few clothes, promenading for the benefit of youths too James-Dean-cool to notice. Had this been a holiday, Fischer would have been content to sit for hours, getting all the inconsequential news from his oldest friend and in return offering what few gems life in North Yorkshire could provide. It was what old men did, what old men had earned the right to do after living lives shaped by more dislocations than most generations would ever know. He couldn't say that it wasn't entirely his own fault that he had yet to be welcomed into that blessed fraternity.

'What have we done to deserve this portion of crap?'

Startled, Fischer looked at Holleman, but his gaze was blank, resting on something at the opposite side of Marienplatz. 'She has nice legs. Almost as sweet as Kristin's.'

The owner of the limbs in question wasn't immediately apparent, but Fischer nodded anyway, glad that the conversation had moved on for a moment. He wanted a real drink and might have suggested it, had he not feared that the singular would become plural and then too many to recall. He was conscious of the fact that he been drinking too much since leaving High Scar farm (where available stocks were limited to a magnum-sized consignment of sweet sherry and a half-finished bottle of Advocaat, neither of which he would wish upon a boil), and the side-effects had felt all the more intense after several months of near-abstention. If Zarubin's scheming was going to drag him into another marsh it would be better negotiated without the company of an industrial-strength hangover.

'D'you know what, Otto?'

'Tell me, Freddie.'

'It's a lovely evening, and we're our own men for a while at least. What we need is to get very, very drunk. Everything seems much better than it really is, when you're tasting floorboards.'

Later, when Fischer was trying to make the helicopter blades slow in his darkened hotel room, he recalled the old adage about married couples slowly becoming the same person and wondered if it was applicable also to good friends. To his mind, nothing else could explain these increasingly irritating telepathic episodes.

21

'Oh, my good God.'

'Head?'

'Stomach, mostly. But every time I dry-heave my skull rings like a bell.'

Fischer's own symptoms prevented him from offering the obvious retort. He had awakened from something closer to death than sleep, thrown up almost immediately (thankfully, the room had its own bathroom), tried and failed to keep down a modest breakfast of rolls and black coffee and then called down to reception for more coffee in the hope of settling the crashing waves. It had worked to a degree, but as he and Holleman walked through the Viktualienmarkt. odours from a clutch of food stalls amalgamated into a single, gruesome whole that threatened to topple him once more. Even the unpleasantly onomatopoeic *dry-heave* had almost done it.

They were completing their third circuit of the market. Holleman had arrived early to ensure that Zarubin had no company to the rear, but as yet there was no sign of the man.

'Have you ever known him to be late?'

Fischer cast his mind back across seventeen years. Most of what came to it hadn't been stored in his modest pleasant memory cache, but as far as he could recall the bad news arrived punctually on the whole.

'No. But then, I'm usually summoned to his presence.'

'Yeah, me too. And this is supposed to be important to him?'

'Artsyuk may have detained him. He seems to enjoy talking.'

'Or he's discovered that his house guest plans to gift him much less than he promised.'

'Um.' Absent an abject confession, Fischer couldn't see how that might happen, but he was hardly in possession of all the facts. Zarubin was about to attempt to misdirect KGB funds. Artsyuk was alleged to have some sort of relationship with KGB despite their being, on paper at least, his deadliest enemies. The intended recipient of the soon-to-be-missing money – *Stille Hilfe* – had a relationship with both Artsyuk's RONDD and KGB. Complicating things further, a man who had almost certainly been assigned to following Fischer had been murdered in a Munich street less than forty-eight hours earlier, which must have lit up the nerves of at least one of the interested parties. There were too many opportunities here for something to be said, some casual or deliberate remark, that might expose Zarubin. It might have happened already, in which case Fischer's only remaining task would be to identify the body to the local police. The thought had only just occurred when another one pushed to the front. He didn't believe in fate, or the Spheres, or any other manifestation of a universal equilibrium, yet he had met Zarubin for the first time in a Stettin morgue. It would be a pity, albeit a neat one, if their goodbyes took place in a similar venue.

Holleman was scratching his scalp. 'Shall we wait in the church?'

'Doesn't that defeat the object of your being here? To make sure that he hasn't been followed?'

'Look at this mess. There're at least six ways in the market, and it's packed. I'd need a gang of helpers to do the job. When he arrives he's bound to look for us in the church.'

'Alright.'

The doors to Alter Peter were open. Inside, and despite the heavy foot-traffic in Viktualienmarkt, only three parishioners were attempting to spoil the long view towards the east end. The new arrivals eased themselves into a nave pew close to the south door, made the Sign of the Cross respectfully (though neither was Catholic - or, indeed, a believer), and contemplated their surroundings.

It was another barn-like space, but sumptuously decorated. A vast, ornate canopy dwarfed the altar, and between them and it, large, gilded statues gesticulated grandly from pedestals mounted upon every pillar. In contrast, the walls were whitewashed, dragging the eye upward to a ceiling concealed beneath epic depictions of biblical events.

'It's good to see they didn't waste their money on any of that humble, Christian stuff.'

'It's supposed to uplift the spirit, Freddie. To make folk think about higher things while they're listening to priests mumbling in a language they don't understand.'

'That's a very *Protestant* thing to say, Otto.'

'Actually, I think the Catholics have the right idea. I'd much prefer not to know what it is I'm not supposed to be doing.'

'Ssshhh.'

Sheepishly, both men smiled at an old lady four pews to their front. They sat in silence for the next few minutes, glancing occasionally at the south door, until the lady rose and went to a side-altar, placed money in the box there, lit five votive candles and knelt to pray for the souls of her dead relations. Holleman exhaled slowly and scratched his crotch. Fischer pretended not to notice.

'D'you know, Freddie, this is the second church I've visited in the same week.'

'They're nice places, peaceful. Kristin keeps telling me so, when she's trying to drag me to Sunday service.'

'Has it ever worked?'

'When the boys were christened, and then married. I expect she'll sneak me in a further time when I croak. Not that I'll mind, then.'

'What's the Jewish position on being buried in a Christian plot?'

'No idea. But I don't expect to mind about that, either. Where the fuck *is* he?'

'There's something wrong. He doesn't make plans and then ignore the timing. Even one of Artsyuk's anecdotes wouldn't have made him almost an hour late.'

'Then it's trouble.'

Fischer rubbed his face. Every bad possibility he had been considering returned as a crowd, in a rush. Zarubin discovered, detained, interrogated and quietly disposed of – anything that removed the man's ability to influence events left his unwilling abettors equally powerless. If he was in Artsyuk's hands they had an address at least, but what use was that? How many men were surrounding him? Fischer doubted that he and Holleman could deal with Surly on his own, much less backed by a squad of equally fit, motivated young thugs. And if, by now, Zarubin was in KGB's hands, or *Stille Hilfe*'s, where and how could they even make a start on finding him before someone decided to …?

Holleman stood. 'Why don't you take a seat in the side aisle, where you can't be seen from the door. I'll stand in the porch, and if he arrives I'll give him directions. If I keep station there I can make any suspicious types who don't look as though they'd ever step into a church willingly.'

'Like us, you mean?'

'Yeah. Hell, there he is.'

Zarubin was standing under the south door's archway, holding himself stiffly. He glanced around, saw Fischer and Holleman and moved towards them. Late or not, he took his time, and Holleman's new mail-order leg helped to close the gap between them more efficiently than the Russian's God-given pair. They exchanged a nod in passing, and Zarubin paused for a moment before completing his journey. He sat down in the pew slowly, and pulled a face.

Fischer regarded him carefully. He was pale, more so than usual, and he shifted a couple of times as if trying to find a more comfortable section of the bare wooden bench than he was presently occupying. Eventually he turned to his neighbour, and the manoeuvre brought a slight moan, quickly stifled.

'Not you as well?'

'I'm sorry?'

'I let Freddie drag me to a bar last night. The consequences are with me still.'

'No. I stopped drinking after you left with Strasser. I awoke with a clear head, good appetite and a strange urge to treat myself to a long, brisk walk. Unfortunately, it didn't last.'

'The urge?'

'The walk. I decided to come here via the Isar's left bank, a nice circular route. It was interrupted.'

'By what?'

'This.'

Carefully, Zarubin moved his hand, which had been held against his abdomen. The dark jacket was a little stained, the white shirt beneath it considerably more so, by blood.

'It would be best if we were discreet, but I think that this needs some attention.'

'Christ. Who did it?'

'KGB, I think. A man approached me on the Wittelsbacherbrücke and asked the time. Stupidly, I looked at my watch, and he stabbed me. Fortunately, he was between me and the water, and I was able to push him over the rail.'

'He's dead?'

'I don't know. I doubt it, unless he can't swim. The encounter was seen by at least two pedestrians, though at a distance. So I may be wanted by yet another police force.'

'Are you sure he was KGB?'

'Almost. It's the timing.'

'How so?'

It's only a little more than a day since I killed one of theirs. The one who was following you.'

The doctor treated them to a sour expression for almost the entire time he was treating the patient. He was well-padded, manicured, the sort of physician whose practice didn't take on many knife-wound cases. He had arrived at the apartment with a young man, his driver probably, whose face stirred something in Fischer's otherwise distracted head. He seemed somehow to fit, in a place where nothing should have.

Zarubin bore the cleaning and stitching stoically, wincing only twice during the procedure. This was the first time in their long acquaintance that Fischer had seen him even partially undressed, and was surprised by the older damage to his torso. The obvious penalty for his having defected (the first time) were the missing or stunted fingernails on his left hand, but *that* procedure must have been preceded by an enthusiastic kicking, or at least a beating with a not-quite blunt object.

'The blade missed your kidney, which is fortunate. Without proper equipment I can't say if I've stopped all the bleeding, but there's no obvious further trauma. You should know in a few hours. If you notice swelling, or a duller pain in your lower abdomen than what you're experiencing now, you'd be wise to rush yourself to hospital. Otherwise, rest and take the course of penicillin I've given you. No strenuous activities, and by that I mean anything that isn't just going to bed or the lavatory. For a week, at least.'

'Thank you. What's the charge …?'

'It's all arranged; an old favour, now repaid. I trust my name's not going to get dragged into anything?'

The last was addressed to the young man, who smiled and shook his head. 'Definitely not, Karl. Here, take the keys. I'll be out in a moment.'

The voice did the same thing to Fischer's memory as the face. He opened his mouth to ask the question, but as the doctor withdrew the young man turned to Holleman and hugged him.

'How are you, Uncle Freddie?'

'Old. Angry. Still doing stupid stuff for the wrong people. You remember Otto?'

'Of course. The man who saved us all that day.'

'Hello, Engi. You've grown a bit.'

'In ten years? I hope so.'

'How are your mother and father?'

'Easing off into retirement. Dad says hello. Mum doesn't know about this, of course.'

Holleman grinned. 'She'd rip out our intestines. Rolf's, too.'

It had come as a considerable surprise to Fischer that his usually impulsive friend had thought to make a note of Rolf Hoeschler's telephone number before leaving Trier; a small stroke of genius, or, even more uncharacteristically, of foresight. A friend in a strange city was too happy a resource to overlook, but Fischer had managed it, somehow. Holleman had not, for which at least one party (the stabbed one) owed a large debt of gratitude.

The apartment, emptied of any furniture other than a bed, side-table and curtains, was one of many properties that Hoeschler and his wife owned in the city. It was between tenancies, in a quiet road only a kilometre from the Viktualienmarkt. Holleman had made the call and then flagged down a taxi while Fischer applied the necessary pressure to the wound. In less than ten minutes, the three men had been off the streets, out of sight of anyone looking to finish the job.

Holleman nodded towards Zarubin. 'Do you remember this one?'

Engi frowned. 'A railway waiting room. I don't know why he was there.'

'He was there to take your dad and put him in a place where no-one could ever find him. But he didn't. He put him in a *Volkspolizei* uniform instead.'

'I thought *you* did that.'

'I didn't have the juice, but *he* did. A Soviet uniform and an MGB badge could do a lot, back then'

On the bed, Zarubin touched his dressing and winced once more. 'It was the child with him that made me sentimental that day.'

'Well, the child's just done you a big favour, so it was a good investment. Why were you knifed, by the way?'

'I didn't think to ask the gentleman.'

Fischer grunted. 'It was retribution, possibly. Zarubin killed the one who followed me on my first night in Munich.'

Holleman gaped. 'He did? Why would he do that?'

Zarubin tried to stand, thought better of it and subsided. 'Because the man was probably KGB, not RONDD.'

'Why d'you say that?'

'I too was following Major Fischer. I'd intended to have a word with him before he returned to Artsyuk's house for lunch the following day, but as I approached his hotel I noticed three other interested parties, deployed in a standard surveillance pattern. As long as he didn't emerge he – and I – were safe, but then he did, and one of the three peeled off to shadow him. I did the same, naturally.'

'He just followed me. It's not a capital crime.'

'When you both entered the wine hall I waited across the street. It was almost dark by then, but I saw the other two men arrived. Their comrade emerged from the hall and spoke with them. They withdrew, but not before doing something that worried me greatly.'

'They kissed, passionately?'

Zarubin ignored Holleman. 'One of them handed a pistol to the Major's shadow, and something else. I couldn't see clearly, but after he took them he seemed to be attaching one to the other.'

'Oh.'

'A pistol might be intended for defence. A suppressor never is.'

'It was lucky you were carrying too.'

'I wasn't. I killed him with his own gun. After hitting him, obviously. I didn't want him to be loud, or unhelpful.'

Holleman seemed vaguely impressed. 'I didn't think you'd have the stomach for that sort of thing.'

'I wouldn't say that I have, but something needed to be done, quickly.'

Fischer stared blankly at a blank wall. 'Why would they want me dead? I'd arrived in Munich only a few hours earlier.'

'And what did you do? You visited Artsyuk. You came in from England, as I had a few days earlier. They may have pinned you to me and decided that things were moving in a bad direction.'

'So KGB may be on to you already. I thought you said Artsyuk wouldn't dare betray you?'

'It's possible he's being watched also, and I was recognized. A double agent is trusted by no-one.'

'But now they – whoever *they* are – have a solid reason to kill you.'

'I know. But you could equally be in their sights, as my accomplice.'

'I took the trouble to play the innocent, and all but handed myself in to the police. I think the two surviving members of the team were at my hotel when I returned that night. My loud, scared act seemed to convince them.'

Zarubin settled back on his bed and stared at the ceiling. Holleman turned to Engi.

'How long can we keep him here?'

Engi shrugged. 'As long as you want. Dad says this place hasn't had an enquiry for almost a month now.'

'That's one bit of good news, at least. The other would be that KGB storm the building, once Otto and I leave.'

Zarubin watched Engi depart and smiled wanly. 'Have I over-valued your affection for me?'

'Very possibly. What do we do now, Otto?'

'The man who's been working our strings is out of action. We should go home, to Trier and England.'

'I don't believe your lips have ever formed more beautiful words.'

'Please don't do that, gentlemen.'

'Why not? You've told us next to nothing, and it's come back to bite you. Unless you want that wound to open you can't do more than rest yourself for the next few days. What use could we be to you now?'

'I've been thinking about that. Herr Holleman has only one task, which is to keep you safe. I think he can manage that, having had much practise over the years.'

'Bloody right I have.'

'But you, Major, I see no reason why you can't act as my attorney in arranging a forthcoming financial transaction. In fact …'

'No. Absolutely, no.'

'I haven't explained what's required.'

'You don't need to put your lungs to the trouble. It would involve my stepping into the path of stampeding KGB operatives, furiously chasing their lost monies, and your five hundred pound bribe would be largely squandered on a decent funeral for whatever pieces of me remained.'

'I assure you, you won't find yourself anywhere near vengeful parties. Being now helpless I need someone to liaise with my contact at the Banque Cantonale de Genève, a very pleasant and helpful gentleman who's going to divert a payment intended for *Stille Hilfe* into an account that will be emptied before KGB can even know that their funds aren't in Nazi pockets.'

'And you expect this to move as smoothly as a Swiss motion, do you? No unexpected shrapnel dropping into the mechanism?'

'I believe I've addressed the risks comprehensively.'

'Your faith in yourself is admirable. How much are you paying this bank clerk to commit what's more or less a mortal sin in Switzerland?'

'Not a penny. He'll do it *gratis*. Almost *gratis*.'

'For the thrill of the near-fatal miss?'

'For information which I'm able to provide to him.'

'Which is?'

'I doubt it's relevant for …'

'*Everything* is relevant, if I'm going to be conveying it to your man. I want to be able to judge for myself how closely I'm likely to be shaved.'

Zarubin caressed his wound gently, saying nothing. Holleman snorted.

'Don't give him time to make up something.'

'It's alright. I know when he's lying.'

Surprised, the Russian looked up. 'You do?'

'You smirk. You don't seem to be able to help it. It's as if you're daring me to be clever enough to realise I'm being taken for a fool.'

'Then I suppose the truth will have to do. What are Swiss banks very good at?'

'Saying nothing.'

'There's no-one quite like them, is there? They have an impervious reputation for confidentiality, not the slightest qualms about whom or what they do business with and yet maintain an aura of stolid respectability that, against all evidence to the contrary, seems to convince. They are the first recourse for swindlers, thieves, rogue regimes, counterfeiters, charities, grandmothers and nuns, all of whom breathe a little easier knowing that their hard-earned pennies couldn't be safer or better hidden in the Federal Reserve.'

'None of this is a revelation.'

'Of course it isn't. Everyone who fought National Socialism knows perfectly well that a great part of the Reich's plunder lies beneath the streets of Zurich and Geneva still, and none of them are willing to cast the first stone for fear of drawing down scrutiny upon their own arrangements.'

'Like KGB's?'

'Very much like KGB's. Which is particularly ironic, because the Lubyanka is uniquely well-informed regarding the complex arrangements that shield the guardians and ultimate beneficiaries of Nazi loot.'

'Because the Red Army reached Berlin first.'

Zarubin nodded. 'There's a belief among the western Allies that during the final fighting we tried to spare the Chancellery in order to take Hitler alive. There's some truth in that, obviously, but the principal motive was to preserve the records of a criminal bureaucracy. We weren't successful, but elsewhere the Regime's frantic rush to hide its vast misappropriations resulted in partial exposures. In particular, we managed to salvage a proportion of the records of WVHA. From their Headquarters in Lichterfelde, poignantly enough.'

Fischer and Holleman looked at each other, an ugly shard of their shared history having been stirred from the soil once more. They had waged a very brief, almost futile war against members of the SS's Main Economic and Administrative Office during the final months of the war, and its only palpable success had been their survival. Whatever data the Soviets had managed to acquire from the building at Unter den Eichen 126-135, it had to refer to the very worst kind of Nazi plunder.

Zarubin noticed their reaction. 'That's right. Himmler's busy little bees had a strong, affectionate relationship with the gentlemen in the Cantons, and Moscow has the account numbers and transactions to prove it. Incidentally, so do I.'

'How the hell …?'

'Discreetly, over a period of years. Not all of it, of course; but enough to represent a handsome commodity, should I ever be in need of an advantage.'

'But …?' Fischer frowned. 'If you can access some of those accounts, why on earth are you bothering with KGB money? You could walk away with a fortune that you absolutely know won't be followed.'

'I have a conscience?'

Holleman smirked. 'Bollocks.'

Zarubin reddened. 'It was worth a try. The truth is, my friend in Geneva wouldn't cooperate if I attempted to access that particular treasure. He has other plans for it, which my data will facilitate.'

Fischer didn't require more than a moment to find a reason why that might be.

'He's Jewish?'

'He is. And regards the income that Allgemeine SS extracted from the death camps as the rightful property of the state of Israel, if it's to be anyone's. My files will allow him to further the process of repatriation, and in return he'll help me to steal both from KGB and the mouths of modern-day Nazis. You see, Major, you'll be putting yourself in the company of someone with every reason to keep things discreet.'

'What if those modern-day Nazis have a close eye on what they regard as *their* rightful inheritance? I'll be in the bear-pit, armed with a toothbrush.'

'It's hardly likely.'

'It's hardly *un*likely. They have a mighty motive and plenty of Swiss friends who don't want any any traction attaching itself to the concept of war reparations being paid from their vaults.'

Holleman was nodding furiously. 'Damn right. Five hundred English pounds isn't going to get Otto's arse sewn back on.'

'Alright.' Zarubin lay back carefully once more and closed his eyes. For a moment Fischer assumed that the conversation was exhausted, but then a hand raised itself from the wound and waved as if swatting away a gnat.

'Nine thousand American dollars, if you go to Geneva. That's in addition to the banker's draft. And your large, irritating friend here gets two thousand dollars for whatever trouble he thinks he's put himself to.'

Fischer looked at his large, irritating friend, who was nodding even more furiously than before. As far as he could recall the current exchange rate made nine thousand dollars something like four thousand pounds, a mountainous sum, and the hairs on the back of his neck redoubled their efforts. If the total trove was in the region of forty thousand dollars (from which Artsyuk's RONDD were to take a sizeable cut), what would be left for Zarubin? Was the offer a mirror of his desperation? And if so, how dangerous was this really going to be?

He knew what his response should be, but his mouth refused to put into words what the head urged. He had no fund for his retirement, no prospect of building one, no hopes for more than what he had: pulled-up roots, a bed in someone else's home and an occupation that filled lungs with fine, fresh air and hospital wards with chronic back conditions. After more than six decades in the world his estate could be (and often was) stacked neatly in a single suitcase, so it wasn't mere greed that made him think twice about the prospect of having more. Stupidity, perhaps, but not greed.

Holleman was still looking at him, his raised eyebrows and frozen shrug as expressive as if *it probably won't be bad, just a quick in-and-out to hand over some documents* had been tattooed on his forehead. But wouldn't it, and was that all that the famously slippery Zarubin needed him to do?

'You might also oblige me with a small favour before you leave for Geneva.'

Here it is.

'I'm supposed to be Artsyuk's house guest still, but this hole in my gut would require an explanation. It would be helpful if you called to tell him that I've been dragged away suddenly upon the matter we discussed. That's all. He's been expecting it, so he won't be suspicious. You'll give the impression that you have no idea what the message means, obviously.'

Fischer relaxed slightly. He could also give the impression that, having delivered the message, he was leaving Munich and going home, forever. Anything that made Artsyuk and his pet thug believe that Otto Fischer was no longer on object upon which attention needed to be squandered was all to the good. If ordnance was incoming, he preferred it from one direction only.

Christ. I'm going to do it.

He picked up one of the many blood-soaked swabs that the good doctor had forgotten to take with him, grimaced and dropped it. 'Your Jewish friend in the bank – is he Mossad?'

'No, a Swiss-born citizen. I get the impression that he believes his country has a deal of penance to do. And what better sort of penance than that which empties its deep pockets?'

'And draining Nazi gold from their vaults also deprives its intended beneficiaries?'

Zarubin nodded. 'Whoever they might be.'

Fischer sighed. If a flight from Munich to Geneva could be arranged without a potential audience; if he could get from the airport to his handover, back again and leave unnoticed; if he could then go home, wait for the large cheque in the post and live comfortably ever after without needing two extra pairs of eyes and a high, electrified fence …

If, if, if. 'When do I go?'

'Now would be ideal.'

23

The aircraft – a Lufthansa Caravelle – had hardly levelled off before it began its long descent towards Cointrin airport, and Fischer hadn't made a start on identifying which if any of his fellow passengers (a pool of some twenty-five souls) might be the one with evil intent. None of them seemed interested in him (which, of course, was no reassurance); most of their heads were buried in the paper content of whatever business was bringing them to Geneva, from which even the stewardess' offer of coffee and *spitzbuben* failed to prise more than two gentlemen with ample bellies.

Fischer's own business was accommodated in a thimble-sized container in his breast pocket, the detail being committed to microfilm, a medium appropriate to its sensitive and potentially ruinous content. Having no briefcase, he stood out uncomfortably from this present herd, but he reassured himself that his face hardly needed assistance in that respect.

His nerves had been singing for hours. He had passed on Zarubin's message at Artsyuk's gate, trying (and failing) to discern more than utter indifference in Surly's expression when he mentioned his imminent departure for England. The taxi journey to Munich-Riem was expensively tortuous, taking in several sudden detours at his request, a precaution that the efficient but heavily populated check-in hall rendered pointless. For all he could judge, he might as usefully have worn a monk's cowl or been carried shoulder-high through the terminal building.

He fastened his seat-belt without hearing the command and looked out of his window. Cointrin had a magnificent setting, framed by pine-clad mountain ridges on one side and Lake Geneva on the other, its long, low, single terminal building set parallel to the only runway. It would have been pleasant to see this as a normal visitor, rather than the on-edge, semi-fugitive he somehow always contrived to be when travelling. Perhaps there needed to be another category, an addition to the politely-indifferent question asked by passport control – is this business or pleasure, or chronic flagellation?

The 'plane landed smoothly and taxied almost to the terminal gate. Disembarkation was immediate, and, carrying only his flight bag, Fischer showed his passport and was waved through. An enterprising taxi driver intercepted him as he reached open air and bundled him into an old but clean Daimler. He gave the address provided by Zarubin – La Voie-Creuse 43, Varembé - and was relieved to be delivered to the building in less than eight minutes. It was a false, shallow comfort, but the more speedily his business could be conducted the safer Switzerland would feel.

He was deposited outside a recently-constructed apartment block, nondescript but substantial and surrounded (this from his driver, a

German-speaker) by an assortment of foreign diplomatic establishments that serviced the Palais des Nations nearby.

The apartment of Rudolph Kaplan was on the third floor. Fischer presented himself at the concierge's door, had himself announced and then took the stairs rather than the tiny lift. A young man was waiting for him, propping open the door from the well to the third-floor corridor. He was dressed casually but smartly in a sweater, shirt, trousers and leather shoes, the sort of ensemble affected by someone who prefers to give the impression that relaxation was only ever taken so far. He offered a nod, but no smile.

'Fischer?' It was a question, but the gentleman was turning away before it could be answered, expecting to be followed. His door was halfway down the corridor and ajar; he stood back, checked the view both ways and waved in his guest.

A cursory glance around the apartment told Fischer that he wasn't dealing with a lowly bank clerk. It was modern, open-plan, and, by his modest expectations, quite vast; furnished in a clean, Scandinavian mode, almost bereft of ornamentation, and if the occupier hadn't been standing next to him he would have guessed that he was looking at a show property intended to celebrate contemporary living without the inconvenient messiness of life itself. He couldn't recall having ever seen a pharmacy with less clutter.

The only domestic note was an odour of freshly-brewed coffee, though he doubted he would be offered any. Kaplan's manner suggested that he wanted their transaction done quickly and the evidence removed as far from him as possible thereafter. Fischer was happy to oblige. He withdrew the tiny canister from his breast pocket and held it out.

'Do you want to check it?'

'I haven't a reader here. The transfer to the new account won't take place until tomorrow, so I have plenty of time to ensure that it's what was promised.'

'Right. I'm not supposed to take anything back with me?'

'My thanks, if you would. Some coffee?'

Fischer pretended to check his watch, though his return flight didn't leave for almost ninety minutes. He was pleased that he had been asked, and not just for the sake of the coffee itself, welcome though it would be. It was rather that Herr Kaplan might make conversation and say something – anything – that could offer clues as to how dangerous the return journey between La Voie-Creuse 43 and High Scar Farm was likely to be or become.

'Yes, please. You have a very nice home.'

Kaplan accepted the compliment quietly, as if it were more a statement of the obvious, and went to the kitchen area. On an island-counter a briefcase sat uncomfortably, a lonely token of untidiness. As he passed by its owner lifted and stood it against a high stool, a quick twitch of two fingers checking that its lock was secure. For a moment, Fischer wondered what other matters the Israelis were casting an eye over, and then chided himself. He was already horribly over-informed regarding business of which he wanted and needed no part, and clueless about what lay beyond the near treeline.

He accepted his coffee and sipped it for as long as he could bear the silence between them. Kaplan seemed in no mood to chat, and whatever questions, doubts or fears he might have about his arrangement with Zarubin, he didn't seem to think that his guest was able to address them. Eventually, and rather than burn his mouth trying to drain the cup as quickly as possible, Fischer cleared his throat and tried something a little larger than small talk.

'How well do you know Herr Zarubin?'

'I don't. He first contacted me by letter several weeks ago. Since then, we've spoken twice on the telephone. That's been the entirety of our relationship.'

'And yet you're involving yourself with him in something that isn't without risk. Has someone else given you a character reference?'

'I doubt that anyone could provide something adequate in that line, not for a former senior KGB officer.'

'So he's been frank with you?'

'On that, at least. And one other thing. When he wrote to me he mentioned that KGB had files on several employees at my bank who might be malleable, for various reasons. My name is among them, apparently.'

'You needn't say more …'

'No, it's alright. Three years ago, I was employed by Züricher Kantonalbank. On my own initiative I contacted an Israeli organization and provided them with information regarding long-standing money transfers from Zurich to Buenos Aires. I can't say that any of it was useful, but they were grateful and asked if they might approach me in future. I agreed. Unfortunately, it seems that this exchange was discovered, though I can't say how. A gentleman with a Russian accent put himself in my way and told me that his employers wanted me to know what they knew. When he wrote to me, Zarubin described him in some detail, confirmed that he was a KGB operative and predicted that they would make a more forceful approach at some point. Apparently, Swiss bank employees are regarded as something of a catch. I was grateful for that information.'

'And now he's giving you more of what Mossad want.'

'For my help in the other matter, yes.'

'You're arranging a re-routing of monies, I understand. How can that be done without your being discovered?'

'It can't. I've set up a new transaction code that will send a payment intended for a certain recipient to a new account, which, I imagine, will be cleared out within an hour of its arrival. The bank handling that account will, as a matter of course, electronically confirm reception of the sender's notice of payment. The confirmation is almost instant, so I shall intercept and misplace it. Clearance of funds will take three days, as always. By which time I shall be gone.'

'Gone?'

'From my employment at Banque Cantonale de Genève. From Geneva, in fact, and from Switzerland. I'm about to perform my own personal *Aliyah*. Hopefully, with what you brought in that capsule I'll be made welcome.'

'You're going just like that?'

'It's hardly an impulse. My family witnessed the Sho'ah from a safe distance, and in considerable comfort. Since then I've made a substantial career doing what Swiss bankers do, which is to absolve oneself of the process of enrichment whatever circumstances permit it. Perhaps I can do a little better, if I try.'

'So this was a plan?'

'It was an intention of sorts, but your comrade Zarubin provided the necessary push. For several days I've been packing what I can realistically take with me, and storing it in a couple of station lockers in …'

Kaplan looked around and smiled for the first time. 'I don't believe this place has ever been so tidy. No doubt prospective tenants will feel dreadfully intimidated, when they see it.'

The admission made Fischer's keen sense of shabbiness lift a little. He picked up his travel bag.

'I should get back to Cointrin. May I ask you something?'

'What is it?'

'You don't know me, yet you've told me things that put you at risk. Why?'

For a moment, Kaplan seemed surprised, as if he hadn't considered the point, but then he tried the smile once more. 'I haven't been able to speak of them to anyone else, and decisions this big need at least some air. As to telling *you*, that wasn't a concern. When Zarubin mentioned that you were coming in his place he gave me a description, and you'll forgive me if I say that you aren't someone who might be mistaken for someone else. He also told me that he didn't know of a man, dead or alive, who could be trusted more. And that, I suppose, *is* a character reference.'

When Zarubin mentioned ... The day's eventful passages had been distracting, but amid the blood and swabs Fischer had noticed that the Rolf Hoeschler's vacant apartment didn't possess a telephone. He doubted very much that Zarubin's belly wound would have allowed him search for a public booth, and he was almost certain that the man didn't have access to carrier pigeons.

'When did he tell you this?'

'During his second conversation with me. Three days ago.'

I really am going to kill him.

24

'This *is* food, yes?'

Holleman's mouth was full, so he couldn't answer immediately. He chewed, moved the main mass around his mouth to get a better grip, chewed a little more and then risked swallowing. He managed, just, not to choke, but the tears and spluttering required a further few seconds to bring under control.

'It's …. the best! You can't get it in southern Germany, usually. The Tommies brought the taste, and Berliners gave it life. Go on, try a bit.'

'What's it called?'

'Currywurst. The fellow on the stall told me that he and his brother came down to Munich to steal a march on the competition. They're from Spandau, originally.'

'Ugh.'

Zarubin's face twisted as he tried to process the taste. Holleman tutted.

'Don't be a girl. Didn't you Ivans try to break through to India last century, to take it from the Brits? If you'd succeeded, curry would be the Russian national dish by now.'

'Then I must thank the Thin Red Line for saving us from ourselves.'

'I would have thought you'd be used to it, after two years in London.'

'I've managed to resist the odours that Indian restaurants emit. This is quite foul. When you go out again, could you find something plainer for me? I worry my wound will open if I vomit.'

'Alright. I'll finish that, if you like. Keep the fries that haven't got sauce on them.'

'None of them haven't. Here.'

'Yum. Have you taken your antibiotics?'

'Yes, father.'

'Good boy. Uncle Otto would nag, otherwise. What time is he due back in Munich?'

'If his 'plane is on schedule, just after nine pm. You had better meet him at the airport.'

'Yeah, I thought that. I'll watch out for other interested parties.'

'Bring him straight here. I need to know what our Swiss friend said.'

'Straight here via a dozen crafty detours?'

'Obviously. Now, listen. The money transfer from Moscow to the Church's Geneva bank account takes place tomorrow. The onward transfer – the one that will be diverted – will occur almost instantaneously thereafter but take three days to reach our bank in Munich. Once it's in the account it will have to be withdrawn immediately. That will be a busy day, therefore.'

'But you've been punctured. Busy isn't something you can do.'

'I know. Fortunately, I took the precaution of authorizing another named payee when I set up the account. All he needs to do is turn up with the account details and his passport.'

'And that would be Otto.'

'A Portuguese citizen, name of Olavo Guzman, yes.'

'You're getting your money's worth out of the poor bastard.'

Zarubin sniffed. 'As he'll be taking possession of about forty thousand dollars, I believe I'm showing my absolute faith in his integrity.'

'Or your aversion to taking a head shot from a passing car.'

'When I set up the account I made certain that I wasn't followed to the bank, and believe me, I know how to do that. I used a dead man's identity, someone who was never of the slightest interest, or even known, to KGB or any other agency; who'll return to his forgotten grave when I burn the passport. If he's sensible, Major Fischer will retire Olavo Guzman too, but in light of what he's being paid it's hardly a brutal sacrifice.'

'How will he get back to England, if he has no passport?'

Zarubin shrugged. 'He can make a leisurely passage to the French coast, taking in a number of good hotels and fine meals, and then bribe a fisherman to convey him across the Channel. I understand that it's a short journey, notwithstanding your failure to manage it during the late war.'

Grudgingly, Holleman nodded. 'He can stay with us in Trier for a while. Until KGB get tired of chasing their arses.'

'Well then, it'll be like a holiday for you both. Meanwhile, my good friend Artsyuk will receive funding for his little organization, the neo-Nazis will be biting the carpet, KGB will be furious but not know who to be furious *at*, and I ...'

'Yeah, what will you do?'

'... don't know, as yet. I conceived this idea to escape one situation but haven't considered a new one, for the moment.'

'You'll need to get far enough from your old workmates to not risk a reunion.'

'KGB has a long reach. Perhaps I should rent Strasser's old rooms in Paradise, Nova Scotia, or follow that great exodus of your countrymen to Latin America. A modest house in rural Argentina – what could be more pleasant?'

'That's not a bad idea. After the Eichmann business I imagine the pampas property market's flooded with Tyrolean-style chalets.'

Zarubin smiled, and winced. 'It was a joke. My boredom gland is extremely active, unfortunately. Some people can stare at a wide, empty vista for hours and find fulfilment, but ...'

His voice trailed off, and he studied the wall opposite his bed. Holleman was no great judge of emotions and their manifestations, but if he'd been obliged to pin Zarubin's mood he would have fallen somewhere between pensive and ... nothing at all. Unlike his friend Otto he had never wanted to understand the man's mind as much as bury an ice-pick in it, yet they had spent enough time in each other's company during the late '40s for some things to seem more usual than not. Whenever he played with loaded ordnance he was animated, even super-charged (as some few, fortunate men can be on a battlefield, and even fewer who choose to take on a mountain overhang). Whether that was merely adrenaline, a symptom of his arrant self-regard or the euphoria that an escape from everyday dullness can bring was beyond Holleman's ability or desire to judge; but as far back as he could recall it had been reliable, and punctual. Today, it was missing in what was undoubtedly action. Zarubin was flat, listless or detached, his head somewhere other than on the problem he had created and worked.

A knife in the gut can do that, mind.

Zarubin the preening, the unbearable, was preferable to his moody incarnation, particularly when more than his own feet were poised above the fire; when, in fact, other, blameless toes had been invited by him to try their luck in the heat. Holleman didn't mind so much for his own tender parts; he was only half-engaged in whatever business this was, and could (and would) retire promptly if the temperature rose uncomfortably. But Otto had let himself be led and then dragged to it, and was in need of more than Zarubin the half-here.

'It's only a shallow wound.'

'What?'

'It'll heal nicely. In no time.'

'Are you now an amateur physician?'

'You seem distracted by it. I was being reassuring.'

'Were you? Strangely, I find your diagnosis less than convincing.'

Holleman sighed, and picked up his coat. 'I'll go and fetch Otto. Give me some money.'

'What for?'

'A taxi, to the airport.'

'Isn't there a bus?'

'I don't know, and I'm not going to waste time finding out. You can deduct it from whatever my cut's going to be.'

'Take it from my wallet.'

Holleman went to the table, extracted a twenty and tucked it into his trouser pocket.

'I'll get you something to eat on the way back. Bread? Cheese?'

'And some fruit, please. Enough for breakfast also.'

Holleman left the apartment building without being seen (he managed to convince himself of this after some twenty minutes of tortuous side-stepping and back-tracking) and then walked almost a kilometre further before managing to flag down a taxi. By that time even his comfortable new leg was beginning to chaff at the stump, and on the way to Riem he surreptitiously loosened it in order to rub the offended article. Fortunately, the journey from drop-off point to airport cafe was a matter of a hundred metres and one escalator, and enough customers waiting for previous flights had abandoned their newspapers and magazines for the time to pass quickly.

The flight was eight minutes early, a pleasing oddity. They met on the main arrivals concourse and gave each other no more than a nod's worth of greeting. During the brief journey back to the rank, Fischer noticed it and paused.

'You're limping again.'

'Yeah. I got cocky and imagined I was a distance runner. Come on, before the queue for taxis gets too long.'

They joined it only four places from the front. A few bodies to the rear, a middle-aged gentleman in a raincoat and fedora gave them more attention than two strangers would have expected or deserved. He had noticed the wounded face on the 'plane, and inevitably, it had dragged up unpleasant memories of the war. He had been at the Front for almost three years, and never managed to come to terms with the indiscriminate fortune that kept one man whole while disembowelling the one next to him. He had killed, of course, often at close enough quarters to see the fading surprise on a victim's face. That hadn't bothered him too much. It was what men had done since they first found a reason or excuse to fight each other. But the scale of what had happened around him, brutally marking the worthlessness of human life, had at low moments made him think that all effort to improve, all striving, was not so much futile as delusional. It had taken a long time for his head to get of that rut.

His career had helped in that process, taking him to places a man from his crushingly rural background could hardly have expected to see. He had worked hard and diligence had been recognized, with steady, unspectacular advancement until three years earlier, when a first foreign posting had been offered. The role was no great improvement on what he'd been doing already, but a chance to live and work in Switzerland wasn't something to think twice about, not with the perquisites it offered. Since then he had found no reason to regret that decision; he only hoped that no-one would think his work was so good he deserved a further promotion that might take him home.

His job was to watch, to listen, to distil a broad mass of mundane human interactions for the small quantities of gold that they carried. It was mundane work but useful, and the mental disciplines that it required were probably responsible for the small excavation he made now from memory. The face and the limp, together, but where, and when?

He shuffled forward in the queue, sifting past assignments, trying to hang an event or location upon a half-recollection, and his mind kept returning to his time in uniform. At first he couldn't understand how that could be possible, but then the insistent drag of his fighting memories gave way to something else - a later time, of disappointment and anti-climax.

But of course Geneva hadn't been his first foreign posting. He had marched west with 1st Guards and remained in Germany after the fascists were crushed, and as ruined as the country had been it still counted as abroad. Being in a front rank formation he and his comrades had behaved honourably and then regretted it. The scum that followed then had raped, murdered and pillaged so efficiently that family heirlooms had exchanged hands for pittances and then been sold on to the Americans for dollars, while the real soldiers were obliged to make do with their miserable pay. Eventually, his regiment had been ordered to return to its home barracks in Rostov Oblast, and in desperation he requested a transfer to an NKVD field unit, hoping to remain where he had a chance of getting into the black market. Unfortunately – or so it seemed at the time - he had been granted his wish and posted to NKVD Special Camp Number 1, formerly Sachsenhausen, in which the dregs of the National Socialist Regime who hadn't been worth hanging were entombed.

Almost four years of boredom followed. NKVD became MVD, and the only opportunity to make money came from squeezing the poor bastards they guarded. He bought their Red Cross bounty for foul Russian cigarettes or cheap vodka, traded their wares outside the camp and painfully built up a tiny pot of western currency. And then, just as he began to make plans for it, the fucking East Germans got their state and MVD officially handed over all their camps on German soil.

The tenth day of January, 1950. He could hardly forget the date, it being of historical importance. Strictly speaking, all MVD personnel should have walked out of the gates that day, but their replacements were learning the art of running a prison system almost from scratch. He and several of his colleagues had stayed on for a week thereafter, drilling the basics into dull, resentful heads and taking shit from arrogant junior officers who imagined that nationhood had somehow freed them from the obligation to kiss Soviet boots. One morning that week, he had stood with a German dolt in one of the two guard towers closest to the main gate, explaining that inmates sometimes chose to commit suicide by proximity to the fence and shouldn't be indulged unless or until they tried to climb the thing. He had almost driven home the point when he noticed the new camp commandant smoking a cigarette outside the gates in the company of a man in an overcoat and *Volkspolizei* cap. Behind them, an old Olympia in lovely condition ticked over, a police driver at the steering wheel.

After a few minutes the commandant had stubbed out his smoke, turned and re-entered the camp, and as he did so a man in shabby civilian clothes emerged – a half-faced man, terribly wounded during the fighting, who had been a resident of MVD Special Camp Number 1 for almost three years past. Seeing him, the *Volkspolizei* cap had moved to close the gap between them; he limped badly but enthusiastically, and they embraced like brothers. Moments later they were in the Olympia, being driven to nearby Berlin, presumably.

It had been an interesting, untypical moment, but nothing that had demanded a reserved place in memory, until now. Yet having dredged it up, he was almost convinced that the fellow in front of him was the same half-face he had known at Sachsenhausen. He could be mistaken, but the accompanying limp had brought past and present together, sharpening his attention, making demands of his intuition. He was *almost* certain that this was the same man.

He should make a report. It might be of no use to anyone, but it wouldn't hurt to demonstrate his assiduity, his fitness for his present post. To whom would he make it, though? All intelligence reports regarding UN missions in Geneva went straight to (and often disappeared within) the Lubyanka, but this concerned two German nationals of unknown circumstances. He considered what might be best – for himself, obviously. He knew a few people at Karlshorst, including *Apparat* Krokhin's second-in-command, Arkady Muratov. Both men were rigorous but approachable, and not inclined to think less of a man for showing initiative. If this turned out to be an irrelevance, he would sooner it be buried and forgotten by someone who didn't stand in his direct line of command; if it wasn't, a word of praise from Berlin-Karlshorst – the foremost of front lines - would look very well on a personnel file.

Being to the rear of the queue, he couldn't follow Half-Face and The Limp, but that didn't concern him. They had met at Munich airport, so they would be in the city or its environs for a while at least.

Perhaps KGB were aware of them already, and that, also, was irrelevant. He didn't care what came next. His only concern was that his prompt response be noticed, and that the people who had posted him to Geneva could reassure themselves that they had made an excellent choice.

25

'I assure you, Major, I mentioned you to Herr Kaplan only in case of an unlikely emergency that kept me from our meeting in Geneva.'

'Yet that emergency occurred. If a flesh wound counts as such.'

'Um, Otto, he's been bleeding on and off for hours now. Properly.'

'No doubt he has a bag of pig's blood tucked under him somewhere. You're defending him, Freddie?'

'I know, it's mad. I just don't see how he might have planned a stabbing. They go wrong so easily.'

Fischer opened and closed his mouth. A knife in the gut *was* an unlikely, messy way to become pretend-incapacitated; it was just that he felt so much better being angry with Zarubin than not. To have one's identity misappropriated, to be lured into an insane plot and then be required to execute the damn thing while its architect directed operations from his bed represented some sort of pinnacle of victimhood, and he had substantially abetted the ascent by not walking away. Worse, having previously resolved not to be moved, swayed, convinced, importuned or otherwise bothered by his principal tormentor he had weakened horribly, telling himself at each marker that he need go no further and then taking another step. He was furious, and realising that his fury should be as much directed at Otto Fischer as Sergei Aleksandrovich Zarubin made him more furious still.

'Otto, you've gone off somewhere.'

'Sorry. So, the money will take three days to clear. What if KGB or *Stille Hilfe* decide to check on its progress in the meantime?'

'Why would they? It's a transaction that's taken place many times over the past few years. Everyone knows that the majesty of international money transfers can't be rushed, and in the Banque Cantonale de Genève the parties can reassure themselves that the very safest, most reliable and discreet measures are being observed. Really, unless someone wants to pore and drool over the figures involved, what point would there be in chasing something they already know to be in transit?'

Fischer nodded slowly. Unless *Stille Hilfe* had run out of cash to feed the office meter they wouldn't be pushing for the money to arrive earlier than it possibly could. He would have relaxed a little, but he'd noticed the frown and slight pause on *Cantonale*.

'How bad is it?'

Zarubin pulled another face and touched his midriff. 'Not agonizing. But moving is better considered than done.'

'You aren't going to be ready, not in three days. Halfway to the bank those stitches will open up, and then what will you do?'

Holleman snorted. 'Give him the good news.'

Zarubin managed a smile this time, the familiar, hateful version. 'I took certain precautions, in case of ...'

'You bastard.'

'Major, I'm sure than even a hewer of stone like yourself has infinite experience of withdrawing money from a bank. All you need do is fill in a slip, present it with your passport, try to sound Portuguese and then wait while the loot is counted out for you. I've prepared the ground as thoroughly as John the Baptist did for Christ.'

'And what happened to both of *them*?'

'Their terrain was a little more perilous than a typical bank lobby. You'll meet with neither a Salome nor Caiaphas.'

'I won't do it.'

'I have no means of compelling you. But if you don't do it, and I *can't* do it, then the money will stay where it is. And when KGB discover that their funds have been misdirected, a degree of hellishness will descend upon this pleasant city. They may not even need to visit us in person. I understand that *Stille Hilfe* employ gentleman with quite esoteric talents, and they'll have equal motive for making an end to us. It will be much easier to gain a head start on trouble if we have our escape planned and the means to achieve it safely in our pockets.'

Fischer didn't need to look at Holleman. His friend had a practical nature, and given that they were both knee-deep in the latrine already he wouldn't see any point in not profiting from it. He breathed deeply, quelling an urge to lunge at the bed and thrust a forefinger deeply into the wound.

'Where is it?'

'What?'

'The bank where I'm expected.'

'Sparkassenstrasse 2. I can give you directions. It's the Stadtsparkasse Bank.'

'And what if my passport isn't sufficient to convince them to hand over forty thousand dollars? Do I demand to see the Manager? Threaten to withdraw your custom?'

'I put that question to them very plainly, and then signed a document authorizing Senhor Olavo Guzman to conduct any and all business on my behalf relating to the account.'

'Aren't there banking rules to prevent transfers of tainted monies across borders?'

Zarubin laughed. 'My dear Major, if there were, the Swiss would go out of business tomorrow. *No questions asked* is not so much their motto as an article of the Helvetian Faith. No doubt they'll be obliged eventually to conform to the world's broader usages, but that time hasn't yet come. At present, pushing money of any dark provenance through a Swiss bank renders it as white as an angel's wings.'

'And if I'm recognized while I'm in the bank?'

'Herr Holleman will be your rear gunner both there and back, to ensure you aren't followed or to warn you if you are. As to being recognized while *on* the premises, I chose this particular bank for a reason. It's Munich's oldest and fustiest financial establishment, used by no known Intelligence agencies, and certainly not KGB. My only worry is that you may need to wear a wing-collared shirt and top hat to gain admittance.'

It had been a faint hope that Zarubin hadn't thought of everything, twice. The correct response to this latest jerk of the strings was outrage, of course; but it was an effort to maintain. As someone who had taken the bait, debated the risk of swallowing it and then presented his belly to the net, Fischer could conceive no good reason not to take the next, final step. The worst of it might be a bullet or a knife; the best would be enough money to make a decent decision about what remained of his life and a ticket to somewhere far, far away from the man best qualified to spoil it. He didn't want to be here, but having been the principal mover of his own misfortune he had at least a small chance to make something of it.

'Your friend Kaplan performs his sleight of hand tomorrow. Another three days pass before we can do anything about it. What happens in the meantime?'

'You'll stay here. Like me, you're too visible to risk outdoors. Herr Holleman can return to his police hostel and attempt to be forgettable. He should come back to us before first light on the morning of your visit to Sparkassenstrasse, but not before. The young man – Hoeschler's ward?'

'His son.'

'Might he oblige us with a further visit, bearing food?'

'If I ask, he will.'

'He can be trusted not to be followed?'

'He was a street kid before Rolf swept him up, remember? In Berlin, in wartime. Ten years old, with *Ordnungspolizei* having standing orders to make the species extinct. KGB couldn't follow him to church on a Sunday if he didn't want them to.'

'Good. We must fight boredom for four days. After that, we'll be wealthy, and running.'

A.F. Muratov scanned the brief report and replaced it on his desk. Having been posted only recently to Karlshorst this was his first walking-barefoot-across-broken-glass moment, and he gave it the attention it deserved.

Was it the same man? His correspondent admitted that he couldn't be sure, but if he was merely indulging a hunch he probably wouldn't have submitted the report in writing. Doubt, in this case, wasn't a warm, comforting blanket, a reason to do nothing. If it *was* the same man, something might be happening.

That damned incident in Berlin, two years earlier, poked them all still. It had been the sort of thing that powerful men, having buried, would have preferred to remain far underground, yet few people at KGB Karlshorst weren't at least partly aware of how it had scorched the arse of his immediate superior, Aleksei Krokhin. He had since held it up (the case, not his arse) as a cautionary tale about operations planned on a napkin and set in motion without adequate intelligence or preparation. So if this *was* the same man ...

Krokhin had to see the report, obviously. After that, decisions had to be made. Was Moscow to be made aware of the sighting? Shifting responsibility from one's own shoulders was always the first, most desirable option; but control of whatever then happened would then lie entirely with the Lubyanka, and the very men who had fucked it up the first time around. The only conclusion that Muratov could or dared draw at this point was that Krokhin would not be pleased with the news.

Not that his was a happy temperament on the best of days. When A.M. Korotkov (the previous Berlin Resident) had died he had been more or less promised the succession, but having served as acting Resident for almost two years now he had yet to receive official paper confirming him in the role. In the meantime, he had been obliged to continue to discharge his not-inconsequential duties as Head of Directorate S (Illegals). Responsibility without status was vinegar, and Krokhin much preferred fine wine.

So, Muratov had to think about how to present this. Something *might* be happening in Munich, and that was never a pleasant combination of words. The city was a bicycle ride from Pullach, where General Gehlen's BND, the Federal Intelligence Service, was headquartered. Its East German equivalent, MfS. had insinuated a significant number of operatives into Pullach, so it was KGB's firm policy to keep a discreet distance from the place. The sudden appearance of this creature with so much history would have rung an alarm bell at the quietest of times, but his face, hideous though it was said to be, wasn't the worst of it. A few days earlier, Karlshorst had received word from London (via the Lubyanka) that a man answering the description of the traitor S.A. Zarubin had left England several days earlier. His intended destination was thought to be … Munich.

Zarubin the black legend. A clear shot at the bastard would of course be a wonderful thing, but more information was needed to ensure that any bullet wouldn't also take off KGB's foot. On the face of it, a recent defector (a senior Kremlin man at that) re-surfacing in a cold battle-zone was begging for an end to his sufferings, but nothing to do with Zarubin could be assumed or met with a standard response. A matter of days after his alleged flight to Munich, a man had been head-shot from behind, classic NKVD-style, in one of the city's streets. KGB would have had no interest in the incident, had the victim not been carrying the Czechoslovakian passport of a deceased infant (this from MfS, who had an operative embedded in the Bavarian Landespolizei). It was exactly what a Soviet agent would have been issued with, given that the Czech border was the closest escape point from Munich. Of course, Zarubin - or his doppelganger - might have had nothing to do with the incident, but the Intelligencer's handbook didn't have a chapter on coincidences. A quick, frantic check had determined that the deceased wasn't officially KGB, but that had been only partly reassuring. It was possible that he was an historic asset, long-forgotten or discarded, an Illegal, a man who had lived among the enemy for years, submerged, German in all but reality, waiting to be activated by Moscow. But then, what if he had been a traitor himself, turned by Zarubin but now surplus to further needs? The very fact of his death could be a trigger moment, the start of a move against Soviet interests. KGB had received seemingly reliable information that neither SIS nor CIA had regarded Zarubin as a potential asset, but what if that wasn't the case? What if he was being worked as part of a bigger operation? If the latter, how the hell could Muratov, Krokhin or the ghost of Felix Dzerzhinsky himself calculate the extent to which it might hurt KGB?

If only Zarubin had chosen to come to Berlin. Even with the wall blocking easy access between the two halves of the city it wouldn't have been too difficult to lift him, even without direct KGB involvement. MfS had infiltrated every level of city government and much of the *Bundesgrenzschutz*, so it would have been a matter of asking the favour of Ruchestrasse and then sweeping over whatever trail his legs made as he was dragged eastwards. Munich was a much harder prospect. A snatch team could be assembled, briefed and put on site within two days, but the footwork necessary to find, watch and pin the target would be a longer, more difficult task, and KGB had little more presence there than their unit at the Soviet Trade Mission.

He began to think of practical possibilities, and had to remind himself that he was being too conscientious. Whether an operation would or could be mounted was not his responsibility; nor, probably, was it Krokhin's. The Acting Resident wouldn't dare *do* anything without Moscow's prior authorization, not on any business that possibly (probably?) involved Zarubin. Their new Chairman, V.Y. Semichastny, had been intimately – in, fact, almost fatally – involved in the operation to prevent Zarubin's defection two years earlier, so he had to be feeling the pain still. Khrushchev himself had stayed KGB's hand at the last moment for God knew what reason, while Krokhin had acted as the hapless go-between at Karlshorst, directing (and then frantically standing down) the squad sent to eradicate the infection. Muratov knew all of this only because Krokhin had embellished his cautionary tale with the gruesome details of that day.

He re-read the report so he could speak without needing to refer to it, and then picked up his 'phone and asked to see the acting Resident at the very earliest opportunity. *Very earliest* was generally understood to mean now if not sooner, but he was aware that Krokhin was over at Russchestrasse that morning, having his monthly meeting with MfS Chairman Erich Mielke (for whom even urgent business had to hang fire). Satisfied that his boss would return the call at the earliest available moment, Muratov tried to apply himself to the day's other calls upon his attention. The big story, one that was dragging itself out, was Kennedy's impending visit to Berlin, a belated response to the raising of the Wall. He was expected to exercise to the full his rhetorical skills, speaking much of visions and aspirations and precisely nothing of substance. As a professional dissembler himself, Muratov could only admire the man, but it was Karlshorst's job to make the visit as uncomfortable as possible. At that moment,

Krokhin was doubtless urging Mielke to use his agents in West Berlin to stir up industrial action, or protests against American encroachments in Africa and southeast Asia. It would all be as futile as an offer of political asylum to any *Wessies* who couldn't bear the presence of the President on their streets, but any chance to embarrass the Amis had to be taken.

And yet, not even Kennedy could shift thoughts of Zarubin and his ugly friend entirely from Muratov's head. If they *were* in Munich together, it couldn't be an innocent visit, however pleasant the city's restoration or excellence of its beers. Pullach's proximity, just a fifteen-minute bus or S-bahn trip from Riem airport, tainted every possible motive other than one that would stir sensitive bowels and kill any chance of post-luncheon naps in the Lubyanka.

His telephone rang. He swallowed hard and lifted the receiver

'What is it, Arkady?'

Krokhin sounded impatient, so Muratov was flattered that he had returned the call so promptly. In as few words as possible he gave his boss the essence of the report, pausing only when a loud *fuck* disturbed his flow. He waited for more but nothing came, so he finished with a lame 'I thought you should know as soon as possible.'

'Yes, that's right.' Krokhin was breathing heavily, and in the background someone was asking (in German) what the matter might be. Muratov could make nothing of a brief, whispered exchange that followed, but it sounded more like an argument than a discussion. Eventually, the heavy breathing returned to the receiver.

'I'll be home in thirty minutes. Be available, will you?'

Muratov, having ruined his boss's day, had no intention of not being available, but the line was dead before he could offer that reassurance. He checked his watch, called in his secretary and asked that tea be brought when Krokhin arrived. Usually, he managed a little banter (she being both personable and witty, qualities not over-represented among KGB's administrative cadres), but something of his mood crossed the space between them and she was out of his office in a moment.

Were his fingernails not manicured he might have bitten them while he waited. Fortunately, his superior improved upon the ambitious schedule he had set himself. Flushed, sweating, Krokhin almost stumbled into Muratov's spare chair and slapped both of its arms.

'What is he doing there?'

'I don't know.'

'Who reported it?'

'Anatol Kuznich.'

'Who?'

Muratov shrugged. 'A minor asset, based in Geneva. Usually, he reports the UN gossip, but he was on a flight to Munich for a meeting at the Trade Mission and recognised the mutilated face. From Sachsenhausen, where he was a guard.'

'He's certain it's the same man?'

'Almost.'

Krokhin pulled a face. 'He has a good memory. Tell him we're pleased.'

'Are we?'

'Are we fuck. But it's better that we know than don't.'

'If I may ask, how close is this man to Zarubin? I mean, they were together in Berlin two years ago, but what else do we have?'

'Not enough. Their relationship almost certainly preceded the time he spent in Sachsenhausen. After that, it's difficult. We know that Zarubin returned from his first defection via Berlin, where the Face was resident at the time, but whether he was involved in it I can't say. And after Beria fell, Khrushchev made sure that no-one got too close to what Zarubin was doing. Serov tried, failed and was shunted to GRU; Shelepin danced around a solution for too long and then panicked when the traitor's second defection commenced. I've told you about the damn mess *that* became, but at least we can say that on that occasion Half-Face was involved. In fact, he was at least partly responsible for ensuring that Zarubin escaped the bullet.'

'A good friend to the General, then.'

'A reliable one, for sure.' Krokhin sighed, leaned forward, picked up and shook the novelty Empire State Building snow-scene paperweight that Muratov had brought home from his United Nations' posting the previous year. Both men watched until the last flakes had settled and then caught each other's eye.

'Right.' Krokhin stood up. 'Everything – *everything* – we think, say or do about this is documented, with copies for Moscow. I'll push this up to First Directorate … no, to Semichastny directly, and he'll decide if he wants to bring in Sakharovsky. Ultimately, this has to be the Chairman's decision, but it's also his old mess that we'll be cleaning up. I have no idea how Khrushchev thinks of Zarubin these days, if at all, but Seminchastny does, I expect - or will do, following a very short conversation with him. *That's* going to determine how final the solution's going to be, obviously. The important thing is, we absolutely do *not* think of taking the initiative, even if it means Zarubin slipping away before we get firm instructions.'

'We do nothing until we hear from Moscow.'

'That's right. We'll respond quickly, diligently and efficiently to orders, but once this report's on its way to the Lubyanka we become as inert as that stupid thing.'

Krokhin's hand waved at the Empire State Building and he sighed again. 'You wouldn't think it possible, would you?'

Muratov assumed he wasn't referring to the problems inherent in raising phenomenally high structures.

'What?'

'Zarubin. The bastard buried Beria, somehow managed to foil the strenuous efforts of that beast Serov to do him the same favour, danced around both Shelepin and Semichastny – two of the cleverest men I've ever met – and now that his arse is finally clear of the snapping jaws he decides to jam it back into the lion's mouth. Either he has no brain whatsoever or the death-wish of someone caught up to his balls in Nadezhda Alliluyeva.'

'Who?'

'Mrs Stalin. Now, get this thing on the wire to Semichastny. And mark it Most Urgent. We don't want him to think we prevaricated.'

27

'Have you heard from Otto?'

'Mm?'

Jonas Kleiber was reading that day's edition of the *Manchester Guardian*, the football pages, for pleasure. He didn't often relax with his nose in a newspaper, but the *Guardian*'s retrospective upon the recently-ended season was unusually pleasing, he being a Spurs fan and his team having finished second in the league, taken the Charity Shield, and - the very pinnacle – thrashed Atlético Madrid in the European Cup Winner's Cup to become the very first English club ever to lift a European trophy. Though not a man to gloat, he had pored over every match report and campaign-retrospective in both the English and German Press for the past three weeks, and was as yet nowhere near wearied of the superabundance of clichés.

Maisie dropped her *Readers' Digest*, having become tired of, and slightly terrified by, an article entitled 'How Safe is Fail-Safe?' She had commandeered the sofa before Kleiber thought to, and was stretched out upon it, showing off her legs to best effect. On the table, the remains of a roast lunch awaited their redeployment to the kitchen, while from a small radio, the organ of Guildford Cathedral was being assailed by someone named Barry Rose (Kleiber hated church music intensely and the organ even more, but his *inamorata* insisted that at least a hint of religion should intrude upon their Sundays).

'Otto. Your mate. Lovely man, had a bad war?'

'Er, no. Don't expect to. He's not what you'd call a natural correspondent. If he needs anything he'll be in touch.'

'What if he's in trouble? You said he might be.'

Kleiber looked up from the apotheosis of Jimmy Greaves and sighed. 'If he is, there's nowt I can do about it, is there? I don't know where he is or who he's keeping company with other than that slippery bugger, Zarubin. I warned him strenuously not to go.' The paper fell to his lap to free up a hand for a plaintive wave. 'He's a grown man, and if he *has* a mind – which I doubt – he's made it up.'

Maisie sniffed. 'But he's like family, darling. And he's done a lot for you, hasn't he?'

'He's shot my nerves to pieces any number of times, if that's what you mean. I don't recall him snatching me from the jaws of death or anything.'

Another sniff. 'I thought you cared for him.'

'I do, my love, tremendously. But when a man decides it's easier to throw himself under every passing bus than not, what can you do? Is there any sherry trifle left?'

Maisie stretched and raised herself slightly to scan the table. 'About a big spoonful, I think. You're getting plump, Jonas.'

Kleiber smiled contentedly. 'It's your fine cooking. When I first met you it was either baked potatoes or corned beef sandwiches. Now, though …'

'I don't recall you thinking much about food when we first met.'

Briefly, a murmur of past depravities stirred the Kleiber libido, but a weight of Yorkshire pudding and roast potato bedded it down again. Besides, she'd got him thinking about Otto, which was not the best way to put lead in his pencil. Despite his pretence of blithe indifference, he'd been hoping for a brief telephone call to reassure him that his friend was breathing still and unencumbered by thumbscrews (or whatever it was that KGB favoured). Days of silence were preying upon his peace of mind, and there really was nothing he could do. He didn't know where in Munich Otto was staying, had no address for this Artsyuk fellow or contacts in the city who might be able to clear the fog a little. If only he'd tied his irritating friend to a chair and demanded details before he fled abroad he could probably relax a little and …

'Did that Russian mention where Otto might be?'

'I never spoke to Zarubin. He only pushed that package through the door, remember?'

'No, the other one who wrote.'

'Eh?'

'I put the letter on your desk yesterday morning. Haven't you opened it?'

Kleiber raised his eyes to the ceiling. If anyone wanted to hide something from him, his desk was the logical location. It was inches deep in research papers, newspapers, bills, receipts and assorted snack wrappers, a small area from which Maisie's neatness-obsession and all cleaning products whatsoever had been banned.

'Boris someone, I think.'

He climbed out of the armchair and went to the desk. As long as no-one added to the mess he knew where everything was, usually. Unfortunately, he had been sitting there that morning, imbibing the glory of Spurs, which meant the letter was somewhere beneath or between just about every sports section in the English- and German-speaking world (the US excepted in both cases).

A rummage became an excavation and then an archaeological dig, and it was only when he bit the bullet and tipped everything off the desk in order to sort it that the blasted thing appeared as if it had been perched on the summit all along. He closed his eyes and breathed deeply, reminded himself that Maisie was a goddess in just about every way other than this, and slipped his thumb into the envelope's flap.

The handwriting was both neat and awful, a painful, crabbed print that, despite the lack of lines on the notepaper, was laid out in as orderly a manner as the Rosetta Stone (which Kleiber feared he might need to decipher it). It took a while to make sense of what he was reading, though the first paragraph told him why that was.

> *My dear Herr Kleiber,*
>
> *Please forgive both the intrusion and quality of this letter. I am not as yet sufficiently familiar with Latin script to attempt to write myself. My assistant, Sandrine, is my hand so to speak, but she tells me that her written English is only adequate. Perhaps together (and with our dictionary) we can convey enough of my meaning to be useful.*

As you will be aware, I fled the Soviet Union almost two years ago with the help of your friend Otto Fischer. Though I hadn't intended to defect, I don't believe that it would have been safe for me to remain in my country, and so I owe Herr Fischer a debt of gratitude. When he visited me a few days ago I attempted to repay that debt in part, but I fear that my desire not to betray General Zarubin made me too circumspect.

The last time I saw the General he told me a little of his intentions and motives. Being as I am one of his few confidants (and unable to offer much practical assistance to his scheme), I believe he was more forthright with me than he was with Herr Fischer.

For several days now I've been recalling my conversation with your friend, and my sense that I didn't say the right things has grown. I have no contact details for him, and though there is one person in Munich to whom I might apply for assistance in reaching either him or the General, I fear that my approach would be damaging to them both. I therefore decided to write to you in the hope that Herr Fischer will call you at some point, and you might warn him.

My specific concern is this:

'What does he say?'

'Sshh, darling.'

As Kleiber continued to read his head became colder, and lighter. A heartfelt *fucking hell* balanced on his lips, but Maisie had long-term ambitions to drag his vocabulary from the gutter and he didn't want her to think she was wasting her time. Never mind, he told himself; he'd been worrying about being worried about Otto, but this changed everything. All that was required of him now was to arrange the funeral – or memorial service, for want of a cadaver. Were flowers appropriate for the latter, or was it more about saying nice things and then getting pissed? He didn't know. Perhaps there was a pamphlet covering the basics, a Bereaved Person's Guide to Doing Death Right …

'Jonas, you're talking to yourself.'

'Am I, Sweet Bits? Here …'

She took the letter and read it, and the frown disappeared as her eyebrows rose towards her hairline.

'Oh, shit.'

'I don't know the man, but he was Zarubin's personal secretary for years, so if anyone was going to hear the truth it would be him, wouldn't it?'

Maisie shook her head. 'He wouldn't just make up. What would be the point?'

'Who? Zarubin or Levin?'

She considered this for a moment. 'I mean the man who wrote this letter. But the other one – why would *he* admit to it if he didn't mean it?'

'Otto says you can't ever know where you are with Zarubin. Which, of course, is an excellent reason to avoid the bastard.'

'Why didn't he? Otto, I mean?'

'Christ probably knows. I think Otto feels he still owes the man. For his wife's life.'

'The tart?'

Kleiber winced. 'He's wrong, obviously. You can't keep paying off the same debt, not forever.'

'He must have loved her.'

'She's been dead for fifteen years. He should have got over her by now. Ow!'

Maisie didn't pull the punch, and Kleiber was still rubbing his bicep a few minutes later when a thought occurred.

'Zarubin bribed Otto to do something, and that something looks like it's going to be almost or actually fatal. He knew that money wasn't important – it was just that Otto would feel himself to be under an obligation if he couldn't return it. That sounds right, doesn't it?'

'I think so.'

'I don't get it.'

'What?'

'I don't *know* Zarubin, but from what I've heard about him he isn't the kind to …'

'He was KGB. What *kind* is that?'

'I mean, he wouldn't lay a trap for one of the few men in this world that he could trust. Would he? Would any sane man?'

'Then what's he doing?'

'Christ probably knows that, too, but I don't. How can we warn Otto?'

'We can't. He'll have to see it for himself.'

Kleiber laughed, though there was no humour in it.

'That's the thing about suicide missions. You can't ever see it clearly until you've been welded into the cockpit.'

28

He would have sneered at it in anyone else, but Zarubin couldn't resist checking his wristwatch for the tenth time. He found no surprises there. Having last consulted it about two minutes earlier, he discovered himself and the universe to be older by about the same quantity.

At this point, nothing is going wrong.

Once more, the reassurance failed to take hold. Today, he was entirely in the hands of other men, and though he had at least half-planned for it (the stabbing apart) he didn't enjoy the sensation. Infants, puppies and Red Army personnel below the rank of captain were content to have their destinies moved by larger, indistinct forces, but Sergei Aleksandrovich Zarubin much preferred to do his own moving. He had known how tormenting this would be, and prescience didn't help at all.

He had mapped out a schedule, allocating minutes to every step of the process, allowing extra for unforeseeable minor delays at each, and the entire thing required two hours and forty minutes, door-to-door. Naturally, it was an exercise in futility, a symptom of his sense of helplessness. *Unforeseeable* couldn't be calculated other than by a hopeful stab into darkness, and what constituted *minor* to a seismologist seemed very much otherwise to a man whose nerves were presently being pan-fried. Still, he had included the likelier possibilities. Traffic might be heavy or diverted due to roadworks, adding considerably to the duration of two taxi journeys; a new clerk at the bank, unused to emptying and closing major accounts, might take his time to decide that he couldn't bluff his way through and seek the advice of a senior colleague; a lost child, pitiably anxious, might intercept and impose himself upon a man notoriously prone to compassionate urges and be led to a police station, where a keen eye, noticing the bulging bag, might well enquire politely as to its contents.

That last seemed improbable, but an anxious mood was always likely to be over-indulged. Three days earlier, he had been a model of calmness and confidence, yet time, and immoveable processes required for monies to clear through banking systems, had worked evil wonders upon his mind. Despite his reassurances to Major Fischer, he couldn't guarantee that one slight misstep by his ally Kaplan, an uncharacteristic degree of interest in the transaction from a button-presser somewhere between Moscow and Munich or an unanticipated new electronic security measure wouldn't bring down the whole thing, in which case his unwilling helper might be walking into a trap carefully set by one of several interested parties (of whom the least dangerous would be the local police).

To spare himself an eleventh bout with the wristwatch he rose carefully from his prone position on the bed and went into the apartment's tiny kitchen. Engi had returned with enough provisions for a week, but not, unfortunately, a supply of tea. Coffee – and the powdered stuff at that – was the only available alternative to tap-water, and it was a measure of Zarubin's impatience that squandering a few minutes upon brewing and drinking yet another cup of the swill seemed preferable to not doing so. His wartime ordeals with Red Army-issue coffee-type product had taught him that the optimal delivery system was via quantities of bread, dipped into the foul liquid and chewed, and in the years since he had found that the addition of a little honey made the whole almost palatable. Fortunately, the young man's patience hadn't been tested by these additions to his shopping list.

Three days in the company of Major Fischer had been a real ordeal, however, and probably for both of them. Conversation, never easy, had faded very quickly, and Zarubin had been unable to resuscitate it. His reluctant accomplice had communicated sufficiently to allow them to share space without coming to blows, but a blind, deaf man could have sensed the ill-will that hung like a thick haar between them. Holleman, returning in the early hours as planned, had been astonished by the near-exuberance of his welcome (particularly as he came bearing no beer).

He had left the apartment at first light, and taken up position at the end of the street. Fischer waited half-an-hour and then followed. He was dressed smartly, having borrowed Zarubin's only tie and hat, and carried a large soft bag over one shoulder. At the apartment door, a brief interrogation confirmed that the bank account number and branch code had been memorized, the security letter (co-signed by Zarubin and a senior bank clerk) and Portuguese passport safely stored in a buttoned-down pocket and an alternative return route to the apartment fully absorbed in the event that Holleman spotted a tail. It took an effort of will on both men's part not to say anything further that might have snapped the final threads of temper.

That had been two hours and twelve minutes ago (Zarubin hadn't been able to resist glancing down at the wristwatch once more), which meant that his pan-fried nerve-ends were due to feel the heat rising. He ate or semi-drank his bread-coffee without tasting it (a small mercy), re-read the previous day's *Süddeutsche Zeitung* that Holleman had brought with him and tried to clear his mind of all but *now*. It didn't work, of course, but the discipline of eating (or drinking) something he didn't enjoy, reading a series of extremely parochial news items and then breathing deeply for several minutes had a dampening effect upon both his pulse rate and intuitive fatalism. What *could* go wrong was impervious to further influence;

what *might* go wrong ceased – for a little while at least – to circle his attention like a hostile horde.

He reminded himself of the things he could rely upon. He trusted Major Fischer to do what was expected of him; he trusted Holleman to be an effective pair of eyes upon Fischer's back; he trusted his own judgement in devising this plan; and he trusted in the power of greed and deception to move other men in the desired direction. If he had any reservations (other than those fed by the countless, dark possibilities he had pored and re-pored over during the past hours), they stood upon the matter of motive – particularly, his own.

Which was why this particular form of strangeness, a dislocation, weighed upon him. He had set himself upon a journey without clear expectations for its ending. He wasn't familiar with self-doubt, nor its power to render clean lines hazy, and he was beginning to understand how a mind not at peace with itself could turn well-shaped plans into fire-fights. Circumstances had made it necessary that he modify his original intentions, but formerly he had always known how to make the best of altered conditions. He was having a first taste of what he suspected was familiar to Major Fischer, for which he felt not only uncomfortable but uncomfortably remorseful.

Guilt. How very irritating. If the day's business hadn't been pressing so heavily he might have smiled. Instead, he checked his damned watch again. Two hours and twenty minutes, almost at the limit of time untouched by incident, almost time to start worrying about what had gone wrong. He was dressed already (more so than since he had arrived, injured, at the apartment), and it was only necessary to pull on his sweater to be presentable. He unlocked the door, stepped into the corridor, and made his careful, painful way down to the lobby. The *hausmeister* was elsewhere, so he took up a position in shadows to one side of the front door, clamped his eyes upon the end of the street and willed Fischer to appear.

He had only just told himself (for the second time) that he was being ridiculous when the object turned the corner. He was walking quickly, head down; he had the bag over his shoulder and seemed to be struggling slightly. Zarubin absorbed this information as a snapshot and then devoted all his attention to the corner. Two minutes later, Fischer had almost reached the street-door and neither car nor pedestrian had yet appeared behind him. Zarubin felt his entire diaphragm relax. At the very least, one flank of their extended Front was secure.

Holleman was not in sight. It had been agreed that he would follow Fischer from the bank as far as the end of the street but then bide his time, watching for suspicious activity and then return to the apartment only after dark. The money would then be counted, apportioned, and the following morning a substantial deposit would be made at a nearby branch of the *Bayerische Landesbank*, at which point Zarubin's obligation to Artsyuk's RONDD would be discharged. He thought about that for a moment. He owed Artsyuk a debt that could best be satisfied in person, but would that be unnecessarily hazardous? He had no way of knowing whether KGB kept more than an occasional eye upon the house in Prinzenstrasse, and it would be foolish in the extreme to test luck that had already been stretched to a gossamer consistency. Yet such a gift, to be offered so impersonally, seemed ...

His thoughts were interrupted by Fischer, barging through the apartment's front entrance and stomping towards the stairs without noticing the other man. A polite cough halted him; he turned, glared and dropped the bag.

'You stupid bastard!'

'Wait. Upstairs.'

Fischer picked up his cargo, followed Zarubin to the third floor and said nothing until he was in the apartment. The glare remained fixed to his face, and it was testament to its intensity that it sat equally well on both sides, the good and the ruined.

'How much?'

'How much what?'

'How much money was supposed to be in your account?'

'Whatever approximately forty thousand US dollars is in deutschmarks. If past deposits have been maintained, that is.'

'Oh, they've been maintained. Would you like to count it?'

'Of course, but …'

'The bag's full, and Schöner's face is on most of the German notes. They ran out of those – or rather, they wanted to keep a sensible reserve in case another customer walked in before closing time. So I said yes, US dollars would be fine for the rest, and if you run out of those, British currency wouldn't be too insulting. It took a while, but at least the establishment didn't need to close its doors early. You know what a run on a bank can do.'

'How much?'

'The transfer was a total of just over one hundred and sixty two thousand dollars, equivalent. I was asked several times if I was *quite sure* that I wanted it all, and that if I did, shouldn't they call someone to provide an escort. A police escort, that is.'

'Mother of God.'

Fischer rubbed his sweat-sodden forehead. 'I don't know if you imagined that forty thousand dollars would be too modest a sum to stir KGB to a tantrum, but four times that amount might do it. They'll probably area-bomb Munich, to get the job done properly.'

KGB funding went to a lot of places, and it was spread thinly. Currently, their largest donations were made to a clutch of African liberation fronts, and, of course, Cuba; but several recent speeches made by members of the Praesidium had mentioned the need to counter growing American involvement in south-east Asia. Zarubin knew perfectly well that Khrushchev wouldn't open the cheque-book on demand, that economies would have to be made elsewhere, particularly among older investments that promised uncertain or longer-term returns. Perhaps *Stille Hilfe* were being offered a final, tempting opportunity to pass on a little information about their German donors before Moscow cut off their funds entirely. Or perhaps this was a private arrangement – one of the Nazis looking to pad his retirement in return for a discreet discussion. Either way, it had the odour of a fond goodbye.

Zarubin held up a hand. The gesture felt as useless as it must have looked, but he needed time to rethink those few assumptions he'd felt fairly certain about.

'I had no way of knowing that the transfer would be so ...'

'Fatally substantial? Of a magnitude to invite fire from just about every direction? KGB, *Stille Hilfe* – who the hell won't be looking for us? We've given the uglier half of Bavaria enough motive to hunt us like the last rat in a barrel of terriers. I haven't told Freddie yet, I didn't get the opportunity. He's gone back to his police hostel with a spring in his step and no idea that he's never going to draw his pension. Christ, I'm babbling.'

Fischer collapsed into an armchair. Zarubin picked up the dropped bag, slipped the buckle strap and peered tentatively into it. The bills were wrapped neatly and secured with rubber bands (probably the bank's entire supply) and ordered by denomination. It would need to be deposited carefully, in relatively modest amounts, and with at least a dozen banks that dealt routinely with sizeable foreign transfers. It would all take time, and time had become tight. In absolute terms, KGB's total budget for subsidies to foreign friends was quite massive, but not CIA-massive. Fischer had guessed correctly: the *Stille Hilfe* donation had been chosen because it was long-standing and therefore routine; large, but not spectacular. The loss of forty thousand dollars would have stirred them, of course, but balanced against the need to recover the monies would be an imperative not to break cover wantonly. Zarubin had been counting upon the time required to balance that equation to get himself and his reluctant assistants out of harm's way. But one hundred and sixty thousand dollars bought an entirely different set of priorities. Within hours – minutes, perhaps - of the theft being noticed and its routing identified, every resource in southern Germany would be activated to recover the loot and expunge the thieves. If assets were lost or compromised in the process the damage would be considered later, by committee.

So he and his merry men had to run, but when? To do so immediately would give them a head start, but if their flight was spotted they would be pinned as the likeliest suspects. If they waited, using this apartment as their bunker for the next few days, KGB might drag some other poor bastards into the frame. That would offer a finite opportunity for the real perpetrators, but how could they know when to move? When they finally broke cover the hunting party might be waiting, guns reloaded and raised, ready for pheasant.

His mind was always clearest when he didn't have company, yet pushing Fischer out of the front door wasn't an option now. He needed to give himself space to consider the possibilities, but he couldn't be sure whether that was caution or prevarication. He could of course admit everything – *everything* – to the man in the armchair and hope that two good minds could find the answer that eluded one of them; but he wasn't sure that Fischer, in possession of all the facts, wouldn't be inclined to do KGB's job for them. There was a very fine line here, and as yet he couldn't locate it clearly.

'I assume you have a selection of brilliant alternative moves prepared in case it all goes to fuck? As it has, obviously.'

Fischer was looking at him wearily. He had cooled down in more ways than one, and for a moment Zarubin feared that it was the calm of a man awaiting the final word from a line of rifles in front of him. The handkerchief had been folded and placed neatly on the small table in front of him, a small nod to order (one that a hand was preventing from wandering away). Insofar as his face was capable of being judged conventionally he looked drawn, older, a better match for his bought-me-down clothes than when he left the apartment earlier that morning. Something invigorating, a mood-rattling reminder of the brighter possibilities was needed, and precisely nothing came to Zarubin's mind. He looked down at the bag's contents once more, willing the many depictions of Herr Schöner, that man of great mental gifts, to provide inspiration.

'Nothing? Nothing at all? Well, may I make a suggestion?'

'Please.'

You must know some KGB people in Munich.'

'There are surprisingly few. The Lubyanka came to an agreement with MfS years ago, to do nothing that might interfere with or compromise *Stasi*'s impressive penetration of BND Headquarters at

Pullach. I think a small handful of KGB men do low-level work at the Trade Mission, but that's it.'

'Then you might make contact with one of them, anonymously. Tell him where he can find a bag full of money and suggest that his superiors bless their good fortune and put aside thoughts of retribution. Tell him that the nameless idiots who took it are very, very sorry, and regard themselves as changed men.'

'It's good that your sense of humour hasn't failed you at a difficult moment. Major.'

'On the contrary, it seems to have abandoned me. I can't think of a way we can survive this, short of reversing as much of it as possible.'

'Obviously, I had no idea of the true amount, but the execution was flawless ...'

Fischer winced. 'You had to use that word?'

'... and we have no reason to suppose that KGB will discover who did it. Not for a few days, at least.'

'They'll have my description within hours. I'm not a blade of grass in a lawn, am I?'

'You have enough former comrades with equally poor luck to make an identification uncertain. It gives us a little space.'

'And you? Are you certain that KGB don't know you're in Munich? If they do, they won't assume I'm anyone other than Otto Fischer, the traitor's erstwhile, clog-headed dogsbody.'

'Dogsbody?'

'A drudge, a menial. Royal Navy usage, eighteenth-century.'

'You've not entirely wasted your English exile on walls, then.'

'I *hadn't*, until now. But a single round from a Makarov's going to make all my labours pointless, unless you can think of something to deliver us from that finale.'

Chairman Semichastny's schedule was a heavy one, and it was almost twenty-four hours after his receipt of a most urgent memorandum from the Berlin Resident that he found time to read it. What constituted *most urgent* was a matter of opinion, of course, but Krokhin wasn't the sort to churn out memoranda to show what a busy fellow he was. Had Semichastny not been dragged away on a matter so important that it defied any official classification of urgency he would have made time for it immediately, and once he read it through he was as one with its author's opinion.

A routine report had reached the Lubyanka the previous week, stating that a man answering Zarubin's description had been seen boarding a flight from London airport to Munich. Given the man's distinctive appearance – particularly the shock of blond hair – Moscow had been inclined to regard the information as reliable. No alarm bells had rung at the time; there were no delicate KGB operations in movement in the city or its environs, and given the fact that none of their Western competitors had chosen to pick up the prize when he defected two years earlier, it seemed likely that his capacity to do damage was limited. Naturally, a zero-risk opportunity to put half a magazine into his treacherous head would have been seized upon, had it presented itself; but Munich was famously off-limits to speculative ventures. The matter of Pullach overrode all lesser concerns.

But the appearance in the same city of a man with the same facial wounds as Otto Fischer (Semichastny needed to refer to old files to remind himself of the name) set the bells pealing loudly. What Fischer *was* to Zarubin – an ally, employee, unwilling servant or pair of dirty hands – remained unknown, yet it seemed from what history KGB had managed to disinter that every time they came together some scheme was being played out. *This* time, a man with what very well might be a KGB-issued passport had died on a Munich street, shot from behind. Had that been Zarubin, or Fischer, and if so, why? Why would they light themselves up for no good reason? And if there was one, what could it be?

Semichastny needed to know who the dead man was, and what he had been doing that night. He needed their people in London to sniff out an already-cooling trail and uncover Zarubin's movements and contacts prior his flight to Munich. As a matter of urgency, he needed Krokhin to have a difficult, delicate conversation with Erich Mielke, to put him on notice that, despite KGB's sincere reluctance to compromise MfS's Pullach operation, it might become necessary to put men into the area at short notice for the sort of job that was almost certain to draw attention. The only guarantee he could offer (a shaky one at best) was that the target would be removed from the city's environs before an extreme solution was applied.

He was still considering the implications, and what triggers would incite the worst of them, when his intercom buzzed. He frowned at the device. His secretary knew not to put through anyone unannounced unless it was a member of the Council of Ministers (at least), and even then she would first knock on the door and ask if he was able to take the call. He picked up the receiver.

'Comrade Chairman, we have a problem.'

Oh, wonderful. Semichastny recognized the caller's voice immediately. Yuri Bodrov, head of KGB's Department for Financial Planning, had a larynx honed by an eighty-a-day habit and a seven-year stint in a Sibirsky work camp, during which time he had donated half a lung to the war effort. His rehabilitation after Stalin's death had been partly compromised by his refusal to play the Moscow game of sniffing the air and bending as the wind arrived, but his accountant's talents and a reputation for reliability had been appreciated by Semichastny's predecessor and friend Aleksandr Shelepin, and to those qualities the present Chairman could add the man's reluctance to cover his arse by having all decisions rubber-stamped in advance. He got on with his job, ruled his little kingdom efficiently and tended not to want to be noticed. If he was calling to report a problem, it probably wasn't something trivial.

'How much of one?'

'Enough for to it to be discussed in person, as soon as you can find time.'

'Now, then. Come up.'

Bodrov was in his office within three minutes, even before Semichastny had thought to order tea. He had a large folder tucked under his arm, at the end of which two nicotine-stained fingers clamped the inevitable, unfiltered *Belomorkanal*. Hastily, Semichastny pushed a near-redundant ashtray towards the supplicant's side of his desk.

'Thank you, Comrade.'

'What is it, Yuri Petrovich?'

Bolkov sat, sighed, put his folder on the desk and scratched his nose with the freed hand. 'Some of our German friends. They haven't received their quarterly pension.'

'Is it our fault?'

'No. The payment was made on time, through the usual accounts. It didn't reach theirs, though.'

'Which friends are they?'

'The fascists.'

'*Stille Hilfe*? That's been going on for …?'

'Over nine years. It gets a little worse. We temporarily upped the payment three months ago – that's to say, this was the first, higher tranche since we made the decision. Because of the embezzlement.'

Semichastny recalled the discussions. One of *Stille Hilfe*'s accountants – a brave or reckless man – had made off with a substantial portion of the organization's funds after a large gilt investment had been realised. They traced him to Argentina (obviously), but their local friends couldn't put a hand on his shoulder before he disappeared into the interior. First Directorate had urged that the opportunity be taken to meet the shortfall and then call in the favour when the West German government most needed to be embarrassed. At the time, the equation had seemed advantageous, but none of its variables had factored in a further theft.

'Have they got *another* embezzler, for God's sake?'

Bolkov shook his head. 'The funds never reached their account in Thuringia, so no, it isn't possible.'

'Where did it go? Presumably, we can trace it?'

'We *should* be able to. At the moment, the Swiss can't identify the recipient account, but they say it will be a matter of hours. Obviously, we can't apply pressure because they don't know they're dealing with KGB.'

Semichastny leaned back and closed his eyes. 'Alright. How much are we missing?'

'Our payment was denominated in Swiss francs - a little in excess of seven hundred and eight thousand of them. About one hundred and sixty two thousand American dollars.'

'That's …'

Bolkov grimaced. 'In the region of five percent of our current quarterly budget for foreign friends.'

'Fuck your mother!' Semichastny had served in the Red Army for a matter of months only before returning to university, and he was not usually comfortable with the casual obscenities of the common *soldat*. An expert on the delivery of foul language would have found nothing forced about this latest effort, however. It was heartfelt. If anything, it understated his strength of feeling, and it took an effort to leave it at that. He swallowed.

'Yuri Petrovich, is there any – *any* – chance that the perpetrator organized this from the transaction's Moscow end?'

'One of ours, you mean? No. We clear funds through two banks before they cross into the Swiss financial jurisdiction, to ensure that our fingerprints are on nothing. It would be quite impossible for someone here to arrange a diversion at the other end without attaching some incriminating instructions that would be flagged at several points. Personally, I believe the interference occurred at the last possible moment – that is, immediately before the money was due to arrive in the Orthodox Church's account prior to its onward transmission to Germany.'

'The priests didn't see it?'

'No. I had to ask – I think they were terrified – but they responded immediately. They had expected the payment, but it never arrived.'

'The bank …?'

'The *Banque Cantonale de Genève*. Yes, they definitely acknowledged receipt, so it seems they have a problem with one of their employees - and probably a senior one, given what it would require to divert funds through internal transaction coding.'

'Can we get to him? Or her?'

Bolkov frowned. 'It would be difficult. Firstly, no bank – least of all, a Swiss bank – is going to admit that they're not secure, so we'll get zero help from them. Secondly, the person who did this is almost certainly running already, so we'd be trying to catch up without knowing in which direction we should be sprinting. It would take an inconceivable piece of luck to find him. Or Her. We should be looking for the accomplices at the other end of the transaction.'

'You think others are involved?'

'Definitely. The moment the diversion was noticed, *Banque Cantonale de Genève* would have requested the receiving institution to reverse the onward payment. The fact that they've owned up to the incident means that they couldn't reverse it – that someone had been ready to empty the recipient account the moment the loot arrived. The mystery is how the fellow in Geneva managed to mask the diversion until the clearing process had taken place, but I assume we'll never be enlightened. His employers will be anxious both to cover it up and devise a method to ensure it's never repeated.'

'But whoever helped him may be vulnerable.'

'I've taken the liberty of asking Simonov to call through to your office the moment Geneva identifies the recipient bank and informs the Church. We'll then at least have a geographical starting point.'

Semichastny tapped the table as he thought through the consequences of this. The stolen amount was sufficiently large to draw questions from the Intelligence Liaison Committee that reported to the Council of Ministers. As far as he knew he had no enemies on the Committee, but it would be a strange creature indeed who wouldn't at least enjoy the discomfiture of the KGB Chairman and possibly seek to use it to bring the organisation under closer, more tiresome scrutiny. KGB was Khrushchev's child, and those who circled around him these days, plucking away slivers of his power, could make it his embarrassment also. Semichastny owed much to the First Secretary, but he had no intention of risking his own ...

Geneva.

Hurriedly, he grabbed the Karlshorst memo from his desk and scanned the second paragraph once more. The half-faced man had been seen on a flight from ... Geneva. He dropped the paper, closed his eyes and sat back. Bolkov waited, but the KGB Chairman didn't seem to want to come out of his little coma, not even when his telephone rang. Eventually, and because he was expecting a call himself, he ignored protocol, stretched across the desk and lifted the receiver.

'Arkady, yes, it's me. Ah, thank you. Get the address, will you?'

Bolkov replaced the receiver carefully. 'That was Simonov. The Geneva Bank has discovered where the money went. It was to a bank in …'

'Munich.' Semichastny opened his eyes.

'It was, yes! How …?'

'I thought of the worst possibility and just said it. You'll have to excuse me, I have quite a few calls to make. Keep pressing the Swiss bankers for information, even if there's little chance of getting anything useful.'

'Right.' Bolkov stood, and paused. 'Forgive me, Comrade Chairman, but I wish to state that I'm certain that none of our people could have anticipated this.'

'Don't worry, Yuri Petrovich, your team isn't going to be blamed. It's in the nature of unpleasant surprises that they jump out of their dark corners without giving notice. Ask my secretary to come in as you leave, will you?'

In what had once been his sitting room, E. N. Artsyuk rummaged through one of several tall piles of newsletters, each of them a legacy of his calls-to-arms years. Every editorial, every analysis of the then-current state of Soviet politics and almost every article upon the lives of Russian émigrés, on freemasonry, Jews, victims of show-trials and a host of subjects drawn from the archives of the Russian Information Bureau (another of his creations) had been his work. The name Artsyuk did not, of course, appear anywhere within this titanic body of literature; his *nom de plume* (he considered it rather a *nom de guerre*) was Evgeny Derzhavin.

He was proud of Derzhavin's corpus, without ever falling into the vanity of believing that it had made a substantive difference to anything. The Soviet Union endured, while the dreams of monarchists, social democrats, fascists and Holy Russian exceptionalists were as beaten down now as at any time during Stalin's sanguinary reign. His success he measured only upon the grounds of his having survived the best efforts of NKGB and MGB to erase him and his work, and then the reluctant accommodation that KGB had offered to keep him out of their active files. He had dared to go to Moscow, twice, to negotiate the truce that had held ever since, and if the price of it was an occasional piece of treachery he comforted himself that no other friend of General Vlasov could claim a similar achievement (mainly because they were dead to a man).

He often spent hours here, re-reading his past essays in the clutch of titles he had founded – *The Voice of the Sovereign*, *Sovereign Call*, *The Will of the People* and *Nabat* – and finding, on the whole, that there was nothing he would have said differently, or more concisely, or with less venom. He and his young assistant Vasili (who wrote his own articles under the pseudonym Mosichkin) had attempted to be the voices of a hundred causes (only a few of them their own) that Bolshevism had hoped to have silenced forever, and if their readership had never been vast it was nevertheless pleasing to know that an archive of the other Russia had been created and would endure, possibly beyond the death of the Soviet system itself.

Artsyuk had given up hoping that it would occur in his lifetime, but to a man who saw the arc of history in its true dimensions this was not a tragedy. He had removed himself only from a brief moment in his ancient nation's story, and who could say that he might not have done the same in some other, kinder age? He was by nature a contrary man, cut from a stubborn cloth, who in the last century might have found a home with one of the many societies fighting Romanov tyranny – as a foot-soldier of the *Narodniki*, perhaps, or even People's Will. Or would he have gone entirely the other way, fearing what might succeed a bad system, and fought instead with the Black Hundreds to preserve it? One would have to experience the times to know what mark they could leave upon a man.

Vasili didn't play such idle games with his own posterity. He was a child of the *Holomodor*, his father shot at their farm gate, the starving mother fled with her only child to Bulgaria, and then Turkey, and then fascist Germany, where the boy's already feral anti-communism found a ready welcome and the means to channel it. He had been too young to serve in the Wehrmacht until the war's final days, but then had resisted the urge to flee the Soviets once more and hid instead in the ruins, doing favours and odd jobs for Red Army soldiers and cutting their throats whenever the opportunity presented itself. Vasili had no inclination to ponder alternative histories beyond the single matter of whether his mother might have survived, had he not fled the consequences of a final murder and found a home in the American Sector. One didn't need to be a Freud to see what head-damage that abandonment did to the young man even fifteen years later.

The head came around the door as Artsyuk searched for an elusive article on the Miller Case he'd written about a decade earlier. As usual, its owner was dressed entirely in black - an affectation picked up in a cinema, probably, but usefully intimidating given that RONDD's budget hadn't ever run to providing adequate security for its leader. All monies received were spent in the service of regional offices the organization maintained in Europe, the US, Latin

America, Australia and even Taiwan (the Kuomintang being every bit as keen to see the end of communism as their counterparts from Russia). The 'offices' on the whole comprised just one or two fellow-travellers working out of their own, rented homes, but propaganda was expensive however it was done. Vasili's brooding presence at Prinzenstrasse 46 was a great comfort, therefore. The young man was also an industrious administrator, a competent author (though the titles of his pieces were often so long that the articles themselves were little more than reiterations), and, when necessary, a ready volunteer for dangerous tasks. Artsyuk aside, he was probably RONDD's most valuable asset.

At present, he was dealing with the day's mundane business, it being the post and whatever telephone calls came through. A small pile of envelopes in his hand were being frowned at, and he didn't look up as he spoke.

'Otto Strasser called about ten minutes ago. He'd like to speak to you this morning, if possible.'

Artsyuk sighed. 'I'm beginning to regret my generosity. He won't rest until he has the money in his pocket.'

'I don't know why you offered it. He needn't have known anything about Zarubin's donation.'

'He doesn't know the source. As for why, it's prudent to keep Strasser sweet.'

'Is it? He isn't *anyone* any more. He hasn't been taken seriously since his party collapsed.'

Artsyuk looked up from his search. 'I know. But there's something *fortunate* about the man. To have been there at the start, to have given Hitler the shits, successfully survive a dozen attempts to crush him and then come home with nothing clinging to him, it's astounding. Other than Mikoyan, I can't think of a more persistent survivor.'

'You hope it might rub off?'

Artsyuk smiled. 'A little of his luck couldn't hurt. In any case, the poor bastard's extremely grateful for the pittance we're offering. And he knows enough people from the old days still to make himself useful, if necessary.'

Vasili grunted and lifted one envelope from the pack. 'This is from London, our friend the Archpriest. It was franked two weeks ago, so God knows where it's been since.'

Artsyuk allowed an eyebrow to rise not quite enough to make it seem that he cared much, one way or the other.

'We haven't heard from him in almost a year. I hope he's not looking for donations.'

'I shall tell you momentarily.'

Vasili slit the envelope with a knife, removed a single sheet of paper and scanned it. As he did so the bored expression on his face shifted with almost pantomime swiftness to something between disbelief and utter wretchedness. To this, Artsyuk responded with a little more emotion.

'For God's sake, what is it?'

'It's …' the younger man looked up. His eyes were filling, a sight entirely unfamiliar to his friend. 'He says that Stanislav Kudrin is dead, murdered in his home, and that the man suspected of it …' The face hardened once more; '… is Zarubin.'

'What? Impossible!'

'Why? He was KGB once. Who would have a better motive?'

'But … Stanislav hasn't been a threat to the Bolsheviks for more than forty years! Why on Earth should they send – Christ, a *general*, of all people – to do the dirty work?'

Vasili waved the paper in Artsyuk's face. 'An ex-general, condemned to a traitor's death in absentia, no doubt. If he wanted to go home, or at least to stop looking over his shoulder, what better way to commute the sentence than to assassinate one of the Soviet Union's abiding enemies, an easy target, elderly and unprotected?'

Artsyuk shook his head. 'I ... no, I can't believe it. Why would he flee to us, known friends of Stanislav? It makes no sense at all.'

'If he's running from the police and can't yet return to Moscow, he has to hide. He's offering us some of the money he intends to steal to deflect from his guilt, or because he thinks we're greedier than we are loyal. He's a clever man, a snake.'

'But ...' Artsyuk consulted a portion of the floor between two piles of newsletters. 'Are there no other suspects?

Vasili glanced at the letter. 'The Archpriest doesn't say so. What he *does* say is that Zarubin had been in financial difficulties, and that Stanislav had helped him, with money and accommodation. *And* he was seen at Stanislav's apartment only hours before the body was found. No-one else was noticed there.'

'It's ... not enough to convict the man.'

'We aren't a judicial process, are we? It looks like he did it, and we have a chance to do something about that. For God's sake, Evgeny, Stan was one of your oldest friends!'

That was undeniable. They had met in Paris, in the 30s, when Artsyuk was a young idiot looking to martyr himself for the cause (gloriously, that is, not by any simple, efficient means such as boarding a train to Moscow and volunteering his political opinions to the ticket collector). At that time, Stanislav Kudrin was already an august fixture on the émigré scene, a real aristocrat among the shabby dispossessed who had merely been born to the station. One of the few surviving veterans of the bloodiest clashes of the Civil War, he attracted forlorn nostalgists and impossible schemes of reconquest like a ripe plum draws flies, yet he was generosity itself to those who needed food, shelter, a dose of backbone or just kind words to carry them through strange days. To Artsyuk he was almost a surrogate father, though the angry, tiresome boy had done nothing to earn it that his older self could recall. Kudrin donated to him a spare bedroom in his apartment, and introduced him to those few Russians who had any sway still in their community of exiles. He also took him to favourite haunts in the Marais, in which establishments Artsyuk quickly came to understand where the older man's tastes lay. Most nights, at least one pretty young man would return with them to the apartment, and though Kudrin never tried his luck with his lodger (or allowed others the same opportunity), it took no great leap of imagination to realise what was going on.

Artsyuk took advantage of this kind but disturbing hospitality for almost six months, but soon after finding trial employment as a translator in a small publishing house south of the river he became involved with one of the firm's secretarial staff, a girl two years older and a decade more sexually experienced than himself. Her own apartment was much smaller than Kudrin's and far less fashionably sited, but Artsyuk promptly accepted the offer of her bed and moved his few belongings out of the Marais. Naturally, his occupancy ended the moment she tired of his enthusiastic but unpractised technique, and soon after that his employer (her father) added to the favour; but a quiet, desperate word with Kudrin brought enough money to take a lease on a small office in Montparnasse with a loft space above that served as a bed sitting-room. From there, Artsyuk built his first Russian-language leafleting operation.

Kudrin's patronage continued. He secured donations from leading members of Paris's Russian diaspora that helped to carry the embryonic venture through several teething disasters, and, when war came, he exercised some shadowy influence that kept the now-naturalized Artsyuk from being conscripted into the French army. The German occupation was, predictably, a comfortable time for the émigré community, and both Kudrin and Artsyuk trod the fine line between keeping their new masters amenable and alienating the mass of their French acquaintances who wanted the occupiers wiped from the face of the Earth. A few pamphlets on the bestial excesses of Stalinist rule were wholly financed by the Germans and distributed widely, but Artsyuk declined to offer a published opinion on the Jewish Problem despite his own pronounced antisemitic proclivities. Liberation brought no problems for either man, and once the military presence on the streets had settled down Kudrin asked Artsyuk's help to disinter a small hoard of gold coins from its hiding place in Père Lachaise cemetery. The younger man quietly booked this token of how close their friendship had become, and, a few months later, suggested that they both relocate to western Germany, it having become the obvious front line in the struggle against international communism.

Kudrin had refused. He felt that was too old now to be in any sort of front line, but he gifted Artsyuk the funds to make his own eastern translation possible. In the years that followed, the establishment of RONDD and its manoeuvres with or against its sister anti-Soviet organizations meant that contact between the two men was intermittent, and Artsyuk was surprised when his friend relocated to London in 1951 (complaining that the émigré scene in Paris was now a near-necropolis of begging corpses). Still, their correspondence, if infrequent, remained affectionate; Artsyuk was able to chart the slow growth of RONDD and its less-than-successful efforts to galvanize anti-communist sentiment in southern Germany, while Kudrin offered no substantive news but plenty of excellent gossip from London's Russian exiles in the wastes of south Kensington and Knightsbridge.

At some moment during the mid-50s, Artsyuk experienced an idle but significant revelation about his old friend and mentor: that not once, during all their long conversations, had Kudrin ever let slip any information about how he had acquired his wealth. He had spoken often about the Civil War, of course - the great men who'd tried and failed to stop the Bolsheviks, and the survivors' flight from their homeland. Of his miraculous transformation from penniless refugee to amiable patron of struggling compatriots he had said nothing, however, nor even hinted at it. Artsyuk tried and failed to recall if he'd ever attempted to broach the subject (so many of those conversations had been heavily fuelled by vodka), but having been such a fortunate recipient of that generosity it probably would have seemed impolite, even to drunken sensibilities.

As the sixties approached, contact between them slowed and then ceased. Artsyuk hadn't been surprised by this. The false dawn of Khrushchev's succession and repudiation of Stalin's excesses had raised hopes tremendously among the diaspora, but as it became clear that reforms would go only so far a heavy despondency fell upon many of the first-generation émigrés (who came to realise, finally, that they were never going home). Depression and its inevitable part-relief, alcoholism, overtook a generation; pawn shops prospered, cemeteries filled with cyrillic-scripted tombstones, the modern age turned and moved on and Stanislav Kudrin, it seemed, had passed into history.

And then, only weeks ago, a surprising resurrection: a single, brief but promising letter from London, and now Kudrin was really, brutally dead. Artsyuk looked at Vasili. The filled eyes had overspilled, and he was breathing deeply, gasps that might soon become sobs. It was almost embarrassing, but more than that, it was interesting. Artsyuk had hardly ever discussed Kudrin with Vasili, but he knew that the two had known each other for a time before the older man left Paris. Until now, he hadn't suspected the nature of their relationship, and that surprised him. Why on Earth hadn't he assumed that, like so many other pretty youths, Vasili hadn't charmed and been charmed in turn by their mutual friend? Kudrin's natural habitat had been the demi-monde of the *golubój*, and for sure, Vasili had never looked at a woman with more warmth than he might a statue.

Artsyuk prided himself on being able to read others, but clearly he'd failed in this instance. It wasn't his business, of course, but he might have made more of it had he known. At the least, he would have encouraged Vasili to keep a line open to London and perhaps press gently when funds had fallen short of what RONDD needed (as they so often did). Given present circumstances it was a wretched thing to wish for, but the Cause came first, always.

What should I say?

Artsyuk put a hand on Vasili's shoulder. 'He was a great spirit, the best of us. Avenging him is an overwhelming urge, but we can't put all our trust in the Archpriest and the British police force. Zarubin may be the only suspect, but that doesn't mean he did it. He was seen at Kudrin's apartment, that's all.'

Vasili wiped his eyes. '*If* he did it, I'll cut out his heart with a kitchen knife, slowly.'

'And I'll help you. But only if there's proof of it.'

'How do we find proof? We're in Munich …'

'And so is Zarubin. When he brings the money to us we'll confront him.'

How much?'

'I've told you twice now, Freddie. The third time won't make it any better.'

'We're dead, then.'

'We appear to be, yes.'

Holleman tossed his head in Zarubin's direction, as if the object itself was too dull, deaf or absent to respond.

'Has *he* thought of anything?'

'Amazingly, no. I think the prospect of vast but very brief wealth's overwhelmed him.'

'*Muschi.*'

Zarubin looked up. 'I accept your criticism. I hadn't anticipated this.'

'I'm a criminal.' Holleman shook his head in disbelief. 'Me! A lifetime devoted to upholding the law – well, devoted to drawing a policeman's salary – and now I'm on the run. At my age. With this leg. Fuck.'

Fischer shook his head. 'If it's any consolation, you won't be running far. They'll want their money back quickly, and messily.'

'Right.' Zarubin had been slouching on the bed, but now he sat up abruptly, ignoring the stab in his side. 'Look at what's in our favour. KGB don't yet know that we did it, and they have very little presence in Bavaria, unless things have changed greatly during the past two years.'

'Things might have. They have, money-wise.'

'A decision to increase a donation is a simple matter. Flinging clandestine resources into a hostile state isn't – particularly when your principal partner doesn't want you to do anything that spoils their own operations. No, they won't be able to respond immediately, unless …'

'What?'

'They ask MfS to do the business for them. But they won't.'

'Too humiliating?'

'You can't possibly imagine. Eric Mielke would want to know why his people were doing it, and once he did, do you think he'd *ever* let Moscow forget about it, or stop calling in the favour? So it's also to our advantage that KGB will need to come to Munich in force to do what's necessary without MFS knowing about it. Or with their agreement, which won't be offered enthusiastically. And don't forget our other blessing.'

'We're old? Dying doesn't matter so much?'

'We have resources, a bag full of them. It isn't like we're about to be chased barefoot through the streets'

Fischer grimaced. 'So we can escape in a chauffeur-driven Maybach. A decent marksman won't miss that, either.'

'I was thinking more of bribes and deflections.'

'Bribes I understand, but …'

'Strategic expenditure, to make eyes follow something or someone other than us.'

'We fit up some other poor bastard?'

'Not quite. We could plant rumours and enough money to give them legs – a large donation to the Orthodox Church, for example. Which will also help to ease my conscience, of course.'

Holleman gaped at him. 'Eh?'

Fischer gestured at Zarubin. 'He stole from their London branch.'

'And, perhaps, to one of the many extinct organizations that want the Soviet system buried. I'm particularly fond of the memory of the *Mladorossi*.'

Fischer tried to recall his last conversation with Boris Levin. 'Weren't they betrayed by their own leader?'

'Yes. Their rising from the dead will rattle tea-cups in the Lubyanka.'

'Would they believe it?'

No, but it's one of those possibilities that has to be checked out, and that buys us time – which, obviously, is the point of it. We need to remove ourselves from this apartment in a manner that leaves few footprints. No trail of evidence links *Oberrat* Holleman to me that isn't at least a decade stale, so I think he can go home to Trier in safety. Obviously, it's no longer feasible that you accompany him'

'I'm not going anywhere without Otto …'

'You have little choice. My error regarding the money has made him something of a prize catch. No doubt his unusual face was committed to memory at Munich and Geneva airports, and though it's not unique I suspect that as soon as my own recent movements have been established, KGB will close all other enquiries. If they find the slightest hint of a trail to Trier, your family will be at risk.'

Fischer was tiring rapidly of having his future argued by others.

'England will be safe, surely?'

'If you remain in the bleak north, possibly. They can't search for you forever, and as you have no fixed abode, no relatives and your wages – I assume – are paid in cash, I doubt that their normal methods would locate you. But London would be too dangerous to consider, and your acquaintances, however much they'd regret it, couldn't help but be a permanent gap in your armour.'

'Christ.' Fischer rubbed his eyes. 'I can't live in Germany, England's a fraught prospect and my time in Portugal almost certainly rates a mention in one of KGB's files. Is there anywhere you'll leave for me that's safe?'

'Again, I apologize; but don't lose heart. There are many regimes where no communists dare go, even in the heat of a chase. Spain? Ecuador? Paraguay has a wonderful climate, apparently …'

'Please, stop. I have no intention of living among expatriate National Socialists.'

'Well, I'm sure we can think of somewhere.'

'*I'll* do the thinking, the planning and everything else. I don't want you to have the slightest idea where I've gone. That way, you'll be spared the temptation to involve me in anything, ever again.'

Zarubin pulled a face and nodded. 'With ten thousand dollars, you'll have a wide choice.'

'You offered me nine.'

'A modest bonus is appropriate, I think. And I'll double the *Oberrat*'s stipend.'

'Which leaves a hundred and fifty thousand dollars, or thereabouts. After giving Artsyuk his pittance and financing a deflection or two, you'll still be rich. Are you going to open a hotel? Play the tables at Monte Carlo?'

'I'm going to fix something with it.'

'What?'

'Never mind. I suppose we should move, get out of here while KGB's collective aneurysm is clouding their thinking.'

'To where?'

'We'd be welcome at Artsyuk's house, but it's possible that my presence as his guest may have been noticed already. How certain are you that your old friend Hoeschler's wife would be loath to assist us, if we were to present ourselves at their door and beg for sanctuary?'

Fischer looked at Holleman, who was attempting to smother an obscenity.

'Reasonably certain. She has far too much of the wrong sort of past to want to open old doors. And I'd remind you that she's a former confederate of Myasnik the Butcher, and may therefore feel much less grateful than her husband for your past mercies.'

Zarubin shuddered. The prospect of what the cold, unhuman General-Quartermaster Myasnik might have inflicted upon him had provided an excellent – the only - spur for his first defection, to

America. He doubted that Frau Hoeschler carried any sentimental memories for the old brute, but she wasn't likely to welcome the man who had tried as anyone to put him in an execution cell.

'We'll not trouble the Hoeschlers further, then.'

'Wonderful. What's left?'

Zarubin's brow cleared. He was holding his side but didn't seem to be in any pain. The other hand rested upon his inheritance, as if readying it for several urgent businesses, or posing for the portrait. For a man who was wilfully inciting a host of injured parties (God, the Lubyanka, and a substantial proportion of Germany's surviving fascists), his apparent lack of anxiety for what loomed did little to reassure his unwilling abettors.

'As I see it, gentleman, if we can't shift ourselves immediately we should do so later. Very much later.'

'How much later?'

'When we can be fairly certain that KGB have given up – on finding us in Munich, at least. Then, I'll risk a visit to Artsyuk, give him his money and we can depart for whatever new lives await us.'

Holleman gaped at him. 'But that could be weeks.'

'It *will* be weeks, I imagine. Two or three of them, at least. You could go now of course, Herr *Oberrat*, all the way back to Trier. But you won't, apparently. Make yourself useful, then. When it's dark, go and find that pleasant young man Engi. I need a few books, and we all need more food. I'll make a list. And alcohol – beer, wine, vodka. Some delicacies would be nice; whatever Bavaria is noted for, if anything. Tell him not to worry, we're in funds.'

'Do you have your passport, Jonas?'

'I have Volker Dreb's passport, my love.'

'Whose?'

'He was a young man who died in my camp, of bronchitis, in January 1946. He'd lost or eaten his *soldbuch,* and a few of us suspected he'd borrowed the name from someone else. Anyway, the British tried to inform his family but couldn't locate them, so I assumed it was safe.'

'What was?'

'To use his identity. Otto went through a phase of forging passports, don't ask me why. But I thought he might as well do the same for me, for when I was a fearless reporter in the Congo or wherever, and didn't want to be made by the local warlord. Look, it's perfect …'

Maisie took the passport, examined it closely, sniffed and handed it back. 'Why don't you use your real one?'

'I don't want anyone - *anyone* - knowing that Jonas Kleiber is within the same polity as that sod Zarubin, just in case.'

'Oh. Do you have enough shirts?'

'For two days? I should think so.'

'You're going to stay out of trouble, aren't you?'

'It's my only ambition.'

'I mean, you won't get into a fight, will you?'

Kleiber laughed. 'You have strange ideas about me. During the war I fought for a total of fifteen minutes, Which is to say, I wandered around for a quarter of an hour, dragging my rifle, until I found a nice English soldier I could surrender to, bless him.'

'So you'll just …?'

They had rehearsed it four times already, but Kleiber, grateful that Maisie had acquiesced to his mad little adventure, wanted her to be entirely at ease.

'I'll just find Otto, tell him what Mr Levin wrote and suggest that he get his arse out of Germany as quickly as possible. I'll yell that last bit over my shoulder as I run back to the airport.'

'Good. You've got the address for his hotel?'

He nodded. Thanks to Levin, he'd known at least which city Fischer had flown into. Even so, it had taken the best part of a morning, calling every small hotel in the centre of Munich, before he'd located his friend. It had taken so long because he recalled Olavo Guzman only after about half the establishments had already told him no, they had no Otto Fischer staying with them. He found Senhor Guzman less than twenty minutes later, and his delight had lasted as long as it took the voice on the other end to mention that the gentleman's belongings were in his room but they hadn't seen him for four days.

Kleiber tried to tell himself that Otto would have returned to the hotel by the time he arrived; that he wouldn't be out and about still, and definitely not kidnapped, or dead. A brief discussion, heartfelt thanks offered and they'd both be on a flight to London by the following morning at the very latest. And then he recalled how plans, stratagems, hopes, expectations and anticipations fell to shit when the name Otto Henry Fischer was written into a plot. If a KGB assassination unit wasn't in place already, or a bubonic outbreak had changed its mind about sweeping down from the Carpathians towards Munich, BEA flight 843 might just dive vertically into the leading man's hotel room instead of carrying on with its precious cargo (one Volker Dreb) to Riem airport. That's just how it was, or almost, usually.

He looked at Maisie, who was watching him carefully. During the initial, trying-to-impress phase of their courtship, he had regaled her with tales of his previous adventures - well, Otto's mainly, but he flattered himself that he'd always been around, ready to help if needed. He regretted that now. Though his narratives had emphasised the triumphant (that is, non-fatal) outcome of their struggles, she must have reached certain conclusions regarding the awful luck of a man who never tried to fall into harm's way but managed rather consistently to do so. With hindsight, he realised that he should have confined himself to hints of dangers faced and overcome, with a manly refusal to dwell upon the detail.

'Are you *sure* this is the best way, Jonas?'

Of course he wasn't sure. Anything that dragged him from his pleasant routine introduced an unwelcome degree of uncertainty, even when the cause wasn't Otto. The misfortune of having been born into an age of conflict and catastrophically opposed political doctrines had long struck him as brutally ironic, given that his temperament inclined fervently towards the metronomic passage of days, years and decades unmarked by bright splashes of arterial fluids. Some might have called it a lack of iron in his spine; others, a subconscious yearning to return to the womb. And it was Jonas Kleiber's considered opinion that if they did they could all just kiss his ...

'I can't think of another option, sweetheart. He needs to know what we know before it's too late to do anything about it.'

'What *can* he do, though?'

This was firmer ground, and Kleiber felt almost confident about his ignorance. 'Otto always manages to think of something sharp when it really matters. And he's lucky.'

'Lucky? You're joking!'

'I mean, for a man who could find and slip on the only wet patch in a drought, he always seems to land right.'

Maisie sniffed. Like many people who believed wholeheartedly in evil luck, she suspected the other sort was a myth.

'Tell him from me that he has to come home, now.'

'I'll be telling him that anyway. But I'll say that you said so. There's my taxi.'

Kleiber had considered driving Brünnhilde to West London airport and leaving her in the parking garage there; but English drivers, even when they weren't stressed or late for a flight, seemed to have no spatial awareness when it came to other people's chassis. He picked up his travel case and kissed his beloved tenderly. 'I'll call you when I get there.'

She thumped him gently. 'Yes, you bloody well will.'

The taxi driver was a cheerful Jamaican who hardly drew breath during the brief ride to BEA's West London Terminal on Cromwell Road. Kleiber made appropriate noises whenever a slight pause in the narrative suggested a response was expected, but otherwise rested his eyes on passing traffic without seeing any of it and thought about what he was going to say to Otto. At the terminal he navigated the brand new electronic booking facility, pocketed his tickets and boarded the airline coach for London Airport. Fortunately, it was half-empty, and he was able to find a twin seat, barricade himself against potential neighbours with his travel case and drift back to the problem.

You daft bastard came to mind most quickly, but its many previous deployments had ever failed to do the job, however accurate the diagnosis. *Otto, think of me for once. Maisie will kill me if someone kills you* was a better bet, but its efficacy would depend entirely upon the depth of shit that his friend already stood in. A heartfelt plea to someone with a muzzle already pressed to his neck wasn't going to do the trick.

He was still trying and failing to conceive an effective argument that, miraculously, wouldn't depend upon as-yet unforeseeable circumstances when the coach pulled up outside the Europa Terminal and a smart young lady in BEA livery herded her charges into the building. At that moment Kleiber placed all thoughts of Otto Fischer in a mental locker and allowed a familiar state of terror to seize his attention. He hated flying, the more so as he did it more frequently. He had been told that familiarity would lessen the ordeal, but that struck him as absurd. Someone with a snake phobia, dropped into a pit of the buggers for, say, 24 hours, would not become habituated to the experience, but rather driven to the edge of insanity or beyond. While he couldn't say that he was *quite* phobic about air travel, his confinement in a pressurized metal tube invariably focussed his entire anima on imagined moments of impact and what they would do to the human body. It wasn't the height, or the velocity, or even the limited volume of the space he occupied; it was his inescapable surrender to the skills and mood of two complete strangers in the cockpit, either or both of whom might recently have discovered that their loved ones were sleeping around.

He hadn't ever spoken of his agonies to Maisie. A few months earlier they had flown to Ireland, to a wedding of one of her friends that she absolutely couldn't miss (Kleiber had tasked her resolutely on the point). A combination of sleeping pills and alcohol had managed to dull the torment to something he managed to pass off as indigestion (outward journey) and a migraine (Blighty-bound), so she mistook him still as a seasoned traveller, an internationalist, someone who crossed continents with as little concern as most folk crossed the road.

The statistics of air-travel, the infrequency of plummeting, didn't move him. Russian roulette gave you an 83.333 percent chance of surviving your turn, but a rational mind couldn't help but dwell upon the other 14.666. For all the thousands of aircraft that crossed the skies daily with no more fuss than a London bus traversing the Strand, it was the occasional graphic photograph of wreckage strewn across several bucolic hectares that wouldn't shift itself from his mind's eye (when he was in the air, that is, or about to be so).

This is for Otto had sounded noble in his mind's ear for as long as his journey had been a distant prospect, but now that it loomed horribly, *Bugger Otto* assumed a greater resonance than it should have. He recalled his numerous wise exhortations about not trusting this Zarubin fellow, his sage observations regarding the man's previous form and Otto's apparent acknowledgments thereof that had altered nothing. That being the case, would even the revelations from Herr Levin that Kleiber was about to deliver have any better effect? Wasn't this flight just a waste of time and effort?

Fortunately, his line of thought hadn't developed to its logical conclusion before the 'plane's wheels left British soil and brought him to more immediate concerns. For the next three hours, he tried and failed to absorb any of the content of the airline's complementary lifestyle magazine and then concentrated upon the back of the seat in front of him. Two glasses of wine helped quell the shakes a little, and he had the sense to refuse the in-flight meal; most helpfully, the turbulence that seemed to save itself up for whenever he climbed into an aircraft did no more than shiver the Tristar's wing-tips a couple of times. By the time the pilot announced that they were only fifteen minutes out of Munich, he had almost convinced himself that he was going to survive the ordeal. Unfortunately, as semi-calmness returned so too did considerations of shit, depth and gun muzzles. Was he already too late to do any good? He had to *find* Otto before he could give him the bad news, but what if he needed a spade to do that? Hell, the men who planted him might still be patting down the soil, in which case they'd hardly begrudge giving him some company.

By the time wheels touched tarmac once more, Kleiber had concluded that he'd been wildly blasé about how serious this might be. From what Levin had written it was clear that he had put himself in *some* danger by the very decision to come to Germany, though the precise nature of the threat couldn't yet be known (and he very much wanted to remain in a state of ignorance). He was moving towards something that had fangs, but was it an irate tabby or a puma? He didn't like cats much. And he definitely didn't like big, mauling cats.

He was playing with animal metaphors still as he entered the terminal building, and, distracted, joined the slow queue for non-German passport holders. After a few minutes he realised his mistake, picked up his bag and scurried across to the shorter, faster-flowing domestic control. About ten bodies behind him in the original line, a man glanced up disinterestedly at the manoeuvre and then returned to his perusal of a Polish-language guide to Munich and its many charms. He had come in on a flight from Warsaw, as had two others, a Russian and a Ukrainian, who stood some way (but separately) to his rear. No-one watching the line could have imagined that the three were acquainted, or had any inkling of each other's presence in the city, the continent or the firmament itself.

This was entirely intentional, and it was only due to the short lead-time and urgency of the operation that they had arrived in Germany on the same aircraft. Each of them was a craftsman, one of the best of his kind, an artist; and while the loss of one of them would have been a great blow to his employer, that of all three would have been catastrophic. In fact, it would probably have been several years before KGB could have put together another team who had the ability to make a stone-cold execution look like an accident, or at least the work of someone else entirely.

Curiously, after a day that counted as possibly his second-worst ever (never discounting that infamous one, two years earlier, when he had been strung out on a line between the Lubyanka and an insane street operation in West Berlin), Aleksei Krokhin found himself enjoying the very next morning immensely. What made it better still was that it flowed as the natural consequence of the previous day's truly awful passages, consequences that bit the guilty party on his arse.

Yesterday, Semichastny had called before he'd had a chance to sit down and drink his tea. Go and see Mielke, he'd been told, and make him sweet. Krokhin knew exactly what it was that needed sugaring, and had only just managed to quell a sincere *fuck*. With eight words, the head of KGB had managed to wash his hands of a filthy job of his own making and pile it into his subordinate's lap.

So, how would it go?

> *Dear Comrade Mielke, do you recall our sacred undertaking to never compromise your painstaking efforts to place a finger in BND's collective fundament? Well, you'll laugh, but it seems we may need to do just that, quickly and messily. You see, we failed to deal with a sticky problem two years ago (yes, that one, I'm glad you recall)*

and now it's returned to embarrass us – in Munich, of all places! So, what do you say to us putting a squad on the city's streets, offing the problem in question and then skipping out again, leaving you to try to keep the lid on the ants that will explode from Pullach? Yes, I imagine that at least some of your people there might be compromised. I know, it would be a shame. But there it is.

Really, Krokhin couldn't think of another way to put it that wouldn't be entirely dishonest. Back when Stalin had first allowed the Democratic Republic its statehood, MfS had been KGB's infant, coddled carefully in its crib and allowed no length of rope with which it might injure itself. But in the years since, the organization had grown massively both in size and expertise, and given that no Russian could penetrate a German institution as easily or effectively as a German, operations against General Gehlen's kingdom at Pullach had quickly become the exclusive purview of *Stasi*, while the KGB presence in Germany devoted itself to countering CIA plots and finding ways and means to prise the Allies off German soil. It was a policy that kept boots off toes, the only sane way to avoid clashes that would aid only the enemy.

And now Semichastny was going to risk all of that, to bring down one man. No doubt his previous failure to get Zarubin nagged at him, particularly as Khrushchev himself had gripped his shoulder as it happened, holding him back. Now, of course, the General

Secretary's displeasure was not the sanction it had been; the Cuba debacle had weakened him, shrinking the space between his authority and that of the pack that followed. The greyer, more cautious men were slowly slicing off tranches of his power, and though they agreed entirely with his insistence that KGB should serve Soviet foreign policy rather than make it, it seemed to Krokhin that Semichastny was being allowed a little more head these days.

Why, though? Was it part of the broader effort to prise the peasant's calloused hand off the delicate business of foreign relations? A case of KGB taking the initiative tentatively to see how much advantage might be taken of the present lack of strong leadership? Or was it that Semichastny had decisively thrown in his own hand with the men who wanted Khrushchev gone? Krokhin decided that he liked the dramatic flavour of that possibility. It was something Tolstoy might have written – the young protege, turning on his once-beloved master, ready to push in the first knife when it came to the moment. Whether that gory tableau was likely he couldn't say, and didn't want to. As acting-provisional-possibly-might be Karlshorst Resident he didn't enjoy anywhere near the level of authority that would allow him to know what was going on in Kremlin corridors. In situations like this (a *this* about which Sakharovsky, Head of KGB's First Directorate, was not to be involved, apparently), being tucked safely into the third tier of who should know what was definitely for the best.

However, Semichastny had spoken; so Krokhin had cursed quietly, made an appointment and gone to Ruschestrasse to see Mielke. He put the case as simply as he knew how, tried to seem regretful but not quite the supplicant, and then waited for the storm to break.

Which, gratifyingly, it didn't. On past form, Mielke might have been expected to chew the carpet and call down the blessed spirits of his dear old friends Stalin and Beria to witness the trials to which he was being subjected. In turn, Krokhin would have made appropriately sympathetic noises but offer nothing that might be construed as a willingness to back down. Yet that dance hadn't commenced. Instead, Mielke had sat silently for a while, his lips pursed, and then nodded.

'Markus Wolf will need to be involved.'

The statement was so self-evident that, for a moment, Krokhin wondered why it had found air at all. For years now, Wolf had run virtually all non-domestic operations, leaving his boss to do what most suited his tastes, which was crushing the Enemy within (a predilection he had nurtured in Moscow, where, due to his efforts, any number of German communist exiles had found a bullet; and then in Spain, applying himself to destroying the anti-Stalin soft-left within the International Brigades). Munich was foreign territory, and MfS's penetration of Pullach was wholly Wolf's responsibility and achievement. Yes, he *had* to be involved in this.

Clearly, Mielke was doing the other thing that came naturally to him: covering his arse. If KGB's intended operation went wrong, MfS would be dragged into the mess, and its boss was ensuring that the splash-radius would stop short of his shoes. Wolf was a hundred times the intelligencer that Mielke could ever be, but hell, it was better to let an invaluable subordinate fall (together with a brilliant operation) than give Walter Ulbricht any excuse to rearrange the chairs in the Politburo.

Wolf would froth at the mouth when he heard what Semichastny wanted, but he didn't have the power to do more than limit the damage as best he could. Probably, he would demand that the job be made to look as much like an accident, a gang-murder or a good old fashioned disappearance as would keep Pullach's nose from twitching, and Krokhin would agree to it, earnestly, knowing that he had no way to make good his commitment. He regretted that dishonesty. The two men had a good relationship, and usually managed collisions of jurisdiction as well as they might be. It would be a disaster, for KGB as much as MfS, if the man's authority and prestige were to be damaged by what was coming.

And what was it for? For some reason, Semichastny had decided that the solution to the Zarubin problem had to be applied now, not at some better time and far less sensitive location. There was something that Krokhin didn't know about the business, and though he didn't *want* to know, it was to him that Wolf would direct his undoubtedly pertinent questions, the first of which would almost certainly be *Aleksei, what the sweet holy fuck is going on?* And *Markus, I can't really say* wouldn't do, not at all.

Krokhin wasn't sure – had never been sure – exactly where he stood with Semichastny. His unsteady appointment as Resident at Karlshorst had been made by the man's predecessor, Shelepin, and if he disagreed with that decision he had never hinted at it. He was never less than entirely professional in his manner, but that was as much a barrier as a courtesy. He didn't bother with small talk or pretend a *faux* interest in his subordinates' lives, and if he was capable of relaxation it happened a long way from eyes and ears that might have enlightened the other ranks in KGB. On the two occasions that Krokhin had made an attempt at conversation, Semichastny had replied in kind, and in such a precisely proportionate but distant manner that the other man felt a little like a British *krestyanin*, standing in the front line at a Royal walk-about.

Still, he would have to try to engage his boss once more, to make it clear that if he was going to continue to be the contact point between Moscow and MfS in this matter (and, of course, it was his day job to be just that), he needed to be fully briefed on why so much was being risked for a problem that appeared to have a number of possible solutions, none of which needed to be applied urgently. A bullet would do very well for Zarubin, but why did it have to be now, and in Munich of all places?

'It probably wasn't KGB.'

'Mm?'

Fischer was reading a history of Bavaria, one of a number of books kindly loaned by Rolf Hoeschler (presumably to distract the reluctant occupants of his apartment from wanting to kill each other). He was presently filling in his scanty knowledge of the ducal period during the breakup of the Carolingian Empire, a tumultuous period of shifting fortunes that quite confused him – as, probably, it had those who'd been obliged to suffer them. He placed a finger on the text and looked up.

Zarubin was lying on the sofa, his arms crossed, staring up at the ceiling.

'The fellow with the pistol, waiting for you outside the wine bar. And my being stabbed subsequently. I don't think it was KGB in either case.'

'Who, then? Artsyuk's people?'

'No. He'd have no reason to want you dead before he knew what business you had with me. And why would he risk upsetting me, the man who'd just offered him a lot of money?'

'We know that he's a turncoat, passing things to KGB. They might have demanded it.'

The ceiling had a face pulled at it. 'Artsyuk works for himself. He feeds the Lubyanka enough gossip about the émigré community to earn a modest pension and keep them off his back, but he'd no more be their finger on the trigger than swear allegiance to international communism. In any case, KGB wouldn't know that you were here, working for me, not on the day you arrived in Munich.'

Fischer scratched his nose. 'Who does that leave, then?'

'A very old friend. Comrade General Serov.'

'GRU?' Fischer sat upright. 'Why? And why now?'

'*Why* hardly needs an answer. Any opportunity to bring me closer to the grave would be seized upon. And he knows that you're one of mine.'

'I'm *not* one of yours.'

'You know what I mean by that. As to why *now*, I suspect he's run out of time.'

'He's dying?'

'He's been sacked. I mean, *really* sacked. Three months ago, I spoke to one of the few people at SIS who'd give me the time of day. He was Sovbloc, of course, and passed on gossip that Serov had recently received a reassignment, to Turkmenistan, as assistant to the Military Governor there.'

'What has he done to deserve that?'

'When SIS were debriefing me they asked me a lot of questions, as you'd expect. A surprising number were with regard to one man, a GRU Colonel named Penkovsky. Did I know him? Was I aware of any personal or professional problems he might be having?'

'What did you tell them?'

'Nothing. I said I'd never heard of him, which wasn't quite the truth. After Serov was transferred out of KGB to GRU I made it my business to find out what new friends he was making at the Aquarium in case he decided to seek an early revenge. Penkovsky's name was mentioned - a bright young man who had caught Serov's eye and was considered to be on the up.'

'Why didn't you mention this to the British?'

'Because they had too many questions about him for me not to guess what their interest was.'

Fischer considered this for a few moments. He might have asked and saved himself the trouble, but he preferred to remind Zarubin that he could think for himself still.

'They had him?'

'If they'd *had* him, they could have formed their own judgement. I decided that he'd been turned and was working for them, but in place still, at the Aquarium.'

'That would be a spectacular coup.'

'It would. But our good friend Boris Levin also heard something, in September last year. One of his old Kremlin colleagues got away from his minders during a trade delegation visit to Italy, claimed asylum and ended up in London, where he was grateful to see a familiar face. They had lunch, swapped gossip and no doubt recalled the old days as being sweeter than they were.'

'What gossip?'

'About everyone on the top floor of the Lubyanka biting their fingernails. It was something to do with GRU, but no details other than that all their field operations had been suspended temporarily. That was in June, I think. A month later, an unnamed GRU Colonel was tried very speedily on treason charges and executed.'

'Penkovsky?'

'Probably. And Serov, well, you don't get to survive one of your favourites crossing the fence. Hence Turkmenistan.'

'Yet he had one particular piece of business outstanding.'

'That I'm breathing still.'

'So, the fellow at the wine bar wasn't going to shoot me?'

'Almost certainly, yes. But not until you'd told him where I was.'

'Yet he died. How did you come to get a knife in the gut?'

'Obviously, the two men waiting at your hotel when you returned that night were the same men I'd seen with him earlier. They didn't believe your little deception, or at least not so much as to *not* follow you to Artsyuk's home the next day. I assume one of them was waiting for me to emerge; when I did, he followed me to a convenient location and tried to make Serov a happy man.'

'I still don't see how he failed.'

'GRU don't like improvisation. They're military, Soviet military, and initiative is always discouraged. He and his friend probably couldn't contact Khodynka for instructions, so I had his nerves on my side. Still, if he'd used a gun I'd be dead.'

'I wonder why he didn't.'

'I assume he wanted to make it look more like a street robbery than an assassination.'

'Because MfS's operation at Pullach might have been compromised?'

Zarubin snorted. 'GRU have never given a fuck about MfS. Back when he was KGB, Serov would have done, but losing the Chair detached him from that relationship. No, it's rather that whoever's trying to fulfil Serov's last wishes doesn't want KGB to know that GRU are doing things in Munich that haven't been cleared by the Kremlin. They probably don't want the rest of GRU to know, either. Their new Director - and whoever *that* is he certainly won't be one of Serov's friends - would probably kill them with his bare hands if it came out.'

It all sounded feasible, and Fischer didn't feel at all reassured. It took a great deal of skill to put yourself in a place where both KGB *and* GRU wanted you dead, and for different reasons.

'Do you think these people are looking for you still? For us?'

Zaurbin touched his wound gently and examined his fingers. 'I doubt it. They've messed it up twice and lost a man. If I were running this, the least I'd do is pull them out and rethink it. After all, they have no idea where to look next.'

'Hell, for a moment I worried I might be unlucky. Is Artsyuk safe?'

'GRU must know that he's under KGB protection. They won't dare touch him.'

A fist knocked on the door three times, then twice, then once. Fischer unlocked it and stood back as a heavily laden Holleman staggered in.

'Christ! There's enough here to feed the Stalingrad pocket.'

'You weren't seen?'

'Nah. I waited behind the front door until Engi backed up the van and then helped him unload it. The old dear who lives across our corridor was going out, so I gave her a cheery smile.'

'Poor woman.'

'Yeah, some things don't wear off. Weisswurst!'

A link of white sausages fell out of their paper wrapping onto the polished parquet flooring. Zarubin tutted and shifted a foot to avoid one. This was their second delivery from *Casa Hoeschler*, and their old friend was attempting to make their confinement as pleasant as it might be. They had tea, coffee, alcohol, rice, pasta, several kinds of cheese and pressed meats and a large slab of dark chocolate, for which Engi had refused all payment (much to Fischer's amusement, given that Zarubin could have bought any or all of the shops the supplies came from). None of it was likely to dim the spectre of a vengeful KGB, but the comfort of several hearty meals lay between the condemned men and a bullet.

Holleman had reached the bottom of the box, the former contents of which were strewn around it. He looked up.

'I've been thinking. We're safe here, right?'

Zarubin shrugged. 'I can't see why we wouldn't be.'

'Still, it would be good if we could keep an eye on the street when Engi comes, to make certain he's not been followed?'

'It wouldn't hurt.'

'But our windows face the wrong way. Give me a thousand deutschmarks.'

'You're going to put in a mezzanine?'

'I'm going across the corridor to see the Old Dear when she gets back from the shop. Her apartment faces the street. I'll offer her the money and ask that either me or my ugly friend be allowed to sit at her window for an hour each day.'

'And the reason?'

Holleman tapped his nose. 'Police business. I'll wave my warrant card.'

'It's Mecklenburg issue.'

'And she'll bother to read it?'

'I suppose not. It's a good idea.'

'Then, we can twist Rolf's arm to take enough money to buy a couple of portable radio transceivers, so that if one of us spots something we can warn Engi before he gets out of the van and gives away the location.'

Zarubin sighed. 'Let's not get too ambitious. Radio signals can be traced.'

Holleman sniffed. 'I'm just trying to cover the risks. Anyway, kill-squads aren't going to be travelling with suitcase-sized electronic tracking units, are they?'

This was self-evidently true, but Zarubin was tired of being out-thought by the least intelligent person in the room (it was a reminder of how dull he became when forced to stare at ceilings for any length of time). He returned the sniff, but said nothing in case it provoked yet another useful suggestion.

Fischer had been looking out of the sitting-room window, down on to a garden area enclosed by the rear aspects of other apartment buildings. He turned around.

'I've been wondering about something.'

Zarubin raised an eyebrow and waited.

'I don't disagree that waiting here until KGB give up the chase is probably the only option remaining to us. But how do we know when that moment comes? We took a lot of their money, so I expect they'll keep it up for a while. If we move too quickly they may be waiting – at airports, train stations, my hotel and anywhere else they have a chance of picking us up. If we wait too long before running, what then? We may be giving them time to put in more resources, or ask more questions of people who know us. Rolf and Mila live in Munich, they're both in KGB files and someone may eventually get 'round to going over old leads, in which case Engi might just bring them straight to us. My point is, how can we know when best to move?'

Holleman grunted. 'We can't.'

'No. And I think that our dear friend here realises that.'

Zarubin offered both men his blankest face. 'There are no certainties.'

'Of course there aren't. But you should seem more anxious about that than you appear to be. You went to a deal of trouble to set up this scheme, and to drag me into it. That weeks of planning have come to this game of chance can't be what you wanted.'

'It's what it is. We're trapped here for the moment, but we have KGB's money and they have no trail to follow. The situation could be considerably less satisfying.'

'It might *be* so, soon. The moment we pack our bags and step into the street, for example.'

'Jesus.' Holleman climbed up from the floor, where he had been sorting the foodstuffs. 'Give me the money. I'll go and see if the old lady's back.'

Zarubin counted out a thousand deutschmarks. 'Ask her for a receipt.'

'Why, for f …?'

'Because it's what police would do - that is, if we lived in a world in which they paid for the use of a window rather than just demanded it. If she signs for the money she might think we're not gangsters. And please, warn her about the Major's face.'

35

'I'm sorry, Sir, but we haven't seen Herr Guzman for several days. He's reserved his room and left some luggage with us, so we're expecting his return. When, though …'

The receptionist offer a mildly regretful shrug. The young gentleman seemed very disappointed, almost upset, and the airline tag on the handle of his small suitcase suggested he'd come a long way to hear the bad news.

'Perhaps if you left a message for him, and a number where you can be contacted?'

Jonas Kleiber, facing the wreckage of his over-optimistic strategy, shook his head. This wasn't to refuse the offer (he'd hardly heard it), but the only way he could register his frustration without opening his mouth. He very much feared that anything he might say wouldn't be fit for delicate ears.

Eventually, and for want of anything resembling a back-up plan, he cleared his throat and tried to convey a little less anxiety than he felt.

'Would you have a room available, just for tonight?'

The receptionist consulted his bookings. He knew very well that half his rooms were presently unoccupied, but it wasn't something a good hotelier would want to advertise. After a brief survey of the options he looked up.

'A basic single, or small double with a view on to the street?'

'I'll have the view, please.'

Kleiber handed over his passport, filled out the booking form and (determined as he was to leave as little evidence of where, precisely, he might be) asked if he might settle his bill with cash. He took his key and went up to the third floor, where it opened a door into a snug, neat room with an excellent view of Sporerstrasse, along which he hoped fervently he would soon see the approach of Otto Fischer – hale still, even hearty, and ready to evacuate upon receipt of Boris Levin's intelligence.

He could feel his heart racing, and he had to remind himself once more that a man who had been snatched in the street (or gunned down in it) wouldn't have had the time or opportunity to reserve his room beforehand. But that didn't necessarily mean that Otto wasn't dead. It was perfectly possible that he'd made his arrangements, stepped out and then been shot. Or kidnapped. Or arrested. Or …

Maisie would want him to telephone to say he'd arrived safely, but when he told her that Otto hadn't returned she'd just demand that he turn around and come home, and he couldn't do that, not yet. He had to go a little further at least before fleeing. It was what would-be heroes did. What else he would do he hadn't yet decided, because nothing had occurred that wasn't more useful than wandering the streets of Munich, hoping to bump into his friend. The city proper had a population of a million souls (and God knew how busy they'd been in the suburbs), so the chances of a fruitful saunter were next to zero. A slightly better strategy might be to visit bars and restaurants with a photograph of Otto (he had a snap of the two of them in *The Flowers*, taken by Maisie's sister the previous year) in hopes of his unforgettable face ringing a bell or two, but he suspected it would take weeks to cover the entirety of Munich's famous night-life and all the while the body might be decomposing gently. He could search the hospitals, but that would be useful only if the damage were accidental rather than inflicted, while the police ...

Rolf Hoeschler. He had met the man only twice: a decade ago on the streets of Berlin, the day the east of the city had risen up against its government, and again two years ago, in Bremen, at Otto's premature funeral. He and his wife lived in Munich, and ... Kleiber dragged his address book from his inner jacket pocket and flicked through it ... they had exchanged telephone numbers. It was what one did in a sad, maudlin mood, wanting some way of keeping the deceased party's memory alive but knowing that nothing would ever come of it.

Would Otto have contacted Hoeschler? Kleiber had no idea how close they were or had been. He *did* know that Hoeschler, like Freddie Holleman, had once been police in East Berlin and under Zarubin's occasional authority, though that could equally impose a sense of obligation or make him run like hell to avoid contamination. A man might want to help a friend, but would he risk dragging himself and his family into the ...?

If the two men hadn't spoken, if Hoeschler and his wife were safe and oblivious to what was going on, telephoning him wouldn't be any sort of favour. As much as Kleiber wanted to find Otto, as helpless as he felt himself to be at present, doubling or trebling the body-count would be a bloody awful solution.

Reluctance to do harm was a noble sentiment, and for a few minutes he felt quite pleased with himself; but he soon saw it for the conundrum it was. Otto *had* to be told what Boris Levin knew, and if Hoeschler was the only possible means of delivering the message it came down to a simple choice. Either Kleiber put potential risk in the way of a man he hardly knew or washed his hands of an undeniable danger to his oldest friend.

Thinking around it didn't multiply his options, so he went back down to reception, to one of the public telephones in the foyer, and dialled the number in his book. The receiver at the other end was picked up within moments. A man's voice, speaking quietly, and just the one word.

'Yes?'

'Hello, is that Herr Hoeschler?'

'It is.'

'This is Jonas Kleiber. You may recall …'

'I do. Is it about our friend?'

'Yes, Otto. I've come to …'

'Don't say anything else. Where are you?'

'The hotel – Otto's hotel. It's just off Marienplatz, the …'

'Yes, I know. Go outside and wait to the left of the entrance. In about fifteen minutes a small white van, driven by a young man, is going to pull up. Get in. He'll take you where you want to go. Goodbye.'

Hoeschler's telephone manner might have seemed abrupt or even rude, had everything he'd said not been delivered in a whisper. For some reason it both worried and reassured Kleiber, and he didn't think of not obeying his instructions. The alternative was a hopeless wait, a humiliating retreat to London and then all the time he needed to hate himself while Maisie's sad, regretful gaze twisted the knife in his coward's gut.

Outside, light rain was falling, so he pressed his back against the hotel wall and waited.

Sporerstrasse was a thoroughfare, but traffic was sparse even in late morning. He tapped his jacket, knowing the letter from Levin was safely tucked in its breast pocket. He'd read it so many times that he could have thrown it into a bin and recited the contents to Otto, but the artefact itself would reinforce the message more effectively than the slightly desperate, wheedling tone he'd employ despite every effort not to. He'd only just satisfied himself that the object hadn't leapt from its place when a white van pulled up in front of him.

A well-built young man leaned across from the driver's seat and opened the door.

'Herr Kleiber? I'm Engi. Get in, please.'

Kleiber recalled the name and relaxed a little. If Hoeschler had sent his own son it wasn't likely that they were driving into danger, at least not any that was apparent. He glanced to either side (offering any potential observers ample proof of some form of guilt) and climbed into the van.

'Have one of these. They're Belgian. Uncle Freddie asked for some.'

Engi was offering a paper bag. Kleiber took a chocolate from it, put it into his mouth and had begun to enjoy the taste when the words registered.

'Freddie Holleman? He's *here*?'

'With Otto, yes. And the Russian one.'

Shit. How could he tell Otto about Zarubin if the subject in question was sitting on his shoulder? He didn't know sign language, had no idea how to code messages and doubted very much that his powers of telepathy (which worked sometimes on Maisie when he wanted a cup of coffee) would be of any use in a desperate situation. Unless he could get him alone for five minutes ...

Kleiber turned to his driver. 'Where are they?'

'In one of our rental properties. It's not far – ten minutes, perhaps.'

It was a surprise, but a small relief also, that Holleman was in Munich. Even a leg short of a sprint he was fearsome, and fearless, and Kleiber was perfectly aware that his own arrival couldn't add anything to Team Otto's defensive perimeter. But who had brought him here? Otto himself wouldn't have wanted to drag a friend into one of Zarubin's plots (particularly a friend with such extensive experience of his previous efforts), which left the plotter himself. In which case, the perimeter might be punctured already.

Engi was driving slowly, checking his mirror constantly and taking more turns than Kleiber – admittedly, a stranger to these parts – felt to be necessary. Nervously, the passenger began to examine the terrain as it passed by, trying to find malice in the manoeuvres of other vehicles, the occasional lingering stare of a pedestrian who shouldn't be interested in a plain white van, and felt his pulse begin to race once more.

Seeking distraction, he cleared his throat and tried to ask a question without seeming overly paranoid.

'How did you know I was Jonas Kleiber?'

Engi's eyebrows rose slightly. 'You said that you were.'

'But I might have been lying. I might be KGB.'

'I don't think so'

'Why?'

The younger man glanced at his passenger. 'My dad gave me a good description.'

'What did he tell you?'

'An under-nourished Eddie Cochran.'

Pleased, Kleiber turned to the view once more, but it was slowing. The van pulled up at the end of a street, Engi switched off the engine but made no move.

'Are we there?'

'Almost. We wait five minutes, to make certain we weren't followed.'

'Oh.'

During what seemed to Kleiber to be the next fifteen minutes at least, the younger man checked his rear-and wing-mirrors every few seconds, paid careful attention to the only four pedestrians who passed by and wrote down the registration numbers of several cars parked nearby. When he was satisfied that they were unobserved he turned the key and drove for about two hundred metres more before slowing and parking outside an apartment building.

'Here we go. Could you bring those two boxes, please?'

Lifting the others himself (it struck Kleiber that both men's faces were almost concealed by their burdens), he shouldered open the entrance door, nodded at the *hausmeister* as he passed his office and led the way to the third floor. A door opened into a corridor of six apartments, three doors per side; Engi went to the middle one to his left, shifted his load to free a hand and knocked three times, twice and then once. The door opened immediately.

The large, unlovely bulk of Freddie Holleman half-emerged to relieve Engi of his burden As he took it he half-turned, saw Kleiber, gaped, laughed, turned back into the apartment and whispered in a half-shout.

'You'll never guess what's for supper.'

Back at the hotel on Sporerstrasse, Karl the evening manager had started his shift. His predecessor's notes told him that two new guests had taken rooms, that the leaking pipe in the kitchen's roof-space had been repaired and that Frau Becker, a regrettably frequent patron, was complaining once more of noises behind her headboard that, in her opinion, were almost certainly made by large rodents. Of course they were; those sections of the hotel that has survived the bombing were almost two hundred and fifty years old, no-one knew what or how many spaces lay behind the walls and Munich's ancient sewers had been hosting the species *en masse* for as long as human waste had been propelled there. For reputation's sake the admission couldn't ever be made, so it had long been a calvary of duty managers to calm the old lady with allusions to venerable plumbing that didn't quite cross the line into outright lies.

Karl sighed and took a sip from his first coffee. As he put the cup down a man took up position in front of him. He was wearing a dark suit and a serious expression that added to an already quite intimidating face. He nodded by way of announcing himself and produced a warrant card, which Karl immediately recognised as belonging to the *Bundeskriminalamt* and therefore to be taken very seriously. He returned the nod with what he hoped was an appropriately concerned manner.

'May I help?' (a stupid question, but he couldn't think of anything better suited to the moment)

'I hope so. We're looking for a man we believe to have come to Munich in the past few days. I can't tell you which name he's travelling under, but he isn't difficult to miss. This photograph was taken about two years ago. Please look carefully.'

Karl examined the photo, for which any degree of *care* was hardly necessary. He returned it.

'Yes, that's Herr Guzman, he's staying with us. He arrived five days ago, I believe. May I ask …?'

'I'm afraid not, but he should be regarded as dangerous. Which room is he in?'

'Thirty-two. But he isn't there.'

'Do you know when he might return?'

I'm afraid I don't, no. He paid in advance for a number of days to keep the room. We haven't seen him since … Tuesday, I think. I can check that.'

'Please do. He didn't say why he had to go away?'

'He mentioned business, that's all. And I don't know where he was going. He seems a pleasant fellow, apart from his wounds.'

'Don't be deceived by that. I'm going to give you a number. If he calls or returns, we need to know immediately. It's a matter of the utmost importance.'

Karl took the card and straightened slightly. 'Of course. I'll let my colleagues know.'

'Thank you. Goodbye.'

Outside, the man in the suit nodded at a Mercedes-Benz parked on the other side of the narrow street, turned and walked towards Marienplatz. The car followed and stopped around the corner, where he climbed into the last available seat. Two others were occupied by human rears and the fourth by a large holdall containing two partially disassembled SVD sniper rifles from the very first production batch of 300 units. They had been released by Izhmash only four weeks earlier, but already the occupants of the Mercedes could claim to be ranking experts on its use. As to whom might be the model's first victims, Sergei Aleksandrovich Zarubin and Otto Henry Fischer were, entirely unwittingly, currently leading the small field by a considerable distance.

The moment he returned to Karlshorst from his meeting with Eric Mielke, Krokhin had called Markus Wolf's office to discuss the delicate business in Munich. Regrettably, Mielke had omitted to mention that his subordinate was in Prague that day, liaising with his StB counterpart on strategies to resuscitate the Austrian Communist Party's moribund political fortunes (forlorn as their hopes might be). He was expected back in Berlin late that evening, so Krokhin, feeling unusually ill-disposed towards his own boss in the Lubyanka still, decided that the business could wait until the following day.

He slept badly, allowing his thoughts to be crowded by the problem of how he was going to explain KGB's looming operation, and before dawn he was up, dressed and clearing his schedule for the morning. He called Wolf at home as soon as decency permitted (though not before he'd taken his own breakfast), and they arranged to meet at Ruschestrasse at 9am. Fortunately, Wolf didn't care to ask the purpose of the appointment before he hung up.

Krokhin replaced his own receiver, lifted it again and asked his secretary to bring some tea. It was only just back in its cradle when another call came through. For a moment he thought about not answering, and then about the circular he had composed the previous week, reminding his staff that the telephone was an instrument of communication, not an unmusical interruption that might be ignored at discretion. He sighed and picked it up.

Five minutes later, the receiver snug in its place once more, he cursed his luck, the day and telephonic technology. Most of all, he cursed KGB Director V.Y. Semichastny for straining every mental sinew to find new ways to torture an assiduous, painstaking subordinate. It appeared that putting him in the impossible situation of explaining to the two senior men in MfS an operation whose rationale he didn't himself understand wasn't quite pain enough. A further twist was necessary, to ensure that any blame for missteps fell heavily upon the one person who wouldn't have pulled on his boots in the first place, given the choice.

Semichastny had been amiability itself, which put Krokhin on his guard immediately.

'Ah, Aleksei Alekseivich, how are you?'

'Very well, thank you, Comrade Director.'

'Splendid. Is the sun shining in Berlin this morning as it is in Moscow?'

'Drizzle, I'm afraid.'

'A shame. I'm calling because I've been thinking …'

Oh, fuck.

'… about the Munich operation. You'll recall our last attempt to solve the Zarubin problem?'

I'm not likely to forget it, ever. 'Yes, the interception in West Berlin.'

'An unfortunate initiative, hastily conceived and implemented hopefully. Its principal flaw, of course, was that a field operation couldn't be directed effectively from the Lubyanka. I had misgivings at the time, but the First Secretary wanted both a close grip upon the proceedings and an early resolution. The results spoke for themselves.'

This self-absolving analysis was so precisely the opposite of what Krokhin knew to be the case that for a few moments he was speechless. It was common knowledge, that when Shelepin had been head of KGB and Semichastny his deputy, the older man had needed regularly to apply the brakes to the latter's impulsiveness. Krokhin suspected that only Khrushchev's patronage (which, ironically, had cloaked Zarubin also at the time) had saved him from bearing all the blame for the debacle.

'With that hard lesson in mind, it's apparent that we'll need strong direction of this operation from a forward post. More importantly, it will be extremely necessary to keep Mielke and Wolf reassured and informed, which, given that you're ideally placed to do just that, makes the choice of coordinator simple. I know this is late notice, but the speed with which the task was put together makes it a moot point anyway. The team in Munich have been informed that you are the first point of contact, which means that you'll have the honour of passing on the good news. You needn't be anxious; we've sent the best men available, they understand their task precisely and it's been more than emphasised that subtlety and discretion are paramount. Their escape point has been determined already. It will be via Passau and Freyung, then across the border into the Sumava, where the Czechs will be waiting to provide laundry services.'

In the pause that followed, Krokhin might have refused to touch the thing and then braced himself for the consequences. He might have negotiated, asked whether his successful supervision of this mess would at least result in his long-overdue written conformation in the post of Karlshorst Resident. At the very least, he might have asked what contingency resources would be put in place should a firefight erupt in the streets of Munich, one of their men go down and someone or something unequivocally identify him as KGB. But all that came to mind in the moment was a tiny point of confusion among all the rest.

'The Sumava?'

'A national park, part of the Bohemian forest. It's where the German Bohemians used to live, and so is almost uninhabited these days. It acquired its new name only recently.'

So now, Krokhin was not only going to see Markus Wolf to explain how KGB were about to trample upon the most sensitive part of MfS's operational anatomy, but that he himself would be doing the stomping. Wolf might have been apprised of the business already by his boss, but it was more likely that Mielke (who, like most self-proclaimed iron men, was a coward also) preferred to have Krokhin deliver the bad news. Wolf would ask a lot of pertinent, pointed questions about timing, resources and how the team planned to make it look like anything other than one or more assassinations by agents of a hostile power. Most definitely, he would ask *why*, and why *now*, and *why Munich* of all places, and to each of these Krokhin would be able to answer *really, Markus, I haven't a fucking clue.*

Naturally, Wolf couldn't object, much less insist that the operation be cancelled. If KGB said it was imperative that it go ahead, that there was no viable alternative, MfS would have to swallow their objections and pray that their long, successful infiltration of Pullach wouldn't be compromised by the shitstorm that would descend should things go wrong. But really, coercion wasn't the way to maintain a relationship that both parties valued, and if it *did* go wrong there would be consequences. MfS would almost certainly decide to play awkward from that moment onwards, and the first to feel it (and most painfully) would be the entire KGB presence at Karlshorst. Intelligence sharing would almost certainly dry up, the special police units guarding the complex might be withdrawn or charged to KGB at a fully built-up rate, and, worst of all, the DDR's political leadership would have been given every incentive to intensify their efforts to sabotage Willy Brandt's campaign to become West German Chancellor and implement his policy of reconciliation with the Soviet Bloc (which KGB were very keen to encourage). To put it another way, Krokhin might earn his official confirmation as Berlin Resident and then discover that it was the very last thing he wanted.

'Why did you bring him?'

Zarubin was trying not to appear annoyed, and failing. Holleman had managed to stop gaping at the apparition, whose mouth was open as if to offer enlightenment but hadn't, as yet, engaged itself.

Unmoved by the frown, Engi shrugged. 'My father said that I should. He's brought a message, for Otto.'

Jonas Kleiber cleared his throat on cue. 'Where *is* Otto?'

Holleman gestured towards the apartment door. 'Across the corridor. He probably saw you coming, so …'

On cue, Fischer stepped in. He didn't try to disguise his exasperation, but the effect was somewhat spoiled by the large cake he was carrying. Holleman's face brightened.

'Oh, good! She said she was baking today.'

Keeping his eyes on Kleiber, Fischer handed the bounty to his large, hungry friend.

'Jonas, what the hell are you doing?'

'I have some news.'

'What is it?'

Kleiber glanced at every other face it the room, and then back at Fischer's. 'It's … confidential.'

'Couldn't it wait until I returned to London?'

'Not really.'

Fischer breathed deeply, trying to contain his temper. He had been dragged – through his own fault, he didn't complain – into a situation of some danger, one that could hardly be eased by the arrival of a man who preferred to face peril with an eiderdown over his head. He was fond of Jonas Kleiber, but mostly in placid circumstances.

'Alright, come outside.'

In the corridor, Kleiber delved into his jacket pocket, removed Levin's letter and handed it to his friend without comment (not that he could have thought of anything that might have done justice to the content). Fischer read it quickly and closed his eyes.

'I wish he'd said all of this when I saw him last.'

'I suppose he feels some loyalty to his old boss.'

Fischer waved the letter. 'If he's right, what would be the point of *loyalty*? Never mind. Listen, I'm very grateful for what you've done, but you're going back to the airport, now. Get on the first 'plane to London, and don't mention anything to anyone except Maisie.'

'I can't. I've booked into your hotel.'

'They have your passport?'

'Of course.'

'Shit.' Fischer sighed. 'Go and get it, tell them something's happened and you have to leave. Pay for tonight's room, then get out, back to England.'

'What about you?'

'I'll follow as soon as I can.'

'You swear?'

'As fervently as I know how. Go and say goodbye to Freddie, and ask Engi if he'll give you a lift to the hotel.'

Within five minutes, Kleiber was back in the van, struggling with a powerful sense of deflation. His heroic mission was over already, and he sensed he'd made himself as welcome as yeast in a damp groin. Otto had thanked him, but it hadn't sounded convincing even to someone who needed very much to hear it. Still, his moral duty was done, Maisie would be proud of him and no-one other than himself could know what an effort of will it had taken for him to do as much as he had (little though it seemed to be appreciated). He told himself that his conscience was now not only clear but had been drenched in spring water; that men could show their courage in different ways, some of which didn't quite meet the accepted definition, and …

'I'll drop you here, to be safe. Your hotel's just across the Platz. See? Over there.'

Engi pointed a finger, Kleiber followed it, nodded and climbed out of the van. He was trying to think of something offhand but slightly memorable to say that would subtly hint at his coolness in difficult situations, but before anything came to mind Engi had returned the nod, revved the engine and pulled away.

Kleiber walked the circumference of Marienplatz, wanting to gather at least a couple of pleasant memories of Munich to relate to Maisie. A cafe stood almost at the corner of Sporerstrasse; he sat down at an outside table and ordered a coffee, allowing himself five leisurely minutes before he began his frantic retreat to England. As he waited to be served he scanned the immediate terrain, noticed something and then turned his attention to his knees.

His first thought was that it might be clinical paranoia. Already agitated, his condition had been made worse by the sense of urgency that Otto had piled on to him, so it was hardly surprising that he was imagining stuff. But then he looked again, carefully, pretending to find interest in a dozen directions yet always coming back to Sporerstrasse and two men, standing fifty metres apart, who seemed not to know each other but who maintained a steady, casual vigil both ways down the street, as neatly as if they had been synchronized cameras.

Of course, they might have been entirely innocent loiterers, separately waiting for their girls or a lift, but to Kleiber's eye and mind they looked suspicious; in fact, they looked to be ... he sifted the lurid argot of his English hack colleagues ... *proper tasty geezers*. He wouldn't have given much for his chances in a brawl with either one of them, even if they agreed, sportingly, to fight from their knees. And now he came to think about it, there was something in their look, their manner, that seemed institutional, and it wasn't universities or sanitoriums that came to mind. On another day, in another city, he might have told himself that they were none of his business and shouldn't ever become so; but here, now, he felt a resurgence of that fucking sense of obligation he'd only just managed to argue away.

Never mind. It would require that he add an extra leg to his taxi ride, that was all. A quick detour to warn Otto about the ambush, and then the airport, a couple of stiff ones in the passenger lounge to calm his nerves before boarding his flight. He picked up his coffee, drank it too quickly and burned his mouth, dropped some money on the table and pointed himself towards hazard. They couldn't know who he was, but even so he felt his cheeks heating as he approached and passed the first of them. It took an effort not to look up, but a momentary inspiration made him put a finger in a nostril and excavate it. No-one had ever, in any of the hard-boiled novels he'd once been addicted to, picked his nose in a tight spot. Or in any other situation, for that matter.

He turned into the hotel foyer, and safety. The receptionist who had first welcomed him was at the desk, writing something on his shift calendar. When he looked up he started slightly, as if he hadn't heard his customer's approach. He smiled, turned and reached for the correct room key.

Kleiber cleared his throat. 'I'm afraid I've been called away, so I shan't need the room. I'll pay for tonight, naturally.'

'Oh dear. Well, we hope to see you again soon, Herr Kleiber. Shall I make up the receipt while you collect your belongings?'

When Kleiber had gone upstairs, Bernhardt the duty manager allowed his diaphragm to relax. He had spoken earlier to his colleague Karl, who told him of the police's interest in Herr Guzman, the terribly mutilated Portuguese gentleman who spoke perfect German. In turn, Bernhardt had mentioned the arrival of Herr Kleiber and his query regarding the gentleman, so Karl immediately telephoned the number he'd been given to pass on the information. Now, Bernhardt had his own duty to perform, and luckily, it wouldn't be too onerous. The policeman had returned promptly to the hotel following his conversation with Karl and taken a seat in reception. A nod was enough to bring him to the desk, and four words to fully apprise him of the situation.

'So, what did he want?'

Almost forty minutes had passed since Kleiber had made his hurried farewell and departed, and Holleman's question was put as if the matter were a trifle hardly to be recalled. Fischer, grateful for the pause, had used it to concoct something vaguely plausible.

'Advice. He's been offered a permanent position by *Der Spiegel*, but he'd need to be based permanently in Germany and he's not sure that he wants to leave London. He thinks his girlfriend won't give up her job there.'

'And he needed to get on a 'plane for that?'

'The offer's going to lapse. He said he'd found which hotel I was staying at, but of course when he telephoned – three times – I wasn't available. He only thought of Rolf Hoeschler once he was here. It might have saved him the trip.'

'Oh. It's only a job, though. I thought he was rich?'

'He's comfortable, money-wise. But he wants to be a respected journalist more than anything.'

'Daft lad. No-one respects journalists.'

'And yet they think very highly of themselves.'

Zarubin coughed. Both men turned, but he didn't speak. He was kneeling on the floor, stooped, sorting the loot into neat piles which he was securing with elastic bands and placing into plastic pouches.

'You seem to be falling in love with your retirement fund.'

Zarubin looked up. 'I'm trying to ensure that the three of us are going to be able to carry it all without anyone suspecting, otherwise we'll need to worry about more than KGB when we leave.'

The question of when and how they would move still hung, unanswered, in the space between the three men. As varied and pleasant as their diet had become, this state of self-internment was becoming less bearable as each day dawned. The group mastermind had the only bed, a nod to his old rank and present affliction. Fischer and Holleman slept on the floor, each cushioned only by a camping mat and single blanket. For them, rising each morning was an opportunity to count the muscles in their backs and shoulders and grade them by refusal to function. To pass their waking hours they had plenty of reading material, but there was a limit to the enjoyment to be derived from doing next to nothing when the necessity of action pressed more urgently by the hour. What KGB might be organizing while they hung in their self-imposed stasis was hardly to be imagined, yet imagine they did, constantly. Fischer had been enjoying a recurring vision of cross-fire from several well-prepared sniper positions, guaranteed to achieve one hundred percent casualties in the killing zone. Now, he could add a prior mugging to that delightful tableau.

'Will it fit in our pockets?'

'It should do, without bulging. No bulges is very necessary.'

Holleman snorted and lifted his trouser leg. 'My old, hollow leg could have carried most of it, but this one's not made for swag.'

Zarubin sniffed. 'Putting our precious cargo into the slowest ship in the convoy wouldn't be the wisest choice.'

Another snort. 'The exit velocity from a sniper rifle is about eight hundred metres per second. You think you can out-sprint a bullet?'

'Our plan is not to put ourselves in front of assassins. Didn't I make that clear?'

Fischer stared down into the enclosed garden area behind the apartment building. He was tired of being here, tired of not knowing what Zarubin was planning (if anything), tired of a weight he'd thought had gone forever. There was a wall in Yorkshire, a modest, harmless thing that needed tender care, and he'd abandoned it to take a step from one good life back into a poorer, familiar state. He'd begun to tell himself that at least this was a salutary lesson, not ever to be repeated, but then recalled that the lesson had been absorbed and rejected before, several times. He was here precisely because experience hadn't left sufficient wounds to deter him (which, as any mirror could tell him, was profoundly ironic). It was much too late to do anything with the revelation, other than make him realise that in another life he might have made a magnificent mine-clearer, or bottom-of-the-bill prize fighter.

Down in the garden, two old ladies sat on a bench, silently enjoying their small patch of countryside in the city. Behind them, an open service door, the type secured by a down-bar from the inside, stood ajar. That was probably against regulations, but as a breed *hausmeisters* tended to be quiet-life sorts who were happy, usually, to indulge their tenants' minor infractions. On the other hand, old ladies were fully sensitive to all real and imaginary dangers, and he was certain that the two specimens he was watching would never, ever forget to pull the door shut behind them when they went indoors.

He turned to his still-bickering comrades. 'I'm going to do a shift at the front window. I'll tell Frau Walter the cake was wonderful.'

Holleman looked hopeful suddenly. 'Ask her if she ever puts her hand to a chocolate torte, will you? Or buttercream, I could live with that.'

'Jesus, Freddie. You haven't finished this one yet.'

'I know, but hell, she'd cater for us full-time if we asked. She almost fell down when I gave her that thousand marks.'

'I'll mention it.'

Fischer opened the door, in which was framed the curiously unwelcome form of Jonas Kleiber, hand half-raised to announce himself. The apparition swallowed visibly, and took a step back.

'What …? No, come in,'

Pulled physically into the apartment, Kleiber staggered and then, righting himself, looked around the room as if something within its walls might explode. Zarubin and Holleman stared speechlessly at him for a moment, and before the storm could break he blurted his business.

'I know, I know, hotel, airport and then England. But there were two men there – the hotel, I mean – and they weren't just hanging around. Big, ugly bastards who knew how to keep a street covered but not look the part. I didn't know if you were going to go back there (this to Fischer), so I thought you had to know. That's it. I'll go now. To the airport. I've got a taxi outside, waiting. Sorry.'

Fischer sat down on the wing of the room's only armchair and shook his head. 'It's too late. They've followed you here.'

'Me? How would they know …?'

'If they have any sense they would have put the hotel staff on alert for me or anyone looking for me. They'll have shown police warrant cards, probably. What was the first thing you said when you arrived?'

'I … asked for you.'

'Of course you did. And no hotelier's going to keep that to himself, not with a potential international criminal staying in one of his rooms. If you haven't been made by now the big ugly bastards aren't doing their job.'

'Then I've … oh, shit.'

'They'll be outside now, waiting for you, me or Zarubin to show ourselves. You can't go.'

Holleman grunted. 'They don't know *me*. I could leave, go around the block and come at them from behind.'

'With what, a stern reproof? They have to be armed, obviously, and there'll be two or three of them at least. KGB won't have sent fools, not on this sort of errand, so they'll be expecting trouble whichever direction it comes from. In any case, we don't want you to be seen. You're the only one they don't know by sight, and we can use that when …'

'What?'

'When we get out of here.'

'How the sweet f …?'

'First, we need to identify them. I'm going into Frau Walter's, to slide around the wall, peek through a curtain and watch the street. Freddie, you go downstairs, to the *hausmeister*'s office. Wave your card and ask to use his telephone. We need to let Rolf know not to send Engi again until we need him.'

Holleman looked appalled. 'What about food?'

'We have enough for a day or two, and if we're reduced to eating nothing but cake, it won't kill us.'

Kleiber had been listening quietly, but *day or two* shook him from his abject misery.

'I can't stay here. Maisie will panic.'

'If you leave now, you'll never get home. They can't know who you are, but they certainly aren't going to risk letting you bring help. You'll be followed, and somewhere between here and Riem airport they'll pick you up. They can't yet be sure that Zarubin's in this building, but after a few minutes' special treatment you'll be happy to confirm it. And once they're done with you …'

'Oh, Christ!'

'For the moment, I don't believe they can do anything. Probably, they'll try the police thing with the *hausmeister*, but he doesn't know which apartment we're squatting in, and there are, what, twenty in this building? They can't do a door-to-door because we'll hear them coming and it would all be too messily public, so it's going to have to be surveillance. They'll set up in a room across the street if they can, and then it's a question of sitting on their arses, waiting for the curtains opposite to open and close. One by one, they'll scratch the apartments on that side, and after that we'll be out of time.'

Holleman frowned. 'Why? They'll still need to check the other ten apartments, the ones that don't look onto the street.'

'And to do that, they'll get into one of buildings behind us, and set up somewhere that looks down onto the garden, which is the only escape route remaining to us. We may have a day, but probably less.'

Krokhin had given strict instructions that any calls from Munich prefaced by the word 'Radius' should be put through to him directly, wherever he was and whomsoever he was with. And then he waited, nerves stretched, unable to concentrate fully on the very many other important calls upon his time. For almost forty-eight hours, he half-listened and made no definitive decision on any matter brought to him by one of his subordinates. Naturally, they began to suspect that something was going on, down or up.

Inevitably, when the call came he was in the sports club showers, having played five straight games of badminton in an effort to distract himself. A frantic half-towelling and an astute secretary's re-direction of the call to the club reception (which was swiftly cleared by security staff) meant that the other party was hanging on for no more than two minutes. Even so, Krokhin had a brief, panicked premonition that some foul twist of fortune would leave him holding a dead line.

'Father here.'

'Radius. We may have located the packages. Someone asked after the badly-wrapped one at his hotel and then went to an address nearby. That was three hours ago, and he hasn't emerged.'

'Do we know who he is?'

'No. But he came into Munich from the little land across the little sea, as did the packages. He's a German national, according to the hotel staff.'

'I see. This is hopeful. What are your next steps?'

'Confirm that the targets are in the building. It's residential, eighteen apartments, the rear enclosed by similar. We're watching the main entrance, and a room's been secured on the second floor directly opposite. The tenant is on holiday, we identified ourselves to the concierge as police and demanded his discretion.'

'Good. I assume this can't be done where you are?'

'No. We're overlooked, so there'd be witnesses. We intend to remain out of sight, wait for one or both of the targets to emerge, follow, secure and remove them to a site outside the city. There are ample woodlands within an hour's drive.'

'Ideally, the evidence will never be discovered, or at least not until decomposition has made identification uncertain. You're using Soviet ordnance?'

'Of course.'

'I ask because I know that some of your colleagues prefer the American product. In this case, however, secure all shells post-mortem. We don't want to point a finger at ourselves.'

'Understood. What about the money? Do we secure and bring it with us, or are other arrangements being made?'

The money? Krokhin stared at the wall in front of him. Semichastny had so many good reasons to want Zarubin out of the world that he hadn't wondered about the precise motive, only the perplexing need to have the thing done now, and in Munich. But if it was about *money*, several uncomfortable questions arose. Zarubin had it, obviously, otherwise Radius wouldn't have needed to ask what he should do; but whose *was* it, and why was it of concern to KGB? Krokhin could see only one answer.

This operation had to be concluded swiftly because damage could be done otherwise. Had Zarubin robbed a bank, or cheated a casino, or embezzled from an investment fund, Semichastny might worry that the man had acquired resources that would enable him to be even more of a pain in the arse at some future date; but it would hardly make him so anxious as to risk KGB's amicable, productive relationship with MfS by drawing eyes to the immediate neighbourhood of their German brethren's most spectacular success.

This was the worst sort of money problem, therefore – KGB's money. That traitorous bastard Zarubin had opened the vault, helped himself and slipped away before he could be swatted. How the hell could he have done that? He couldn't, of course; the money had been in transit, to one of the many good causes that couldn't afford to buy their own rifles, explosives or electorate, and his hand had snatched it in mid-flight. *That* was why Semichastny wanted a swift resolution. It was an embarrassment, an insolent coup that would make KGB look ridiculous should it reach daylight, and he hadn't been Chairman nearly long enough for his reputation to absorb the jibes.

'Father?'

Krokhin thought quickly. If he took charge of any recovered money and assumed responsibility for its return, Semichastny would know that he knew everything, and that could be good (his discretion proved in the most practical manner) or very bad (some people really didn't enjoy being found out). If he told Radius to take full responsibility, he would have put a little distance between himself and potential shrapnel – unless, of course, the team was intercepted by highway robbers, or lost the loot, or had their loyalties tempted beyond endurance and absconded with it. In any of those cases, the Berlin Resident might be first in Semichastny's list of grudges to be satisfied.

No, he told himself, don't imagine things that you can't influence. He had been handed a poisoned chalice, so the less he sipped from it the better. He cleared his throat.

'Your task is to carry out the exercise and withdraw as quickly and as quietly as possible. A handover somewhere in transit will introduce complications. Secure whatever you find and cross the Czech border with all speed.'

'Understood. I'll call one time more, to confirm the result.'

'Good. Let me add something. General Zarubin is not to be underestimated. It may be that your approach has not been noticed by him and his friends, but please don't trust to that. Until he's covered in soil, assume that anything that can go wrong may very well do so.'

'We're never overconfident.'

'Excellent. I look forward to your report.'

Krokhin replaced the receiver in its cradle. The sensible thing would be to call Semichastny immediately, confirm that things proceeded as anticipated and give absolutely no impression that he was either sanguine or shitting himself about the outcome. This had been dumped upon him for want of a better fool, but it was by definition a test that he had to pass. And there was another consideration, part of the same test yet not necessarily complementary to its success. He picked up the receiver once more and dialled a direct number.

'Markus, hello, it's Aleksei. I have some good news. The business I mentioned has progressed. The objects have been located, I believe, and all care is being taken to ensure that everything will proceed calmly and quietly. There is, however, a possibility that a third package is involved. Yes, I appreciate that complicates matters, which is why I called. Our intention is to remove everything from the vicinity of Munich before resolving things, and obviously, three packages would make that more difficult to achieve. Sensitive to your concerns, we sent in only three workmen to do the job. They're very conscientious, but perhaps if they were to be supplemented by, say, two or three of your local people, the work might progress more smoothly?

'I know, it isn't what we agreed; but since then, I've come to understand why this job has been arranged at haste, and with such little notice. I'm not authorized to offer details. Let me just say that the damage has been considerable and the repairs need to be put in hand as a matter of great urgency.'

There was a long pause at the Ruschestrasse end of the line. Wolf hadn't wanted this operation to go ahead, but now he was being offered a chance to influence its course. The opportunity didn't come without barbs, and almost certainly he would see it for what it was – a way for Krokhin to partially cover himself. If MfS were linked to the operation and for some reason it went wrong, blame would have to be apportioned; if it was a brilliant success, the Berlin Resident's reputation would rise equally in Ruschestrasse and the Lubyanka; and if Semichastny was angered by the prospect of Markus Wolf (and, therefore, Eric Mielke) getting dangerously close to the true reason for this mad scheme, what could he say or do? If he'd wanted discretion he should have told Krokhin everything before putting him in charge of it. There were many ways in which a man could murder his own prospects, but failing to be telepathic wasn't yet one of them, even within the Soviet system.

The silence dragged while Wolf tried to work every possible consequence of saying yes or no, and Krokhin, pleased with his rather clever idea, didn't try to rush him. He knew already what the answer would be. Of course the German spymaster would get involved; how could he not, when the alternative was to let outsized KGB boots tramp horribly close to his most sensitive crop? It hardly mattered how many men he committed. Even one would be enough to …

'Just one man, to observe only, unless it becomes necessary for him to intervene to ensure the operation's success.'

'That's very helpful, Markus, thank you. I'll get an address for you, and let the team know that he's on his way.'

'Once I have it, he should be there within the hour. He's in Munich already.'

'Very good. And again, thank you.'

Krokhov clicked the receiver cradle with a finger and asked his secretary to connect him to Semichastny's office. For once, he was very much looking forward to the coming conversation, in which he would be the innocent yet assiduous bearer of good and unexpectedly bad news. It was a small, petty triumph, but he wasn't going to let that stop his enjoyment. After all, how often did a man get the chance to piss in the KGB Chairman's teacup?

'Well?'

'I didn't see anyone hanging around on the street. There's a pair of almost-closed curtains on the second floor across the way. They haven't moved since yesterday, as far as I know.'

Freddie Holleman was putting on his shirt. He had been in Frau Walter's apartment for almost an hour, with only his vest covering his ample upper body. This indecent display, so ruinous to her reputation, had been made necessary by secret police intelligence (hurriedly conceived by Fischer) that the felons they were after were becoming watchful. Subterfuge was required therefore, and the officer warned her that, in addition to his regrettable state of undress, he would be obliged, while standing openly at her window, to yawn and scratch his arse occasionally (though only with great reluctance).

Despite her strong misgivings, Frau Walter had sent him back to his colleagues with a freshly-baked loaf, to which Jonas Kleiber was helping himself. He looked up.

'If the curtains haven't moved, perhaps it's just that the tenant's away?'

Two of the other men in the room regarded him with mild contempt; the third, Fischer, shook his head. 'No-one leaves curtains like that if they're going out. They close or open them fully. But a curious person needs to keep their eye on someone without being seen themselves.'

'Oh. But I thought you didn't want them to make Freddie.'

'Not in our company, we don't. But they've had a good view of someone who doesn't a damn about being seen, and in whatever state. He isn't going to raise suspicions.'

Holleman grinned. 'I found it strangely enjoyable.'

'Degenerate. It's strange that they've not put men at each end of the street.'

Zarubin stood up, and, as was his unconscious habit by now, gently touched his wound. 'No, it isn't. They can't do this in the normal way. We're in Munich.'

Holleman's eyebrows went up. 'So?'

'So Pullach.'

'You think Gehlen's boys will give them a rough time?'

'I think that *Stasi* won't want anything happening that might draw the wrong sort of attention. When I ran two years ago, they'd already infiltrated almost every department at Pullach. God alone knows how compromised BND is by now.'

'Really?'

'Field intelligence is the only area in which the DDR entirely outclasses the Wessies, and it's very much to do with what leeway their respective regimes allow. For every man that Gehlen's managed to put into MfS, they've sent fifty his way. I only wish KGB had managed the same with CIA and SIS. That is, I used to wish it.'

Fischer felt a first, tiny tremor of hope. 'So KGB are going to have to be discreet about this. That helps us, doesn't it? We can assume that they aren't going to shoot on sight unless we first allow ourselves to be herded into a dark alley. Which means they'll need to snatch us, and take us somewhere quiet.'

Holleman grimaced. 'We get a nice car ride first. It isn't much.'

'Isn't it? If you want to do a job quietly, without being noticed, how many people do you send?'

'Not many.'

'No. Three or four, at most. They assumed they were coming for Zarubin and me. But now they've made Jonas also, so it's messier than they'd like it to be. What if …'

'What if what?'

'We invite Rolf and Engi for supper this evening? And a couple more of Rolf's larger employees?'

Holleman nodded slowly. 'Yeah, that would help. But even if we leave as a crowd, they can follow. And sooner or later they can pick you off.'

'Not if we leave in two directions, from two exits. There'll be, say, eight of us. We'll tell Rolf to bring some hooded jackets. They won't know who's gone where, will they?'

'Two exits? There's only one, the front door. The fire escapes all lead into the back garden, and that's enclosed.'

'I spoke to Frau Walter earlier. She has a friend in one of the other buildings that enclose it. If we ask nicely, she'll have her open one of its fire doors, so some of us can exit onto another street.'

Zarubin smiled. 'Excellent, Major.'

'If we don't … Jonas?'

'Bugger it up?'

'Yes, that. If we don't, we can be a hundred kilometres from here by dawn.'

'No. I need one more visit to Artsyuk's residence.'

For Christ's sake, why? Your donation to his RONDD was only conceived to stop him ratting to KGB. Now they *know* that you took their money we can just run with all of it.'

'That would be ungracious. I intend to keep my word.'

'So that a pathetic group of exiles can continue to put out anti-Soviet propaganda that nobody reads? Or is it to keep Artsyuk's fine wine cellar well-stocked? You'd put yourself in further danger for that?'

'He can be of a little more use to me. Your concern is touching, but believe me, I intend not to fall into KGB's hands.'

'Do you? Really?' Fischer glanced at Kleiber (who was giving him a cartoon-meaningful stare), drew Boris Levin's letter from his jacket and handed it to Zarubin. 'That isn't what our good friend told us.'

The letter was read for the second time that day. Zarubin replaced carefully in the envelope, and, smiling, returned it.

'Poor Boris. He isn't cut from a hero's cloth.'

'He may not be, but he's as observant as any man I've known. You told him that you were going to Germany, and that you might not survive the trip.'

'Actually, I said that I might not be able to return.'

'And that you valued his friendship. From your mouth, that reads like more than just goodbye.'

'I was embarking upon something uncertain. Stanislav's murder and my assumed part in it required that I put myself in others' hands, and quickly. Had I been able to do this from London the risks would have been much more measurable. Perhaps I should have said nothing to Boris. He worries too much.'

'You …' Fischer shook his head. 'You've dragged us all into a pit, you can't see its bottom or how high the sides might be, and you think that his anxiety might be misplaced? If he'd told me what you'd said to him I would have taken his excellent advice …'

'And mine', murmured Klieber.

'… yes, and yours, too.'

Holleman snorted. 'I called you a fucking idiot.'

'Thank you, Freddie. You were entirely correct.'

Zarubin held up his hand to ward off the general consensus. 'I am *not* planning an elaborate suicide. It's true, I appear to have overstepped the mark, but I had no idea that KGB's patronage of *Stille Hilfe* had become so generous. If I had, I would have chosen some other fund. In any case, here we are. Major, I like your suggestion. Tonight, we leave in such a way as to confound our assassins, and if by some unhappy chance I fall subsequently into KGB's hands, what can I tell them about you, other than that you're far from here?'

'Well …'

'Herr Holleman, please go down to the *hausmeister*'s office, telephone your friend Hoeschler and ask him to arrive about ten pm – it should be fully dark by then. It would be of great assistance to us if he, his son and two more gentleman could come separately, in two vehicles, yes?'

Grudgingly, Holleman nodded. 'While I'm on the 'phone, will we need guns?'

'By all means, let's encourage them to shoot us out of hand.'

'It was a serious question …'

'Though it would be fascinating to hear you make the request of Herr Hoeschler in the *hausmeister*'s presence.'

'Alright! Jesus …'

Fischer cleared his throat. 'Freddie, Jonas and I should go in the van. Once we're clear, we drop off Engi, give him a good price for it and disappear. You and Rolf …'

'Ah, no, Major.' Zarubin said it almost regretfully, and the hairs on the back of Fischer's neck came to attention. 'There's an extremely important – and entirely safe – task that only you can discharge. My last request to you, I promise.'

'Why can't you do it?'

'Because it wouldn't be credible, coming from me. I'll explain in the car. Or van. Whichever it is, you and I will leave via the other building.'

'Because if our friends see two men who aren't us emerging from the front door, they won't dare follow them for fear of missing us. And if they don't see us they'll have to ask themselves whether we were ever here at all.'

'Precisely.' Zarubin waved casually at Holleman and Kleiber. 'Let's keep them alive, though, if we can. Now, the money.'

He removed several note-filled plastic pouches from the swag-bag and handed them to Holleman, who took them gingerly.

'This is more than you said.'

'It is. About thirty thousand deutschmarks.'

'It's too much.'

'You have grandchildren?'

'Four.'

Zarubin removed another plastic pouch and held it out. 'It would be nice for them to have a start in life. The *wirtschaftswunder* isn't so *wundervoll* that a following wind won't help. Herr Kleiber.'

'Yeah?'

Another pouch emerged. 'This should cover your recent costs, I think.'

'I don't need it. Really.'

Fischer shook his head. 'He doesn't. He's quite wealthy.'

'Yes, but he's going to do a favour for me. You have Boris Levin's address?'

'I do.'

Then please give this to him, with my best wishes.'

Kleiber took some time arranging the loot in his pocket, patting it down and checking the results in a mirror that hung over the fireplace. Then he turned, frowning.

'What about Otto?'

'What about him?'

'You owe him more than anyone, after all the proverbial you've shovelled in his direction.'

'Of course I do. I shall *settle up*, as the English say, once we're out of here.'

'Why not now?'

'Because I couldn't do it *now* without offering too many clues as to what comes next, and I'd prefer not to do that in case the gentlemen outside decide to snatch you, against all logic.'

Kleiber blanched. 'Oh.'

Holleman sighed. 'I'll go and 'phone Rolf, to tell him he's got a busy evening.'

'Wait.' Fischer rubbed his chin. He was almost satisfied that what they had agreed upon made the best of a poor situation, but the recent succession of cakes from Frau Walter's clever hands had put him in mind of icing, and how it made a good thing better. 'Let's think just a little more about this.'

41

A thinly-built, unmemorable young man introduced himself only as Michael, and in turn was introduced to Tomasz and Arman. Slight nods were exchanged, no hands were offered; the newcomer glanced briefly around the room and took in all the expected evidence of a short surveillance operation – binoculars, hand-transmitter, a thin roll-up mattress, portable gas-stove, tea, milk, sugar, three mugs, several crushed paper bags strewn across the parquet floor and a Makarov 9.2mm pistol sitting on a Scandinavian-style ash sideboard.

'There are three of you?'

'Gennady is around the corner, a first-floor apartment, watching the rear. None of the ones we can see from here are possibles.'

'Right. Transport?'

'The silver Opel in the street, fifty metres to the right.'

'No sight yet of the packages?'

'No.'

'You're certain they're in there?'

'Not certain, no. But the one asking after them at the hotel went in yesterday and hasn't emerged.'

'Your orders?'

'To acquire, remove and dispose of two packages.'

'And the one asking questions?'

'If he becomes a problem, yes. Otherwise, we concentrate on the two, whether they leave separately or together.'

'Not quite straightforward.'

'We've done easier. Not being able to put them down right away complicates things. You brought your own transport?'

'An Auto Union, four-seater. I parked it at the end of the street, about one hundred and fifty metres.'

'That will help us, your orders permitting.'

'I'm to monitor your operation and assist if circumstances require it, at my discretion. Above all, to ensure that this looks anything other than what it is.'

'Ours also. Usually, we try to make it seem like a criminal gang reprisal, an execution, but we don't know enough about Munich's underworld to make that feasible.'

'It would call down all kinds of attention. The city's had no significant organized crime since the *ringvereine*.'

'So, we make this a simple disappearance, of men who've been here for a few days only, no bodies to be found now or later. Who's going to know?'

Michael relaxed slightly. 'That sounds right. So it's a question of waiting.'

'When is it ever anything else?'

'You've been given no time frame?'

'We were told to get here on wings. There were no other constraints. We expect them to move at night, obviously.'

'Let's hope it's tonight, then.'

Tomasz grinned. 'Someone warming your bed, is there?'

'Not any more. I brought coffee and *schrippen*.'

'Good man.'

Arman checked Gennady's status on the hand-set, Tomasz brewed coffee and they took turns to monitor the street from the darkened room. A family entered the target building as dusk faded, followed almost immediately by two young girls in BCP uniforms. An hour later, an elderly woman departed the main entrance, made her arthritic way to the corner and disappeared around it. Just before 9pm, two young men approached the building and stood for a few minutes, arguing outside the entrance, and went inside. None of these events caused the KGB men to make a note in their watch diary. At 9.25, a black Mercedes-Benz 190D drew up at the entrance and waited, the driver remaining at the wheel, engine running. Quickly, both Tomasz and Arman donned outdoor jackets and checked their pistols; the latter picked up a set of keys, unlocked the door and stepped out. His colleague turned to Michael.

'You should wait. Here, introduce yourself to Gennady. Tell him we're on the street, ready to follow if we make the targets. If that happens, we'll call with a location within the hour. Clear up the room and bring him, if you will.'

'Right.'

Michael made the call to Gennady and then picked up the binoculars. He had only just focussed on the entrance across the street when two men exited the building. One of them was a young'ish, slim-framed man in a smart jacket; the other older, larger, uglier and dressed for gardening or a walk over rough ground; both walked to the waiting Mercedes-Benz and stood for a few moments, scanning the street in both directions before getting in. Immediately, the car pulled away from the kerb and moved westwards. Michael lifted the transceiver and was about to call Gennady to give him the news when Tomasz burst back into the room. Without a word, he passed one to the other.

The Pole made the call, identified himself and listened for a moment, 'Yes, I know. Arman will have the car at the entrance. Follow them. We'll be behind you, three minutes at most.'

Michael was already clutching his car keys. 'What?'

'The two who came out the front were decoys – the skinny fellow who asked after half-face at the hotel and a big bastard who's been showing himself off at a window opposite. Gennady's confirmed that the packages are leaving the back way, through the garden. He's almost outside already, they won't get away. Come on.'

The two men moved quickly but quietly, evacuating the room and leaving all evidence of their occupation where it was, to be discovered upon the return of the holidaying tenants. Taking their time on the street, moving deliberately rather than in such a way as to be noticed, they were in the Auto Union in less than two minutes. There was no need to rush now. Gennady and Arman would radio directions, making no move to take the packages until the team had reassembled and could make the snatch clean, efficient and discreet. They were all adept at this, and now that the waiting was over the worst of the job was behind them.

The hand-set buzzed once more. Tomasz put it to his ear, listened, said 'right' and turned to Michael. He was almost smiling.

'They're moving east, towards the river, on Fraunhoferstrasse. Slow and steady, unaware of what's behind them. Doing our job for us.'

Michael eased the Auto Union out into thin traffic, keeping his eye on the speedometer. He was a native of Munich and knew its roads as well as any taxi driver. He'd feared that this assignment, suddenly gifted to him and bearing all the marks of a rushed, half-considered clutch at something, might be his ticket to the blunt end of a professional cul de sac, but he couldn't fault how it was being handled. Tomasz was giving him constant updates from his colleagues, and it was obvious already that the unmarked van was heading towards, if not to, Riem airport. *Slow and steady.* Michael considered Preysingstrasse, looping up to Einsteinstrasse and putting the Auto Union between the van and its destination. There was ample green space south of Zamdorf, between the edge of the metropolis and Riem, where the snatch (or, if it became necessary, the executions) could be done without witnesses. Within the hour, the packages would no longer be a problem to anyone, and he could report to Ruschestrasse in expectation of something more than shit sticking to his reputation.

He put his idea to Tomasz, who considered it briefly, nodded and spoke to the man on the other end of the transceiver. Michael pushed down on the accelerator, taking the Auto Union to the edge of the speed limit. On Preysingerstrasse there was less chance of being stopped by the police than on Einsteinstrasse (the main artery into Munich from the east), but he wasn't going to tempt fate. If the white van didn't speed up he would get ahead of it. If it did, it might well be pulled over, giving the pursuers all the time they needed to arrange things. Either way, he was feeling better about this than at any moment since Markus Wolf had given him the bad news personally, some two hours earlier.

Five minutes after the Auto Union pulled away from the kerb, two men stepped out of the front entrance of an apartment building that had been the subject of considerable attention that day. Both wore hats; the one to conceal his starkly blond hair, the other to make less of a face that a myopic village idiot could hardly fail to recall in detail, should it be required. They walked briskly to the end of the street, turned two corners and approached a Mercedes Benz 190D that had been waiting, its engine running, for almost twenty minutes.

Three men occupied the vehicle already, but what had already made the model such a favourite of German taxi drivers was its capacious interior, and the newcomers had no difficulty finding ample room next to the skinny young man who had been keeping a lonely vigil in the rear.

'Hello, Rolf. Thanks for the ride.'

The driver twisted in his seat to offer the unforgettable face an old-fashioned look.

'Well, this is hellish, Otto. Couldn't you have stayed dead?'

For an unanticipated reunion of very old friends, conversation was thin. Rolf Hoeschler's attention was wholly on the roads and traffic, while the three men behind him gazed at the passing scenery and kept close company with their own thoughts. Even Freddie Holleman disturbed the silence with no more than occasional grunt as he attempted to find a comfortable position for his new leg and the stump it clasped.

The Mercedes Benz was approaching Allach, where slave labourers once toiled to produce fine porcelain for their entrepreneurial SS masters. Fischer had wondered whether Hoeschler might be taking them to his home, but he recalled that it was a Neuhausen address, and they had driven too far be in the inner city still.

'Where are we going, Rolf?'

'Augsburg. It's far enough away that KGB won't …'

'No. We can't leave Munich just yet. Not the Major and myself.'

Hoeschler regarded Zarubin coldly in his rear-view mirror. 'Your right to give orders ended a long time ago. What's he up to this time?'

The last was addressed to anyone in the car other than the Russian. Holleman shrugged slightly. 'Robbing his old colleagues. Of a lot.'

'And you dolts volunteered for duty?'

Fischer coughed. 'I'm the only dolt. Freddie and Jonas did their best to convince me of it.'

Hoeschler shook his head. 'You shouldn't be allowed out on your own.'

'I know. How's Mila?'

'Fine, glad to be easing off the pedal, finally. I haven't told her anything about this.'

'We assumed not. Is Engi driving your van tonight?'

'I couldn't persuade him not to. But the two men I sent are fairly capable.'

'Against KGB assassins?'

'They're ex-police, both armed. They're leading the Ivans towards Riem and the airport. If the bad men want to do the business discreetly they'll need to wait until the van reaches green space. But it won't get that far.'

'Where is it going?'

Hoeschler half-turned and smiled. 'Zamdorf police station, their old gaff. A quick left turn off Einsteinstrasse, and before the Ivans know what's happening the chance will be gone. If you're not leaving Munich, where am I dropping you?'

Zarubin leaned forward in his seat. 'Major Fischer and I need somewhere to hide, just for tonight. We'll be gone tomorrow, I promise.'

The car slowed and pulled in to a bus halt. Hoeschler stared up at the network sign for a few moments.

'Alright. We have another unlet property, in Obermenzing. I'll take you there after I've dropped off Freddie and Jonas at the local s-bahn station.'

Kleiber glanced at Holleman, not wanting to be the first to sound relieved. 'Where will that get us?'

'Ingolstadt. Change for Stuttgart, and home.'

Holleman shook his head. 'I'm not …'

'Yes you are, Freddie.' Fischer put a hand on his shoulder. 'You can't do anything else here that won't complicate things. If we can take our tormentor's word I have one more thing to do. After that, I'll be out of Germany faster than a November swallow, I promise.'

'And if you can't take his word?'

'I think I can. I believe I know what's coming.'

Zarubin looked at Fischer but said nothing. A man who had just been slapped down and insulted might well have taken offence (particularly from those whose fates he had once dangled), yet none of it seemed to move him. He was almost entirely with his own thoughts still, and Fischer's suspicions strengthened.

At Obermenzing s-bahn station, Kleiber thanked Hoeschler quietly and got out of the car. Holleman whispered something in their driver's ear, patted his shoulder and turned to the back seat.

'Otto, can I have a word, please?'

Fischer followed Holleman to the rail of an empty taxi rank. The bigger man had already pulled a cigarette from a pack and was lighting it (as far as Fischer knew, he had given up the habit early in

1945, his extra little push for the war effort after the Red Army crossing the Vistula). His face was flushed, which only ever happened when he was about to do or say something entirely out of character.

He drew deeply, coughed, and spoke quietly.

'Listen. I don't know if you're going to be breathing by tomorrow evening, but if you are, and if you can still walk, get away, far away. Don't tell me, or Jonas, or anyone else – and by *anyone else* I mean Zarubin, first and last – where you're going. Don't *ever* say. That other life's a dream as long as your pockets are loaded with stones from this one.'

'Freddie …'

'Shut up. Starting again means just that. You need to lose everything that's *this* and live what's left of your portion without looking back or pining for stuff. The Nazis they've caught, every one of them, held on to some fatal piece of the good old days and lit themselves up. Christ, that cock Eichmann even gave taped interviews in case anyone forgot what he'd done. No-one cares enough about you to put on a show-trial, but the way you make your own foul luck, being guilty of anything hardly matters, does it? If you leave even a toe in the past a bullet's going to find you, eventually.'

'He's right.' Kleiber had crept up and listened to every word. 'I've never known how, but you attract shit like white shoes. You have to break the habit, and it shouldn't be difficult. You have no family, no ties other than to us …'

'And we don't like you anyway.'

'Thank you, Freddie.'

'… and now you don't need to count your pennies, as the English say. You can do just about anything you want.'

'But what *do* I want? To leave no mark, anywhere? To be something carried in a breeze?'

Holleman shrugged. 'It'd be a comfortable, warm breeze.'

Kleiber tapped his chest. 'Look at me ...'

Obediently, the two older men regarded the slight, unhealthily pale prospect in front of them.

'I left Germany, my homeland, on my own, without any friends or family in England. But I've made a place for myself, haven't I?'

Fischer frowned. '*The Flowers*?'

'Fuck off. I have a home, a girl who quite likes me and a job I enjoy most days. The thing to do, Otto, is to take the blank sheet and make a mark on it.'

'That was almost profound, Jonas.'

'I'm being serious. Who knows what could happen, if you do? Be a watch-repairer in Auckland, or a gramophone restorer in Marrakesh. Or, once you're settled in Cape Town, 'phone Earl Kuhn and get his advice on setting up a record shop. Just don't tell him where you are.'

They stared at him earnestly, willing a future to recommend itself. He was touched, and frustrated. A fresh start was a myth, a wraith; the one thing that couldn't be left behind was the self, which meant that every new step taken over virgin soil would be inescapably tainted by the weight of old lessons not learned. It had worked for Jonas Kleiber only because he had been young enough not to have yet laid down a store of regrets; for Freddie Holleman, the abiding presence of a strong wife and a vague understanding of what the Assyrians did to wilful Israel were ample discouragements to revisit past idiocies. Fischer had neither the latitude of youth nor an excellent spouse to tempt any *new* into a new life, and if there was any lesson to be drawn from recent history it was that the legs that had carried him to the edge of countless precipices were fully operational still.

He was tired, and the conversation best finished. He nodded. 'Alright.'

'Really?'

'What else can I say, Freddie?'

Holleman's mouth opened and remained that way. He was unconvinced, but had nothing with which to reinforce the most, best advice he had ever offered. Kleiber sighed, looked around and tugged Holleman's sleeve. A passenger train was pulling slowly into the station from the direction of Munich.

'We should go, that may be the last one tonight. Good luck, Otto. Please don't write.'

Holleman wrapped his arms around Fischer and almost crushed his rib cage. 'Take care, mate. Send us a blank card every other year, to let us know you're breathing.' He wiped an eye with his fist, coughed, turned awkwardly and followed Kleiber into the station.

The journey from Obermenzing station to the apartment took less than three minutes. Hoeschler drove slowly, smoothly, saying nothing until they had parked and entered the building (a five-storey, mixed residential and retail structure stretching almost the length of a block). Soft, piped music wafted them through the warm foyer and into an elevator.

Fischer regarded his unlovely reflection in the polished wall. 'Do you own all of this, Rolf?'

'The building? Yeah. As we've sold off and bought new properties in recent years, the trend's been to go for fewer but bigger.'

Zarubin stirred. 'Lower overheads, less maintenance, more profit.'

Hoeschler's eyebrows rose slightly. 'When did you become a capitalist?'

The question hung there, unanswered. The elevator door opened on to a fifth-floor corridor, where the same music (an adagio from a forgettable violin concerto) played them into the apartment. Even in its unoccupied state it looked to be beyond the means of all but a minority of the city's working population, an open-spaced hangar with every modern fitted convenience, deep carpets and bland but tasteful artwork mounted sparingly. A log-effect gas fire was embedded into one of the walls, flanked by two American-styled wood and leather armchairs on metal pedestals Making a boundary between them and the kitchen area stood a long, low radiogram, and, surrounding it, open-case shelving to host a future tenant's record collection.

Fischer couldn't imagine a place more suited to his own domestic tastes. 'Very nice.'

'Do you think so? Mila put it all together. I worry she has it in mind for when we retire.'

'You don't like it?'

'I don't like where it *is*. When I give up the work detail I want a big garden, and fields around me. Here, the key. When you leave tomorrow, lock up and push it back under the door.'

'Thank you. Rolf ,,,'

'Yeah?'

'For everything, these past few days.'

'Ach, it's what comrades do. There's food in the fridge, and beer. Wine if you prefer, in a rack at the end of the island.'

Hoeschler shook hands with both men and left without saying more - another excision, a further delicate paring of flesh from something reduced to little more than what was needed to keep bones in place.

Zarubin took off his jacket and dropped it on to one of the expensive leather chairs. 'I don't believe that Herr Hoeschler is fond of me.'

'I wonder why that might be.'

'He has a good life these days. One could say that my not having had him shot put him in the way of it.'

'Your logic is singularly stretched.'

'Shall we drink to our new wealth?'

'Only if we can talk about it also.'

'Why should we do that?'

'Because it's a small part of what's not quite right about any of this. A good place to start.'

'It isn't important.'

Fischer went to the kitchen area, opened a few drawers, found a corkscrew and went to examine the wine rack. He found just two bottles, both clarets, neither notable nor objectionable. He removed one and began to open it.

'It isn't, is it? From the moment this began, your interest in the loot hasn't been what I'd expect from a thief, particularly one who steals from extremely dangerous people. It made me think that you were doing this for the thrill that mountain climbers or lion hunters chase; but then, you don't seem thrilled either. If you were merely suicidal you might have put yourself beneath a bus with far less inconvenience. And if your intention was to goad your former colleagues I imagine you've collected enough career-destroying gossip to do the job without needing to place yourself so close to the noose, bullet or gulag. This is actually very good.'

He poured a glass for Zarubin, who took it, sniffed the wine but didn't drink. 'So, why am I doing this?'

'Because you didn't kill Stanislav Kudrin.'

'I told you that I didn't.'

'I know, but I don't read minds and you have a habit of saying things that aren't true. Actually, I decided very quickly that you *weren't* the murderer, but ...'

'Why, if I may ask? My virtuous demeanour?'

'You don't have the belly for it, not the real thing. I'm sure you've signed any number of warrants that other people executed – in every sense. And you did plug that fellow outside the wine-cellar, so you're not too virtuous to do kill. But to do it with your hands would require a quality you've never demonstrated, to me at least.'

'Which is?'

'Feeling. And strangulation in particular requires a depth of it. You would have had to grab a throat and squeeze while you watched the twitching and the eyes clouding over, feeling the legs kicking, and extreme human intimacy isn't your thing. Besides, I couldn't see a motive.'

'I had none. In fact, acknowledging what you say about me, Stan Kudrin would have been one of the very last people I might have summoned the inclination to kill. I owed him a great debt.'

'He was generous.'

'I don't mean the money and mattress, although both were very necessary. He gave me something else - a precious gift.'

'His memories, of your father.'

Zarubin's wine glass shuddered, tipping enough of its contents to horribly stain the expensive white carpet beneath his feet. He looked down at the damage blankly, then at Fischer.

'How could you know?'

'A young priest in London who believed you to be guilty of the murder. He told me that Kudrin had known General Zarubin during the civil war, though they were of different factions. We should get some water on that.'

After ten minutes of gentle effort (entirely Fischer's), the stain was a dull patch that had an equal chance of disappearing or becoming indelible. Had he shown any interest in the process, Zarubin might have been a mute overseer, but he somewhere else, his lips moving occasionally in conversation with his thoughts. One of them stirred something, and he cleared his throat.

'I didn't know my father. I have a vague memory of his presence, but even that might be fostered by the wish that it should be so. My mother's recollections were entirely partial, of course, so I grew up with stories of a noble soul, a hero, a tragic moralist. My uncle would never speak of him, not even to damn his eyes, his politics or the harm he did to his brother's career. Stanislav Kudrin was the first person to speak to me of a recognizably whole creature, someone who might have walked in the world as men do, rather than a demigod, or demon.'

'They were friends by choice, enemies by circumstance.'

'Many Russians could have said the same, at that time. The finest compliment Stan paid my father was that he reminded him of himself, a man struggling to keep upright in violent waters. They couldn't agree on what should come next, of course. My father wanted a socialist republic; Stan a constitutional monarchy on something a little more old-fashioned than British lines – a Romanov monarchy, of course. They agreed to disagree, which was a momentous thing in those days. Their common ground was that the greatest tragedy for Russia would be a Bolshevik victory, and that stopping it would take alliances of men who couldn't abide each others' preferences. Insofar as it might be said of anyone, I believe they were both visionaries.'

'How well did they know each other?'

'Enough to be at ease with their very different backgrounds and aims. At one point they spent two days together in a house in Rostov, trying to hammer out something that would last beyond the next local battlefield. Naturally, they failed. Behind each man were less intelligent, blinkered people with the rank and authority to impose their own wishes. You know the result. My father was one of the thousands who fought, failed and then disappeared during the Boleshevik reckoning; Stan Kudrin fled into exile when the last hope for victory died.'

'And you went on to serve the Bolsheviks.'

'I was never committed to any cause, though my uncle managed to straighten out my idiosyncrasies before they did me harm. His connections got me into NKGB.'

'And you got him into an early grave.'

'Where he belonged, the bastard. My mother had died some years earlier, cutting the last link between a father and his son.'

'Which Kudrin reconnected, in a modest way.'

'More than modestly. As I say, the debt is great.'

Fischer noticed it, and nodded. 'You didn't kill him, but someone did. Was it KGB?'

'Probably. Almost certainly. He was harmless, but represented a tradition of resistance they prefer expunged, given the choice.'

'I wonder how they found him.'

'He didn't use a pseudonym, or otherwise try to conceal himself.'

'Then it's surprising he wasn't removed earlier.'

'He hadn't been active for some years. His work in Paris would have exposed him to more danger, but he and his colleagues took precautions back then.'

'I suppose someone just noticed an opportunity, and took it.'

'Yes.'

'I believe you know who, and why.'

'What makes you say that?'

'The debt *is* great, you said, not *was*. You haven't discharged it and he's dead, but you see a possibility still for retribution. It's why you're here.'

'How did you know?'

'Kudrin died, you were the only suspect, so you had to flee. Why the hell would you choose to find sanctuary with a man who's probably betraying his own people to KGB?'

'He invited me, as a guest, before Stan died.'

'Because he wanted to gain further favour with KGB by handing over one of their most irritating arse-itches.'

'That's what I assumed when Boris Levin told me of his letter. But then I offered him money, quite a lot more than KGB were ever likely to push his way. His organization is always desperately short of funding.'

'That's *how* you did it, not why. A thousand alternative options would have recommended themselves more strongly, with no need to hand over a large part of the loot you planned to steal. You had absolutely no motive to go to Artsyuk, of all people. Except one, that is; the one that makes the matter of money irrelevant.'

'Which is?'

'It was Artsyuk who betrayed Stanislav Kudrin. You're going to repay your debt to the old man by killing his Judas. It's the only conceivable reason for you to risk being in his company.'

Zarubin smiled thinly. 'And how would I do that, with his fearsome young bodyguard – and, possibly, several others - hovering between me and him?'

'I think the answer to that has much to do with the final, perfectly safe little task you have in mind for me.'

'And you'll oblige me?'

'I will. But I'll need an address.'

44

KGB Chairman Semichastny was called out of his quarterly presentation to Sovmin, a discourtesy that his prior apology and hint at great matters moving quickly he sensed had only partly eased (their granite faces were unreadable, their sense of self-importance legendary). He hurried to the nearest secure telephone as quickly as wouldn't make his anxiety noticeable, had the room cleared and dialled the Resident's number at Karlshorst.

'Well?'

At the other end of the line, Krokhin cleared his throat. 'The packages were not collected.'

'Why?'

'We had four men in place – our three and Wolf's local agent. They faced a minimum of seven, and probably eight, brought in late. With two vehicles, it wasn't difficult for them to decoy their pursuers. From what I hear of how it went, the team couldn't have performed more efficiently. We needed more resources in place. That, of course, was not acceptable to our friends at Ruschestrasse.'

'There are no clues as to where they …'

'No. The vehicle assumed to be the objective stopped at a police station near Munich's airport. Three men emerged, none of them identifiable. By now, the packages might not be in Germany, or even Europe. To be frank, the team can't say for sure that they were ever in the apartment building under surveillance. Perhaps our men weren't even decoyed, only distracted by something that looked like something else'

'Perhaps you should have …'

Semichastny paused. He'd almost been glib, as frustrated men often were to their subordinates. *What* should Krokhin have done? His analysis was entirely correct: for a snatch to go smoothly, quietly and without attracting notice, the targets had to be located precisely and overwhelmed instantly. For four men to take two from a group of seven or eight would require that the others were neutralised, which meant a great deal of bloodshed and its inevitable publicity. And if they couldn't determine even that Zarubin and his twisted-faced accomplice had been in the area at the time, what success might have been hoped for?

The question made him consider the entirety of the palpable information they had, and whether he had allowed his eagerness to end Zarubin warp his judgement. KGB in London had sent in a routine report that someone resembling the traitor had boarded a flight to Munich. Even if the sighting had been confirmed, might

Zarubin have departed the city immediately following his arrival? Otto Fischer's appearance a few days later had been noticed and notified by a low-level operative courtesy of a ten-year-old memory, and Holy God alone knew how many badly mutilated Germans were walking the streets still (courtesy, not least, of the Red Army). One event had magnified the relevance of these sightings - the subsequent diversion of a large KGB donation to one of the hold-out fascist organizations and its relocation to a Munich bank account. To Semichastny, that had been one coincidence (in the literal sense of the word) too many. And yet coincidences (in the commonly-used sense) *did* occur. To date, there had been no reliable sighting of Zarubin *in* Munich, and no-one had been able to get a description of the person who withdrew the stolen monies before KGB had a chance to reclaim it. Even so, the whole was sufficiently compelling that he might have placed a bet upon this being Zarubin's doing. The problem was, he *had* bet upon it, and now they had nothing – no money, no packages, no idea of where to look next.

'*What* should I have done, Comrade Chairman?'

There was a slight catch in Krokhin voice that sounded like impatience, or even irritation. It shouldn't have been there, of course, but Semichastny's conscience was not entirely unmoved by the man's predicament. Three years ago he had gifted him a turd with orders to sugar it, quickly. Krokhin had failed (by the same token, so had Semichastny and his predecessor, Shelepin), and it was clear that he felt the episode to be a drag-weight upon his career. In fact, he was mistaken, and if his acting Residency at Karlshorst was never going to be confirmed it was for an entirely different reason. Appointed hastily following Korotkov's untimely death, he had since discharged his duties conscientiously and efficiently, and to date no-one had expressed the slightest reservations regarding his work. If anything, he had been a little too successful in juggling his several responsibilities. The Berlin Resident's first and last loyalty was to the Lubyanka, but he was also the principal daily liaison between KGB and MfS, and Semichastny had formed a firm conviction that Krokhin had become too close to Markus Wolf. Wolf was a good man, as good an intelligencer as anyone in KGB; but he reported to Erich Mielke, whom KGB regarded more as a problem than an ally. Mielke was a dinosaur, an unrepentant Stalinist for whom Khrushchev's reforms – *any* reforms – were a betrayal, a step away from the pure path of Bolshevism. The passing of the age of mass denunciations and show-trials, of the necessary periodic cleansing of the Intelligentsia's troublesome gene-pool, was to him a matter of infinite regret. Like the Chinese, he considered the modern Soviet Union to have lapsed into heresy, and if (unlike the Chinese) he didn't dare say as much, the hugs and kisses he exchanged with Semichastny at their infrequent meetings were no warmer than those he might have offered to CIA Director John McCone. With Krokhin he was a little less unbending, and sometimes even polite. It may have been that he appreciated the effort the Berlin Resident made to massage MfS sensitivities, or perhaps it was merely a fling at

Moscow, to mark his unmentionable disapproval of the times and their new mores.

So Krokhin had tainted his chances at Karlshorst by doing his job as well as he could, and Semichastny wasn't going to blame him for that. That he had been entrusted with this latest near-impossible task was a sincere compliment to his talents, though he would hardly see it that way. As for harming his career, this damn business was so far from ever seeing daylight that nothing would or could appear on his record, nor even move eyebrows if ever a question was raised regarding him. KGB was not so over-blessed with assiduous, intelligent heads of department that the traditional reward for failing to work miracles – a bullet to the head *pour encourager les autres* – was an option, much less the preferred one.

Semichastny sighed. 'I can't say, Aleksei Alekseevich. You were presented with a difficult situation, at very short notice.'

'Then may I ask if you can tell me why we had to move so quickly?'

No, of course you may not. Nevertheless, Semichastny paused. He wanted as few people as possible within the organisation to know how they had been swindled like village idiots, but it occurred that absolute secrecy couldn't be maintained. Whoever had taken their money – Zarubin, a rogue banker or an enterprising gang of Genevese street urchins - it needed to be recovered, preferably before KGB's funding discussions for the next triennial commenced. He could hardly ask his best overseas operatives to be vigilant if he didn't tell them what it was they had to be vigilant about, nor hope that some preternatural intuition move a sighting of the guilty party to be reported promptly. Krokhin had no connection with or authority over the network of illegals that KGB ran in the Federal Republic, but as a friend of Markus Wolf he could expect to be passed useful information picked up by any one of the army of MfS operatives who burrowed industriously through its institutions. A long shot, perhaps, yet worth the risk of confiding in one man, a man whose future career lay firmly in Semichastny's hands.

'This is, of course, in the strictest confidence, not to be shared with anyone at Karlshorst.'

'I understand, Comrade Chairman.'

'It appears that we have been embarrassed …'

After the call ended, Krokhin let out all of his breath, as if he were in deep water and trying to finish it quickly. He had guessed correctly about the money, and he wondered now how good or bad their failure to recover it might be – for himself, of course. Semichastny had admitted everything, which was encouraging, given that people who are about to be blamed for something aren't usually made privy to its awful secrets. The piquant *but*, however, was that it had been one A.A. Krokhin who, however innocently, had set the operation moving by reporting the sighting of Otto Fischer to Moscow. A sacrificial goat had therefore volunteered itself, should one become necessary. Semichastny's tacit absolution had been *too* tacit to sound more than provisional, and in any case a telephone conversation wasn't a document that could be produced at a trial.

Continue to liaise with Markus Wolf. Ask that descriptions of Zarubin and Fischer be circulated to MfS agents in major West German cities and sightings reported to you quickly.

It sounded like Semichastny had given up. Could he bury the loss of a hundred and fifty-five thousand roubles in KGB's operating budget? In theory it was possible. Since his predecessor Shelepin's swerve to Africa, they had been pouring money into revolutionary causes there that rarely emerged from the bush, much less submitted accounts for monies disbursed. It was generally accepted that donations to these groups were likely to buy as many expensive cars as grenade-launchers; that the only real short-term return upon the investment was the increased brutality that western-backed regimes would inflict upon their fractious subjects to cowe them. With some careful book-keeping, even a large discrepancy might be kept from being noticed by the time-servers on the Finance Committee.

No. Krokhin wasn't close to Semichastny, but a relatively new man at the KGB helm wouldn't (he tried to think of another nautical metaphor, but all that came to mind was Damocles) want a sword hanging over his head – the chance, however thin, that someone on the Committee might act out of character and wake up. This was something else. If it *was* something, and not just surrender.

But why would it be surrender, unless ... he recalled his thoughts on Semichastny's loyalties: where they lay, and where they might wander if the wind changed direction. He was Khrushchev's protege, and three years earlier his scheme to stop the traitor's defection had been stifled at the last moment – literally, the *last* moment – by his mentor. Back then, Khrushchev's word was law, but since Cuba his coat-tails had been grabbed by several hands belonging to members of the Central Committee, most notably those of Kosygin and Brezhnev. How hard those hands pulled, how effectively they prevented Khrushchev from going his own way, was *the* issue of current Soviet politics.

Semichastny was walking a thin line, therefore, between loyalty to the man who had put him in the chair and not being seen as the First Secretary's creature by those who might soon be making appointments of their own. He had failed in his (second) attempt to get Zarubin, but only he, Krokhin, and, probably, Markus Wolf, knew it as yet. If he didn't put it right, and quickly, that dangling sword ...

Had two edges. Zarubin had also been one of Khrushchev's proteges, and not only was he a traitor to his country but now an embezzler of KGB funds also, a living taunt. Hamstrung by MfS's insistence that KGB not compromise their operations in the Federal Republic, Semichastny had tried to stop him and failed. Whose fault was it that Zarubin still breathed – his, or that of the man who had prevented him doing the job three years ago?

Naturally, he couldn't say as much; not until Khrushchev was so close to falling that criticising him was less a suicide note than a declaration of loyalty to his successor (whoever that was). Was KGB's Chairman playing that long a game? And if he was, what should or could Krokhin do?

Nothing, obviously. If he even twitched, either Semichastny or one of the parties the man was hoping to impress would arrange something messy, and final. He had been played himself, so closely associated with this latest failure that he would stand or fall with his boss (or fall anyway, once it became clear to whom the latter would owe his future career). There was literally nothing to be done, other than watch it play out.

Zarubin had won twice now, and Krokhin had lost upon precisely the same ground. He sincerely wanted to hate the man, but a degree of naked admiration got in the way. That anyone could defect and return, contrive to bring down the Soviet hierarchy's psychopathic wing (Beria and his successor Serov), rise through the ranks of KGB while remaining his own man, defect once more and then (very probably) swoop back in to steal a fat pension from his former employers constituted an epic of effrontery that deserved the deployment of an entire directorate to study. In fact, an organization with far greater self-awareness than KGB (or any other intelligence agency, for that matter) might consider putting aside history, swallowing its ire and offering handsomely-paid tenure to the man. One couldn't eradicate an infection without understanding it fully.

'It's … more than I expected.'

Artsyuk was attempting to keep his delight hidden, but one hundred thousand dollars was making it very difficult. He glanced down into the bag and back up to Zarubin's face several times, as if doubtful than his benefactor really intended the gift, or fearful that it might lose corporeal form if he took his eyes from it for too long.

'The rewards were significantly greater than I'd anticipated. It seemed wrong not to share my good fortune. Besides, it's all to a worthy cause.'

A hint of doubt momentarily clouded Artsyuk's expression. 'Really? I wouldn't have thought the struggle was something a former KGB General might have found sympathy for.'

'You forget that my father died for his almost-democratic principles, and that my mother longed for nothing more than a full Romanov restoration. Perhaps this is my apology to them, for turning out bad.'

Artsyuk laughed. 'It's a handsome apology. I was hoping that your donation would allow us to weather a few more years of relative penury, but with this we can actually build something. Vasili will be delighted.'

'Where is he?'

'I sent him out, to meet a prospective donor – that is, to beg an elderly émigré to mention us in her will. It's pitiful, but that's what we've been reduced to these past …'

His eyes returned to the bag's contents once more. '… this really is wonderful! Thank you, Sergei Aleksandrovich.'

'It's my great pleasure. Now, I must be going.'

'No, please! We should have a lunch, to celebrate. I can find two marvellous bottles of champagne, the last of a venerable …'

'Thank you, but no. I have a very busy day, and I don't want to spoil your triumphant moment with Vasili.'

The smile remained, but Artsyuk's eyebrows furrowed. 'How could you possibly do that?'

'By bleeding on your carpet. He's a fearsome young man, and I don't think I want to test his temper.'

'How could you possibly do that?'

'He was a close friend of Stanislav Kudrin, I believe?'

'How did you know?'

'Kudrin mentioned him to me, rather fondly. I think Vasili was the last of his conquests before age and a sense of the ridiculous caught up with him.'

'Ah. Yes. I believe they knew each other in Paris. I still don't know why you imagine he wouldn't want to bless the ground you walk upon, after this.'

The bag moved slightly, though it was too heavy to raise fully. Zarubin shrugged.

'He won't be too kindly disposed towards the man who killed Kudrin, once he hears of it.'

Artsyuk's mouth dropped open. 'But you didn't ...'

'No, I didn't, but you wouldn't know that unless you knew who did. You arranged things so it seemed that way, though - no, please, I'm not offended. Had I been in your position I probably would have done the same. It would have been a magnificent double-coup, and put you in KGB's very best books. I'm also aware that I brought it on myself, to a degree. Or at least, I nudged you a little along the path.'

'Path?'

'You heard that Kudrin had offered me his hospitality? That he'd given me a roof and a bed?'

'Yes, he wrote to me, to say that he was harbouring a senior KGB man and that the rest of his congregation thought he was mad. It amused him greatly. That's why I wrote, inviting you to Munich.'

'To make a new, dangerous friend?'

'Of course not. Stan Kudrin was a very rich man, but he'd given up on RONDD. He didn't believe that we could do anything more than was useful for the cause. I was hoping to persuade you to talk to him, to open his wallet once more.'

'I might have done so, but then he died, badly, and I was suspected of the crime. It was KGB, of course, putting right a very old wrong as far they were concerned.'

'Artsyuk nodded slowly. 'Yes, that's what I thought.'

'Of course it is. You told them where he was. You told them where *I* was too, or so you thought. But I'd moved out of his apartment already, otherwise two bodies would have been found there.'

'Why would I do that?'

'Because you've been dancing with KGB for quite a while now. You keep them at arms' length, I suspect, but with RONDD dying on its feet you probably felt you had to explore what options remained to you. Your relationship was mentioned at a Kremlin meeting that I attended some years ago.'

'Did you tell him …?'

'No. I think it would have broken Stanislav's heart, if he knew. He complained of what he called your pestering, but he regarded you as a friend still, a solid comrade. Clearly, you didn't return the sentiment.'

Artsyuk had the small, thin grace to flush. 'Believe me, I regretted the necessity. KGB had paid me several small sums and were pressing for something in return. I couldn't think of anyone of sufficient importance in the Munich or Paris émigré communities whose exposure and removal wouldn't come back upon RONDD. Poor Stanislav had exiled himself from his fellow exiles, and was giving all his money to the damn church. He seemed …'

He paused, and swallowed. 'You don't appear to be taking his death too badly. I mean, this …'

He raised the bag once more. Zarubin pulled a face.

'He was nothing to me. I was grateful for his hospitality, but the price was heavy. His reminiscences were interminable, and he felt no need to censor the detail of his amorous adventures, though knowing perfectly well that I'm not of his persuasion. Certainly, I was shocked by his death, but there was a degree of relief also, that I had escaped the assassin. Who was he, by the way?'

'I don't know his name. My KGB contact in Berlin told me that they had an illegal in Paris, a long-term resident of the city who affects to be an émigré himself. Apparently he arranged a trip to London on some pretence of business there.'

'Ah. The armoire.'

'I'm sorry?'

'Someone came looking for me, I believe, after Kudrin died. He had a *pretence of business* and might have bagged three victims, had I been at a friend's shop when he called to appraise a particularly ugly piece of furniture. No doubt my absence – on both occasions - also preserved the proprietor's life.'

'I know nothing of that.'

'No, and as I say, I hold no grudge. Had I been in your position, neglecting to mention that a senior KGB defector was also available for removal would have seemed a criminal omission.'

'And yet you contacted me the day after Stanislav died, to accept my invitation. Weren't you worried I'd betray you again?'

'No, for three reasons. First, bringing in a KGB assassin to do the business here, in Munich, would put you perilously close to exposure, and I'm sure that there are plenty of people in RONDD – not least, Vasili - who would be very unforgiving, were they to be enlightened. Second, I assumed that my offer of money would be very amenable to someone whose organization lives so close to the bone. Third, following Kudrin's death I needed to escape both England and KGB, and it struck me that the very last place the latter would look for me was the household of the man who'd betrayed me so recently. The money was intended, not least, to prevent a repetition.'

That Artsyuk might be offered pieces of silver *not* to be a Judas made him wince once more, but he didn't repeat the apology.

'I can assure you, Sergei Aleksandrovich, that this gift puts me in a state of imperishable loyalty to you. They can torture me and I'll say nothing.'

Zarubin smiled politely and glanced at his watch once more. 'Well, my new life begins today, so this must be farewell. Though perhaps when the Soviet Union falls you'll invite me for lunch?'

'One that Belshazzar would envy, I promise! And …'

'Yes?'

Another loving glance caressed the money in the bag. 'May I ask – to whom did this belong?'

'You may not. Knowing will make you vulnerable, and me also. I'll say only that no-one deserves more to be robbed than the victim. Your conscience is clear. Goodbye, Evgeny Nikolaevich.'

The house stood almost at the end of a cul de sac of staid, comfortable properties, a sore thumb poking the eye of its neighbours. Its redundant wooden facings (an attempt to bring a rustic air to suburban Munich) were sorely in need of repainting, the front garden was monstrously overgrown and the fence which tried unsuccessfully to contain it offered several points of ingress to stray dogs, adventurous children or passing burglars. Unlike other houses in the street it had no name plate on the gate, but Fischer would have put money on the missing article bearing the words *Better Days*.

He knocked on the front door (hinges for an ornamental knocker survived; the object did not) and waited as a series of muffled noises within suggested that the occupier was not quite ready to receive. Eventually, the door opened a few inches, paused and then swung wide.

Otto Strasser was half-dressed, a collarless shirt untucked from corduroy trousers, socks but no house shoes and a piece of toast, half-eaten, hanging from the hand that wasn't holding the door. He looked surprised, but a smile spread across his broad, ugly face.

'The other Otto! Come in, we're having breakfast.'

It was the Imperial 'we', there being no-one else in the house, a shabby, dark, untidy house whose days of glory had probably departed sometime during the Weimar years. They waded through the hall, negotiating piles of pamphlets, relics of the effort to get Strasser's Deutsch-Soziale Union into the modern German consciousness. Similar signs of political activity had cluttered Artsyuk's house, but whereas RONDD's proceedings at least proceeded still (if until now on a tight budget), here the literature bore a thick, dusty patina of neglect. Strasser didn't seem to be moved by its silent reproof; tsking, he barged a little more room for his guest with a knee, holding his toast high so that it wasn't polluted by rising particles.

'Just shove it out of the way, none of it's important. I use it for lighting fires in cold weather.'

The kitchen was another sort of mess, with half a day's pots, pans and plates protruding above the sink's rim and a rich variety of organic material smeared across most of the working surfaces. Strasser glanced around, grimaced and turned to Fischer.

'I don't often have visitors. Please try to ignore the worst of it.'

'A lived-in room.'

'It's that, for sure. Tea?'

'Please.'

Strasser found an impeccably clean teapot and two matching cups, boiled a kettle and waved Fischer to one of only two stand chairs. A few moments later, he brought a ridiculously delicate tea-tray to the table, hitched his own chair beneath him with a foot and lowered himself and his load smoothly into place. It seemed a very practised manoeuvre.

He poured the tea, passed Fischer his cup and patted the table.

'Well, you've now met the real Otto Strasser, the sad pretender. I was about to say that I recall you seeing me in my best suit last time we met, but that would be pathetically dishonest. It's my *only* suit, which I keep carefully covered in a plastic sleeve upstairs.'

The frankness was so raw, yet so amiably offered, that Fischer hardly knew how to respond. It did occur, however, that the reality of Strasser's condition made his task a great deal easier. He sipped his tea, replaced the cup and cleared his throat.

'I assumed that you and Herr Artsyuk have some sort of financial arrangement.'

'He's a friend, or as much of one as our circumstances allow; but his own business consumes what little he raises.' Strasser pulled a wry face. 'I don't complain. I eat enough, my rent is paid by an old comrade and my children visit occasionally. There aren't many of the original Munich gang who can say the same. Who can say anything at all, in fact.'

'You were there at the birth of National Socialism, it's said.'

'Not quite, but both my brother and myself had very low Party numbers. Lord, when I …'

'What?'

'Never mind. I've bored a thousand people with this speech.'

'Bore one more, if you would.'

Strasser sighed and examined his teacup. 'When one thinks back, events acquire an odour of inevitability by reason of having happened. The things that Hitler did, the beyond-mad adventure that he set the entire German nation upon, it's as it some natural force ordained that it should have been so. But if you'd seen what I saw, lived through the Party's early struggles, you'd understand that there were a hundred ways it might have gone. Obviously, we underestimated the bastard; but if one or more of a certain group of us had resisted a little harder, or trusted him a little less, or saw more clearly how fucking broken he was, we could have buried him long before – even *slightly* before – he could no longer be touched. There wasn't just the one opportunity. If we had moved decisively before the Hitlerites won the strategic argument in '26, the little swine would have ended his life begging on a street in Linz. Gregor had another chance, in '32, when Von Schleicher offered him the vice-chancellorship. Did you know that?'

'I've heard it. I didn't know if it was true.'

'It is. If Gregor had accepted, we would have had the Wehrmacht behind us. Half the Party would have followed – power is much more seductive than the tongue of even the best orator – and we could have had Hitler smothered at a conveniently discreet moment. But my brother allowed himself to be bullied by the comrades into refusing the offer. He quit the Party in disgust and went back to his old pharmaceutical trade, thinking he was safe. He wasn't. Two years later, Reinhardt Heydrich put a bullet in his neck in a police cell and let him bleed out like a pig. You may imagine how I celebrated eight years later, when I heard that Heydrich himself had died in agony, but it was a thin revenge. The Strassers' NSDAP would have led Germany into no unwinnable wars, no catastrophe. There would have been a more equitable distribution of the national wealth, certainly, the Prussian taint diluted and a loose federation of sovereign German states established, though with common a economic and foreign policies. Perhaps fewer Jews would have found a path into public office, and there would have been encouragements for them to emigrate to Palestine ...' Strasser smiled; '... but nothing to shit-stain our posterity.'

Fischer scratched his ear. 'You paint it rather prettily.'

'Believe me, we wouldn't have allowed that Weimar nonsense to continue. Germans need a strong hand, one that slaps down our stupid urge to talk everything into everlasting circles. I don't doubt that we would have filled the prisons in short order, and disappeared the worst offenders – it would have been a rigorous, closely-regulated regime, but no spit-flecked insanity. However ...'

Strasser waved a hand around his little domestic Reich; '... opportunities not taken have brought me to this. Affectations of propriety, thanks to a good tailor – yet to be fully paid – and a very few friends to help with rent and potatoes. I shall probably disgrace myself by asking if you might like to contribute to the cause as you leave.'

'To which I will say that, if I had a life's-motto, it would be Fuck all Causes.'

'Ha! A noble sentiment, but quite out of its time, I'm afraid.'

'You speak of friends; earlier, you named Artsyuk as such.'

'He's been hospitable.'

'Did he tell you that RONDD was expecting a mysterious donation?'

'Yes, and that I would receive a modest sum from it.'

'May I ask how modest?'

'He promised a thousand marks. He said it would have been more, but that the total donation wasn't much.'

'Not much?'

'He didn't offer a figure, but I sense it's in the region of ten, fifteen thousand marks.'

'Then you may be surprised to hear that this morning, a gentleman I won't name went to see Artsyuk. He took with him a bag containing the equivalent of almost one hundred thousand dollars.'

For a few moments, Strasser's mouth moved to no effect, so Fischer pushed the blade into the wound. 'I don't know Herr Artsyuk, of course; but he impresses me as a very plausible gentleman, a necessary quality in his chosen life, I suppose. I expect he made you his friend to impress those few remaining German fascists who don't regard you as a traitor - or, possibly, to demonstrate his magnanimity to the many ex-Wehrmacht veterans in his own organization. Either way, a thousand marks is a fair indication of your worth to him, your value as a dinner guest. I suspect you can pull fascinating anecdotes out of your hat until the taxis arrive.'

Strasser was a big man, probably as old as Fischer yet only slightly overweight and powerful still. He might have taken the words as a slight (honestly though they were meant), but as he sat at his shabby kitchen table he seemed to close in upon himself. There probably weren't many nights during which he didn't stare up at an unseen ceiling and measure the distance between his once-ambitions and present state, and this latest slap couldn't have brightened the view ahead. He looked at his hands, his tongue pressed to the side of his mouth as if he couldn't trust it at present.

Fischer sensed that his welcome had more than run its course. He stood and pushed back his seat.

'Artsyuk doesn't know it, but the money isn't his benefactor's to give away. It belongs to KGB, and they're extremely keen to recover it. It strikes me that anyone with information on its present whereabouts might stand to earn a significant recovery fee, if he knows who to approach. I put the question to my friend General Zarubin, who suggested that the best, safest ear belongs to KGB's

Berlin Resident, a man named Krokhin. Apparently he's discreet, loves the German people as much as any Russian could and has nothing of the old-style NKVD bastard about him.'

Fischer reached into his pocket, removed a piece of paper and placed it on the table. 'This is the number for the main switchboard at Karlshorst. I imagine that if a man were to ask for Krokhin by name and say that it concerns a recent incident in Geneva, he'd be put through very quickly. Were that man to introduce himself as an old enemy of the Soviet Union's greatest enemy, he might expect a good hearing. You'd be surprised how many old-style Germans remain in KGB's good books.'

Rue de Vaugirard, 5th Arrondissement, Paris.
Two months later.

The antique shop was as old as anything it sold, a venerable relic of that period of the Restoration when the chattels of beheaded aristos began to find their way from hiding places or the mansions of their purloiners into the light of day, to be snapped up promptly by those who had done very well from the late Empire's many appropriations. Its present owner was known to be a refugee from a different Empire, erased in 1917 but mourned still by many adopted Parisians of a certain age. He had a noble name, which he refused either to venerate excessively or to play upon, and this had earned him a deal of respect among that section of the Russian émigré community who quietly believed that one's antecedents were the only measure of a man's present worth.

He had conducted business from Rue de Vaugirard for almost a quarter of a century, and his reputation as a man who could find the most esoteric pieces was unrivalled. A search for a pristine blackamoor *gueridon* would need only a brief telephone call to satisfy; an understated, barely-gilted *ormolu* perhaps an hour's mining of M. Golitsyn's rolodex; while a rare bamboo *indiscret* with intact, original upholstery might raise an eyebrow or goad a gentle sigh, but a day's patience would almost invariably be rewarded by the discovery of a prime example. His clientele was not large, but it knew what it wanted and had the means to pay for it. Old money, new money, questionable money and even those charged with keeping the Élyseé Palace fashionably unfashionable had his address, and none had been disappointed.

M. Golitsyn enjoyed his work, but it was a fine, comfortable lie. His real, almost-forgotten name was Grigor Avdeyev, though no-one in France (and very few people who didn't work in the Lubyanka) knew him as such. He had learned French in Moscow, studied Fine Art in Leningrad and picked up more practical, physical skills as his other job had required. He was an Illegal, a man who had passed for something else on enemy territory for almost half of his life to date. He lived modestly despite his handsome profits, avoided close friendships (though several people who regarded themselves as such would have been wounded to hear it), paid cash to strangers for his occasional sexual releases and fed a steady stream of information on the movements of his compatriots-in-exile to the Soviet Embassy on Boulevard Lannes. Occasionally, Moscow required him to follow up one of his pieces of intelligence with a rigorous gesture that put the fear of God or Bolshevism into the target's surviving acquaintances, but his distant, hands-off handlers were loath to overuse him. An effective, supple Illegal was a rare commodity; the majority, having immersed themselves in alien cultures, raised families who knew nothing of their pasts, gradually became what they had once pretended to be and rarely performed to expectations when activated. M. Golitsyn was the exception, an illusion perfectly preserved as such, and far too valuable to risk on routine matters. Only once in recent months had he been required to prove his enduring expertise, and he had done so to the full satisfaction, even admiration, of his principals in First Directorate, KGB.

Usually, he opened his shop late, having a habit of breakfasting well at a pâtisserie at the top of Rue Mouffetard and then walking it off in the company of a couple of *gauloises* (filthy things, but in no way inferior to the *belomorkanals* with which he had coughed his way through military service). Today, however, he was at his premises before 9am, being preoccupied by the matter of a velvet *crapaud* armchair that a persistent customer absolutely needed for her Avenue Montaigne apartment. He had found two pieces that might suit, but one of them required restoration while the other was true green, and the old bitch had insisted upon emerald. He was waiting for a 'phone call from Marseilles regarding a third possibility, and didn't want to miss it.

A customer – or, rather, a browser – stepped into the shop before he had a chance to boil the kettle. The man crouched briefly to examine a group of three *jardinières* arranged on a console table, and it was only when he rose and turned to offer a belated smile that M. Golitsyn noticed the terrible burns, dark red with age, that had almost erased the right side of his face. Long familiar with war trauma (both observed and inflicted by his own hand), he wasn't so gross as to react visibly. He returned the smile no less pleasantly than if his caller had been a nymph, and was about to ask if he might be of service when the creature gestured around the small showroom.

'I probably know the answer already, but I'm looking for an armoire, unpainted, mahogany if possible.'

His French was reasonably good, but with a distinct German accent. M. Golitsyn inclined his head slightly to one side and pulled his face in the Gallic manner.

'Unfortunately, I have nothing at the moment. Had you asked some weeks ago, I might have been able to help. I saw something very much in that line, and had a prospective customer for it. He pulled out, though, so I saw no reason to make the acquisition. If you leave me your name and contact number, I can certainly make enquiries.'

'Thank you, but I'm only in Paris for a day or two. Never mind, it was worth a try. Good day to you.'

When the gentleman had gone, Golitsyn went to make his tea and hunt down a few biscuits. He had only just brought his paltry breakfast into the shop and placed it by the telephone when the front door bell rang once more.

Fuck your Mother!

He sighed, straightened his legs before his arse had a chance to touch the chair, painted on another welcoming smile and turned to greet the latest impediment to a satisfactory morning, at which point all thoughts of any sort of morning fled. He recognised the man at once, having received a good photograph and instructions only three months earlier; but his pistol was in the desk drawer some metres away, and his hand had only just begun to reach for the antique circumcision knife he kept in his pocket for what-if moments when the cosh came down on his head. He collapsed to the floor, unconscious before he could feel its impact.

His assailant put the weapon next to the teapot, stepped back, took off a cheap plastic shower coat that he had purchased at a kiosk a few minutes earlier and placed it over the fallen man's head. Retrieving the cosh, he knelt and struck down, hard, three times more. When the last twitch had faded he rose and allowed his breathing to slow. A glance in a massive Napoleon III mirror on the wall confirmed that no blood had splashed onto his shirt or suit, and force of habit made him run a hand through his strikingly blond hair (though hardly a strand had been disturbed by his exertions). A further glance took in the entire room, which, other than for a single detail, would have raised no suspicions or alarms. Satisfied, he went to the door, grasped the handle, turned and regarded the corpse.

'My friend swore that I wouldn't be able to do it. He's very perceptive, usually.'

An hour later, the blond assassin and the half-faced man were sitting outside a café in the Marais' Jewish neighbourhood. A cafetière and a plate of palmiers half-filled their tiny table; they had waved away the latter, but, being ignored by their waiter, had since picked at the pile while watching passers-by in the manner of idle tourists.

When the palmiers were almost a memory the assassin brushed crumbs from his lap, plucked a small leather bag from out of a bigger one and placed it on the empty seat between them. His companion noticed that the busy hand was still shaking slightly, but he said nothing. He leaned across, unfastened the buckle and regarded the contents for a few moments. His only eyebrow, having risen, remained there.

'This looks to be all of what remains.'

'Less three thousand. It will get me to where I want to be and give me options.'

'And where is it you want to be?'

'Somewhere I can hide in a sea of blondness, unnoticed.'

'Scandinavia?'

'Probably. You?'

'I don't know yet.'

'Perhaps you should consider the matter, urgently.'

'I didn't mean that. At the moment I *know* only that I'm going to my bank to deposit this and draw some travellers' cheques. And then I'm going to Orly, the Air France ticket desk. After that, I can't say.'

'Why? Haven't you …?'

'I'll ask what they have – unfilled seats, cancellations for today or tomorrow. And then I'll flip a coin.'

The assassin smiled. 'So I can't get it out of you, even if you wanted me to know.'

'Which I don't, obviously. Surely you want more of this? You've given me almost forty thousand dollars, it's far too much.'

'An impartial judge might say that it's owed. I don't need more. If a man in his early forties can't start again with a fat wallet then he isn't really trying. To be blunt, your weight of years makes new beginnings more difficult, and capital will be … convenient.'

'But not this …'

The shaking hand waved away the objection. 'I have no use for it.'

The half-faced man considered the leather bag for a while after zipping it and then placed it in his holdall, an item he had purchased the previous day at La Samaritaine. 'What changed? You had a plan to make money, plenty of it. And then …'

'And then Stan Kudrin was murdered. My friend - one of only two, perhaps three, I've ever made. It smothered an urge, and replaced it with something else.'

'A moral obligation?'

'Are you teasing me, Major?'

'No. You'll allow me to be surprised, though.'

'I apologize for bringing you into this. My plan was – it *became* – stupidly dangerous, and your involvement, previously desirable, became necessary.'

'You needed more hands to move the cash?'

'I needed help with something that's not familiar to me. For want of a better word, you are *constant*, Major, and I am not. Until recently I didn't think of it so much as a virtue as the heel with which you were dipped in the Styx. Stan made me realise its nature, what it was *for*; but following his death I feared that constancy to constancy might be beyond me.'

'I was the chaperone for your journey into grace?'

The assassin laughed. 'Put that way, it seems absurd. Perhaps the help of a steady hand was necessary for me to negotiate an unfamiliar journey.'

From the south came a faint peal, the bells of Saint Paul-Saint Louis. The half-faced man counted off eleven, reached for his holdall and stood. For a few moments he paused, looking around Rue des Rosiers, and wondered what made it seem different today. He knew the street fairly well, having favoured the area over the past few weeks as he slowly found his bearings. The Marais was comfortable, shabby, less combed and trimmed than most of the rest of central

Paris; it had something of what had once made the less reputable parts of Berlin interesting, and had he not carried a weight of dangerous history he might have considered it as yet another possible new home. Today, though, he felt as if he were viewing it through a long lens, and more dispassionately than it deserved. He was seeing detail, not the whole, carving off shards for memories yet to be laid down, of a place to which he could never return.

Inside the cafe, someone switched on a radio, a yé-yé station to entice a younger clientele to lunch. The moment, such as it was, passed into another sort of history, and he turned back to his manipulator, his tormentor, his friend.

'Goodbye, then.'

Author's Note

The various Russian émigré and German recidivist organizations mentioned in the text existed, and their idiosyncrasies have been described as accurately as possible. In the 1950s, E.N. Artsyuk formed and led RONDD, which attempted to revive and consolidate various near-moribund émigré factions. Nevertheless, there is strong circumstantial evidence to suggest that he attempted to negotiate a personal reconciliation with the relatively reformist Soviet regime that emerged after Stalin's death. While the present author has perhaps overstated his willingness to betray his fellow émigrés, it is hardly conceivable (given KGB's eagerness to stamp out the last remnants of anti-Bolshevik resistance abroad) that he would have been permitted to visit Moscow upon at least two occasions during the early 1960s and then return to West Germany thereafter had he not offered something substantive in return. A matter of months after his final such visit, he was killed in the streets of Munich, apparently by a hit-and-run driver.

As mentioned in the author's note at the conclusion of 'Working the Dead', KGB Chairman V.Y.Semichastny, one of the generation of bright young apparatchiks promoted by Khrushchev to replace many of Stalin's appointees, played a major role in bringing down his former patron. In 1965, it was he who confronted Khrushchev to tell him that he had lost the confidence of the Council of Ministers and had no choice but to stand down. However, Semichastny did not long survive in post thereafter. Regarded still as Khrushchev's 'man' by the new regime, he was removed from office in 1967 following KGB's bungled attempt to kidnap Stalin's daughter Svetlana, who had defected to the USA. He was replaced by Yuri Andropov, who remained in that post until 1982, when he succeeded Leonid Brezhnev as General Secretary of the Party. After his dismissal, Semichastny served as Deputy Prime Minister of the Ukrainian SSR until his retirement in 1981. He died in 2001.

A.A. Krokhin continued in his uneasy semi-official capacity as KGB's Berlin Resident until 1966, when he was appointed to the less prestigious but undoubtedly less stressful role of KGB Section Chief at the Soviet Embassy in Paris.

Otto Strasser's role in bringing down Artsyuk is the author's fiction, though details of his prior career given in the text – not least, the huge reward on his head and Hitler's persistent attempts to have him assassinated – are a matter of record. Following the collapse of his NSDAP-successor party, the Deutsch-Soziale Union, he lived quietly in Munich until his death in 1974.

Printed in Dunstable, United Kingdom